continued . . .

TRACY ANNE WARREN

Happily Bedded Bliss

THE RAKES OF CAVENDISH SQUARE

A SIGNET SELECT BOOK

SIGNET SELECT
Published by New American Library,
an imprint of Penguin Random House LLC
375 Hudson Street, New York, New York 10014

This book is an original publication of New American Library.

First Printing, March 2016

For more information about Penguin Random House, visit penguin.com.

ISBN 978-0-451-46923-6

Printed in the United States of America
10 9 8 7 6 5 4 3 2 1

Penguin
Random
House

*For everyone who has known
the joy of the special bond
that can only be shared
with a beloved animal companion.*

Chapter 1

Gloucestershire, England
September 1818

L ady Esme Byron hiked her sky blue muslin skirts up past her stocking-clad calves and climbed onto the wooden stile that divided the vast Braebourne estate from land owned to the east by her family's nearest neighbor, Mr. Cray.

Cray, a widower near her eldest brother Edward's age of forty, was rarely in residence and never complained about her trespassing on his land; since her childhood, he'd let her traipse across it almost as if it were her own. Not that Braebourne didn't provide plenty of beautiful vistas to explore—it did, especially considering that her brother owned nearly half the county and more besides— it was just that Cray's land possessed a lovely natural freshwater lake that sat at a perfect walking distance from the house. The lake attracted a rich variety of wildlife, so there was always something fascinating to sketch. Plus, no one ever bothered her there; it was quite her favorite secret place when she was looking for an escape.

She jumped down onto the other side of the stile, taking far more care of the satchel of drawing supplies slung over her shoulder than she did of her fine leather half boots. She wobbled slightly as they sank ankle-deep into the mud, then stared at her ruined boots for a few seconds, knowing her maid would give her a scold for sure. But as she was always able to talk dear Grumbly around, she shrugged away any concern.

Grabbing hold of the fence, she unstuck herself one boot at a time, then scraped the worst of the mess off into the nearby grass. Turning with a swirl of her skirts, she continued on to her destination.

As she walked, she angled her face up to the sun and sighed blissfully.

How good it was to be home again after weeks in London.

How wonderful to be out in the open once more, free to roam wherever she liked, whenever she liked.

A tiny frown of guilt wrinkled her dark brows, since technically she was supposed to be back at the estate helping entertain the houseguests visiting Braebourne. But all seven of her siblings and their families were in residence, even Leo and his new bride, Thalia, who had just returned with celebratory fanfare from their honeymoon trip to Italy. With so many Byrons available to make merry, she would hardly be missed.

Besides, they were used to her penchant for disappearing by herself for hours at a time as she roamed the nearby woods and hills and fields. She would be back in time for dinner; that would have to be enough.

An exuberant bark sounded behind her and she glanced around to see her dog Burr leap the stile and race toward her. She bent down and gave his shaggy golden head a scratch. "So, you're back, are you? Done chasing rabbits?"

He waved his bright flag of a tail in a wide arc, his pink tongue lolling out in a happy grin. Clearly, he was unapologetic for having deserted her a short while ago so he could hunt game in the bushes.

"Well, come along," she told him before continuing toward a stand of trees in the distance.

Burr trotted enthusiastically at her side.

Nearly ten minutes later, they reached the copse of trees that led to the lake. She was just about to step out of their protective green shelter when she heard a splash.

She stopped and motioned for Burr to do the same.

Someone, she realized, was swimming in the lake. Was it Mr. Cray? Had he returned home unexpectedly?

Soundlessly, she peered through the leaves and watched a man emerge from the water—a man who most definitely was *not* Mr. Cray.

But who was most definitely *naked*.

Her eyes widened as she drank in the sight of his long, powerfully graceful form, his pale skin glistening wetly in the sunlight.

A quiet sigh of wonder slid from between her parted lips, her senses awash with the same kind of reverence she felt whenever she beheld something of pure, unadorned beauty.

Not that his face was the handsomest she had ever glimpsed—his features were far too strong and angular for ordinary attractiveness. Yet there was something majestic about him, as if a dark angel had fallen to earth. His tall body was exquisitely proportioned: wide shoulders, sculpted chest, long arms, narrow hips and sinewy legs, even the unmentionable male part of him that hung impressively between his heavily muscled thighs.

Clearly unaware that he was being observed, he casually slicked the water from his dark hair, then walked deeper into the surrounding area of short grass, which she knew was periodically trimmed by the groundskeepers.

She caught her lower lip between her teeth, her heart pounding wildly as she watched him stretch out on his back across the soft green carpet of grass. With a hand, she motioned again for Burr to remain quiet. She did the same, knowing that if she moved now, the mystery man would surely hear her.

One minute melted into two, then three.

Quite unexpectedly, she heard the soft yet unmistakable sound of a snore.

Is he asleep?

She smiled, realizing that was exactly what he must be. Of course she knew she ought to leave. But even as she began to ease away, he shifted, his face turning toward her. One of his hands lay on his flat stomach, one ankle tucked under the other at an elegant angle.

And suddenly she couldn't leave.

Not when she was in the presence of such splendor and grace; it was as if the universe had decided to give her a gift.

I simply have to draw him.

Without considering her decision any further, she sank quietly onto a fallen log nearby that provided her with a sheltered, yet excellent view of her subject. Burr settled down at her side, laying his chin on his paws as she extracted her pencil and sketchbook from her bag and set to work.

Gabriel Landsdowne came abruptly awake, the late-afternoon sun strong in his eyes. He blinked and sat up, giving his head a slight shake to clear out the last of the drowsy cobwebs.

He'd fallen asleep without even realizing. Apparently, he was more tired than he'd thought. Then again, that was why he'd come here to Cray's, so he could spend a little time alone, doing nothing more strenuous than taking a leisurely swim and lazing away the day. He could have done the same at his own estate, of course, but visiting Ten Elms always put him in a foul humor.

Too many bad memories.

Too many unwanted responsibilities on behalf of a place that had never brought him anything but pain. For the most part, he left Ten Elms' management to his steward, since he rarely set foot over the threshold, but invariably there was some matter or other that would crop up requiring his attention. There was also his house in Cornwall and his town house in London, both of which put claims on his time and attention, but he never minded seeing to those properties. They were his and his alone, with none of the taint of the past to sour his habitation.

Yet he'd grown tired of his usual haunts of late—and

his usual companions and their seemingly insatiable craving for debauchery.

Even the devil needed a holiday every once in a while.

When his old, and far more respectable, friend Cray mentioned that he was going hunting in Scotland—an activity Gabriel did not enjoy—Cray offered Gabriel the use of his house in his absence. Knowing that Cray House was a place none of his regular crowd would ever think to find him, Gabriel had accepted. He'd actually left London without so much as a word to anyone, instructing his butler to take the knocker off the door and say only that the master was away at present and not receiving.

Wouldn't his ribald set of cronies laugh now to see him doing something as prosaic as taking a solitary afternoon nap? Then again, he was out of doors, stark naked, so they would most certainly approve of that.

Smirking, he stood up, brushing an errant blade of grass from his bare buttocks. He was about to cross to the stand of bushes where he'd left his clothes when he heard a faint rustling sound behind him. He turned and stared into the foliage.

"Who is it? Is someone there?" he demanded.

The only answer was silence.

He looked again, scanning the area, but nothing moved; no one spoke.

Maybe it had been the wind? Or an animal foraging in the woods?

Suddenly a dog burst from the concealment of the trees, its shaggy wheaten coat gleaming warmly in the sun. He was a medium-sized mix of no particular breed, part hound, possibly, or maybe retriever. He seemed well fed, so it was doubtful that he was a stray. Then again, mayhap he was skilled at poaching birds and rabbits from the bountiful reserves of game in the area.

The dog stopped and looked at him, eyes bright and inquiring but not unfriendly.

"Who might you be, fellow?" Gabriel asked.

The animal wagged his tail and barked twice. Then, just as suddenly as he had appeared, he spun and disappeared into the trees once more.

In that instant, Gabriel thought he spied a flash of blue in the woods.

A bird?

The dog must have sensed it and gone off to chase.

Gabriel stared for one last long moment, then shrugged and turned to gather his clothes.

Chapter 2

"'T is high time you got home, my lady," Esme's maid scolded as Esme hurried into her bedroom nearly fifteen minutes after the dressing gong had been rung. "I was on the verge of sending one of the footmen out to fetch you. Och, and look at those boots. What new mischief have you been about this afternoon? Tromping in the mud again, I see."

The older woman's face creased into a scowl that put Esme in mind of a wizened prune.

"Oh, don't carry on so, Grumbly," Esme said with a coaxing smile, using the old nickname she'd given Mrs. Grumblethorpe when Esme had still been in leading strings. "I went for a walk, then stopped at the stables afterward to check on Aeolus. His wing is still healing and he needs food and exercise twice a day."

Aeolus was a hawk Esme had found in the woods a couple of months earlier, shot with an arrow. She'd nursed him through the worst and hoped the bird might be able to fly again with enough time and care.

Grumblethorpe tsked and turned Esme around, her fingers moving quickly to unfasten the buttons on Esme's mud-stained dress. "You and your animals. Always worrying over some poor, misbegotten creature. Rabbits and birds, hedgehogs and box turtles. You're forever dragging something back, to say nothing of all the cats and dogs you've brought with you into the house."

Esme let her maid's words roll harmlessly away.

Despite Grumblethorpe's noises of disapproval, Esme knew she liked the family pets. She just didn't approve of having so many of them in her mistress's bedroom at once. Still, it was an old battle and one the lady's maid had given up waging long ago.

Good thing too, since four of Esme's six cats—who had all started life in either the Braebourne stables or as strays she'd rescued—were snoozing in various locations around her room. They included a big orange male, Tobias, who was curled up in a cozy spot in the middle of her bed; Queen Elizabeth—a sweet-natured tabby, who was lounging in her usual window seat; Mozart—a luxuriously coated white longhair who luckily loved being brushed; and Naiad, a one-eyed black female, whom Esme had rescued from drowning as a kitten. Her other two cats, Persephone and Ruff, were out and about, seeing to their own cat business.

As for the dogs, Burr lay stretched out on the hearthrug in front of the fireplace. He snored gently, clearly tired after their recent adventures. And joining him in the land of dreams was dear old Henry, a brindle spaniel who was curled up inside a nearby dog bed lined with plush pillows that helped cushion his aging joints. Handel and Haydn, a pair of impish Scottish terriers, were absent. She suspected they were on the third floor playing with her increasingly large brood of nieces and nephews. The dogs loved the children.

Still making a few noises that were true to her name, Grumblethorpe stripped Esme down to her shift and bare feet. She carried away the soiled garments, leaving Esme to wash up with the fresh water and towels that had been laid out.

As Esme dipped her hands into the basin of water, her thoughts turned again to the mysterious naked man at the lake and the drawing of him that now resided in her sketchbook.

A warm flush rose on her skin, together with a tiny secret smile. He truly had been . . . magnificent. Better than any of the Greek statues she'd ever seen.

But her interest in him had been strictly artistic, she assured herself. She was an artist and he had been her chosen subject. If he happened to be pleasingly shaped, and if she happened to have taken extra care in her rendering of certain intriguing body parts, well, she had only been doing justice to the artwork, nothing more.

Even so, she was grateful he hadn't realized that she'd drawn him. Some people didn't like having their likenesses sketched—although considering that he'd been swimming naked, he didn't strike her as the bashful type.

Thank heavens, though, for Burr. For a few seconds, when she'd been turning to leave, she'd feared that her accidental Adonis had spotted her. But Burr had dashed out and diverted his attention so that he hadn't known she was there.

Picking up the bar of honey-scented soap, she lathered her hands and began to wash. As she did, she speculated again on who he might be. Certainly no one who lived in the neighborhood; she would have remembered a man like him. So why did she have the strangest feeling she'd seen him somewhere before? For the life of her, she couldn't place him.

Oh well, it would come to her eventually—or not. She wasn't going to concern herself. After all, it wasn't as if their paths were likely ever to cross again.

Just then, Grumblethorpe came back into the room with Esme's evening gown and silk slippers in hand. Realizing she had no further time to ruminate, Esme began to bathe in earnest.

In far less time than one might have imagined, Esme stood clean, elegantly coiffed and attired in an evening gown of demure white silk—presentable for company once again.

She'd hoped with the Season over, she might be able to put all the entertaining behind her for the year. But then Claire had decided to host one of her autumn country parties, inviting the usual gathering of friends and family, in addition to a few new acquaintances from London.

Esme sighed inwardly, wishing she could spend a quiet evening with just the family, then retire early with a good book.

Instead, she straightened her shoulders, fixed a smile on her lips and headed downstairs.

"Might I have the pleasure of procuring a beverage for you, Lady Esme?"

Esme glanced up from where she sat on the end of the long drawing room sofa and into the eager gray eyes of Lord Eversley.

Only minutes before, the gentlemen had rejoined the ladies after dinner, strolling in on a wave of companionable talk and the faint lingering aromas of cigar smoke and port wine.

Esme had been half listening to the other women's discussion of the latest fashions when Lord Eversley approached and made her a very elegant bow.

He'd been seated next to her at dinner; she'd found his conversation both pleasant and interesting. He was an attractive man, personable, well-mannered and intelligent. He was also heir to an earldom and a fortune that was impressive even by her own family's standards.

In short, he was everything any sane young woman could want in a husband.

So why wasn't she falling under his spell?

She couldn't even claim the excuse of disliking him; she liked him quite well. He was nice. He had a good sense of humor, and as a friend, she had no quarrel with his company.

But marriage?

Instinctively she knew there should be something more—a spark, a flicker of passion, to say nothing of love. And that, above all else, was the problem. Perfect as he was, he simply wasn't the man for her.

Yet out of all her suitors during this year's London Season, Eversley had been the most attentive. She'd done her best not to encourage him. She had even tried a time or two to actively *discourage* him. But if he had one fault, it was his bone-deep streak of stubbornness. Which, she supposed, accounted for his decision to accept Claire's invitation to come to Braebourne for a fortnight of shooting and entertainment.

As for her sister-in-law Claire and her sister, Mallory, and their rather badly disguised attempt to further a relationship between her and Eversley . . .

She ought to be cross with them; really she should.

But she knew they only meant well. She could hear them now, whispering as coconspirators. *But she so clearly likes him. We all like him; even Ned approves. The only thing those two need is a gentle nudge, a bit of time on their own, and the wedding bells will be ringing.*

And that was the trouble.

Claire and Mallory were happily married—as were all her siblings now except her brother Lawrence, who just laughed and shook his head whenever anyone brought up the subject of matrimony. All any of them wanted was for her to be happily married too.

Which was sweet in one way and exasperating in another. If only the lot of them would believe her when she said that she wasn't interested in a husband.

Not right now at least, and not for a good long while, if she had any say in the matter.

Luckily, her oldest brother, Edward—despite his approval of Eversley—was in no hurry to get her off his hands. He'd assured her before the Season had even begun that she was to take her time and marry only when, and if, she wished. He was quite content to let her remain at home for as many years as she liked.

Someday, she knew, the time would come when she would need to marry. Until then, she would have to find ways to avoid the overtures of interested young men, especially the thoroughly eligible and clearly deter-mined Lord Eversley.

She smiled and nodded toward her nearly empty teacup. "Thank you, Lord Eversley, for your kind offer, but I am very well refreshed at present."

"Ah," he said, linking his hands behind his back while

he took a moment to regroup. Suddenly his eyes brightened. "A walk, then, perhaps? The gardens here at Braebourne are quite splendid, even by lantern light."

There it was, alone in the gardens. She wasn't falling for that trick.

"Indeed the gardens are lovely. But again, I must refuse. Another time perhaps? I have walked a great deal today, you understand, and my feet are far too weary for another outing tonight."

Her feet were never weary—everyone in the family knew she could beat paths through the fields like a seasoned foot soldier—but Lord Eversley didn't need to be apprised of that fact. Hopefully none of her family was listening and would decide to give her away.

Yet apparently someone else *was* listening.

Lettice Waxhaven—another of the London guests, who happened to have made her debut along with Esme this past spring—leaned forward, a fierce gleam in her pale blue eyes. "Yes, where were you this afternoon, Lady Esme? We were all of us wondering what could be so fascinating that you would vanish for the entirety of the afternoon."

Esme hid her dislike for the other young woman behind a tight smile. Why her mother and Lettice's mother had to be old childhood friends who had been unexpectedly reacquainted this Season, she didn't for the life of her know. But owing to the renewal of that friendship, Esme found herself far too often in Lettice's company.

"I was just out," Esme said. "Walking and sketching."

"Really? Pray tell, what is it you sketch?" Lettice asked as if she were actually interested—which Esme knew she was not.

But quite without warning, she was caught up in unbidden memories of the lake and the drawing she had done of the naked sleeping man. She blinked, grateful for the room's warmth, since it disguised the flush stealing over her neck and cheeks.

"Nature," she answered with a seemingly careless

shrug. "Plants and animals. Anything that takes my fancy at the time."

And, oh my, had the glorious stranger taken her fancy.

"Lady Esme is quite the accomplished artist," Lord Eversley said with enthusiasm. "I had the great good fortune to view a few of her watercolors when we were last in Town." He smiled at her with clear admiration. "She is a marvel."

Lettice's mouth tightened, her eyes narrowing. It was no secret—at least not to Esme—that Lettice had long ago set her cap at Lord Eversley and that so far he had failed to take notice of her. Esme would have felt sorry for her were she a nicer person.

After a moment, Lettice rearranged her features into a sweet smile, as if realizing she'd let a glimpse of her real personality show instead of the usual falsely pleasant mask she wore. "Oh, I should so like to see your sketches. Perhaps you might show them to us?"

"Yes, Lady Esme," Eversley agreed. "I too would greatly enjoy a chance to view your newest work."

"That is most kind," Esme said, hedging. "But I suspect you would find my efforts disappointing."

"Impossible," Eversley disagreed. "You are too good an artist to ever draw anything that could be termed disappointing."

"You give me far too much credit, Lord Eversley. What I drew today amounts to nothing of importance. Just a few random studies; that's all."

A nude study of an unforgettable male.

Sleek limbs corded with muscle.

A powerful hair-roughened chest.

Narrow hips.

Taut buttocks.

And his face . . .

Planes and angles that begged for an artist's attention, rugged yet refined, bold and brilliant.

Captivating.

"Truly, they're mostly rubbish, and I have no wish

to offend anyone's eyes with the viewing," she said, hoping Eversley would take the hint and let that be the end of it.

Instead, he persisted. "You are far too modest, Lady Esme. Why do you not let me be the judge?"

"Who is modest?" her brother Lawrence said, turning his head to join the conversation. A few of the others looked around as well.

"Lady Esme," Eversley explained. "Miss Waxhaven and I are trying to persuade her to show off the sketches she did today, but she is too shy."

Leo, Lawrence's twin, laughed from where he sat next to his wife, Thalia. "Our Esme? Shy about her art? That doesn't sound likely."

"Yes, she's usually raring to share," Lord Drake Byron agreed.

"That's because even her bad drawings are better than anything the rest of us can do," Mallory said before she shot a glance over at Grace. "Except for Grace, of course. No offense, Grace, since you are a brilliant artist too."

Her sister-in-law smiled. "None taken." Grace looked at Esme. "Do let us see, dear. I know we would all enjoy a glimpse or two of your latest efforts. I particularly love the landscapes you do."

Cheers of agreement and encouragement rose from those gathered in the room.

Esme's chest tightened. "No, I couldn't. Not tonight. Besides, my sketchbook is upstairs. It's far too much bother to retrieve it right now."

"It's no bother," Edward said. "We'll have one of the servants fetch it." He glanced over at the butler. "Croft, please ask one of the maids to collect Lady Esme's sketchbook and have it brought here to the drawing room."

"Right away, Your Grace." The butler bowed and exited the room.

No! Esme wanted to shout and wave her arms to call Croft back.

But it was too late. Any further protestations on her part would look odd, drawing speculation about why she was so adamant that no one see her sketches. When her siblings said that she had never before shown a great deal of modesty concerning her work, they were right.

Still, this could all turn out fine, so long as she didn't panic. In the main, her sketchbook contained renderings of birds and animals, field flowers, trees in leaf, and the landscapes for which Grace had shown a partiality. The sketch of the man was at the back of the book. So long as she was careful, she could show only the innocent drawings in the front.

All too soon one of the footmen walked in, her blue clothbound sketchbook in hand. She leapt to her feet and hurried across to take it before anyone else could. "Thank you, Joseph."

Quickly, she clutched the sketchbook against her chest, collecting herself. Then she turned to face the waiting company.

"Here we are," she said brightly as she crossed to resume her seat. "Since you all wish to see, why don't I just hold up the drawings rather than passing the book around?"

Slowly she cracked open the binding, careful to go nowhere near the back pages. She thumbed through, looking quickly for something she hadn't already shown her family.

"Ah, here we are," she said, relieved to have found a new sketch. "I drew this of the hills toward the village earlier today."

Actually, she'd drawn it the previous week.

She held up the book, fingers tight on the pages.

Murmurs of appreciation went around the room.

"Lovely," Lady Waxhaven said.

"Astounding," Lord Eversley pronounced. "As I said before, you are a marvel, Lady Esme. Show us another."

"All right."

Bending over the book again, she found another new sketch, this one of her dog Burr lying under a tree.

She held it up, eliciting more positive remarks and smiles. From everyone except Lettice Waxhaven, that is. Lettice's innocent mask had slipped again, her eyes filled with a bitterness that made her look as if she wished she'd never started this.

Well, that makes two of us, Esme thought.

Esme showed them one last sketch of farmers working in the fields, then closed the book, holding it on her lap. "There, you have all had your art exhibition for the evening. Now, enough about me. Please go back to whatever you were doing before, talking and drinking and enjoying the evening."

"Thank you, dear, for sharing your beautiful drawings with everyone. But Esme is right," Claire said with a broad smile. "Let us make merry. Perhaps a game of cards or some dancing? I should dearly love to hear a tune."

"That sounds wonderful, Duchess," Lettice declared, openly enthusiastic. Her gaze went to Eversley. "Do you enjoy music, my lord?"

"Indeed," he said. "Mayhap you could play for us, Miss Waxhaven? You're quite accomplished on the pianoforte as I recall." Then he turned to Esme. "Lady Esme, what about you? Would you care to take to the floor?"

Lettice Waxhaven's face drained of color.

Esme actually did feel sorry for her—and rather cross with Lord Eversley for being so obtuse. She stood, intending to refuse him. But before she could, Lettice stalked forward and deliberately bumped into her shoulder, though Lettice did a good job making it look unintentional.

The sketchbook flew out of Esme's grasp, pages fluttering wide before the book spun and skidded to a halt on the floor.

She bent quickly to retrieve it, but Lettice Waxhaven's loud gasp let her know it was already too late. Everyone else was turning and looking too.

Breath froze in her chest, her thoughts tumbling wildly one over the other as she tried to think exactly how to explain the page with the gloriously bare, unforgettably gorgeous male specimen lying open for all to see.

"What in the nine circles of Hell is that?" Lawrence said, his voice so loud she jumped.

"I believe we can all see *what* it is," Leo answered, his face wearing the identical look of shock and dawning outrage as his twin's. "The only thing I want to know is how we're going to kill him."

"Kill who?" Esme squeaked, suddenly finding her voice.

Leo and Lawrence's gazes swung her way, while the rest of their family and friends looked on.

"Northcote." Leo said the name like it was a curse.

"Our neighbor from Cavendish Square," Lawrence finished.

Chapter 3

Gabriel poured himself a fresh brandy and leaned back in his chair. After taking a swallow of the alcohol, which left a fiery tang in his mouth and throat, he returned to his reading.

A fire crackled in the library hearth. The comfortably masculine, book-lined room was scented with a mixture of leather, parchment, woodsmoke and lavender.

Earlier, he'd considered venturing out to see what female sport might be had in the nearby village. But in spite of his admittedly strong sexual appetites, he'd come here for several days of rustication, not with the intention of trolling the local taverns in search of fresh bedmates.

He could find that sort of company anywhere, and lately he'd begun to grow bored with women who were easily had. Frankly, he was bored even with the ones who weren't so easily had.

Naive virgins were strictly off-limits, of course, since they always expected a ring to accompany any deflowering, and he had no intention of falling prey to matrimonial shackles.

As for virtuous widows and repressed wives, now, they could be interesting game, especially the ones who needed a bit of coaxing before surrendering to the lustful desires they claimed not to have. Such women had long been a favorite hunting ground of his.

But recently, even they were leaving him cold.

Perhaps after years of determined debauchery, he was becoming jaded. A few of his former paramours had even accused him of cruelty, claiming he'd ruthlessly seduced them only to cast them aside with barely a backward glance.

But he felt no remorse. He believed in pleasure for pleasure's sake and always left his partners thoroughly satisfied; there were never any complaints when it came to the sex itself. It was only later that matters sometimes grew unpleasant, particularly with the ones who fancied themselves in love.

They weren't, of course; love was a delusion, a kind of temporary insanity that polluted the brain and the bloodstream, ravaging its unwitting victims like a disease until the fever eventually broke.

It wasn't as if he had no understanding of the compulsion. He'd experienced the insanity of love once himself in his youth. But luckily he'd been shown the perfidious nature of the emotion, the shallow core of what was ultimately an excuse for self-delusion and personal debasement.

He sighed and drank more brandy, aware of the terrible ennui that plagued him. A hollow emptiness that nothing seemed to fill, not even the hot, mindless pleasure of sex. Of course he wasn't about to turn celibate; he had lost neither his mind nor his basic male needs. But clearly he would have to find other means of entertaining himself.

He would also have to seek out fresh ways to antagonize dear uncle Sidney, other than hosting scandalous orgies at his town house, adding to his erotic art collection, and seducing the young wives and daughters of his uncle's friends and political allies.

Pissing the old man off, now, that truly was one of life's greatest pleasures.

He tossed back the last of his brandy, then returned to his book. He'd just turned a page to begin a new chapter when a heavy knocking echoed from a distant part of the house.

He glanced up at the clock and saw that it was nearly

midnight. Who would be banging on the front door at this hour? Well, whoever it was, Cray's servants would send them on their way.

He'd barely had time to read another page when he heard the unmistakable sound of raised voices.

Men's voices, several of them.

Then there were hurried footsteps.

A quick rap came at the library door. It opened without his permission, and in rushed the butler.

"Forgive the intrusion, my lord," the servant said in a breathless voice. "There are several gentlemen here to see you. I explained to them about the late hour and that you are not receiving, but they are most insistent."

"Did these gentlemen state the nature of their business?"

The butler shook his head. "No, but they are—" He paused and visibly gulped. "One of them is the Duke of Clybourne. The others are his brothers and his brother-in-law, Lord Gresham."

They were men of whom he had heard but whom he had never met. Actually, the only members of the Byron family with whom he was acquainted were Lords Leopold and Lawrence, who were his neighbors in London. He knew that Braebourne, the great country estate of the Byrons, abutted Cray's lands, but since he wasn't here to socialize, he hadn't bothered to pay calls on any of the local aristocrats or gentry. Given his dreadful reputation, most of them likely wouldn't have welcomed a visit from him anyway.

So why the late-night call? He couldn't fathom a reason. Unless they were here to carouse, but that seemed as unlikely, given the circumstances, as the visit itself.

He set his book aside. "Very well, show them in."

"That won't be necessary," said a voice deep and rich with natural authority. "We decided to let ourselves in." The dark-haired man, who Gabriel presumed must be the Duke of Clybourne, flicked a glance toward the hapless butler. "You may go."

The servant bobbed his head and fled.

One of the other men shut the door. Gabriel began counting Byrons—there were seven, or rather six, if you didn't include the brother-in-law. They were all tall and powerfully built, and they were all wearing hard, angry expressions, even the twins, who were usually grinning or making some humorous jest over their latest scheme.

No, this was definitely not a social visit.

Gabriel gave no outward sign of concern as he rose slowly to his feet, his own great height putting him an inch above even the tallest of them. "Good evening, gentlemen. Lawrence. Leopold. Perhaps one of you might be so good as to do the introductions. I presume these are your brothers."

A muscle ticked in Leo's jaw—at least Gabriel thought it was Leo, since it wasn't always easy to tell the twins apart; the two men looked so much alike.

Lawrence's eyes narrowed and for a minute Gabriel thought he might refuse. "Lords Cade, Drake and Jack Byron," Lawrence said, gesturing toward each one in turn. "Edward, Duke of Clybourne, and our brother-in-law, Adam, Lord Gresham."

Gabriel inclined his head. "I would offer all of you refreshments but I have the feeling you are here on more important business. So, what may I do for you?"

Leo's eyes flashed and he took a step forward as though Gabriel's words had unleashed some self-imposed restraint. "You smug bastard. How dare you act like you have no idea why we've come. Or are you going to claim next that you didn't have any idea it was her?"

"Her? Her who? Obviously this has to do with a woman." He folded his arms. "You'll have to enlighten me further, since I know a great many hers and sometimes it's difficult to recall one from another."

"Why you—" And suddenly Leo leapt the distance between them, his fist connecting with Gabriel's jaw before he even knew the blow was coming.

His head snapped back as he absorbed the punishing blow. His own fists instinctively came up, deflecting a second punch, which would have landed in the center of his gut. He shifted stealthily out of the way and readied himself for more.

He'd heard about Leopold's boxing prowess but had never been on the receiving end of it before. Now he knew why even formidable men thought twice about crossing Leopold Byron.

Before the fight could escalate further, two of his brothers, Jack and Drake, caught Leo around the chest and arms and wrestled him back.

Leo struggled. "Leave off. I'm not finished with him yet."

"You can pummel him to bits later," Jack said, "and it will be our pleasure to join in, won't it, Drake?"

"Indubitably," Drake agreed.

"But only after we're done talking to him," Jack said.

"What's there to talk about?" Leo shot back. "It's plain enough what he's done."

Lawrence pounded one balled up fist into his other hand. "I'm with Leo. Punishment first, then a hearing, once Northcote's regained consciousness, that is."

"That's not very lawyerly of you," Gabriel said. "Don't I at least deserve a chance to know of what it is I'm accused? Innocent until proved guilty and all that."

Lawrence shot Gabriel a furious glare. "Since we're not in a court of law and I'm not acting as counsel, I believe I can set the finer points aside in your case." He smacked his fist into his cupped hand again. "To think I considered you a friend, only to find out you would do such a no-good, reprehensible thing. This is beneath contempt, Northcote, even for you, and that is saying a very great deal."

"Let me go," Leo demanded in a voice that was nearly a growl. "Let me hit the stinking blackguard just one more time."

"Are you sure only once will do?" said Lord Cade, glaring menacingly.

"Yes, I'd say several times more seems fitting." Adam Gresham tightened his fists, his knuckles popping.

Gabriel tensed, raising his own fists another defensive inch higher in case Leo broke free, or one of the others decided to have at him instead. He took a moment to assess his adversaries. The older Byron brothers, and Gresham, were unknown quantities, but they all looked to be lethal in a fight.

As for Lawrence, there was a curious kind of irony in their present circumstances considering the two of them had once fought side by side in a bruising tavern fight that had landed them both in gaol. Lawrence was a seasoned fighter and Gabriel knew not to underestimate him any more than his twin. But he could handle himself, having participated in his own share of dirty, bare-knuckle street fights and vicious brawls over the years. He'd rather not fight Lawrence, or Leo, come to that, but he would if necessary, even as badly outnumbered as he was.

"I'll take you on, all of you, if that's what you want," Gabriel challenged. "Seven to one. I'll make book on those odds."

"I'm going to tear you apart, Northcote!" Leo struggled anew against his brothers' hold; Jack and Drake suddenly looked as if they just might set him loose.

"Enough!" the duke ordered with a crisp authority that quieted everyone in an instant. "We will hear Lord Northcote out and see what explanations he can offer for his actions. Then we'll decide how best to vent our collective fury. Even I would not be averse to a good old-fashioned horsewhipping; or mayhap some boiled tar and goose feathers might be better."

Damn, Gabriel thought, *but Clybourne just might be the most dangerous one of them all.*

Leo gave a low grunt of frustration but ceased his struggles, while Lawrence lowered his fists to his sides. The rest of the men stood down. Satisfied that Leo was no longer going to attack, Jack and Drake released him.

Slowly, Gabriel relaxed his fighting stance as well, letting his arms drop to his sides. "So, let's hear what it is all of you think I've done. Or should I amend that to say *who* I've done, since you made mention of a 'her.'"

The other men bristled.

Jack's eyes flashed fire. "Why, you loathsome son of a—"

"Quiet," Clybourne ordered in a hard, smooth tone that cut through the impending chaos. Once everyone had calmed again, the duke fixed Gabriel with a glacial stare. "I'm going to enjoy making you suffer for your insolence. Now, tell me how you come to know my sister."

"Sister?" Gabriel scowled, racking his brain as he flipped quickly through his extensive list of current and former sexual partners. "Lady Mallory, do you mean?"

"Lady *Gresham*," Adam Gresham shot back. "And what do you know of my wife, sir? How dare you impugn her reputation when she is an angel and wholly above reproach."

"Yes, so I hear. The lady and I are scarcely even acquainted. I admit that I may have danced with her once, years and years ago. Is she ginger haired?"

"No, she most certainly is not."

Gabriel shrugged. "Well then, there you are. I guess I do not know her, after all."

Gresham made a sound like an angry bear.

"Calm yourself, Adam," Clybourne told his brother-in-law in a low aside. "Mallory is not at issue here, and it's clear he does not know her."

"Then he ought not to have even mentioned her name," Gresham said.

Gabriel briefly lifted his eyes to the ceiling before focusing again on the duke.

Clybourne looked back. "We are speaking of our other sister."

"And what is her name?"

"Lady Esme."

Silence fell, the others clearly waiting for his reaction so they could pounce again.

But he didn't have one. "Sorry, I'm afraid I don't know her either. She's not a ginger, is she, by any chance?"

Cries of outrage erupted.

"Bastard!"

"Blackguard!"

"Liar!"

"Lord Northcote," Edward Byron said in voice so cold it could have frozen the Thames, "you are walking a very fine line. We all know you are lying and that you *do* know our sister. Tell us how it is you came to meet her and how long this"—the duke briefly closed his eyes as if he were in pain—"liaison has been going on. Was it at Cavendish Square? Did you see her perhaps when she was visiting one of her brothers, or Lady Leopold, and formed an acquaintance?"

Gabriel grew abruptly annoyed, his hands turning to fists at his sides. If there was one thing he disliked, it was being accused of deceit. "As I've told you already, I do not know her. I have never met Lady Esme Byron. I don't even know any women named Esme."

He shot looks at Leo and Lawrence, meeting their eyes. "The pair of you know me, at least a bit. Do you honestly believe I would seduce your sister? Your unwed sister, I presume, since there has been no mention of a cuckolded husband demanding we trade pistol fire at dawn. No, black as my reputation may be, and I in no way dispute the fact that it is every bit as bad as rumor claims, I am not in the habit of pursuing naive young girls."

The twins gave identical frowns and exchanged looks with each other. Their silent debate went on for several tense moments before they returned their gazes to him.

"Very well, if it is as you say," Lawrence stated in the erudite rhythms of a trained barrister, "and you take pains to avoid romantic dealings with innocent young ladies, then why is it our sister happens to have a drawing of you in her sketchbook?"

Gabriel stared. "Does she? How very peculiar."

"A *naked* drawing!" Lawrence added.

Gabriel took a moment to digest that particular revelation. "Are you certain it's me?"

"Of course it's you," thundered Leo. "You're not all that difficult to recognize."

"Show him," Clybourne ordered.

One of the others came forward, Lord Cade, if he

remembered correctly. The man walked with a slight limp, courtesy of an old war wound, he thought. "Here." Cade held open a sketchbook.

Gabriel glanced at the picture, which was surprisingly well-done. "A fine likeness. But the drawing appears to be of a flock of sheep in a field. Although I do agree that they're all naked except for their natural woolly coats."

Cade looked down, scowling heavily. "No, not that one." He flipped to the next page. "This one." He held the book out again.

This time Gabriel saw what they were all talking about as he looked at a drawing in which he was very plainly the subject—and in which he was indisputably naked.

Again, the picture was exceptionally well drawn, the artist having captured his likeness with considerable skill. Astonishing skill, actually, if this was indeed the work of an untrained young woman.

He studied the scene, noticing that he was asleep and out of doors, a pastime in which he rarely engaged. In fact the only time in the past couple of years that he could recall falling asleep bare-arsed and lying in the grass was earlier today after his swim.

A frisson of memory went through him of seeing an odd, lightning-quick flash of blue there in the green woods. He'd also thought he'd heard something in the trees that surrounded Cray's lake, a dry snapping sound as if someone had stepped on a twig. But then he'd been distracted by the dog and had forgotten all about the noise.

But now that he thought about it all again, the truth hit him like a brick to the head. By Christ, she must have been there, this Esme Byron. The little sneak had to have been spying on him as he lay asleep in the grass, observing him like some Peeping Thomasina while she drew this sketch.

Now it was his turn to scowl.

"Well?" demanded Lawrence, as the others looked on expectantly.

"Obviously that is me," Gabriel said. "I cannot dispute that fact. But the drawing was done without my knowledge or consent. I went swimming this afternoon and fell asleep afterward. Lady . . . Esme must have come upon me while I was unaware."

"Oh, please, give us some credit," Cade scoffed.

"You expect us to believe that load of horse chestnuts? You had 'no idea.'" Jack jeered, arms crossed over his chest.

Drake regarded Gabriel with a kind of intense scrutiny that unexpectedly made him want to squirm.

"Pity we aren't in London, so I could have access to my equipment," Drake mused aloud. "I've been conducting some promising experiments using electricity. I'd love to see what results they might produce when it comes to truth telling."

"Give me a list of what you need," Adam said. "Surely we could cobble something together."

"Yes, I'd be happy to send a rider to Bristol for any necessaries," Gresham offered.

Clybourne's blue eyes twinkled; he was obviously amused by the turn of conversation.

As for the twins, Leo and Lawrence exchanged another set of speaking looks.

"Could she have done?" Lawrence said in a low voice.

"It would be like her—," Leo agreed softly.

"And she was out today—"

"Yes, but surely she must have considered . . . ?"

Leo shrugged. "You know how she is."

"But of all the coincidences. Him here and her—"

"I know. What deuced bad luck."

"Hellfire."

"And damnation."

Everyone else had gone quiet as they did their best to follow Leo and Lawrence's disjoined conversation.

Gabriel glanced at the duke, who wore an expression that was agonized but curiously resigned.

"Just to clarify," Edward Byron said, his own gaze shifting to Gabriel, "this lake where you swam. It's on Cray's land?"

"That's right."

"And you believed yourself to be alone?"

"Yes. I had no notion your sister was there, observing and drawing me. At least not until—"

"Yes, until?"

He told them about the odd flash of blue, the sound and the dog.

"There was a dog? What did this dog look like?"

He described the animal.

A collective groan went through the room.

"Sounds like Burr," Jack said.

"Must have been," Drake agreed.

"I suppose, then, that we're to believe him?" Cade said.

"Yes, I rather think we must," the duke said, "particularly since Esme denied knowing Northcote. She told me it was not what we were all imagining and that I was overreacting. I must admit I was scarcely in the mood this evening to hear her out, so I sent her off to her room. Now I realize I ought to have stayed and listened to her more closely."

The duke fixed Gabriel with a penetrating stare. "You give me your word as a gentleman that you have never in your life met my sister Lady Esme?"

"Yes. I swear I have never met her," Gabriel said. "As for my word, you may have it, though my reputation as a gentleman is admittedly suspect."

Clybourne sighed and nodded. "Well, at least I can rest easy knowing you did not seduce our little Esme after all. However, this changes nothing about what must come next."

"Next?" Gabriel asked, not entirely sure he liked this new conversational direction. "What do you mean by *next*?"

"I mean that as soon as the arrangements can be made, it will be my unfortunate duty to welcome you to the family."

"What!" Gabriel felt the blood drain out of his cheeks. "Now, see here. I have no intention of marrying your sister."

"Intention or not, that's exactly what you are going to do. Lady Esme's sketch of you was seen by the guests at the house party my wife and I are currently hosting, which means she is now quite thoroughly ruined.

"Had the incident occurred in front of the family alone, I might be persuaded to let the matter end here. But several of the witnesses are not the sort who can be trusted to hold their silence. So although it pains me, since I had hoped for a love match for my youngest sister, it seems that you and Esme will wed."

"And if I refuse?"

Adam Gresham and the other five Byron men stepped forward as one—a united front.

"Refuse?" the duke said. "We won't let you refuse. I'm afraid, Lord Northcote, that your fate was sealed the moment my sister saw you and put her pencil to paper."

Chapter 4

Esme tossed back her bedcovers the following morning, having barely slept. The incident with her sketchbook kept replaying itself over and over again in her mind, along with the expressions on everyone's faces, which ranged from shock and dismay to anger, disbelief and even titillated amusement. The latter belonged to Lettice Waxhaven, who'd looked so puffed full of spiteful delight it was a wonder canary feathers weren't sticking to her lips as she smiled.

The worst of all, though, had been the look of sad disappointment on her mother's face, as if Ava Byron couldn't believe her youngest child would be capable of committing such a shameful, headstrong act.

And then there'd been Edward . . .

After the guests had been hurried off to their rooms, he'd marched her into his study. There, she'd tried to explain that it wasn't what they were all imagining, that there was nothing between her and the man in the drawing—this Lord Northcote, whom she'd never even met. She'd simply found him intriguing from an artistic point of view and had sketched him.

"It wasn't anything sexual," she'd said, not sure if Edward had heard more than every third word of her hurried speech.

But he'd heard that last part, his clenched jaw actually making a popping noise as he'd launched into a blistering tirade that had left her silently quaking in her slippers. When he'd ordered her to her room, she'd been only too happy to go.

Now here she was, like a prisoner waiting to learn her fate. But in the meantime, unless someone had locked her inside her room—she went across and tested the door just to see if it would open, and it did—she wasn't going to sit idly by, worrying the day away until her family decided to share what was sure to be even more unpleasant news.

Her brothers and Adam had gone out last night, riding away in a furious thunder of horses' hooves. Had they gone to find and confront Lord Northcote? And what was he even doing here in the country, seeing he was Leo and Lawrence's neighbor from London?

No wonder he'd seemed vaguely familiar to her. She must have seen him getting in and out of his coach or climbing the front steps of his town house on one of the rare occasions she'd visited Cavendish Square. She'd noticed him—how could anyone *not* notice him?—but she obviously hadn't realized exactly who he was.

Well, she certainly knew now.

Did he now know what she'd done, this man who was still a stranger to her? Edward had kept her sketchbook. Had they shown Northcote the drawing?

But she didn't want to think about all of that right now, she told herself as she moved over to the washstand. Later would be soon enough. *Much, much* later, if she had her druthers.

Since it was too early to ring for her maid, she washed and dressed on her own, donning an old, well-worn gown of brown cotton that she was able to fasten herself. She brushed her long dark hair and tied it back with a plain green ribbon rather than struggling to put the heavy mass up in pins.

She'd tried learning to do her own hair in the past but had never mastered Grumblethorpe's knack for anchoring the long, thick strands in place. To date, her own efforts were nothing short of disastrous, so tied neatly and left to hang down her back would have to do despite any impropriety. And after last night, not pinning up her hair seemed the least of her sins.

She left the room, with her black-and-white kitty, Ruff, Elizabeth, Naiad and Persephone—a spotted gray-and-white shorthair—following on her heels in hopes of getting breakfast. As for her other two cats, she knew they must be out hunting rodents and birds rather than waiting to go down to the kitchens with everyone else.

Burr and old Henry, who had climbed with a stiff gait out of his basket, joined the furry entourage, tails wagging and tongues lolling as they descended the stairs. The Scotties were probably asleep in the nursery, happy to wait to see what tidbits the children would sneak them during their breakfast in another hour or two.

A couple of sleepy servants were in the kitchen when she entered, one lighting the coals in the stove while another filled kettles with water to warm. They exchanged friendly greetings with her, then went about their duties, used to her comings and goings and her menagerie of pets.

Charles, a footman who had once worked on his father's farm and who loved animals, appeared and came over to help her prepare dishes of boiled chicken and brown rice for the cats and dogs waiting eagerly at their feet.

When guests were staying, Charles often assisted with the care of her furry brood. Without asking, he set to work, even taking a few moments to gather fresh meat scraps for Aeolus, her wounded hawk, and cut-up apple and beetroots for Poppy, a convalescing rabbit who had an injured leg. He gave her several more apple quarters for the horses, who got jealous if she didn't bring them treats as well.

Once all her cats and dogs were fed, Esme set off for the stables, laden pail in hand, Burr trotting at her heels. She stopped along the way to chat with the gardener and his assistant, who gave her some timothy grass, comfrey and lavender to supplement the hay she regularly fed Poppy. They also showed her a dormouse nest in one of the flower beds but promised not to harm any of the inhabitants.

If only her cats would promise the same. Tobias, in particular, was a good mouser, who in addition to mice caught an occasional vole or bird, which he sometimes left in her bedroom as tribute. Mrs. Grumblethorpe and the maids were always horrified whenever they found one of his little "gifts." But as sad as the dead animals made her feel, Esme couldn't get angry with Tobias. He was just being what he was—a cat. Still, she hoped he left the dormice alone.

She went on, stopping first at the rabbit hutch to tend to Poppy. The young rabbit kicked as she was lifted out of her pen but then grew quiet as Esme cradled her in her lap and checked her wound. One of the local children, who'd found her and hadn't wanted her eaten for supper, had brought her to Esme. Esme suspected a fox had done the damage to her leg, which seemed to be healing nicely. After rubbing a specially made salve into the wound, Esme returned the rabbit to her hutch, changed her water dish, and set her munching happily on her breakfast.

Next was Aeolus, who was housed in a corner stall in the barn, well away from the rabbit hutch. The majestic hawk blinked his brilliant tawny eyes and clicked his beak in greeting, permitting Esme to inspect his injured wing. His wound looked pink but healthy and was healing as well as could be expected. She fed him, taking a moment to watch as he tucked into his meat scraps with enthusiasm and drank from the water basin she refilled.

Satisfied with the bird's progress, she went out into the main section of the stables, careful to close and latch the top and bottom doors to Aeolus's stall behind her.

"Good morning, Lady Esme," called one of the grooms in a friendly voice.

"Good morning, Pete."

"They're all waiting for you," he said, nodding toward the horses, who one by one were sticking their heads out of the tops of their stall boxes. A couple tossed their heads and pawed the ground; one whinnied in excitement.

Esme laughed. "Good thing, then, that I brought lots of apples."

Pete smiled and ambled away to continue his work.

She began making her way along the stalls, stopping to greet each horse like an old friend, and to pet and feed them an apple quarter or two.

As she did, she talked to the grooms as they passed. She knew each of them by name; a few she'd known since childhood, including the head groom, Ridley, who'd set her on her very first mount—a pony named Pollux—at age three.

She was relieved when none of them gave her curious looks or made mention of last night's debacle. Of course they wouldn't since they were all too well trained to ever gossip about Byron family business—at least not within earshot of the family. On the other hand, they must surely know something of what had occurred last night, particularly given the fact that Adam and all six of her brothers had saddled horses and ridden out unexpectedly into the night.

She gave a tiny sigh when she finished giving a treat to the last horse, aware she was delaying so she wouldn't have to return to the house just yet. She wasn't looking forward to coming face-to-face with her family. She didn't want to endure the inevitable rounds of questions and lectures, or worse, see the disapproval and disappointment shining in their eyes. She already knew she'd let them down, most especially Edward and her mother, who had always supported and indulged her independent, wayward habits.

In London, she'd overheard more than one matron decrying what they considered Esme Byron's inappropriate eccentricities, aghast that she was allowed so much personal freedom and the ability to voice opinions they considered unsuitable for an unmarried young woman barely out of the schoolroom. But her family always stood by her, proud of her artistic talent and uniformly deaf to the complaints of any critics who might say she needed a firmer hand.

What must Ned and Mama be thinking now? Were they regretting that they had not listened to those critics? Wishing they'd kept a tighter rein on her activities rather than letting her venture out as she chose?

But she would have gone mad being constrained and confined the way she knew most girls her age were. She could never have borne the suffocating restrictions, the smothering tedium of being expected to go everywhere with a chaperone in tow, or worse, being cooped up inside doing embroidery or playing the pianoforte.

In hindsight, she admitted that she should never have done the drawing of the beautiful naked stranger—or rather, Lord Northcote, as she supposed she ought to call him now that she knew his identity. She ought to have turned her back the moment she'd seen him lying there in the grass, rather than give in to the temptation to capture his likeness on paper.

But it wasn't all her fault. Her sketchbook was private and not meant for public consumption. If Lord Eversley hadn't insisted on seeing her drawings and if Lettice Waxhaven hadn't maliciously bumped into her and sent her book flying, none of this would be happening. Really, when she thought about it, Eversley and Lettice Waxhaven were the ones to blame, not her.

That was another reason she was loitering in the stables longer than necessary; she didn't want to cross paths with any of the guests, most particularly the Waxhavens. She expected all of them would be departing today, given the uproar. And what better opportunity to start spreading gossip?

But what did she care if they flapped and crowed? She'd done nothing so very dreadful. She was an artist; she'd drawn a picture. Admittedly it was of a naked man, but once everything was explained and put in the proper context, people would see that it was a great deal of fuss over nothing. It wasn't as if she and Lord

Northcote were lovers, engaged in a torrid, clandestine affair. They'd never even met—well, not in the accepted sense of the word at least.

But therein lay the difficulty. Would everyone hear about the drawing and assume the worst? Would they think Northcote had seduced her and ignore the truth? She frowned, having the sinking feeling that she knew which version of the story the *Ton* would believe.

But her siblings had been embroiled in scandals before, and they had all successfully weathered the storms. She would surely come through this latest hiccup too with no lasting harm.

And if I do not?

There was no point at present in ruminating over what-ifs.

She knew she ought to return to the house to change her attire, have breakfast and endure whatever scolds and cross-examinations were likely on today's schedule.

Instead, she dawdled, wandering back to the stall where her mare was kept. Unlatching the door, she went inside, stopping to pat the animal and croon softly to her. The mare's ears pricked up, and her velvety brown eyes glazed with pleasure as Esme scratched her on the forehead and neck and down along her withers.

Esme was about to go to the tack room to obtain a currycomb, brush and hoof-pick to do some grooming when one of the stable lads appeared.

"'Scuse me, my lady," the boy said, "but we thought ye'd want ter know that tha' new stray, the black one wot's been hangin' 'bout, looks like she's ready ter have her kittens."

"Abigail?"

"Aye, if tha's wot yer callin' her. She's settled in ter a corner of tha' feed room in the haymow."

"Of course I want to know. I'll go check on her now. While I do, see if you can find a good sturdy box, medium sided and broad; an herb box would do nicely. And some soft blankets and laundered rags. She and her kittens might feel more secure in there for the first few weeks, at least until the babies open their eyes."

"Aye, Lady Esme."

"Oh, bring me a pan of clean warm water too. You never know when there might be trouble during a delivery. I want to be ready to help if need be."

As the boy hurried away with his instructions, Esme did the same.

Chapter 5

Gabriel nearly turned back as he rode toward the Byron family's palatial estate, Braebourne. It wasn't too late to change his mind. He could still return to Cray's house, pack his bags and leave the area.

He'd never even met this Esme Byron. It was utter insanity to think he was on the verge of doing the gentlemanly thing and proposing marriage to her.

Ridiculous girl. The blame for this entire fiasco lay squarely in her lap. What had she thought she was about, spying on him as he relaxed in the altogether, then being idiotic enough to immortalize her sneaking ways by means of pencil and paper?

Were she anyone but the damned Duke of Clybourne's sister, he would have shrugged the whole thing off and left the brazen chit to twist on the end of the noose she'd made herself. But as Clybourne and his band of formidable brothers had explained most insistently last night, they weren't giving him the option of refusing.

And sadly, they didn't need a set of pistols to enforce their edict. Not only did they know who he was and where he lived, they also knew scores of influential people who could—and would—make his life an utter misery.

The heads of all the reputable banks in London—and several disreputable ones as well—would, he was told, be asked not to do business with him should he fail to do the right thing by their sister. Since the Byrons were on friendly terms with both the Rothschilds and financial wizard Rafe Pendragon, he could well see how it wouldn't be difficult for them to turn every bank in the city against him, including the one that held the mortgage on his London town house. Although the farms and tenant housing at Ten Elms brought in an adequate income, it was far from a grand fortune and insufficient to settle his debts should they be called in all at once. Of course, the irony was that as viscount, he was due to receive a large trust fund should he marry. Despite the financial enticement, he had always resisted before, unwilling to shackle himself in an unwanted union.

But even if the money were not an issue, the Byrons had also informed him that they would see to it he was cast out of Society. Not that he'd ever been warmly welcomed among the *Ton* in spite of his title, but still he was received everywhere, able to set foot in whatever great house he cared to grace. He suspected he would even be admitted to Almack's, that hallowed bastion of propriety that he'd always avoided like a case of the pox, had he ever seriously decided to look for a bride.

Laughable now to think that he'd never actually had to change his mind about remaining a lifelong bachelor. Instead, he was apparently caught tight in the parson's noose and by no less than a girl upon whom he'd never even clapped his eyes.

As for Lady Esme, he wondered at her game. Was she really just some foolish young woman who'd drawn a naughty picture and gotten caught? Or had she done this deliberately, lying in wait to trap him into a marriage he most definitely did not want? God only knew many eligible misses had tried—and failed—in the past to do exactly that.

He supposed he would shortly have an opportunity to decide just how duplicitous the future Viscountess Northcote seemed to be.

He ground his teeth together at the thought.

Even now, in spite of the ruin he would surely suffer at the hands of the Byrons, he felt it might be worth calling their bluff and walking away. He'd heard Vienna could be quite nice this time of year.

Then he remembered that the Rothschilds had their fingers in finance there too, assuming he could withdraw sufficient funds from the London banks in time to escape to the Continent in the first place. But did he really want to live as a refugee, denied his home and his friends, all over his refusal to marry some silly, imprudent chit?

No, it would appear that he was well and truly caught.

But if he was, then so was she; he'd make sure she remembered that fact after the wedding ring was on her finger.

At least he could take some grim pleasure in knowing just how furious his uncle would be; the taint of scandal alone would drive him mad. The Byrons might be a wealthy, powerful family, but they were almost as infamous as he was himself. In fact, before being "reformed" by love and several supposedly happy marriages, the Byron men had been known as unrepentant rakehells, raising skirts and eyebrows wherever they went. If there ever was a family of black sheep, it was the Byrons. Fitting, he supposed, that he would soon be joining their ranks.

But first he had to propose—assuming that pretense was even required under the circumstances. She had to be expecting his arrival. For all he knew, she was in the drawing room at this very instant, preening in front of the mirror to make sure her dress and hair looked just right.

Lord save him if she was.

Heaving a sigh at the prospect, he rode on toward Braebourne.

Esme plunged her hands into a bucket of clean water, barely aware of the blood and other unmentionable substances staining the front of the apron she'd donned for the birth. But it was all over now, mother and babies doing well—all five of them!

She'd had to help a bit with the last two kittens, who

had been slow at coming into the world. But finally they had emerged, snuggling, blind and deaf, as newborn kittens were, against their mother so she could groom them clean and urge them to drink their first meal of mother's milk.

All five tiny, adorable kittens—two tabby-striped, two black and one white—had eaten and were sleeping contentedly with their mother in the warm blanket-lined box Esme had prepared for them. Abigail had eaten a small amount of the minced chicken Esme had sent to the kitchens for; then she too had dropped off to sleep, exhausted from the exertion of having given birth.

Esme smiled down at them, already thinking about various friends and neighbors who might be willing to adopt the kittens once they were old enough to be weaned and settled in new homes. And, of course, a few of her siblings might have room in their homes for a new feline addition. The older of her nieces and nephews would want to see the kittens. Once they did, she suspected they would be begging to take home their favorites.

For tonight they would remain here in the feed room, but tomorrow she planned to move them to a more secluded part of the stable, where they would be in no danger of getting underfoot as the grooms did their work.

After one last look at her furry charges, she turned away and headed toward the main stable doors. The sky was a brilliant blue, the sun warm and bold, making her realize that the hour was more advanced than she had thought.

Her stomach panged and she became abruptly aware of just how famished she was. If she was lucky, she might be able to wheedle some tea and biscuits out of Grumbly. Otherwise, she'd have to wait for nuncheon, which was never served earlier than one o'clock.

She walked toward the house, not bothering to stop and look as she cut through a break in a high hedgerow and stepped out onto the graveled drive. A pounding of hooves came to her ears seconds before she saw the massive gray stallion thundering toward her. She cried out and instinctively raised an arm to shield herself from what was certain to be a brutal blow.

But it never came, the rider reacting so quickly that he slowed the animal's speed and shifted his mount's direction in the blink of an eye.

The horse whinnied and reared, great equine hooves slashing the air only inches from her head. The man turned the frightened horse again so that when the stallion's legs came back to earth he was well clear of her, the rider having controlled his mount with a skill that was nothing short of awe-inspiring.

Esme stared wide-eyed, her breath coming in quick, shallow gasps as she willed her heart to stop beating like a tom-tom. She pressed a hand to her hammering chest and gazed up, then up again.

Good heavens, it's him! The man from my drawing.

Only he was wearing clothes this time—and one of the darkest, most furiously menacing scowls she had ever seen, which, considering her six devil-take-the-hindmost older brothers, was saying a great deal.

"Are you injured?" he barked in a harsh tone. "Have you suffered any harm?"

"No, I—" She took a moment to assess her health. "I am well, physically, at least."

"A state for which you have my quick reflexes to thank. What in Hades' name did you think you were doing, darting out from between those bushes like that? My horse and I nearly ran you down, you idiot girl."

Whatever guilt Esme had been feeling for her part in the near accident vanished with the words "idiot girl." Her arms dropped to her sides, her fingers curling into fists.

"I was taking a shortcut to the house," she said in clipped tones, "which would not have been a problem had you been riding at a less reckless pace."

"Reckless? I was cantering. That is hardly a dangerous speed."

"It is when you are traveling on an unfamiliar lane and fail to watch what is in your path."

"That was not a matter of not watching. I would have spotted you with plenty of time to spare had you not leapt out of that hedge like some deranged rabbit."

"Oh, so now I'm deranged *and* an idiot, am I?"

He shrugged. "As you say. It is good to know you are willing to admit your own failings."

"Why you—you—" Her fingers balled tighter at her sides.

She wanted to tell him exactly how ungentlemanly she thought him but couldn't come up with a term vile enough. If only he would climb down from his horse, so she could express her feelings without having to crane back her neck. She was getting a crick just looking up. And to think she'd once found him appealing; she liked him far better naked and asleep.

"Yes? Go on? What is it you wish to call me?" he drawled in a rich baritone.

She resisted the urge to flush as he raked his tawny-eyed gaze over her. Judging by his expression, he clearly found her lacking in that regard as well. Not that she could entirely blame him, given her shabby attire, which was only made worse by the begrimed apron she still wore. Then there was her hair, which trailed untidily down her back, a few damp tendrils clinging to her forehead and cheeks due to her recent efforts at helping to deliver Abigail's kittens.

"There are any number of choice terms I could apply to you," she said, "several of them involving the barnyard. But since most of them would be an insult to the animals living there, I shall refrain from saying them aloud."

His lips twitched, his fierce eyes glittering with a dangerous light, as if he were caught somewhere between anger and amusement. "Cheeky piece, aren't you?" Then to her astonishment, he winked. "Hurry on to wherever it is you were bound. I shouldn't wish to make you even later in resuming your duties, or to be the cause of you suffering any punishment, however deserving of it you may be."

Her lips parted, no sound coming out.

She was still contemplating his remark and the erroneous assumption that she was a servant when he touched a finger to his tall beaver hat, pressed a knee to his mount's side and set off again—at a gallop, she noticed.

For a moment, she stood watching him disappear up the main drive toward the front entrance of the house. Then she came back to herself, once again remembering the time.

Hurrying forward, she moved across the lane and onto the lawn, her destination a quiet side door in the east wing that the servants always left unlocked for her use.

As for Lord Northcote and his unexpected arrival, she tried hard not to think about it at all.

Chapter 6

.

"More tea, Lord Northcote?" asked Claire, Duchess of Clybourne, from her place on one of the elegant drawing room sofas.

Gabriel was seated in a surprisingly comfortable armchair across from her, his nearly empty china cup balanced on his knee. "Thank you, but no." He set the cup and saucer aside, his gaze straying toward the mantel clock and the ever-lengthening morning; he'd already been here an hour.

"I cannot think what must be keeping Esme," the duchess said, her own gaze darting toward the clock. "I'll just go check on her, shall I?"

Jumping to her feet, she left the room.

But her departure had not left Gabriel alone; the various Byron brothers were scattered throughout the space like a royal guard, and a silent one at that.

The duke was reading a newspaper, making no attempt to conceal the fact that he was present merely to ensure that Gabriel made good on his promise to do the honorable thing, regardless of how little the term actually applied in his case.

Cade, Jack and Adam Gresham were playing a quiet game of cards at a table near the windows, while Drake sat on a chair near the fireplace, periodically penciling notes onto a small pad.

As for Leo and Lawrence, they were still cross with him and had spent the past hour shooting identical glares his way in between foraging trips to the tea tray. Between the two of them, they'd eaten most of the scones and biscuits and virtually all of the lemon curd.

Gabriel would likely have found the situation amusing had his circumstances not been so patently lacking in humor. Not for the first time, he considered standing up and telling them all to go bugger themselves, that he wasn't marrying their impetuous chit of a sister after all. But seeing as he was outnumbered again, and in Byron home territory this time, he thought better of the plan. Chances were good the brothers would tackle him before he made it halfway out the door.

And so he sat and waited.

And waited.

Arrogant minx. Who does she imagine herself to be, keeping me kicking my heels like this? Oh, that's right, he reminded himself as his gaze strayed to Clybourne, *she thinks herself a duke's sister; that's who.*

Impatient with sitting, he got up and wandered over to the set of windows at the far end of the room. The Byron brothers all looked up for a moment, then, assured he wasn't trying to make an escape, went back to their own activities. Gabriel stared out across the beautifully manicured lawn with its mature trees and lush flower beds. The long front drive stretched off in an earth-toned ribbon that wound away as far as the eye could see. As he recalled riding up the drive, he thought again of the servant girl he and Maximus had nearly trampled.

He wondered where she was now and what duties she was performing. Based on the stained apron she'd been wearing, he suspected she worked in the kitchens.

She'd certainly been a pretty little thing, with her clear alabaster and rose-tinted skin, stormy blue eyes and small round breasts that had thrust enticingly against the worn fabric of her bodice. Even if she could do with a good dose of caution, he'd found her intriguing—and desirable.

She'd been feisty as well, surprisingly so. Servants

were usually far too afraid of losing their positions to ever directly confront a member of the aristocracy, and yet she'd fearlessly gone toe-to-toe with him. He'd rather enjoyed trading barbs with her. It made him wonder what she'd be like in bed. He bet she'd give him a damn fine ride, with enough spirit to keep him guessing what might come next.

He smiled to himself. Perhaps once all this engagement nonsense was resolved, he would seek her out. A bit of extracurricular sport might be exactly what he needed to smooth out the rough spots in his mood.

With a silent huff of exasperation, he wondered how much longer his "intended" planned to keep him waiting.

Annoying little baggage.

Without warning, the drawing room door opened and in walked what appeared to be an entire gaggle of women, the skirts of their brightly colored gowns shimmering in rainbow hues. He stared, doing a quick head count, and realized there were eight of them in total. Good thing the drawing room was large; there were so many people inside it now the duke and duchess could have hosted a party.

Are they all Byrons—or Byron brides at least? He assumed so, recognizing three of the ladies—Claire; Ava, the dowager duchess, whom he had met briefly on his arrival; and Mallory, Lady Gresham. But which one of the others, he wondered, was the elusive Lady Esme?

He moved forward, looking from face to face. Then abruptly he stopped, as if he'd walked into a brick wall, his gaze falling on a dark-haired young woman he most definitely had never expected to see in this room.

"You!" he exclaimed, his eyes widening.

For there she stood, the servant girl about whom he'd just been fantasizing—only she was clearly no servant, but rather an elegantly groomed young lady of class and refinement. She was clean and tidy now, dressed in a pale pink silk gown with matching slippers. A darker pink ribbon was threaded through her upswept sable curls, her skin radiating a healthy, youthful glow.

She lifted her chin and looked him squarely in the eye. "Yes, me, the deranged idiot back once more. How do you do again, my Lord Northcote."

All around the room, Esme's brothers got to their feet, looks of suspicion and speculation ripe on their faces. Mama, Claire, Mallory, Sebastianne, Grace, Meg and Thalia looked puzzled as well at this unexpected turn of events. Upstairs, while they'd been gathered in her rooms, waiting for her to finish bathing and dressing so they could coax her to come downstairs rather than slip out of the house again, she'd said nothing to them about her unexpected encounter with Northcote.

Why she'd decided to say something now, even she wasn't entirely certain. Although mayhap it had something to do with coming face-to-face with Northcote again; when she was around him, her usual reserve seemed to fly straight out the nearest window.

"What is all of this? I thought the two of you were unacquainted," Edward said, clearly not about to let her comment go unremarked.

"Except in a semibiblical kind of way, of course," Jack piped. "Naked drawing and all that, you know."

Edward shot him a quelling look. "Thank you so much, Jack, for that illuminating, and completely unnecessary, explanation."

Jack grinned like an impish little boy instead of a married father of four. "Anytime, Ned. Always ready to help."

Across from him, his wife, Grace, shook her head, an amused little smile playing on her lips, which she did her best to hide. Jack met her eyes and waggled his brows. She covered her mouth with a hand and glanced away.

"So, which is it, Northcote?" Lawrence said in a far less amused tone, his arms crossed over his chest. "Do you and Esme know one another after all?"

"What he means is, were you lying to us last night so we wouldn't beat the stuffing out of you?" Leo's fierce expression was identical to his twin's.

"We can still beat the stuffing out of him," Cade suggested with a militant gleam of anticipation in his eyes.

"Most definitely." Jack rubbed his hands together. "Shall we take him out to the gardens? Or maybe the woods would be a better spot?"

"Or there's always the lake," Drake mused. "Give him a good dunking. Headfirst, I think."

Cade nodded. "There's an old army tactic using a sack and bucket. We could—"

"Boys, that will do," the dowager duchess interrupted in a soft, yet implacable voice that quieted the lot of them instantaneously. "Lord Northcote is our guest and there will be no more of this unpleasant sort of talk."

Around the room, eyes lowered. "Yes, Mama," came a chorus of deep male voices.

Apparently satisfied, Ava Byron turned her focus on Northcote. "Now, my lord, do let us clear up this matter so as to eliminate any further confusion. Do you know my daughter Esme or not? Given your exclamation on seeing her when we entered the room, she did not appear to be unfamiliar to you."

Esme waited, refusing to look away when his gaze shifted to meet hers.

"You are right," he said, his tawny eyes still locked with hers. "She is not unfamiliar to me, but only because the lady and I had a rather unexpected encounter earlier today. She darted out from behind some bushes and dashed straight into the path of my horse on the drive leading to Braebourne."

"I did not dart or dash; I *stepped*," Esme clarified, "and had his lordship been riding at a less dangerous pace than a full-on gallop, he would not have had occasion to nearly run me down."

He arched one sardonic brow. "Had I been riding as swiftly as you claim, rather than at a steady canter, I would never have been able to stop in time to avoid a collision."

"Actually, it is your horse who stopped in time, but

since he cannot testify to such matters we shall have to agree to disagree."

"Yes," Northcote said with wry amusement, "it seems there will be no meeting of the minds on this topic. As for the outcome, luckily no lasting harm was done to any of us—you, me or my uncommunicative steed."

"Yes, very lucky indeed."

She fell silent, only then remembering that they had an audience, as her family looked on with acute interest.

Northcote had apparently not forgotten, however, as he turned back to the dowager duchess. "So, you see, ma'am, I am both acquainted—and yet unacquainted— with your daughter. She is known to me through happenstance rather than introduction. I give you my word that until today, I had never laid eyes upon her."

"Thank you, Lord Northcote," Ava said. "I am sure we all appreciate your candor."

From the expressions around the room, not everyone seemed to agree. The dowager turned toward Esme. "You and I will talk later about this dangerous predilection you seem to have for taking shortcuts through the shrubbery. You were returning from the stables, I presume?"

"Yes, Mama. I had been seeing to Abigail and her brood. I told you about them, remember?"

"And so you did. Curious you omitted nearly being felled by Lord Northcote's horse on your return, but as I said, we shall speak on this later."

Esme nodded and lowered her eyes.

"Well," Edward said, picking up the conversation, "now that we have gotten all that out of the way, allow me to introduce you to my sisters-in-law." He nodded to each woman in turn. "Northcote, this is Margaret, Lady Cade; Sebastianne, Lady Drake; Grace, Lady John; Thalia, Lady Leopold; my sister Mallory, Lady Gresham. The duchess and dowager duchess, you already know."

"Ladies, a pleasure." Northcote bowed.

"And, of course, my youngest sister, Lady Esme, but then, as we have just ascertained, the two of you have met already."

"Even if he claims not to remember the first time, since he was asleep," Lawrence murmured in a quiet aside to Leo that nonetheless carried the length of the room.

Edward turned his glare on Lawrence.

Lawrence stuck his hands into his pockets. "Sorry, but I'm still reserving judgment."

"Yes, well," Edward continued, "now that we've all been reminded of the reason for Lord Northcote's visit, perhaps we should get on with today's business. Let us give Esme and his lordship a few minutes to converse. Ten ought to suffice, I would think."

"What?" Esme said, watching in sudden alarm as the others began to exit the room, even Mama. Surely they weren't going to leave her alone with Northcote, who stood observing the exodus with sardonic amusement.

"Mayhap I ought to remain?" said Mallory, uncertainly.

Esme reached out a hand to her sister. "Yes, do, please."

"Come along, sweet," Adam told his wife as he slid an arm around her waist. "This will be handled more easily without an audience. And she's safe enough; we'll be just next door." Gresham directed the last comment Northcote's way.

The viscount lifted a brow and smiled.

Mallory hesitated another few seconds, then squeezed Esme's hand, her blue-green eyes filled with compassion. "You'll be fine."

"But—"

"We shall return shortly," Edward told her, his tone resigned and strangely sad.

Before she had time to question—or plead with—any of them further, they had gone, closing the doors behind them. She drew a breath, then slowly turned to face Northcote.

He said nothing for a few moments, his expression enigmatic. "Would you care to be seated or should we do this standing up?"

Do what? she thought, suddenly remembering a few of the more lurid rumors she'd heard whispered about him.

Although they hadn't met during her London Season, she nevertheless had heard his name in passing, always in the context of gentlemen to strictly avoid. The fact that Leo and Lawrence had a town house next to his . . . well, her brothers had wild reputations of their own—most of which she was also supposed to know nothing about. Add to it the fact that her sister and sisters-in-law weren't always careful about closing their doors when they decided to gossip, and she knew just enough to give her pause.

But her family wouldn't have left her alone with him if they had the slightest worry that he might do something untoward. No, her greater concern at the moment was trying not to die of embarrassment, her mind full of memories of the way he'd looked lying naked as he slept beside Cray's lake.

She cringed inside, vividly aware that he must have seen her sketch of him. Was he thinking of that too?

"I'll stand, thank you. But please—" She gestured toward the sofa, silently inviting him to take a seat.

He remained where he was, his hands behind his back.

"I suppose I should begin," she said.

"Should you?" He looked surprised.

She met his gaze, reminded again of how much his eyes looked like those of her hawk—beautifully golden, piercing and predatory.

"Well, yes," she said. "They've all left to spare both of us further embarrassment while I apologize for what I did yesterday. The sketch and all of that, you know."

"Is that why you think I'm here?" He tipped his head, disbelief ringing in his tone. "To receive an apology?"

Her eyebrows drew down. "Of course. Why else would you have called upon me today?"

His eyes narrowed, assessing her as if she was a great puzzlement, one that he had not entirely figured out. "You've really no idea, have you?"

"No idea what?"

"The real reason I was summoned here."

She crossed her arms. "Oh? And what, pray tell, might that be?"

"I am here to do the honorable thing by you. In order to save your reputation, Esme Byron, you and I are to be married."

Chapter 7

Lady Esme's vivid blue eyes widened, her soft pink lips parting on a silent inhalation as she considered his declaration.

"Married?" she repeated. "But that's absurd. We don't even know each other."

"Exactly my own sentiment when I first heard the news," he drawled.

She caught her lower lip between her teeth, drawing his attention there as she gently worked the lush flesh.

Suddenly she freed her lip and waved a dismissive hand. "No, that cannot be. You must have misunderstood."

"I am afraid I misunderstood nothing."

But she was shaking her head before he had even finished speaking. "No, I am certain you are misinformed and that I am here to offer you an apology. My family merely wants to find a way for both of us to remedy the damage caused by this unfortunate situation and put it behind us as swiftly as may be."

Silently, he regarded her, trying to decide whether to be amused by her reaction or merely feel sorry for her obvious naïveté.

"My brothers can all be rather stubborn and hot-tempered at times, I admit," she continued, "blustering and threatening when they really don't mean half of what they're saying. Honestly, they may seem to some like wolves, but in reality they're as kind and gentle as lambs."

Gabriel forced himself not to snort. From what he'd observed, the Byron brothers were all wolf and meant every vicious, bloodthirsty word they'd said. Even his once so-called friends, Lawrence and Leopold, were angry and mistrustful of him despite the fact that he was innocent of any wrongdoing in this case.

Lambs, my eye.

Next she'd be comparing the duke to a harmless bunny rabbit who did nothing all day but sit around nibbling clover and looking for a soft patch of grass on which to sleep. More likely, Clybourne ate rabbits for breakfast—raw and dripping red all over his plate.

Lady Esme folded her hands at her waist, her cheeks the same ethereal pink as her gown. "I am sure words were exchanged when my brothers called on you last night. They can be extremely protective and were greatly upset by the drawing they accidentally saw in my sketchbook. They jumped to the most dreadful conclusions concerning the two of us without giving me any chance to explain. I am genuinely sorry for any inconvenience and alarm you have suffered as a result. I hope you will forgive me, Lord Northcote."

He studied her as a most peculiar sensation passed through him. Sinner that he was, it wasn't often that he found himself in the position of being asked to forgive someone else. Generally, he was the one in need of absolution—although he couldn't remember the last time he'd given enough of a damn to bother seeking it.

"Do not trouble yourself further on my account," he told her. "I assure you I am not worth the effort. Just out of curiosity, though, why did you do it?"

"It?"

"The drawing? Why did you put pencil to paper when you spied me sleeping outdoors au naturel? Most young women would have run away the moment they saw me."

Her cheeks pinkened ever so slightly more, but she continued to meet his gaze, her expression forthright, even a tad defiant. "I am an artist. I draw things that interest and intrigue me. When I happened upon you there at the lake, I felt compelled to capture your likeness."

A slow smile spread over his face. "So I interest and intrigue you, do I?"

"Only from an artistic point of view, nothing more. You might have been a particularly fine ram or perhaps a goat who had strayed from its flock. You were there, so I drew you."

Gabriel's eyebrows arched, uncertain whether she was playing games with him or not. "I can assure you that I am neither a ram nor a goat, although I have been accused over the years of being as randy as one."

This time she flushed.

He bit back a laugh, along with the urge to pull her into his arms and kiss her. He ought to be entitled, after all, considering that he was going to have to marry the outrageous minx, whatever she might currently believe to the contrary.

He was on the verge of reaching for her when a quick tap came at the door. Before either of them could answer, it opened and in walked the duke.

Clybourne looked between Gabriel and Esme, his expression expectant. "Your ten minutes have passed. I thought I'd check to see if matters have been satisfactorily settled between the two of you yet."

"No," Gabriel said.

"Yes," Esme chimed.

The two of them spoke at the same moment, their words overlapping.

Clybourne studied them again. "Well? Which one is it?"

"It is no, since Lady Esme is under the impression that I am here to receive her apology," Gabriel said.

Esme nodded. "Which I have given and which Lord Northcote has most graciously accepted. I know things may be sticky for a time since Miss Waxhaven, in particular, cannot be counted upon to hold her own tongue about what she saw. But, as I was starting to discuss with Lord Northcote, I am sure we can come up with a strategy to deflect the worst of the rumormongering."

Clybourne's gaze shot to Gabriel's. "You didn't explain to her?"

"I tried, but she had other ideas in mind. Perhaps you ought to have taken her aside earlier and discussed how things must be."

The duke glared. "I didn't think I had to; it seemed so obvious. I assumed she knew."

"Apparently not."

Esme scowled as she listened, annoyed at being talked about as if she wasn't even in the room. Still, a lump of dread formed in her chest, one that quite abruptly made her feel rather dim. Had she been the one to misunderstand, rather than Northcote? Surely they didn't mean what she thought they meant? Surely they didn't expect her to . . .

"I am not marrying him, if that's what you're both talking about," she said with dawning horror.

Both men shifted their gazes her way; nothing in either of their expressions proved reassuring.

"There must be some other solution." She rushed on, her mind working frantically. "Nearly everyone in the family has been in one scandalous scrape or another and things have always worked out for the better. I'm sorry that the sketch was revealed; I certainly never meant it to be, but let us not go to extremes. We're Byrons. We'll bluster through. And Lord Northcote seems well up to weathering any storm, are you not, my lord?"

"You are right that I can weather almost anything, Lady Esme, most particularly a scandal." Northcote's voice was deep and surprisingly gentle. "But I believe your family worries that you will not fare nearly so well. Society can be a cruel place to those it believes to have broken the rules, especially young ladies."

His eyes turned a rich gold as they looked into hers. "Innocent though both of us may be of any overt wrong-doing, there are few who will pause long enough to even listen to an explanation. Nor is it likely that any of them will forgive the fact that in your sketch I was naked as the day I was born and that you were brazen enough to draw me that way. People prefer to think the worst and they are sure to believe that something lurid happened between us, however untrue that may be. Sadly as well, my own less than estimable reputation does nothing to alleviate that impression. Quite the contrary, in point of fact."

Esme felt the warmth fade from her cheeks.

Dear God, when he laid it all out like that, no wonder my family was so upset.

Her heart raced like a cornered animal, but one not yet quite ready to accept defeat. She turned a pleading gaze on her brother and moved closer for some semblance of privacy. "But, Ned, you promised. You said the decision to marry would be up to me and that I could choose whomever I liked. You agreed to wait until I meet a man I can love and respect, that nothing would be orchestrated or arranged like it was for you, regardless of how well your marriage to Claire may have turned out in the end."

A look of sorrow darkened Edward's blue eyes, whose color and shape were so like her own. "I'm sorry, Esme. I know what I promised and I fully intended to keep my word. But that was before. You must see that you are ruined and that there is no choice anymore."

"But, Ned—"

He took her hand. "Sweetheart, facts are facts. From the moment that page in your sketchbook landed out in the open where everyone could see, your fate was sealed. Marrying Lord Northcote is the only option. If you do not marry him, I don't believe you will ever marry at all."

She frowned, thoughts racing in desperation. "Maybe I don't care. Would it be so bad if I lived here with you and Claire and the children?"

"Not at all. We would be happy to have you with us forever," Edward said with sincerity. "But I worry that you will come to regret your choice someday, that years from now you will be sorry not to have a home and children of your own."

Edward gave her hand a squeeze, then let go. "There is also the fact that if you refuse this marriage, you will never again be received in Society. Lord Northcote is right that you will be an outcast, and for your sake that is something I cannot abide, not even if it means giving you over to the care of a man of Northcote's questionable stamp."

Esme and Edward both glanced over at Northcote, who stood waiting in polite silence as if he were listening to them discuss the weather rather than debating the positives and negatives of Esme entering into a marriage with him.

She drew in a quick breath, her mind awhirl. "I don't know what to do. I need time to think."

"Unfortunately, time is not something of which we have a great deal," Edward said gravely. "I cannot say for certain what our departing guests will do, but as you already mentioned, the Waxhavens will not hesitate to spread the news. As for Lord Eversley—"

"Eversley? But you needn't worry about him. He likes me, after all."

"He *did* like you. How he feels now, one cannot say for sure. As a gentleman, he may indeed hold his own counsel. On the other hand, I could not help but note that he departed this morning without asking to hear your side of the story."

Esme's fingers curled against her skirts, remembering the shocked look on Lord Eversley's face when he'd caught sight of her sketch of a naked Lord Northcote. Afterward, he'd avoided her gaze, soon excusing himself to retire upstairs. She had not seen him again.

Of course, she'd risen early and left the house, so perhaps he'd wanted to speak with her but hadn't been able to locate her before he departed. Then again, if he'd truly wished to seek her out, he could have asked one of the servants and they would have pointed him in her direction.

But why was she dwelling on Lord Eversley anyway? She'd already decided against him as a prospective beau, despite the not so secret hopes her family may have cherished. And even if she hadn't eliminated him from matrimonial contention, it was too late now to change her mind.

He was gone.

But Lord Northcote was not. Hedonist and self-described libertine though he might be, he was here, apparently ready to do the decent thing and marry her, even if there was little else to recommend him in the eyes of Society.

Her gaze moved to Northcote, a tiny shiver whispering along her spine as she met his steady, inscrutable look. Once again, he reminded her of Aeolus, a keen-thinking predator who would track his prey and cut it down without so much as a glimmer of hesitation or remorse. In a bird, she understood the behavior, which was natural and instinctual.

But in a man . . .

My God, can I possibly go through with this and marry him? He's a stranger and a rather intimidating one at that. Then again, how can I refuse, given the alternative that awaits me?

Because reluctant though she might be, Edward was right; she would regret never marrying, never having a home and children of her own. But did she want them with Lord Northcote, who clearly had little more enthusiasm for this marriage than she did herself?

Hades and hangnails, she thought, *I don't even know his first name!*

"Mayhap Lady Esme and I might have another private minute to talk," Northcote said to Edward. "Then she can give you her final decision."

Edward's brows drew close. "Esme? What do you say? Shall I leave you with the viscount?"

She paused, scrutinizing Northcote for a long moment. Then she nodded. "Yes. He and I should talk again, properly this time."

Edward looked concerned, more so than he had on the first occasion when he'd left them alone. But a few seconds later, he turned toward the door. "We'll all still be just outside."

After shooting a look of warning at Northcote, he exited the room and closed the door behind him.

"So, Lady Esme, here we are again."

Gabriel watched her, wondering what thoughts were flitting through that quick mind of hers. She'd certainly made no effort to conceal the fact that she wasn't the least bit eager to tie the knot with him. He supposed he should be glad to know he wasn't on the verge of marrying a conniving liar who had deliberately led him into a trap. Then again, he hadn't liked the direction the conversation with her brother had taken. Was there another man? A prospective suitor for whom she might harbor tender feelings? If so, that would end immediately. He was no saint, but that didn't mean he would stand idly by and allow himself to be made a cuckold. That had been his father's error; it would never be his.

"What is this about Eversley?" he said, his words easy yet laced with an underlying steel that anyone familiar with him would have known to heed. "Have I a rival of whom I ought to be aware?"

Her eyes rounded slightly at the question. "No. Well, not anymore it would seem. Lord Eversley may have hoped—more than hoped, actually. He danced attendance on me this past spring in London and came here to Braebourne so we could get to know each other better in a more relaxed atmosphere. But amiable though he is, I did not encourage him. Rather the opposite, despite my family's approval of a match between us."

So the Byrons had entertained ideas of a union between Lady Esme and this Eversley fellow, had they? Their disappointment must be even greater than he had imagined.

He narrowed his eyes. "Are you in love with this man and trying to conceal your feelings from me?"

Gabriel waited, studying her for telltale signs of heartache over the would-be lover who had run off and left her in the lurch. If that was the reason for her reluctance to accept Gabriel as a husband, then everything made far more sense; everything, that is, except her decision to draw him by the lake.

Or did she have a naughty streak that she couldn't quite keep tamed and it had gotten out of hand yesterday?

He knew all about naughty streaks.

Esme tipped her head to one side, her eyes a clear, guileless blue. "I'm not trying to conceal anything, Lord Northcote. Lord Eversley was a friend, or so I imagined, and now he is gone."

"You haven't answered my question." Gabriel took a step closer. "Do you love him?"

"No. I love no man." Her fine dark brows drew downward in thought. "Well, except for my brothers and uncles and nephews and several male cousins; them I love a very great deal. I am quite fond of several of the servants as well. But if you are asking if I am romantically inclined toward any particular gentleman, then my answer is 'not at present,' not that it is any of your concern."

He moved another step toward her, putting her within arms' reach. "If I am to be your husband, then who you love is most definitely my concern. As for romantic interests, there will be none, now or in the future, is that understood? I will not tolerate affairs or flirtations with other men from my wife."

A small silence fell.

Something sparked in her gaze. "And may I expect the same of you, should I decide to accept your proposal? Which you have never actually made me, might I add."

His lips twitched, leaving him unable to decide if he should be annoyed or amused. She had a spirit and forthrightness that he could not help but admire.

"You are quite correct, Lady Esme. Everyone would already have us married and yet I have never officially sought your hand. Under the circumstances, I suppose

I thought the exercise moot. However, let us abide by the formalities, by all means. That way there can be no mistaking either of our intentions. Would you prefer that I drop down onto one knee or remain standing?"

"Do whichever you like, Lord Northcote, since I can tell you will follow your own preferences regardless of mine. Before you decide, however, please be so good as to reply to my earlier question."

"And if I choose not to?" he said, making no effort to act as though he didn't remember what she'd asked.

"Then I will take your lack of response as a no and assume that you plan to continue your lascivious ways."

"And what would a little slip of a girl like you know about my lascivious ways?"

"Enough to have heard several rather indecent rumors about you during my time in London. Debutantes have ears, you know, even if they might not always understand everything they hear."

A smile broke across Gabriel's face before he tossed back his head and laughed, his chest moving with a kind of honest good humor the likes of which he had not experienced in a very long time.

It felt good. Almost too good.

Far too quickly, he sobered, gazing into her vibrant eyes, which reminded him of warm, rain-shadowed summer skies. "You are unexpected, Lady Esme, I will give you that. Most unexpected."

"And your answer?"

He said nothing as he considered what she asked. Was he ready to give up his life of loose women and wild debauchery? He'd spent years sampling all that the fairer sex had to offer; would he now be content to confine himself to just a single woman? Admittedly, Esme Byron was exquisite and tempted him as none had for some time. He could already imagine what it would be like to kiss those lush lips and touch that pretty white skin of hers. As for how she would taste, well, he expected she would be every bit as succulent as the finest Château Margaux in his wine cellar.

So was he going to trade away his freedom for a chance to partake of her?

"Very well, if it means that much to you, I shall cleave to you and you alone," he said, his statement coming as a surprise to them both. "But be warned of the promises you make in return. I shall expect you to abide by them all, with no exceptions whatsoever."

She swallowed but did not look away.

Reaching out, he took her hand and lowered himself to one knee. He met her eyes. "Lady Esme Byron, will you do me the honor of becoming my wife?"

Long seconds ticked past before she gave a single jerky nod. "Yes, I will."

Chapter 8

Esme stared, a part of her not quite able to believe that she had just agreed to marry a complete stranger.

Well, not complete, complete, she reminded herself, since she had seen him in his birthday suit, so she at least knew what she was getting there.

Her body tingled to recall.

But as for the man himself, she knew next to nothing about him except for his devilish reputation and sharp-tongued, cynical turn of phrase. For as much as she'd just gone toe-to-toe with him—six bold, fiercely independent older brothers had taught her never to back down from a fight—he still set her ashiver.

Whether in a good way or bad, though, she hadn't yet decided.

And then he was back on both feet, towering above her so that she was viscerally aware exactly how much larger he was; the top of her head came only to his shoulder. Determined to show no vulnerability, she tipped back her head and looked him right in the eye.

What she saw there made her quietly gasp. His gaze was focused on her parted lips, the undisguised hunger she saw there too forceful to mistake, even for a green girl like her.

Slowly, he smiled. "I'll have to give you a ring later. When I came for holiday here in Gloucester, I wasn't expecting that I might become engaged."

"No, nor was I."

His smile widened.

She saw that he had nice, even white teeth; only a single cuspid was slightly out of place. It did not detract from his appeal in the least.

He moved fractionally closer. As he did, she noticed that her hand was still held inside his. She tugged lightly to free herself.

He didn't let go.

"Lord Northcote."

"Lady Esme," he said, the faintest trace of mocking amusement in his voice.

"You may release me now."

"Oh, I will. After we've sealed our bargain."

"What do you mean by that? I've already consented to marry you."

"Indeed, but aren't you the least bit curious to see if we're compatible?"

An electrical charge, rather like one of her brother Drake's experiments, surged through her as Northcote wrapped his free arm around her waist and tugged her to him.

"But we've only just met," she said hurriedly. "I do not even know your full name."

She pressed her palm to his chest to hold him off—his extremely male, remarkably solid chest, which felt every inch as firm as it had looked when she'd drawn him.

"The family name is Landsdowne and I am Gabriel."

"Oh. Like the archangel," she said without thinking.

His eyes crinkled at the corners. "Exactly. Although I've more often been likened to Lucifer, the angel who was cast down to earth. My uncle once suggested I petition Parliament to have my name officially changed so everyone would know me for the devil I am."

Esme gazed up at him, unsure whether or not he was joking. Then before she could consider further, it was too late, his mouth lowering to capture hers.

She'd been kissed only one other time, and that by a cousin the summer after she'd turned sixteen. But comparing that quick, sloppy mashing of lips with the easy, sophisticated heat of Lord Northcote's touch was like comparing a light spring rain to a raging summer storm, complete with wind, claps of thunder and lightning bolts.

He didn't overpower, exploring her mouth with confident thoroughness, as if they had all the time in the world. Gradually, he increased the intensity, his mouth sliding this way and that, angling his head to find the perfect fit. Then, before she had any idea what he truly wanted, he coaxed her lips to part so he could slide his tongue inside. He dipped and sipped, licked and pressed, teasing her in ways that made her thoughts turn to ash. Her fingers opened and closed spasmodically against the fine wool of his coat, and she rocked up onto her toes to get more.

He chuckled low in his throat as he slowly eased away, leaving her momentarily confused and bereft, her body keenly aware of the abrupt loss of pleasure.

His eyes gleamed like gold coins. "You taste every bit as sweet as you look, my dear." He skimmed the back of one finger over her cheek. "Maybe this bargain we're making won't be such a bad one after all."

His words brought her suddenly back to the present, to her surroundings, which, to her mortification, she seemed to have entirely forgotten. He'd had her so enthralled, she suspected the earth could literally have opened up beneath her feet and, so long as he'd kept kissing her, she would never have noticed.

Dear Lord, he really is Lucifer and I'm in over my head.

For a few frantic seconds, she considered taking it all back. It wasn't too late, not yet. No announcement had been made to her family. No promises given that could not be undone. All she needed to do was tell Lord Northcote that she'd changed her mind and would not be marrying him after all. He would understand, would he not? Likely he would even be relieved.

And yet she could not be sure how he might react.

She was used to handling wild, unpredictable creatures, used to gentling, even taming them. But Gabriel Landsdowne was an entirely unknown quantity; a force unto himself, he was unique and without equal in her experience.

If she proceeded with this marriage, what would happen once he had her in his grasp? Would she have any hope of counterbalancing the forcefulness of his personality? Or would he overwhelm her, take what he wanted, then toss away whatever might remain?

She was still weighing that particular quandary when the doors opened again and her brothers walked inside. She nearly went to Edward, nearly hurried into his arms to tell him she would face ruin rather than give herself into the keeping of Gabriel Landsdowne.

But then she glanced up and met Gabriel's eyes, saw the jaded cynicism, the lurking self-derision, as if he knew exactly what she was thinking and expected her to reject him.

And suddenly she could not do it.

Something about him called to her, like one of her wounded beasts, and she could not turn him away. She needed his name and protection in order to keep from being cast out of Society. But strangely, she realized, he just might need her even more.

"Just five minutes more and Mrs. Benson will be finished—won't you, Mrs. Benson?" Mallory told Esme from where she sat in a chair in Esme's bedchamber.

The modiste, who'd made a hurried journey from Bath, mumbled something around a mouthful of straight pins and kept moving at a steady, though efficient pace, as she worked to properly fit the voluminous white gown to Esme's small frame. Her two assistants hovered in the background, ready to lend a hand as needed.

Esme shot her sister a reproachful look, her arms held out at her sides like a living scarecrow. "That's what you said ten minutes ago."

"Good fashion takes time." Mallory gave her an encouraging smile. "Don't you want to look pretty on your wedding day?"

"Not if it means being tortured to death," Esme said. "No offense meant, Mrs. Benson."

"None taken, my lady." The modiste removed a last

pin from her mouth, stuck it into the material, then accepted a pair of scissors from one of her helpers in order to do a little judicious snipping. "If you would just turn half a step to the left, I'll finish this side panel; then you can lower your arms."

"See? You're nearly done." Mallory smiled again.

It was a good thing Esme couldn't reach any handy projectiles or she might have been tempted to lob something in her sister's direction. A hairbrush would have done nicely, or perhaps the rather ugly blue vase on the fireplace mantel that one of her aunts had given her a few years ago and that she'd always wanted an excuse to break.

Usually she and Mallory got along like two green peas in a pod, but ever since her engagement to Northcote, Mallory had behaved in the most alarmingly cheerful manner—one that didn't fool Esme for a moment. It was as if Mallory hoped that by putting on a happy face she could convince herself, and all the rest of the family, that Esme's impending nuptials weren't the hasty marriage of necessity that they were.

She knew Mallory was just trying to make the best of a bad situation, but it was starting to set her teeth on edge.

"Mallory, that will do," Ava Byron murmured in a low voice. "Your sister is under enough strain as it is, and your remarks don't seem to be helping matters."

"What do you mean?" Mallory looked surprised. "I'm only being encouraging, Mama. Fittings have never been Esme's favorite and I'm just trying to buoy her up a bit. Esme knows the last thing I would ever want to do is upset her. Don't you, sweetheart?"

Esme met her sister's expectant gaze and felt instantly contrite. "Of course. Yes."

She mustered a smile.

Mallory smiled back and nodded, reassured. "Despite the gown's age, I think it's going to work out splendidly, do you not all agree?"

Sebastianne, Meg, Thalia and Grace sat in nearby chairs. Two dogs and four cats, who had even less interest in fittings than Esme, lay slumbering around the large room as well.

The ladies gave murmurs of agreement.

"It was a brilliant stroke on Thalia's part to think of using Mama's old wedding gown, seeing as there isn't time to send to London for a new gown," Meg said.

"More practical than brilliant, but thank you for approving the notion." Thalia drew a needle and violet-colored thread through the piece of embroidery on her lap. "It's what comes from years of frugal living and the need to refurbish old clothing so it looks new again."

Sebastianne nodded. "Yes, it's amazing what inventive solutions one can come up with in moments of need."

"You sound like Drake," Mallory teased.

"Or does he sometimes sound like me?" Sebastianne's mouth turned up at the corners. "My husband may be one of the smartest people on the planet, but that doesn't mean he knows everything there is to know. I've taught him a thing or two since we've been married."

"Now, if only you could manage to get him to pay attention at dinner parties rather than drifting off into his own universe," Mallory remarked.

Sebastianne gave a Gallic shrug. "I said *teach*, not perform miracles."

They all laughed. All of them, that is, except Esme and the seamstress.

"You may lower your arms now, my lady," Mrs. Benson said.

"Thank the Lord," Esme murmured under her breath.

"Now, if you will just climb up onto this box so I can do the hem."

With skepticism, Esme eyed the small wooden step that Mrs. Benson's assistant slid into place before her. Sighing inwardly, she did as instructed.

"Oh, you're right about the dress." Grace tilted her head with its glorious crown of red hair, so she could view the gown from a different angle. "By the time Mrs. Benson is finished, no one will realize that the style originally dates back to the 1770s."

Thalia smiled at her new mother-in-law. "It was most generous of you to volunteer your wedding gown. Many women would quail to have their dress altered in such dramatic fashion."

"For a chance to see my darling Esme wear my wedding dress," Ava said, "it is worth any number of alterations. I am simply pleased to find it in such excellent condition after all these years."

All eyes turned for a moment to appreciate the ivory satin sacque dress with its large, heavy skirts, which would once have been draped over a wooden pannier frame, lace-trimmed elbow-length sleeves and a shoulder-to-floor back pleat. Tiny gold flowers were embroidered all over the material, lending the gown a regal cast.

At just that moment, Mrs. Benson cut away several bits of lace from the sleeves and removed a trio of decorative, though now fashionably unnecessary, bows from the stomacher.

Ava drew in a bracing inhalation, clearly fighting not to cringe at the sight of the scissors snip-snipping. "The dress was only gathering dust in its box in the attics. It is exciting to see it out and being given new life again. Besides, it's not as though I'm ever going to have the occasion to need a wedding gown again."

None of them said anything, suddenly reminded of Ava's brief engagement a few years earlier. For those few short weeks, she'd been happier than any of them could remember, as giddily in love as a schoolgirl, when Lord Saxon had abruptly called off the wedding. None of them knew all the details, but rumors had swirled that Saxon had lost his fortune due to bad investments and had gone abroad. Ava hadn't once mentioned his name since then, and everyone in the family was careful not to do so either.

"You oughtn't say that," Grace told her softly. "You never know when the right gentleman might appear and sweep you off your feet."

The dowager duchess smiled wryly. "You are a true romantic, child, and very sweet to think that some gentleman might be interested in a widow of my advanced years."

"You make it sound as if you are in your dotage, which you most clearly are not, Mama," Mallory said. "You're a beautiful, vibrant woman and were you ever to take notice of any of them, I know of several eligible gentlemen who would be delighted to pay you court."

"Indeed," Meg agreed, "just before we left London, Lord Podmoor was rhapsodizing to me about all your exceptional qualities and saying what an utterly charming woman he thinks you."

Ava looked amused. "How very gratifying to hear. Then again, Euphestis Podmoor has always been a fawning toady of the worst variety. I once heard someone say that he would tell a sow dressed up in an orange bonnet how attractive she was and that the color quite flattered her skin."

A flutter of gasps sounded around the room, followed by a couple of snickers.

"Besides," Ava continued, unfazed, "I could never countenance a flirtation with a man named either Euphestis or Podmoor, let alone consider marriage to him. Only imagine the dreadful nicknames that might result. Fezzie, for instance, or worse yet, Poddy."

"There's always Euphie," Thalia chimed with a grin.

"Or what about Po-Po?" Grace rested a dramatic hand against her chest. "Oh, my darling Po-Po, how I long to be held in your arms."

Fresh gales erupted, everyone laughing, even Mrs. Benson and her assistants, who grinned as they continued their work.

Esme joined in as well, her mood lightened as laughter tumbled from her throat like music. Handel and Haydn started barking, the Scotties excited by the noise. Their stubby black tails wagged fast as they leapt up from their dog beds and raced around the room.

Gradually the humor died down but the goodwill remained, her mother, sister and sisters-in-law chatting happily while the modiste completed the final round of adjustments. The dogs quieted too and settled back down to continue their naps.

"Nearly finished, my lady," Mrs. Benson told her in a quiet voice.

Esme smiled her thanks and willed herself to stand still a little while longer. As she did, she let her mind drift back over the hurried preparations that had ensued as a result of her decision to marry Lord Northcote.

Once she'd given her consent, she, Northcote and her family had talked and decided that the wedding should take place as soon as a special license could be procured.

Waiting for the banns to be read by the local vicar was out of the question since the delay would take far too much time and risk further damage to Esme's already tarnished reputation. Better to speed things along and tell any inquisitive souls who might ask that the engagement between Esme and Northcote was one of long standing and that the happy couple was eager to tie the knot.

As for the scandalous drawing that had landed Esme and Northcote in their present fix, it would be explained away as a harmless peccadillo between an affianced couple.

Esme loves to draw and Lord Northcote enjoys swimming—or so the story would go. When Esme quite by accident had come upon him sleeping out of doors, she'd been unable to resist the urge to sketch the man who was soon to be her husband.

It was all completely innocent despite anything you may have heard otherwise.

The hope was that if Northcote and the entire Byron family presented a united front—and Esme and Northcote were wed quickly—the incident would be dismissed as so much taradiddle, to be brushed aside and forgotten as soon as the next lurid scandal arrived to take its place among the *Ton*.

Charged with the task of obtaining a special license, Northcote had left for London two days before. He'd been accompanied by Leo, Lawrence and Cade, who'd gone with him to ensure he didn't sneak off one evening and fail to return.

Yet curiously, Esme wasn't worried that Northcote would run off. She didn't know him well—actually she barely knew him at all—but he struck her as the sort of man who, once he gave his word, stuck to it no matter what.

There was that—and the kiss he'd given her just before he'd left.

"To remind myself what I'm doing this for," he'd murmured as he'd pulled her into his arms in the entry hall under the glowering gazes of her brothers. By the time he'd turned to go, she'd been dazed and breathless, all rational thought scattered under the pleasurable force of his demands.

She trembled now to remember, the memory of his kiss still burning like a passionate whisper against her lips.

No, if anyone might be tempted to flee, it was she. Not because she disliked him, but rather because she feared she might not.

"That's the last of them." Mrs. Benson straightened, then lowered her hands to her sides and took a step back to survey her work.

Esme stood, feeling like a satin-draped pincushion, while her loved ones looked on.

"My girls and I will sew as fast as our fingers allow," the modiste declared with enthusiasm.

Her assistants came forward to help Esme slip out of the gown, much to Esme's great relief.

"Her Grace has been kind enough to provide us with accommodations while we are here altering your dress, Lady Esme," Mrs. Benson continued. "I expect to have enough work completed for you to have a final fitting in three days' time and the completed dress the day after that. As I promised the duchess when she retained my services, your gown will be ready no later than Friday."

Which meant that Saturday would be her wedding day; a day that would irrevocably change her life.

Forever.

Chapter 9

"What do you mean the judge has gone?" Gabriel subjected the Doctors' Commons clerk to his blackest scowl. "I've been kicking my heels around this benighted place for nearly half the day with the assurance that I would be granted a special license, and now you have the nerve to tell me you cannot issue one today."

The functionary, who was clearly used to dealing with irate patrons, met Gabriel's fearsome expression with a stoic look of his own. "I regret to disappoint you, my lord. However, the judge has departed for a prior engagement and will not return until the morrow. I am afraid you will have to come back in the morning."

"Then find me another judge. There must be more than one around here."

"None that have the authority to assist you, I am afraid."

"Give me the direction of the blasted judge I require, then, and I will seek him out myself."

The clerk's mouth tightened as if he'd just eaten a sour pickle. "There is no need to use profanity, nor will such language be tolerated within these walls."

"You call that profanity?" Gabriel scoffed. "If you're going to complain about my language, I can think of far more creative ways to sully your ears. How about bleeding idiotic cocks—"

"What my friend means to say," Lawrence interrupted loudly enough to drown out the remainder of Gabriel's words, "is that Lord Northcote came directly here after a lengthy journey from Gloucestershire and that his lordship would appreciate any assistance you might render in order to help him obtain a special license with the utmost haste."

"We would all appreciate it." Leo gave the clerk a friendly smile and extended a hand. Inside his palm was a folded five-pound note, the amount equivalent to the cost of the license itself. "Any chance we might persuade you to aid us more quickly?"

The clerk eyed the money for a moment, then reached out; the fiver disappeared into the other man's pocket.

"We open tomorrow at nine," he said brusquely. "I suggest you gentlemen present yourselves again at that hour and someone will be happy to help you."

Before Gabriel, Leo or Lawrence could react, the clerk turned and hurried away.

"Hey, you little weasel, get back here!" Leo called after him.

A few patrons and functionaries turned their heads to regard him.

"Did you see? That no-good blighter took my money." Leo started after the clerk but was stopped by the hand his twin laid on his shoulder.

"Let it go," Lawrence told him.

"No, you let *me* go. I plan to throttle him, or better yet, beat him to within an inch of his sorry excuse for a life."

A couple more onlookers, bewigged lawyers included, joined those who were already staring—and listening.

"Much as I agree with you, brother, we have a few too many witnesses at present," Lawrence said.

"Witnesses be damned; that worm deserves his comeuppance." Leo shook off his twin's hold. "We're both lawyers. If he sues, you can act as my counsel."

"It's not a potential lawsuit that concerns me. It's the chance you might end up in Newgate." Lawrence looked at his twin out of a set of virtually identical gold-green eyes. "I spent several hours in gaol this year, if you'll recall, and I don't advise it. Northcote can also attest to the dubious comfort of the place, and that was only a local compter. Newgate's even worse."

Gabriel watched the pair of them, the worst of his own anger dissipating as he listened to their byplay.

"Anyway, if you beat up that duplicitous little ferret, Northcote here will probably never get the damned license, and then where will we be?"

Leo pounded his fist into his palm. "I suppose. But it galls me to let that cretin steal my money. I should lodge a complaint against him."

"Which I would approve were it not for the fact that you were attempting to bribe him. That clerk's a stinking polecat, but he's a smart one, since he knows you aren't going to complain. With this lot it would probably land *you* in trouble rather than him. The judges and most of the advocates here are all so old and outmoded, most of them still think they're living in the eighteenth century."

"Seventeenth, more like," Leo grumbled. "Did you see that old windbag earlier? His grandchildren probably have grandchildren. I wonder if they keep a coffin in reserve in case he drops dead in the middle of the day."

Lawrence grinned slowly, looking like an exact copy of his twin when Leo grinned back.

"Ancient judges and thieving clerks aside," Gabriel said, "I presume we are done here today."

"I'd say so." Lawrence did a quick scan of the room. "Unless one of you has some clever plan for tracking down the judge we need."

"If he frequents gentlemen's clubs and gaming hells I might have some ideas; otherwise, I believe we're out of luck." Gabriel thrust a hand into one pocket.

He knew enough to recognize a lost cause when he saw one. Besides, he was tired and sorely in need of a bath and a change of clothes after two grueling days of almost nonstop travel.

Lord Cade, the fourth member of their party, had

already gone on to Leo and Lawrence's town house more than two hours earlier. The old war injury to his leg had been paining him after the journey, so when it had become clear that the wait for the special license could stretch on for the rest of the afternoon, he'd excused himself and departed. Gabriel wished now he'd done the same, considering today's frustrating outcome.

A bath, a meal and a drink; those would be Gabriel's chief priorities as soon as he got home.

"Gentlemen, shall we give up for now and be on our way?" he asked.

With resignation, Leo and Lawrence agreed—Leo somewhat reluctantly since he was still making noises about going after the "larcenous troll" of a clerk and meting out some well-deserved justice.

The three of them went outside to the waiting coach, which Cade had been good enough to send back, and climbed into the vehicle for the trip to Cavendish Square. Little was said on the ride across town, exhaustion and frustration dampening their usual lively spirits.

Finally, the coach pulled to a stop at the front entrance to Leo and Lawrence's town house. Gabriel was the first to jump down onto the pavement. The twins followed quickly after him.

Gabriel turned to face them. "Well, I wish you both a good evening and shall see you when we reconvene tomorrow to embark on a fresh attempt to secure a special license. Until then, enjoy your night."

"Hold there, Northcote," Leo said. "Where do you think you're going?"

Gabriel arched a brow and sent a significant glance toward the town house next door. "Home, of course. It is where I live."

"Maybe so," Lawrence said, "but we promised to keep an eye on you. Which means you'll have to stay with us tonight."

Gabriel stared. "You cannot be serious."

"If you're worried about the accommodations, don't be," Leo said. "We have plenty of room."

"I am sure your town house is quite comfortably appointed." Gabriel worked to moderate his temper. "However, I have no intention of finding out, since I am not staying there."

Both twins crossed their arms.

"We promised Ned we wouldn't let you out of our sight while we were in Town," Lawrence informed him.

Leo nodded. "Which means you are staying with us whether you like it or not."

Gabriel met their stubborn gazes with an equally stubborn look of his own. "Not a chance. I'm not setting one foot over your threshold."

Leo paused, exchanging a sideways glance with his twin. "Fine. Then we'll stay with you. I'll tell one of the footmen to carry our luggage over. Yours as well, since I presume it's already been taken into our house."

"Your servant most assuredly needs to return my valise. As for you and your baggage, none of it is welcome," Gabriel told them.

The Byron brothers ignored the remark. "What about Cade? Should we have him relocate as well?" Lawrence asked his brother.

Leo shook his head. "Not unless you want to get chewed apart. With his leg hurting and Meg away, we'd be crazy to even suggest it. You know how he gets when she's not around."

"Rather like you without Thalia."

"We *are* still newlyweds, you know," Leo said defensively. "She and I weren't expecting to be apart so soon."

"You weren't expecting to be apart at all."

"No," Leo said sourly. "We weren't."

The twins both turned grim stares on Gabriel.

He stood his ground. "Look, as far as I'm concerned, you can take yourselves back to Gloucestershire immediately, and Lord Cade with you. I've no need of guard dogs, as I informed the duke prior to our departure. I only put up with your presence because it seemed easier than having the lot of you trail after me the entire way."

Gabriel slashed a hand through the air. "I draw the

line, though, at this ridiculous insistence on sharing the same overnight accommodations. I am going to my town house, you are going to yours and we shall meet again come morning."

"I'm afraid we can't allow—," Lawrence began.

"You most definitely can and you will. I've given my word that I will marry your sister and I will honor that promise. If you require more assurance than that, then you are doomed to be disappointed."

Leo and Lawrence assessed him, their expressions alike.

"If you run, we'll hunt you down like vermin." Leo's casual tone was laced with underlying menace.

"And tear you limb from limb when you're caught," Lawrence promised with equally smooth venom.

"If I run," Gabriel said, "you are welcome to give chase. But I swore my oath to your sister and it is her whose trust I will not abuse."

The twins considered him for several seconds more, then nodded, apparently satisfied by what they had heard.

Gabriel was about to turn away when Leo spoke again.

"One more thing, Northcote," Leo said.

"Yes?" Gabriel waited.

"Be careful you don't hurt our Esme."

"If you do, we will kill you." Lawrence spoke matter-of-factly, his calm tone more chilling than a heated threat could ever have been.

Outwardly, Gabriel didn't react. Inside their threat gave him pause, since he was fully aware they meant exactly what they said. Then again, he supposed he should expect no less of men like the Byrons. The twins might appear amiable, even carefree, but as he had reason to know, they were deadly in a fight. When it came to protecting those they loved . . . he wouldn't put any limitations on how far they would go to defend or to avenge. And from what he'd seen, the same could be said for the rest of their family.

Such love and loyalty were traits with which his own family was little acquainted. Nonetheless, they were qualities he admired, envied even.

Gabriel inclined his head. "Duly noted. Now, unless there is something else, I will bid you both a good evening. Please have your servants see to it my luggage is sent 'round."

He turned and took four steps toward his town house.

"Oh, Northcote."

Gabriel stopped and swung around. "What now?" he demanded in exasperation.

Leo chuckled, a familiar twinkle in his eye. "Come by for breakfast. Our cook makes the most excellent blood sausage, fried eggs and cheddar biscuits you've ever eaten. I guarantee you won't regret losing a few minutes' sleep to make the short walk over."

Gabriel had an excellent chef of his own and never lacked for good food. But he realized that the invitation was an olive branch of sorts after all the harsh words that had been spoken between them. Besides being his neighbors, Lords Leo and Lawrence, not to mention Lord Cade, were going to be his brothers-in-law in only a few short days; he supposed it wouldn't go amiss to accept.

"I'll be there," he said. "Seven thirty."

"Make it seven," Lawrence called. "You'll want time to digest."

Three hours later, Gabriel finished the last bite of a delicious sirloin steak with all the accompaniments. A waiter arrived soon after to clear away his empty plate and dust a few stray crumbs from the linen-draped table into a silver crumb catcher.

Earlier at home Gabriel had bathed and changed clothes before heading out to Brooks's club, where he'd ordered a hearty meal and a bottle of rather excellent Burgundy wine.

He'd half expected to find the Byron brothers trailing after him when he'd emerged from his town house a little over an hour after he'd gone inside. But Leo, Lawrence and Cade had apparently decided to trust him to keep his word and had put a halt to their surveillance despite the duke's edict that he not be allowed out of their sight.

After refilling his glass, the nearly bloodred vintage swirling darkly in the candlelight, he leaned back in his chair and contemplated his plans for the rest of the evening.

Normally, when in Town he would have sought out a few of his friends for conversation and cards, or perhaps a visit to the latest gaming hell or to see a play. Later, he would have bid them good-bye and sought out the bed of a willing female to keep him entertained for the rest of the night.

Yet this evening he wasn't in the mood for company. As for finding a convenient bed partner, he'd given his promise not to engage in the pleasures of the flesh with any woman but his fiancée. Technically, he wouldn't be breaking his vow by having sex with another woman since he and Esme Byron weren't married yet. But there was the spirit of the thing to consider, and when put in that light, he owed it to her not to stray.

He snorted quietly to himself and took another swallow of wine. Obviously he'd lost his mind during this latest trip to the country. Not only had he promised to marry a brazen chit he barely knew, but he'd sworn fidelity to her to boot. If his friends only knew, they'd have stared at him in goggle-eyed amazement before breaking into fits of laughter, sure he was having them on.

Really, it wasn't at all like him to be so damned honorable. Usually he was the blackhearted cad, the villain who seduced the girl and left her ruined and weeping while he went merrily on his way. He wasn't the man who did the decent thing.

So why was he this time?

Oh yes, the Byrons and their threats.

And then there was the lovely Lady Esme herself.

He had to admit he was looking forward to getting

her alone again, peeling the fine clothes off her body and introducing her to the addictive world of carnal pleasure. She was innocent; their kiss had shown him that. He hadn't had an innocent in a very long time, not since he'd been a stripling youth himself. For in spite of his dreadful reputation, he wasn't in the habit of despoiling virgins. But he quite liked the idea of despoiling young Esme Byron—more than liked actually, he realized, as his shaft gave a hard, aching pulse of arousal.

Yet was having the chance to tup her—and not just tup her but be the first and only man who would ever do so—really worth the loss of his freedom? He supposed the answer must be yes if the suddenly heated state of his body was anything to go by.

He shifted in his seat and drank more wine, willing his body to calm.

Maybe he should take advantage of the chance to ease his lust tonight. A short drive across Town to a high-class brothel he knew and he would be able to lose himself in the pretty, perfumed arms of a bevy of light-skirts one last time. He was randy enough tonight to entertain a pair, or perhaps even a trio, of eager Cyprians. He could imagine them giggling and jiggling bare breasted, rounded asses exposed as they kissed and fondled and sucked and had carnal knowledge of one another well into the night.

Lady Esme would never know.

But you will know, taunted an annoying inner voice.

He scowled and polished off the last of the Burgundy in his glass.

He was still engaged in a mental battle between his conscience and the libidinous cravings of his body when a man approached who drove all such considerations from his mind.

He forced himself to show no emotion as an older gentleman, with hair so pale a blond as to be nearly white, strode pugnaciously forward and halted roughly a foot from where Gabriel sat. The older man glared, his blue eyes blazing with unconcealed vitriol in his once-handsome, age-lined face.

Rather than acknowledge him or invite him to take a seat, Gabriel raised a hand to signal a nearby waiter.

The man came quickly forward. "Yes, my lord?"

"Another bottle of Burgundy, if you please."

"Of course, your lordship." The servant darted a glance toward the older man. "And shall I bring a second glass for your friend?"

"You shall not," the blond man said in a gruff bark. "This misbegotten whoreson is no friend of mine, and I would as soon drink with a rabid cur as share a glass with him."

Gabriel quirked a sardonic brow. "Just the wine, I believe."

The waiter hurried gratefully away.

"So, to what do I owe the displeasure of your company tonight, Uncle? And here I imagined you off in the country this time of year, gunning down as many birds and scurrying rabbits as you've bullets enough to slaughter."

His uncle Sidney was notorious for indiscriminately hunting wild creatures. He'd been known to kill dozens of birds, small game and deer in a single session, with no consideration for the harm it might inflict on the area's wildlife balance. Worse still, he generally had his cook utilize only a fraction of the kill for himself and his family. He had the remainder thrown away, buried or burned, rather than allowing his staff and tenants, who would have benefited greatly from the fresh meat, to partake.

Gabriel found his uncle callous and repugnant. But then the feelings of dislike between them were mutual, since Sidney Landsdowne had never spared Gabriel so much as a single kind word or thought, not even when he'd been a child.

"Save your bleeding-heart opinions for someone who gives a tuppence worth of a damn." Sidney thrust out his slender jaw and glared down at Gabriel; it wasn't a terribly great distance given Gabriel's height of well over six feet.

The Honourable Sidney Landsdowne was a slightly built, moderately tall man who'd been known for his athleticism in his youth. Yet what he might lack in stature, he more than made up for with his oversized, overbearing personality.

His older brother, Arthur, Gabriel's father, might have held the title of viscount by virtue of birth order, but it had always been Sidney who'd been the real force behind the scenes. He spent years handling all the estate business at Ten Elms that Arthur had been loath to do—which, as it happened, had been quite a lot.

When Arthur died, Sidney had stepped easily into the role of de facto viscount. Although he'd grieved his brother's death, Gabriel knew he'd relished being lord of the manor. His uncle had also become the legal guardian of himself and his older brother, Matthew, who'd been only seven and nine years old at the time of their parents' deaths.

With Matthew far too young to assume his duties as Viscount Northcote, it wouldn't have been surprising for Sidney to have shuffled Matthew aside. But Sidney had doted on his brother's elder son—some might say even more than his own three children—taking Matthew under his wing and teaching him everything he would one day need to know in order to be viscount and manage the great estate of Ten Elms.

Like all the Landsdownes, five generations deep, Matthew had had fair skin, blue eyes and pale blond hair. He'd had the Landsdowne looks too, taking after his father. He'd been Uncle Sidney's golden boy in all conceivable ways.

Then there'd been Gabriel.

Brown haired and tawny eyed, he'd taken after his mother's side of the family, with nothing of the Landsdownes visible in him. He'd been tall and sturdily built as well, and his uncle had taken no pains to conceal his dislike.

From Gabriel's earliest memories, his uncle had despised him, glaring at him as if he were some foul creature, loathsome and unworthy.

For the first seven years of his life, Uncle Sidney had mostly ignored him. After Gabriel's parents died and he came into his uncle's care, he'd thought longingly of those days when he'd been invisible to the older man. Instead of turning his back, Sidney had taken it upon himself to correct Gabriel's so-called willful, despicable nature, disciplining and bullying him unmercifully until Gabriel was old enough to be sent away to school at age twelve.

By the time Gabriel reached his majority, the enmity between him and his uncle had run marrow-deep. Matters had not improved, but rather worsened, when Matthew was killed in a freak accident that had broken his neck and Gabriel became the viscount.

His uncle had been furious when Gabriel's first act as viscount had been to kick his uncle, aunt and assorted cousins off the estate where Sidney had lived and worked for the whole of his life. Sidney had been near incendiary when Gabriel had turned his back on Ten Elms and left it to stand idle and unloved these past ten years. Of course, Sidney never took into account the fact that Gabriel made sure the tenants and farms were looked after, even if his steward did most of the day-to-day management.

Nowadays, Gabriel derived particular satisfaction from tossing his uncle's occasional letters in the fire, the contents of which always redressed him for his lewd, profligate behavior and for failing to take "proper care" of Ten Elms, his birthright and legacy.

"What is it you want, Uncle?" Gabriel said bluntly, already weary of the encounter. "I'd as soon get whatever this is over quickly so I don't have to worry about tainting a perfectly good bottle of wine with your presence."

Uncle Sidney's blue eyes chilled to the temperature of ice. "I'm here because I've heard rumors. Gossip of a most vile and unsavory kind."

"Well, if it's about me, then chances are excellent it's

both vile and unsavory. Wouldn't stand for anything less." Gabriel lounged back in his chair, striking his most indolent pose as he waited to hear more.

"They say you were caught in flagrante with a young woman of good birth," Sidney accused. "That you seduced her to such a debased extent that she actually did a drawing of you in a most indecent state of undress, and out of doors, in the grass, no less."

"My, but how quickly the harpies spread their malicious tidings when they've juicy tattle to share."

"So you don't deny it?" Sidney's eyes wheeled in their sockets. "You admit you despoiled the daughter of a member of the nobility?"

"Why should I say yea or nay, since you wouldn't believe the truth, even if I told it to you?"

"You've got that right, boy." His uncle shook an accusing finger his way. "You're a devil and always have been."

Gabriel covered a yawn with one hand, well used to his uncle's oft-repeated opinions concerning his character—or lack thereof.

"I hear the girl's a Byron, so I suppose her fall from grace should come as no great surprise. That whole family hovers on the constant edge of ruin. Were it not for their wealth and position, they'd have been run out of Society years ago."

"I suppose that's what comes of having one of the most influential dukedoms in the land. Rather helps to insulate one from even the stickiest of social wickets."

Sidney narrowed his eyes. "Well, that girl won't wiggle out from under this peccadillo. Once the tale becomes known at large, she'll never be received anywhere again."

"She will, if she's married," Gabriel said quietly.

"Hah. And who would marry her now?"

"Why, me, of course."

"You!" Sidney's pale eyebrows shot high. "You must be jesting."

"I think not. I asked and the lady has agreed. As

soon as I can procure a special license and return to the country, we will be wed. I'd tell you more, but then you might expect an invitation to the ceremony."

His uncle's expression turned even uglier. "I wouldn't attend your wedding if my very life were at stake."

"In that case, I'll make sure to send you all the particulars. There must be a cliff somewhere in Gloucestershire you could fall off."

Sidney hissed out a breath. "You imagine yourself quite clever, as always, but let me impress a few facts on you. You and your *bride* will receive no welcome from myself, your aunt or any of your cousins. This marriage is a disgrace no matter who her family may be. The situation must indeed be even more desperate than I had imagined for them to marry her off to a vile reprobate like you. You haven't got her with child, have you?"

"No, not that it is any of your business. Contrary to what you believe, Lady Esme is innocent, and I will thank you not to spread your malicious speculation with others of your acquaintance."

"Why? It's what everyone else is thinking already, especially considering her involvement with you. A man who's spent the past ten years making it his goal to tarnish the Northcote title and sully the good name of Landsdowne."

"Surely it's been far, far longer than that, particularly given some of the things father and grandfather got up to."

Sidney's eyes flashed again. "Don't you dare besmirch the memories of those two fine men. You are a shame to their legacy and I wish to God your brother were still alive so I would never have had to see this day."

Gabriel's expression hardened. "I am well aware of your opinion on the subject, sir."

"Then you should also be aware that although I've had little choice but to put up with your lewd, disgusting behavior until now, I will not tolerate any further scandalous acts on your part." Sidney's hands opened and closed at his sides. "Your cousin Gillian is to make her come-out next spring. She is a good child and I'm warning you now that I will not have her chances of making an advantageous marriage sullied by the unholy union between you and the Byron baggage."

A small nerve twitched near Gabriel's left eye. Slowly, he rose to his feet, towering at his full height above his uncle.

Sidney took a step back.

"My fiancée's name is Lady Esme Byron," Gabriel said coldly, "and from this moment forward you will not to refer to her with anything but the utmost respect. Do I make my meaning plain?"

Sidney's thin chest heaved in and out. "I'll refer to her any way I—"

Gabriel closed the space between them and glared down at the man who used to scare and belittle him as no other could. But he wasn't a child now and he was no longer scared.

"You will refer to her as Lady Esme, or Viscountess Northcote once she is my wife. Is that understood?"

Never one to back down, his uncle thrust out his chin. "You can do nothing to stop me from saying whatever I like."

"Perhaps not. But I can see to it that my dear little cousin fails to take next Season. My sister-in-law to be is Lady Gresham. Perhaps you've heard of her? She wields a great deal of influence in certain elite social circles. And lest you forget, one of my other future sisters-in-law is the Duchess of Clybourne. I'm sure the right few words in either of those good lady's ears and poor Gillian will have a sad time in London indeed."

Color slid out of his uncle's cheeks. "You wouldn't."

Gabriel didn't look away. "If you think not, you don't know me as well as I imagined. Something more to consider are the unfortunate circumstances surrounding my parents' deaths. It's an old scandal, but one a few people will surely recall. Once they do, Gillian will have even more trouble on her hands. You wouldn't want that gossip to start early, now, would you?"

Unconcealed hatred burned in Sidney's gaze. Inwardly, Gabriel smiled with satisfaction.

"Oh, and one more thing while we're chatting," Gabriel continued.

"Such as?" his uncle grated from between clenched teeth.

"The Landsdowne jewels. The ones that ought to have come to me on Matthew's death but most conveniently did not. I want them back."

"You've already received everything due you. If you've been careless enough to misplace such priceless heirlooms, it's no one's fault but your own. Or maybe one of your low-minded friends took them when you were too busy fornicating and carousing to notice. I'd expect no less of you."

"Come, Uncle, let's have no more lies between us." Gabriel smiled sardonically. "We both know you are in possession of the jewels and that Aunt Enid has been seen wearing them at various functions over the years. I personally spotted her with great-grandmother's emerald choker around her throat and the diamond tiara on her head at a ball last summer. Until now, I've had no use for jewelry, so I've never pressed for their return. However, in consideration of my upcoming marriage, I require the jewels for my bride."

"Your harlot, you mean."

Gabriel's jaw turned to rock. "What did I say about insults? If you speak ill of her again, I won't be held accountable for my actions."

Sidney's hands fisted as he mumbled something under his breath that might or might not have been an apology.

Gabriel considered forcing the issue and making the old bastard spit out the word "sorry," but he feared such a confrontation might turn physical. Not that he wouldn't have enjoyed giving him the thrashing his uncle had so long deserved, but he was supposed to be helping to restore Lady Esme's reputation, not creating a fresh scandal that might damage it even more.

"I shall expect delivery of the Landsdowne jewels at my town house by midday tomorrow," Gabriel said with quiet authority. "Don't play games and put me to the trouble of coming to retrieve them myself."

While Sidney was stewing over the edict, Gabriel spied the waiter hovering on the far side of the room. "Ah, good. My wine has arrived."

Turning, Gabriel resumed his seat. Only after he was comfortably settled did he look up again. "Good evening to you, Uncle," he said with clear dismissal. "I would send my best to everyone, but I doubt such sentiments would be warmly received."

Sidney's cheeks pinked again, his mouth working as if he wanted to start ranting. Instead he let out a growl, spun on his heels and stormed from the room.

Gabriel waved the waiter forward and let the man fill his glass. Once the man had withdrawn, he drank a long swallow, savoring the notes of aged oak, black currants and cherry in the wine.

Leaning back, he sighed.

The discussion about the Landsdowne jewels reminded him that he was going to need a ring if he planned to wed Esme Byron by week's end. Despite his threats to his uncle, he held out only partial hope that the jewelry would turn up at the appointed time. Assuming it did, he believed there were a few rings in the collection.

But when he thought about giving one to Lady Esme as a wedding band, he wasn't sure he much cared for the notion. As he recalled, they were all heavy and very old-fashioned.

Maybe I should purchase a new ring for her?

Something simple yet elegant.

Yes, that would suit her nicely.

He took another long drink and added a visit to the jewelers to his list of things that needed doing tomorrow.

Until then, however, he might as well enjoy himself at least a bit.

Fleetingly, he considered again whether to go to a

brothel. But the confrontation with his uncle had really rather ruined the mood, and if truth be known, Esme Byron was much too much on his mind—along with the promise he'd sworn to her.

But he hadn't promised not to gamble.

Hooking his fingers around the neck of the wine bottle, he stood and carried it and his glass toward the gaming room.

With any luck, he would win.

Gabriel returned to his town house the following afternoon, a special license in one pocket and a jeweler's box in the other. After a breakfast with the Byron brothers that had proven every bit as delicious as promised, Cade had left on business of his own while Leo and Lawrence had accompanied Gabriel back to Doctors' Commons, where he'd finally been successful in obtaining a marriage license.

He'd refused, however, to let them tag along to purchase a wedding ring for Esme; it was a task he wanted to perform alone. He hoped she would like the ring he'd chosen for her. He'd deliberated far longer over its selection than he'd ever dreamed he might.

With the essential tasks now completed, he and his future brothers-in-law had agreed to depart at first light tomorrow for the return trip to Braebourne. After that would come the wedding, an event on which he was doing his best not to dwell.

Pike, his butler, greeted him solemnly on his entrance, accepting his hat and gloves.

"A messenger arrived with a delivery while you were out, my lord," Pike informed him. "I took the liberty of placing it on the desk in your study."

Gabriel arched an inquiring eyebrow. "What sort of delivery?"

"It is a box. From your uncle, I believe."

He contemplated that surprising bit of information. Was it possible that his threats last night had worked and the old blighter had actually coughed up the family jewels he'd illegally pilfered all those years ago? If so, the old man must be getting soft. Then again, perhaps he actually loved his daughter and was conceding defeat rather than putting her future happiness at risk.

But no, Gabriel thought, rejecting that last idea. The only person Sidney Landsdowne loved was Sidney Landsdowne. It must have been the potential loss of his own reputation that had done the trick. Not even the satisfaction of continuing to thwart Gabriel was worth that kind of risk.

"Thank you, Pike," Gabriel said before walking down the corridor to his study.

On the desk, as promised, sat a long, rectangular wooden box. Gabriel opened it to reveal the Landsdowne jewels, which included three necklaces, two bracelets and several rings that were as ugly and heavy and old-fashioned as he remembered. Compared to the new ring nestled in the black-velvet–lined box inside his pocket, these were monstrosities.

Perhaps he would have them all reset. Yes, that was exactly what he would do. Modernize the pieces into something Esme would like, and something he would like to see her wearing.

Chapter 10

"Oh, just look at you." Ava Byron sighed softly. "You're so lovely, you take my breath."

Esme stood quietly under her mother's regard as Ava surveyed her in all her wedding finery.

As promised, Mrs. Benson had completed the dress on time and it had turned out so well that all of Esme's female relations had exclaimed in delight when they'd gotten their first glimpse of the finished gown.

In order to conform to the current Empire style in fashion, the modiste had raised the waistline so that it fell just beneath Esme's small rounded breasts. Mrs. Benson had embellished further by adding a slender grosgrain ribbon there that matched the exact shade of tiny embroidered golden flowers scattered over the gown's ivory satin. Next she had shortened the sleeves so they were now small puffed caps edged against the arms with more narrow golden ribbon.

As for the long length of material that had once run from shoulder to heel, she'd removed it and used the excess fabric to create a sweeping train that ended in a spectacular half circle that trailed after Esme as she walked. The entire hem was further enlivened by small appliquéd white lace rosettes, whose effect was nothing short of ethereal.

On her feet, Esme wore a soft pair of ivory satin slippers with gold and diamond buckles that had been a last-minute gift from Mallory and Adam. On her hands were long white silk gloves that ended just above her elbows; her lustrous dark hair was pinned and styled in an elaborate upsweep with a few soft curls left to brush in dainty wisps against her forehead and cheeks.

Carefully draped over her head was a waist-length veil of the finest Brussels lace, which had been another present, this one from Claire, and in her hands she held a fragrant bouquet of newly cut, fresh white dahlias, creamy pink hothouse roses and crisp green holly leaves banded together inside a wide white satin ribbon.

However lovely she supposedly looked, she felt rather like an autumn partridge—preened and plumped and ready to be flushed from its covey for the slaughter.

She sent her mother a quick smile, but it was strictly for show. Inside, she was a queasy tangle of nerves. Her hands and feet were as stiff and frozen as icicles despite the warm early-autumn day. As for her heart, it was doing a rapid thump-thump-thump that reminded her of Poppy when the rabbit sensed there might be a predator lurking nearby.

Or in her own case, an enigmatic and keenly dangerous man of whom she knew virtually nothing and yet whom she was very shortly about to marry.

Heaven help me, she thought. She'd been acquainted with Lord Northcote for only the past eleven days, the majority of which had been spent apart while he'd raced off to London and she'd stayed behind to prepare for the wedding.

Truthfully, it all seemed rather like a dream—or perhaps some elaborately bizarre nightmare—with time slipping past in a kind of curious start-stop motion that seemed to fly like a Derby-winning racehorse one minute and creep slower than a garden snail the next.

Last night, for example, she'd felt as if time itself had come to a near standstill, the quiet darkness no comfort as she'd lain sleepless and fretting until very late—or early, depending on one's point of view—and had at long last fallen asleep.

Yet the day before had been the exact opposite. The

minutes had moved like lightning, each moment frenzied and unpredictable, as close friends and family
began descending upon Braebourne—as many as could
be presumed upon to attend the wedding ceremony on
such short notice.

Everyone had agreed beforehand—everyone being
her brothers, brother-in-law, sister, sisters-in-law and
mother, with no consultation or consent from either the
bride or the groom—that a wedding with the full support of Esme's family, however hurried, would be better
than some quiet, secretive affair that people would whisper and speculate about for months to come. A united
front on the Byrons' part would help defuse the scandal
that was already spreading through the *Ton* like a bad
cold. If they were quick enough, and Esme and Northcote were married without delay in the presence of
friends and loved ones, it was hoped the whole "sketchbook incident" would be swept aside and soon forgotten
as nothing more than a bit of amusing nonsense.

So Esme stood now in her bedchamber, preparing
to walk down the wide main staircase to the grand
marbled entry hall. Then it would be out through the
front door to the coach that would drive her the short
way to the Braebourne family chapel, where she'd been
reliably informed her groom was waiting.

She would have preferred to walk rather than ride
but had given up on the idea, knowing how distressed
her mother would be if she got dirt and grass stains all
over her heirloom gown, even if Mama would have considered it in bad taste to outwardly show that distress.

"Ned is ready whenever you are, Esme." Mallory
came into the room, looking radiant in a gown of sap-
phire silk that enhanced the blue in her blue-green eyes.

Despite her earlier annoyance with her older sister,
Esme had asked Mallory to be her matron of honor, to
which Mallory had given an enthusiastic yes. After all,
who else would Esme want at her side but her one and
only sister on this the most important and nerve-
shattering day of her life?

As for walking her down the aisle, Edward would naturally do the honors.

She'd been an infant barely born when their father had died nineteen years ago, so she had no memories of him. She knew Robert Byron, ninth Duke of Clybourne, only through the family stories she'd heard and the grand painting of him by Reynolds that hung in a place of prominence in the Braebourne picture gallery. Ned was her eldest brother, but he'd also served as a kind of surrogate father at important turning points in her life. So he would act today as he took on the duty of giving her away.

Her stomach gave an uncomfortable flip.

She supposed she ought to have eaten more this morning than a single bite of unbuttered toast and a sip of tea, but it was all she'd been able to choke down. She hadn't eaten particularly well last night either, not with all the guests chattering away around her, and Northcote seated across the long table, a speculative look in his eyes as he gazed at her.

Northcote, Cade and the twins had arrived not long after noon yesterday to the barely disguised relief of her mother and sisters-in-law. Edward was more stoic, as Edward generally was, and had done nothing but ask if their trip from London had been eventful; then he'd disappeared into his study.

With so many people in the house, Esme hadn't had an opportunity to exchange more than a few polite words with her betrothed. After dinner there still had been no chance to speak to him, since her brothers, Adam and his friend Mr. Cray—who had returned home unexpectedly and been staggered to discover that Northcote and Esme were to be wed—had taken him out to do whatever it was men did the night before a wedding.

"Most everyone has already gone on ahead to the chapel," Mallory said, breaking into Esme's reverie. "Mama, you probably ought to leave now so you can be seated before the ceremony begins. Claire and Grace are waiting outside in a coach to accompany you. Not to worry—I'll look after our Esme. And Thalia has been gracious enough to stay behind to help with anything last-minute, so she'll ride over with us."

It was only then that Esme noticed the newest of her sisters-in-law standing quietly nearby. She looked beautiful in a gown the orange-gold color of autumn leaves, but then she always looked beautiful.

Ava frowned slightly but finally gave a nod. "Yes, you're right. I ought to be off." She walked forward and bent to press a quick kiss against Esme's cool cheek. "You're going to do splendidly. I love you."

"I love you too, Mama."

And then her mother was gone, leaving her alone with Mallory and Thalia.

She looked at them.

They looked back.

But when she tried to muster another false smile, it just wouldn't come. Suddenly she started to tremble.

"For heaven's sake, sit down before you collapse." Mallory hurried forward and took hold of her elbow to steer her toward the nearest chair.

"But my gown—"

"Your gown will survive; it's you I'm worried about. You aren't going to faint, are you?"

"No. At least I don't think I am."

Mallory made sure Esme was settled in the chair before handing Esme's bridal bouquet to Thalia for safekeeping.

Thalia set it carefully aside on a nearby table.

"I have smelling salts," Mallory remarked, "but perhaps something stronger is in order. Thalia, did you bring it?"

"Yes. I have it right here." Thalia withdrew a slim silver flask from inside her reticule and handed it to Mallory.

"What's that?" Esme eyed the container with suspicion.

"Your saving grace. Think of it as medicine." Mallory unscrewed the cap. "Here. Drink."

The scent of alcohol perfumed the air. "Is that brandy?"

"No, Scotch whiskey," Thalia said. "At least that's what I think Leo put in it last time he refilled the flask. I borrowed it from him this morning. He only carries it when he travels, so he won't even realize it's gone."

"Oh, I don't know—" Esme's stomach churned again, lurching with a slightly sickening tilt this time.

"Drink." Mallory curved Esme's fingers around the metal container. "Or do you want to pass out halfway down the aisle and make a complete cake of yourself at your own wedding?"

Everyone said that Mallory was as sweet as sugar— and usually she was—but there were times when she could be more intimidating than Lord Wellington shouting orders at his troops during the heat of battle.

This was one of those times.

"What if I get foxed?"

"You won't. But even if you do, who will care?" Mallory nudged Esme's flask hand closer to her mouth. "Under any other circumstances, I'd feed you hot tea and Cook's best beefsteak, but in your present state, you'd never keep it down. This is the next best thing. Dutch courage, or so I've heard it called, of which, dear one, you are sorely in need at the moment."

Mallory was right about that. Esme needed all the courage she could muster if she was going to make it through the next few hours. And after that, when she was irrevocably bound in marriage to Lord Northcote and none of her family was around to act as protection?

She gulped, her hands shaking even worse. Well, she would simply have to deal with that when the time came. Maybe she'd keep Leo's flask just in case. Without giving herself another second to consider, she raised the flask to her lips and took a big swallow.

Fire exploded in her throat and she gasped for breath, coughing furiously. Her lungs strained for air and for a moment she wondered if she'd done herself in.

But then Mallory patted her on the back while

Thalia offered her a glass of water. She caught her breath long enough to take a few sips, which eased some of the sting.

"Are you all right?" Mallory continued rubbing her back in soothing circles. "Why on earth did you take such a huge drink?"

"Because you told me to, goose."

Thalia pressed a handkerchief into Esme's hands, which she took gratefully, using it to wipe her mouth and tearing eyes.

"I did not," her sister said. "I thought you would have the sense to sip it."

Esme patted her face, aware of the sudden flush in her cheeks.

"Better?" Mallory surveyed her. "You look better. Your color's back."

And Esme realized she felt better too, now that the choking and burning had stopped. Warmth spread through her, chasing away the earlier cold, which had seemed as if lodged deep in the core of her bones. The shaking was gone as well, her fingers steady against the silver flask she still held.

She nodded. "Yes."

Mallory and Thalia both smiled.

"Have another," Mallory encouraged. "Just a sip this time."

Carefully, Esme followed her sister's suggestion, letting more of the calming warmth slide through her.

Then she took another.

She was raising the flask for one more when Mallory stopped her with a touch.

"That's enough, I think." Gently, her sister took the whiskey away.

"Are you sure? What if it wears off before I get through the ceremony?"

"It won't," Mallory reassured her with a grin. "Now, up you go. Can you stand?"

"Of course I can stand," Esme declared.

But when she did, she swayed slightly and reached

out to steady herself by quickly gripping Mallory's shoulder.

Thalia and Mallory exchanged looks again.

"Maybe this wasn't such a good idea, after all," Mallory murmured. "I should have known she wouldn't be able to hold her liquor."

Thalia laughed. "Well, it's too late now." Reaching out, she took Esme's other arm. "Come along, Esme. Your groom awaits."

But at the reminder, Esme stopped, some of the pleasant warmth disappearing. She looked at her sister, then at her sister-in-law. "I know everyone is waiting," she whispered, "but what if I can't go through with it?"

The other women stopped smiling, their eyes suddenly serious.

"It's only natural for you to have second thoughts considering the circumstances," Mallory said gently. "Is it because he frightens you? It's all right to be honest."

Esme looked at her sister with surprise. "No, of course he doesn't *frighten* me. Why would he?"

Mallory and Thalia exchanged another set of looks.

"Well, despite his undeniable physical appeal, he can be rather formidable," Mallory said. "So, is it because you dislike him, then?"

"No, I *do* like him," Esme said. "At least I think I do. I've hardly been around him enough to decide. But I certainly liked it both times he kissed me."

"*Both times?*" Mallory gave her a speculative look. "I heard about the thorough bussing Northcote gave you in the hallway before he left for London. But when was this other time?"

"The day he came here to propose," Esme said. "It was in the drawing room. He kissed me to . . . seal our bargain."

Thalia studied her. "And you enjoyed it?"

Esme's cheeks grew warmer. "Yes. Shouldn't I have?"

Mallory and Thalia laughed again, each woman looking subtly relieved.

"Of course you should," Mallory told her.

"Especially with a rakehell like Northcote," Thalia added before she turned serious again. "Esme, if I, for even so much as a second, thought you had anything real to fear from Lord Northcote, I would stop this wedding immediately, no matter how socially expedient it is for the two of you to wed. And scandal or no scandal, your family wouldn't be letting Lord Northcote marry you if they weren't certain you would be safe and well cared for as his wife. I even discussed it with Leo when this whole thing began."

"You did?"

Thalia nodded. "I just wanted to be sure of Northcote, since we have met only a handful of times, and then only in passing. But Leo assures me that in all the essentials Northcote is . . . well, perhaps not a *good* man in the conventional sense, but he is a fair one and one who in no way abuses women, children and other creatures weaker than himself. Dreadful as his reputation may be, and there's no denying that it is, you've nothing to fear from him in that regard."

"As I said already, I am not afraid of him." Esme took Thalia's hand. "But you are so kind to be concerned for me."

Thalia gave her hand a quick squeeze. "Of course. We are sisters now."

Esme's heart warmed. She didn't know all the details, but she was aware of a small bit of Thalia's own history and the brutal nature of her first husband, so she understood why Thalia was expressing such concerns.

But those were not her concerns. She wasn't worried that Gabriel Landsdowne would mistreat her; such an idea had never even entered her mind. No, she was afraid instead that he might make her unhappy and in return that she might do the same to him. Marriage was for life, regardless of the happiness it might or might not bestow. It was that knowledge that had her standing paralyzed with sudden angst and indecision.

But she'd promised them all.

She'd promised him.

How could she turn her back on him now? Leave him to suffer the ridicule of his peers when he was doing what many men would never have agreed to do in order to salvage her reputation?

As she had on the day she'd consented to be his wife, she knew again what she must do.

"I'm only being foolish," she said, forcing another fake smile and wishing she could have Leo's flask back for another drink or two. "It's just cold feet. Every bride gets them, right?"

Even the ones who don't consider their grooms virtual strangers.

"You're sure?" Mallory ventured. "Adam and I would be more than happy to have you come live with us. The children would adore it."

"You and Adam would be sick of me in a month's time, two at the most, and you know it," Esme said. "But you're a dear to offer." Esme brushed a hand over the full skirt of her ivory bridal gown, relieved to see that her hands hadn't started shaking again. "No, I'm ready. Let us go put an end to Ned's waiting. He must be wondering what has become of us all."

"Knowing our brother, he probably nipped off to the library for a book to pass the time."

"Or gathered up some estate papers to review."

Esme smiled in agreement, then walked across to where Thalia had laid her bridal bouquet aside earlier and picked it up.

Taking a deep breath, she let her sisters lead the way from the room.

Chapter 11

Gabriel resisted the urge to fidget with his watch fob as he waited at the altar. Lawrence Byron, his best man, stood at his side dressed in the same formal black and white as himself. He might have asked Cray to do the honors instead, since they had known each other for more than a decade. The two of them had met under rather unusual circumstances one evening in London when Cray had been set upon by thieves and Gabriel had charged in to help. They'd been good friends ever since. But until yesterday Gabriel had had no idea that Cray had decided to return home unexpectedly from his hunting trip in Scotland.

As it was, Cray and a pair of Cray's hunting cronies, with whom Gabriel was barely acquainted, were the only ones seated on the groom's side of the chapel. The absence of Gabriel's family was notable. Then again, he'd rather have no one there at all than endure the misery of putting up with his uncle, aunt and pack of irritating cousins. Had she still been living, he would have asked his maternal grandmother to attend. She was the last person on earth who'd loved him without condition or reserve. But Nanna had passed on when he'd still been a boy.

Then there was Matthew. Gabriel had loved his brother and still grieved his untimely death, but their relationship had never been an easy one. As the heir, Matthew had always received special treatment, while Gabriel, the spare, had often been shunted aside and left with the unwanted seconds. Their uncle's marked partiality for

Matthew after their parents' deaths had driven a further wedge between them, one they'd never had time to repair as adults. Still, he thought that Matthew would have gladly stood by his side today as best man.

Shaking off the maudlin thoughts, he glanced again toward the chapel's open oak double doors and the empty drive beyond.

She was late—his bride. No doubt having second thoughts.

I wonder if she's going to desert me at the altar.

He scowled, not entirely sure how he felt about the idea of her reneging at the eleventh hour. Though if she did, he supposed it might be a lucky escape for them both.

From the domed ceiling high above, painted angels looked down from their perch amid cerulean skies and fluffy white clouds. Since entering the chapel, he'd done his best to ignore them, feeling curiously sacrilegious beneath their gazes.

He was just about to give in and check the time on his watch when the sound of gravel crunching under coach wheels came from outside the chapel's main door. Murmurs rippled through the small crowd gathered to attend the ceremony.

The bride was here at last.

He caught a glimpse of ivory satin skirts as Esme stopped just out of his line of sight. He craned his neck for a better view but still managed no more than a frustrating peek. The sounds of low, indistinguishable conversation drifted inside while feminine hands moved in and out of view as her sister and sister-in-law helped straighten her gown and veil.

Then a hush fell.

It was broken seconds later by Lady Leopold as she darted inside. A few kindhearted chuckles erupted as she hurried to take the seat saved for her by her husband, who grinned hugely as she slid in next to him.

Everyone turned their heads to watch the bride's sister, Mallory—the matron of honor—start gracefully down the aisle, leading the way for the bride.

But Gabriel spared her hardly a glance. His eyes were all for Esme, who stood framed beneath the arched doorway, one small gloved hand resting securely atop her brother Edward's arm.

His heart thumped, warmth rushing through his veins with an almost electric pulse. He knew he was staring and he didn't care, a peculiar craving rising within him that was almost primitive in nature.

She's mine, he thought, any lingering doubts about their union falling away.

Silently, he willed her to look at him, to meet his eyes and acknowledge him as the man who would shortly claim her for his own. But her gaze remained lowered behind the sheer lace of her veil, dark eyelashes fanned like downy half circles against her creamy cheeks.

Finally, she reached the altar and stopped, but still she did not lift her gaze to his. Clybourne squeezed her hand and murmured something into her ear that Gabriel couldn't quite catch. She nodded and whispered something back as Gabriel stepped up to take his place at her side.

The vicar, dressed in crisp vestments that smelled of starch, opened the Bible in his hands and smiled at everyone gathered. He cleared his throat. "Dearly beloved, we are gathered together here in the sight of God, and in the face of this congregation, to join together this Man and this Woman in holy Matrimony . . ."

And so the ceremony began.

Esme kept her eyes on her slippers. In spite of the whiskey with which Mallory and Thalia had plied her, she feared that if she looked at Northcote she'd never make it through the next few minutes.

The traditional ceremony continued, the vicar's words swirling like smoke inside her brain, leaving her fuzzy and strangely unfocused.

Or maybe that was the whiskey again. Perhaps she shouldn't have drunk quite so much back at the house. Then before she had any warning whatsoever, she heard her name spoken. Then spoken again. She scowled and forced herself to concentrate, becoming aware that the vicar wanted her to say something. To her relief, she realized that the only response required of her was a simple, "I will."

Despite not being one hundred percent certain what she was actually agreeing to, she said the words anyway. A ripple of quiet relief traveled through those gathered in the surrounding pews.

Then Edward was speaking, answering some other barely heard question of the vicar's.

Suddenly her hand was no longer on her brother's arm. Instead he was placing it inside Northcote's large grip, then stepping away. What was he doing, leaving her alone up here at the altar?

But as she stood there, she became aware of the comforting warmth of Northcote's hand and how the heat of his touch drove the last of the lingering chill from her fingers. She trembled, aware of how strong and sure his touch was, how very male and yet how very unlike her brother's it was.

For after all, tingles never chased through her like quicksilver when she touched Edward, or any of her other brothers come to that.

And her breath never grew oddly shallow in their presence, as if she'd suffered a sudden fall and couldn't quite manage to get her lungs working right again.

And she certainly did not flush, cheeks and neck bursting with heat and telltale color.

Suddenly she was glad for the veil that partially hid her from his gaze—a gaze whose force continued to compel her to look up, to obey his will and do exactly as he wished.

He began reciting his vows, his voice rich and melodic, almost hypnotic, as he spoke words of love and made promises of lifelong devotion that she knew he could not possibly mean.

And yet he said the words, agreed to that final step, which would forever after bind his fate to hers.

Then her turn arrived, only this time she had to say more than two simple words.

"Repeat after me," the vicar told her solemnly.

Concentrating, she took a fortifying breath and began the recitation, promising things she also did not feel but would try her utmost to honor.

She finished saying her vows, grateful that she verbally stumbled only a single time when she had to swear to obey him—which she most certainly would *not* be doing.

Then Lawrence, whose presence she had nearly forgotten about, handed Gabriel the ring.

Gabriel took her hand again and she saw her wedding band for the first time. What with everything having been so rushed, he never had given her an engagement ring, but this one more than made up for its lack. The band was delicate and made of warm rose gold. The stone itself was stunning, a large round diamond surrounded by a circlet of smaller diamonds that glittered like stars. It was as if he'd managed to reach into the sky and pull down a constellation on a recent starry night.

And that's when she finally looked up at him, meeting his eyes as he slid the ring on her finger and recited the last of the vows that made her his wife.

His eyes were blazing, as gold as coins and as penetrating as a midday sun. She shivered again, but this time from a deep, inner warmth that was shocking in its intensity. She pressed her toes hard against the soles of her slippers and fought to hold herself steady.

But she needn't have worried, she realized. Gabriel was holding her tight; he would not let her fall.

Once the vicar had concluded his prayers and finally pronounced Gabriel and Esme "man and wife," Gabriel lifted her veil away from her face, folding it back so he could see her clearly without any interference.

She looked beautiful and very innocent, her vibrant blue eyes wide with what he guessed was shock. Her cheeks were stained pink with more of the nerves she hadn't been able to hide during the ceremony. As for her rosy mouth, her lips were slightly parted and ripe for kissing.

Mine, he thought primitively. *Mine to touch and taste and claim at my leisure.*

He nearly laughed aloud at the realization that she was his wife now, and that beginning today, no one could keep her from him. In his mind's eye, he gathered her to him and pulled her high inside his arms, coaxing her legs to wrap around his waist as he kissed her breathless.

But he supposed he would have to wait until later for such love play, seeing that they were standing on the wedding altar in front of her family. Besides, such antics might cause the vicar to faint dead on the spot.

He smiled down at her and bent to take a quick kiss, regardless of how unfashionable such behavior might be considered among the upper classes, but stopped short when he caught a surprisingly familiar scent on her breath.

"Have you been drinking?" he murmured low, so that only she could hear.

She blinked up at him, rather like a baby owlet who'd fallen out of its nest. "No," she said, then frowned at her own lie. "Well, maybe just a little. I needed something to steady my nerves."

"So you drank your weight in brandy?"

"It was whiskey and I only had a couple of sips."

A slow grin spread over his mouth; then he chuckled, slid an arm around her waist and tucked her against his side.

Turning them both around, he steered her along the aisle, ignoring the quizzical looks of her family and friends, who were clearly wondering what they'd been whispering about.

Just beyond the wide double doors, he stopped and angled his head toward hers to press a quick, firm kiss against her lips. She tasted sweet with the promise of unexplored passion and a delicious hint of the whiskey she'd drunk.

"We'll continue this later," he said, "but that will have to do for now."

Then they were surrounded as the guests flooded from the church to wish them well.

Chapter 12

It might be her wedding day, but Esme was ready for it to be over.

She'd been on her feet for hours and hours—first at the ceremony and then at the reception. Her only real respite had been during the reception nuncheon, where the bridal party and all of the guests had gathered to partake of the sumptuous meal prepared by Cook and the kitchen staff.

Cook had even found the time to create a lavish four-tiered wedding cake with a traditional fruitcake topper that would be saved for her and her new spouse to share in celebration of their first wedding anniversary.

At the moment, Esme couldn't even imagine such a possibility; she could barely believe she was married at all. And yet she had the grand diamond ring on her left hand to prove it and Lord Northcote at her side—large and real and undeniably male.

He hadn't kissed her again as he had outside the chapel right after the ceremony. But brief as their embrace had been, she could still remember the sensation of his lips pressed to hers along with the dizzying pleasure of his touch. Or maybe that had just been the whiskey making itself known, her head hazy from alcohol and nerves rather than from the man who was now her husband.

She shot Northcote a sideways glance where he stood talking with her cousin India and India's husband, Quentin, Duke of Weybridge. Quentin, whom Esme counted

as one of her favorite relations, had once boasted a reputation as bad as—possibly even worse than—that of
Northcote himself, although she wasn't supposed to know
anything about such matters, of course. Given his history,
she supposed she shouldn't be surprised to discover that
Quentin and Northcote were old acquaintances. Apparently, they had even "cut a swath" through London together in years past when Northcote had still been what
Quentin good-naturedly called a "young puppy."

But despite the fact that Quentin was now a loyal, loving husband and father of three who had long since given
up his profligate ways, Esme held out little hope that
Northcote would do the same, regardless of his promise
to remain faithful to her. For unlike India and Cousin
Quentin, she and Northcote had not married for love.

Swallowing a tired sigh, she shuffled her slippered
feet beneath her long skirts and gazed longingly toward
the doorway, wishing she could slip off to her room.

At least there'd been no mention of her leaving Braebourne tonight with her new husband. What with all
the hurry for them to wed, plans for a honeymoon had
been overlooked. Given the circumstances of her marriage, though, going off on a honeymoon seemed rather
ridiculous. After all, honeymoons were for couples in
love like Leo and Thalia, whom she'd caught more than
once gazing at each in the most heatedly intimate way
when they didn't think they were being observed.

What must it be like to be loved, to be wanted, with
that kind of intensity?

Suddenly, she looked up and got a jolt like she'd been
poked with a hot brand when she saw Northcote staring
at her.

She spun around and forced herself to listen more
attentively to one of her neighbors, who was discussing the latest fashion plates she'd viewed in *La Belle
Assemblée*.

Without warning, a powerful masculine arm, one
that could only belong to Northcote, snaked around her
waist and pulled her near. "Every pardon, my dear. I

fear I have been neglecting you. I hope you will for-give me."

Leaning down, he brushed a kiss against her cheek; it burned like fire.

Her neighbor fell silent and stared with a kind of intrigued awe at Northcote. It was as if she'd never quite seen his like before, despite her acquaintance with the Byron men, who all had reputations of their own.

Esme felt rather tongue-tied herself, though not for anywhere near the same reason. "Of course," she managed.

"Excuse me, madam," he said to the other woman, "but I'm afraid I'm going to steal my bride. You don't mind, do you?"

From the corner of her eye, Esme saw him flash the woman a smile.

Her neighbor, the local squire's wife, who was at least fifteen years his senior and likely outweighed him by a stone, let out the most unlikely giggle and shook her head. "No, my lord. You are the groom, after all. Pray steal away."

"How forbearing. Your graciousness is noted and appreciated."

The woman giggled again like some schoolgirl, watching dazedly as Northcote led Esme away.

"You're completely shameless—do you know that?" Esme said once they were out of her neighbor's hearing.

He stopped and turned to face her. "Frequently, but how so on this occasion? Or are you referring to my tearing you away from your companion? You looked glassy-eyed with boredom. I presumed I was doing you a favor."

She tipped her head back to look at him and realized he really didn't know what she was talking about, though surely he must be aware of the almost hypnotic effect he had on women. Then again, perhaps he was so used to getting his way with members of the fairer sex, he no longer noted their dramatic reactions but instead took them for granted.

For a moment, she considered explaining, then decided it wasn't worth the effort. "Never mind. What is it you want?"

He arched a dark brow. "The company of my bride, of course. I thought we might share a dance."

"Thank you, but I would rather not. I am tired."

He studied her. "Hmm, it has been rather a long day, even for a girl of your obvious youth and energy."

"My *youth*," she repeated with a mocking edge, "has naught to do with it. I did not sleep well last night."

"Did you not?" Reaching out, he skimmed a finger along her cheek, leaving another trail of fire in its wake. "Mayhap you should have drunk that whiskey last night rather than today before the ceremony. No doubt it's left you sleepy. Ah well, you can lie abed late tomorrow."

She fought the blush that rose to her cheeks, color that seemed to delight him as a slow smile spread over his mouth.

"Maybe I shall. If you will forgive me, Lord Northcote, I wish to withdraw for the evening."

"Yes, go change your attire. I shall await you down here; then we'll be off."

"Off where?"

"Why, to Cray House, of course. Did no one tell you we are to spend the night there?"

"No, they did not," she said, alarm making her voice go higher.

"Well, we are. The arrangements have all been made. Cray and his cronies have very kindly agreed to take lodgings elsewhere for the night. His wedding gift to us."

Suddenly she didn't like Mr. Cray nearly as much as she had always done. She'd never realized what a high-handed busybody he could be.

"That is most considerate of Mr. Cray." She worked to modulate her tone. "However, he and his friends need not discompose themselves. I am far too tired to relocate tonight and have no wish to do so. I am going to my room and shall see you in the morning. Good night."

Northcote scowled, all hint of a smile vanishing from his face. "You will see me this evening as well. In case it slipped your mind, this happens to be our wedding night."

She glanced around to make sure no one was listening, then leaned closer, her voice dropping to a whisper. "I know very well what night this is. I also know that we are scarcely acquainted with one another and that this marriage is one of necessity rather than personal inclination on both of our parts. Sleep well, Lord Northcote. We shall continue furthering our acquaintance over breakfast."

His eyes took on a look of amused forbearance. "Trying to put me off, are you? I think not. We shall continue furthering our acquaintance tonight in bed, *Lady Northcote*. I can think of no faster or better way for us to get to know each other than lying naked together between a set of sheets."

She gasped, her pulse beating erratically at the images he'd just put in her mind.

He gave her an implacable look. "Now, go change out of that dress and have your overnight things brought downstairs so we can leave within the hour."

She gulped but held her ground, suddenly trembling at her own daring. "No. I am not going to Cray House with you."

A brief silence descended.

"Very well," he said, his voice reasonable.

Too reasonable.

"Truthfully, it makes no matter to me where we consummate this union, so long as we consummate it," he said. "I'll come up with you now, then, and help you out of the gown myself."

He wrapped his arm around her waist.

She shrugged out of his hold. "You will not!"

Several people looked around at her outburst, a couple of them her brothers, who scowled in their direction.

"Don't make a scene, darling," Northcote murmured for her ears alone. "Not at your own wedding."

"I am not your darling."

"No, you are my wife. Or have you forgotten the vows you took today? Among them was your promise to obey me."

"No, it wasn't. I crossed my fingers during that part, so it didn't count."

His lips twitched as if he was suddenly of a mind to laugh.

"Come along, Esme." He took hold of her elbow and steered her toward the door.

"Gabriel, no." She trotted along at his side.

"Ah, so you've remembered my given name, have you?"

They moved out into the hallway, his long strides eating up the distance as he propelled her along the elegant Aubusson hall runner, past niches containing priceless vases full of fresh flowers and magnificent sculptures and paintings done by masters—old and new.

"Please, Gabriel. Not tonight."

He stopped, turning toward her without releasing his hold. "And why not, my dear? Surely I am not so terrible as all that?"

"No, you . . . are not terrible. But still you are a stranger, or very nearly one. I would just like to know you better before we . . . before we are intimate in the way of a husband and wife."

He studied her, a measure of the tension easing from his shoulders. "I confess I forget sometimes just how little you know of such matters. I am not used to dealing with innocents. Rather the opposite, in point of fact."

"Then can we not postpone tonight for a little while?" she said, clutching at the straws he'd just offered her. "Surely I am not the only one of us who is tired. You and my brothers were on the road to London and back with hardly any chance of respite in between. What is one more night when we have an entire lifetime ahead of us?"

"When you put it that way, I suppose it would be churlish of me to insist on exercising my husbandly rights this evening."

She let out a sigh of relief, which drew a look of ironic amusement from him.

"You needn't look so happy about it, you know," he said.

She wiped the smile off her face. "Of course not, and you are most forbearing to agree. Thank you, Lord Northcote. I mean, Gabriel."

"Hmmph. I fear I have just been insulted." Without warning, he took her chin between his thumb and forefinger and bent closer. "I could take it back, you know. I feel quite confident I could have you stripped bare and moaning with pleasure in a matter of minutes, probably even less."

She quivered at his words, afraid he might be right.

"But never let it be said that Gabriel Landsdowne forced himself on a woman, especially one who is his new bride." He skimmed his thumb over her lips, his skin surprisingly rough for a gentleman who supposedly did no manual labor. "You may have your reprieve tonight. But just for tonight. My patience only goes so deep."

"Yes, Gabriel." She smiled, her heart thumping in her breast.

"Be careful, little girl," he warned. "Or else the big, bad wolf might just change his mind and decide to eat you, after all."

Her eyes got wide and he laughed, then held out his arm. "Come, I will escort you to your room."

She nodded and laid her hand on his sleeve.

Before they had so much as turned in that direction, a set of forceful footsteps sounded behind them.

"Esme. Northcote." It was Edward, wearing his most forbidding ducal expression. "Is everything all right? It looked like the two of you were having a disagreement back in the ballroom, then left rather abruptly. I came to make sure all is well."

"Yes, everything is fine between me and my *wife*." Northcote's amused expression vanished as he and Edward exchanged glares.

"What Gabriel means," Esme said, jumping in

before things could escalate further between the two men, "is that he and I had a minor misunderstanding about our accommodations for the night, but we've talked and everything is settled now."

Edward crossed his arms. "Settled how?"

"Cray offered us the use of his house tonight," Northcote said, "but Esme is too tired to make the trip, so we're remaining here at Braebourne."

Edward looked between them. "Exactly as you ought." He turned toward Esme and directed his next words specifically to her. "And that is all? No other *misunderstandings* you wish to share? You may be married to him now, but that doesn't mean you aren't still my sister. You can tell me anything, Esme, anything at all. That is something that will never change."

Gabriel's arm flexed beneath her hand; his shoulders tightening with obvious umbrage.

Her brother's concern touched her, but once again, she found herself leaping to Gabriel's defense for reasons even she didn't really understand.

"There is nothing further to tell," she said in a cheerful tone. "Everything is exactly as it ought to be between Gabriel and myself. Truly. You have no reason to be concerned, Ned. After all, he is my husband now."

Edward studied her for another few seconds. "Yes, he is, isn't he?" His eyes shifted back to Northcote. "You may be my brother-in-law, but that doesn't mean I will cease either my care of, or concern for, Lady Esme. Not ever. She is precious to me and to all of her family. Pray remember that."

Northcote smiled wryly. "Oh, don't worry. I shall. How can I not with nearly the entirety of your family taking every opportunity to remind me of that fact? I believe the only Byron who hasn't made some remark to that effect is one of your cousins, although perhaps he was a footman and I am simply in error as to his identity."

"They haven't been doing that," Esme said on a gasp.

"Yes, they have," Northcote drawled, gazing down at her. "You are greatly cherished, my dear."

She rounded on Edward. "Well, stop it, all of you. Gabriel has been nothing but a gentleman since we first met and I am perfectly safe in his company. Tell everyone they are to cease their warnings immediately."

"Please, my dear, do have a care in your choice of phrasing," Northcote told her. "I am far from 'perfectly safe.' You make me sound like a gelded stallion. I might remind you that I have a reputation to uphold."

Edward laughed. "My apologies, Northcote. I keep forgetting what a gallant defender you have in my sister, however little it may be deserved."

Northcote inclined his head. "If we are done here, Lady Northcote wishes to retire."

Edward sobered again at the reminder of Esme's new marital status. "Of course, do not let me detain you further. This is, after all, your wedding night." He leaned over and kissed Esme's cheek. "Remember that Claire and I are only just down the corridor if you need us," he added in an audible whisper.

"Ned!"

Edward smiled. "Good night, Esme." His eyes hardened slightly. "Northcote."

"Clybourne."

Esme murmured her own good night, watching as Edward turned and started back the way he'd come.

Once more, she and Northcote were alone.

Silently, he accompanied her to her bedchamber. The two of them stopped in front of the closed door.

"Here we are," he said.

"Yes, here we are."

He leaned toward her and met her gaze. "Certain you don't want me to come in with you? We could dispense with the services of your maid. I've been reliably informed over the years that I'm rather a dab hand at undressing ladies. I'm sure I could have you out of that bridal gown in a trice, even with all those petticoats you must be wearing. Just how many are there?"

Her pulse did a quick double beat, her nerves rushing back all at once.

Egad, some of the things he said!

Then again, why should she be surprised when he had so little modesty that he slept naked out of doors?

And I have so little that I drew him that way, an inner voice reminded her.

Her throat squeezed tight. "I'm quite sure I'll manage satisfactorily with my maid."

His tawny eyes gleamed with regretful acceptance. "As you will, my bride. Might I at least be given a good-night kiss? I am forgoing my husbandly rights, after all. It seems only fair I should be granted some sort of recompense for my magnanimity."

When he put it like that, how could she refuse? "Very well. But only one."

"One kiss, hmm? Then I shall have to be sure it's a good one."

Before she could say more, he pulled her to him and bent his head to take her mouth.

Weary though she might be, his touch awakened her in an instant. Fire caught and burned in her veins, the sensation of his lips alone enough to make her ache. He angled his mouth one way, then angled it another, all without once breaking contact. He pressed more insistently, tender yet forceful all at the same time.

When he drew the tip of his tongue along her lower lip in a warm, wet slide, her mouth parted almost of its own accord, as if that part of her knew what it wanted before she did.

His tongue dipped between her lips, tangling against her own before tracing the ultra-sensitive flesh of her inner cheeks, first one, then the other. She shivered, an odd little mewling sound humming deep in her throat.

He smiled but didn't break the kiss. Instead he deepened their embrace, kissing her harder, deeper, compelling her to follow his lead and accede to his demands, whatever they might be.

And she did, nearly mindless with pleasure, her body burning, her flesh feeling suddenly too tight inside her clothes.

Using only his touch, he coaxed her to kiss him back, to mimic his actions so that she was darting her tongue into his mouth, was crushing her lips against his with wild abandon she hadn't realized she possessed.

She barely even felt her feet leave the ground when he picked her up and wrapped one strong arm under her bottom to hold her against him. Her arms went around his shoulders to anchor herself as their kiss continued. He pressed her against the wall, then pressed himself against her.

Even through the layers of her gown, she could feel his need. Even in her innocence, she knew what he wanted. She'd seen animals couple and had at least some sense of what was involved in mating.

Her fear returned.

He was too much, this man.

Too experienced and worldly.

Too carnal and passionate.

Heavens knew how many women he'd been with. Would she be just one more? She was very much afraid that despite the ring on her finger, she would.

Worse, what if she disappointed him? This man she'd just committed herself to for life.

She turned her face away, breaking the kiss, subtly ashamed to hear her own panting breath and to acknowledge her utter lack of control in the arms of a man she barely knew.

Good Lord, even her nipples were as hard as little pebbles inside her dress; she prayed he didn't notice.

"You may put me down now," she murmured.

He met her eyes, staring at her with a knowing look. "If you're sure that's what you want. My earlier offer still stands."

"Down, please." She looked away.

He set her on her feet.

She swayed slightly, relieved that he hadn't let go of her entirely, else she might have fallen.

He set a finger beneath her chin and gently forced her head up so she was looking in his eyes. "Good night, my little Esme. I look forward to continuing this tomorrow. Rest well. You'll need it for everything I have planned."

Her breath hitched, aching in her lungs.

"Y-yes, good night."

Reaching behind her, she turned the doorknob and slipped inside.

She was still leaning against her bedroom door when she heard him walk away.

Chapter 13

Gabriel awakened to the faint gray hues of predawn light and his erection tenting the sheets. He stared at it, then groaned and let his head fall back on the pillow, slinging an arm over his eyes.

He'd gone to bed last night in exactly the same pitiable condition, thoughts of his bride slumbering just down the corridor plaguing both his mind and his body.

When the hall clock had chimed two, he'd nearly given in and gone to her, regardless of his promise to let her have the night to herself. But it was that selfsame promise, and the memory of her softly pleading eyes, that had kept him where he was despite his certainty that he could seduce her into giving herself to him.

So there he'd lain, the long dark minutes creeping slowly past until he'd finally dropped off for a few uneasy hours of rest.

Obviously they'd been spent dreaming of the new wife he wished was in his bed right now. If she'd been there beside him, he would have kissed her slowly awake then slid heavily into her, listening to her sounds of pleasure as he brought them both to shattering climaxes.

He cursed aloud as his shaft throbbed with frustrated need. Tossing back the sheets, he climbed out of bed and padded naked and barefoot across to the adjoining bathing chamber.

He'd been an idiot to have passed up a chance to take the edge off his lust with a courtesan in London.

It hadn't been like him at all, since he'd never been the sort to repress the carnal side of his nature. So why had he this time?

Esme.

Well, tonight should take care of his difficulty, since he fully intended to relieve Esme Byron . . . correction, Esme Landsdowne . . . of her maidenhead. He looked forward to educating her in the ways of the flesh and the marriage bed.

Groaning at the thought, he reached for the pitcher full of water, turned icy-cold overnight. He stepped into the tub, raised it high, and poured.

"Good morning, Ridley," Esme said as she walked into the stables.

The head groom turned from his work with one of the horses, eyebrows rising. "Lady Esme! Beg pardon, miss. I mean, Lady Northcote."

Lady Northcote.

How odd it sounded to hear herself called that. But she supposed Ridley was right. She was no longer Lady Esme Byron. Her new title would take some getting used to, though, as would the idea of being married in general.

Truth be told, it all seemed like an elaborately bizarre dream—a continuation of the wild nocturnal ramblings that had plagued her throughout the night. Lord Northcote had figured prominently in those dreams. So much so that she'd almost expected to find him with her when she'd awakened.

Instead she'd discovered her big cat Tobias curled in a lazy feline sprawl across the pillow next to hers. Northcote had honored his promise to give her the night to herself.

But what of the night that was to come?

Had anything really changed between her and Northcote over the past ten hours? Was he any less of a stranger than he had been yesterday?

She frowned, deciding she would think about the

immediate future later on, after she returned to the house.

After she saw him again.

"So what brings you around here so early, my lady?" Ridley continued. "I thought for certain you'd be sleeping late, seeing what a big day you had yesterday. The lads and I all wish you the very best, by the by. No young lady is more deserving of happiness than yerself."

Esme gave him a wide smile. "Thank you, Ridley. You are all so kind. Thank the lads for me as well."

Ridley tipped his cap. "You may depend upon it."

"Despite all the wedding excitement," she said, "I have animals to look after and they don't much care whether I got married or not. They only want their breakfast."

Ridley smiled. "That's true enough, my lady. True enough. World don't stop for beasts just 'cause humans got personal concerns. But it's your special time. A lady only gets married once in her life and deserves a bit of indulging. The lads and I can handle things for you for the next little while, especially seein' that you'll be leaving soon with your new husband to set up a household of your own."

Her stomach lurched at the idea of leaving Braebourne. But of course Ridley was right again. She would be expected leave Braebourne eventually, probably sooner rather than later, since Northcote had his own estate, his own separate life, of which she would now be a part.

"That's most generous of you to offer to take on extra duties," she said as she fought to repress the sudden wave of panic that rose inside her, "but I've already seen to my own dogs and cats this morning and given Poppy fresh water and new hay. I was just about to drop in for a peek at Abigail and her kittens to see how they are faring today."

"Oh, those kittens are right as rain. Barn cats they may be, but the lads are a fair way to spoiling the lot of them. And Pete in particular has taken a shine to 'em. He's been slippin' in to see them at all hours, and gives their mama a bit extra from his own plate, seein' she's nursing such a hungry brood. Naught to worry about there. Abigail is a grand mouser and an even better mother. We're all glad of her."

"I know you are, but I'll look in on them regardless. They're just too adorable not to watch."

"They are that. Wee balls of fluff what fit right in your hand."

Esme and Ridley shared another brief smile. "After I see Abigail, I'm wondering if you could spare Pete for a few minutes. Aeolus is as healed as I can manage and growing more restless by the day. I'm going to take him out and see if he'll fly. I'd like Pete to assist me."

"So you think he'll fly again, that hawk, what with his wing shot through the way it was?"

"We can only see. He belongs out in the wild, not cooped up in a horse stall."

"That he does. But what if he can't fly? What if it turns out he's too damaged?"

"Then I'll see to his continued care, of course. I would never turn loose any creature who could not care for itself."

"No, my lady, I know you would not. I'll send Pete to you directly."

Gabriel let himself out of his room and walked silently down the carpeted hall.

It was early yet, he knew, too early even for the breakfast service to be laid out in the morning room. Only the servants were up, already hurrying about their duties, as industrious as ants.

He thought of knocking on Esme's door to see if she was awake, but doubted she would appreciate his intrusion. Quite likely, she was still asleep, lost in dreams like everyone else in the house.

He could have rung for his valet to have a cup of hot coffee and a biscuit brought to his room. Instead, he'd shaved and dressed on his own, then set off for the stables.

A ride would help to calm his mind and body in preparation for the day ahead.

Many of the family members who'd arrived to attend the wedding were still in residence, several planning to stay for a few days more, or so the duchess had mentioned in passing.

Then there were all the Byron siblings themselves, their various spouses and offspring, who had already been in residence before the wedding, there to spend a few weeks of early autumn together before returning to their own estates until mid-December. He'd been told they would all converge again for Christmas, as was the established Byron family custom.

Considering that fact, he really did need to make arrangements for himself and his new bride to depart soon so they could spend some time alone. As for the holidays, he wasn't in the habit of celebrating much beyond drinking an extra cup of wassail, but knowing the Byron brothers, they would probably hunt him down if he failed to return Esme to the family fold for the festivities.

His first thought was to take her to his town house in London—but given the gossip presently raging, it seemed unwise, at least not until enough time had passed for the worst of the whispering to die down.

Then there was Ten Elms.

The estate might be his ancestral home, but he'd always found it as grim and smothering as a shroud. Given the additional fact that he'd set foot in the place less than a handful of times in the past decade, it was hardly a proper location to pass the first few weeks of any marriage—even his own unwanted, hastily arranged affair.

Lastly, there was Highhaven.

He warmed to the idea immediately, even though the house on the Cornish coast was little more than a cottage and not nearly grand enough to satisfy the daughter of a duke. Highhaven had been a bequest from his grandmother on her deathbed but had remained unknown to him until he'd been advised of its existence when he'd come of age at twenty-one.

He'd also inherited a small stipend that he'd used to repair and put the old place to rights. He'd hired caretakers as well—an honest, hardworking couple who cleaned and maintained the house when he was away.

He'd always loved Highhaven, the first place in the world that had ever been completely his own. What would Esme think of it? Should he take her there? Show her the breadth and splendor of the Cornish sea and sky? Would she find it as beautiful and peaceful as he did himself?

Making up his mind in that instant, he reached for pen, paper and ink. Quickly, he dashed off a note to inform the Canbys that he and the new Lady Northcote would be arriving in the next sennight, and to make the house ready. Sealing the note, he went to find the butler so that he could be sure the letter would go out with the first post.

Afterward, he headed toward the stables.

He was nearing the adjacent structure when he heard Esme's voice carrying ever so faintly toward him on the wind. He looked to the east at the broad expanse of carefully maintained green lawn, which was bordered on one side by some woods, and found her in conversation with a young male servant. Between them sat the most curious kind of structure, a flat-bottomed wheelbarrow-like arrangement with something huge and cloth draped fastened on top.

As he watched, they carefully edged back the cover on one side to reveal a wooden cage with a large hawk perched inside. The great brown bird had round yellow eyes that gleamed with predatory interest as it surveyed its natural surroundings.

"All right, Pete," Esme said, "let's open the door and see what he does."

Fly away, Gabriel thought, wondering whose hawk it was she was in the process of liberating. Then again, any well-trained bird would return to its master if signaled in the proper manner.

But as he continued to watch, he began to wonder if

the bird was trained at all, or whether it was wild instead, since it wore no hood, bells, or leather jesses. Surely not, since wild birds could be extremely unpredictable and dangerous. Even domesticated hawks had been known to turn savage, if alarmed or mishandled.

What in the blazes does she think she's doing? She isn't even wearing gauntlets.

Gabriel started forward, his long strides eating up yards between them.

"All is well, Aeolus," she crooned to the bird as she drew closer to the open cage door. "Come out and test your wings."

The bird cocked his head and pinned her with a look but didn't move from his perch.

"Come along, sweetheart," she coaxed again. "Time to see if you're better. Don't you want to fly again?"

"Esme! Step back from that cage," Gabriel ordered, careful to modulate his tone so as not to startle the hawk inside.

Three pairs of eyes shifted his way. The servant and the bird regarded him with curiosity, Esme with a frown.

"Lord Northcote, good morning." Her voice was quiet and calm, without the slightest hint of concern. "If you would be so good, please stop where you are. Aeolus doesn't care for people he doesn't know, particularly men."

"Did you not hear me? Come away from there now, before you get hurt." He took three strides closer, hoping to get within arm's reach in case he needed to pull her away suddenly.

"Gabriel, stop," she said, holding a hand out toward him, palm up. "I am fully aware of what I am doing and have everything under control. But that will no longer be the case if you continue to approach. Please stop and step back slowly, out of Aeolus's range of vision."

Inside the cage, the great bird ruffled his feathers and clicked his powerful beak, as if in agreement.

"'Tis true, your lordship," Pete said. "Lady Esme is

a right wonder when it comes to working with beasts. Once ye've seen wot she can do, ye'll think it's magic."

Or insanity.

Gabriel stayed silent, deciding to reserve judgment on the grandiose statement for the time being. Clearly Esme had the servants wrapped so tightly around her little finger that they could gainsay her nothing. But as much as he wanted to hurry forward and snatch her out of harm's way, he also feared provoking the animal. With his jaw clenched, he moved backward, but no farther than needed to put him out of the hawk's sightlines.

Once he was at a safe distance, Esme turned her attention back to the hawk. "It's all right, sweet bird. You're safe. You're fine. Do you feel up to trying to fly? We can always take you back inside if you don't."

Gabriel kept his eyes on Esme, ready to act if needed, as he listened to her soothingly spoken monologue, which the bird couldn't possibly understand.

Yet the hawk calmed, quieting in his cage but still making no move to exit.

"Peter," she said in a near whisper. "Hand me the sleeve, please, then step away too. I'm going to see if I can coax him forth."

"Yes, milady."

The servant did as ordered, handing her a long sheath of cotton cloth lined inside with what looked like leather. It wasn't exactly a gauntlet, but at least she wasn't such a fool as to leave herself completely exposed. The sleeve fastened around her wrist and up over her forearm to her elbow but did not cover her bare hand. With the cloth on the outside, it looked rather like she was wearing a long-sleeved dress.

Gabriel tensed, still not liking the situation. He ground his teeth together and swallowed down the warning that rose in his throat. Suppressing the instinct to rush forward again, he watched her ease her hand inside the cage.

But rather than draw out a bleeding stump, Esme

ever so carefully lifted the bird from the cage, the hawk balanced now on her arm.

She crooned to him again, murmuring encouragements that he almost seemed to understand. The hawk tipped his head, listening to her as he slowly blinked his eyes.

"I shall miss you, Aeolus," she said. "You have been such a good, brave bird. But you are a wild creature and need to be free. I have done all I can to heal you; now you must do the rest. You must fly and make your home in the trees again. You must seek a mate, wherever she may be, and raise a brood of fine little eyases."

She blinked, her voice suddenly thick with emotion. "Go on, now. You're ready. Take flight and have a long, happy life."

She extended her arm fully and gave it an encouraging upward bounce. But Aeolus hung on, turning his head again to look her once more in the eyes.

Then, as if he too had said his good-byes, he spread his magnificent wings and lifted upward. Briefly, he fell back toward the earth, as though still uncertain if he had enough strength in his newly healed wing to make the flight. But then his feathers caught hold of the breeze and he flapped harder. Once, twice, three times, and he soared into the sky. With a profound grace, he flew farther and farther away until gradually he disappeared from sight altogether.

Pete grinned widely, satisfied at the exhibition they had all just witnessed. "Exactly as I told ye, your lordship. Nothing short of amazing. 'Tis a gift Lady Esme has. She understands creatures like none I've e'er seen."

"Yes, so it would appear." Gabriel walked slowly forward, considering his bride from an entirely new point of view.

Briefly she met his eyes before looking away to busy herself removing the leather and cotton sleeve.

The stable hand cleared his throat. "I'll just take this back to the stables, then, shall I?" He gestured toward the cart with the wooden cage fastened on top.

"Yes, thank you for your help." Esme handed the sleeve to the servant.

"Anytime, Lady Esme."

"Lady *Northcote*," Gabriel corrected quietly as he drew to a halt at her side.

"Right ye are, my lord. So used to thinkin' of her the other way, it'll take a mite to get the new one lodged in me noggin. Day to ye, my lord. Lady Esme."

With a tip of his hat, Pete took hold of the cart handles and wheeled everything away.

"Rather impertinent fellow. Does Clybourne not mind?"

"Mind Pete? Not at all. Why, he's one of our best grooms and has an excellent way with the horses, and with the barn cats too. Everyone likes Pete."

"He certainly reveres you. That was a terrible risk you took with that hawk, you know," Gabriel said.

Esme started toward the house. He fell into step beside her.

"Not at all," she said. "Aeolus is far from the first wild animal I have nursed back to health. Over the weeks since I pulled an arrow out of his wing, he's learned to trust me. I find animals are amazingly understanding after you save their lives."

"Not always. Some of them have been known to bite the hand that helps them. So, do I take it you make a habit of rescuing wounded creatures?"

"I do. And lost, abandoned ones as well." She came to an abrupt halt, then turned and looked up into his eyes. Her own gleamed an intense blue. "Gracious, but I never thought to ask. You do like animals, don't you?"

He arched a brow. "What if I told you I do not?"

Her delicate little forehead scrunched tight. "That would present a formidable problem, one that might compel me to ask you for an annulment."

Reaching out, he drew her to him. "Then it is a good thing that I *do* like animals—and not just to eat or wear."

Her frown grew thunderous. "That isn't funny."

He chuckled, then forced himself to be serious again. "No, you're right. It is not. Truly, I was just teasing. All your furry little charges are completely safe with me."

She studied him for a moment, then relaxed, apparently satisfied with whatever it was she had seen on his face. "Do you have any pets, Lord Northcote?"

"Gabriel," he reminded her. "No, I do not."

"Oh, I cannot imagine not having pets. They bring so much joy and comfort. Have you never had any animals, not even as a child?"

His scowl grew more pronounced. "I had a dog once, when I was a boy."

He didn't like to think about Scrapper, a small misbegotten-looking brown terrier, who'd once followed him everywhere and had slept each night at the foot of his bed. Then his parents died and they'd both been left to his uncle's less than tender care.

Scrapper had tried to defend him once during one of his uncle's more vicious whippings. For his loyalty, the little dog had paid the ultimate price. Even after all these years, he could still hear his uncle's enraged voice.

Bite me, will you, you miserable cur? I'll teach you how to show proper respect.

Amid Gabriel's own pleading shouts to stop and Scrapper's furious barks of pain and terror, his uncle had repeatedly brought the cane he'd been using on Gabriel down on the small animal. Gabriel had reached for his uncle's arm and been hurled brutally aside. Scrapper had seemed to go crazy then, growling and snapping wildly despite his injuries, trying still to protect his master. Before Gabriel's horrified eyes, his uncle had grabbed the little dog around the neck and flung him hard across the room. He'd hit the wall with a sickening thud, where he'd lain still, everything unnaturally silent.

Scrapper had never moved again.

Gabriel had been confined to his room for a week for his disobedience; he hadn't even been allowed to bury his dead pet. He'd learned later that Scrapper's body had been tossed into the rubbish pit and burned along with the kitchen waste.

He'd never spoken of him again.

"You only had the one dog, then? You've had no pets since?" Esme asked softly.

He looked down, startled to realize that he'd temporarily forgotten her. "No. Never."

For cruel though it might seem, his uncle had taught him a valuable lesson that day—that life was easier when you didn't let yourself love anything too deeply; that way it didn't hurt so much when it went away.

"Well, we shall have to remedy that," Esme said. "I have four dogs, so you can make up for your lack of pets by enjoying mine."

She eased out of his hold and started toward the house again.

"Four?" He caught up to her quickly, her shorter strides no match for his own.

"Yes, and six cats. I had a hedgehog at one time but the cats kept trying to get at her despite her protective quills. Poor dear, much as I did my best to protect her, she was constantly terrified. In the end, I gave her to a friend, who simply adores her. She's happy and healthy and has an excellent garden plot where she likes to dig for grubs—the hedgehog, not my friend, of course," Esme added with a grin.

Somewhat bemused, he smiled back.

Ten pet animals? To say nothing of any other creatures she might have secreted away in the stables and on the Braebourne grounds.

Good Christ, maybe he was the one who ought to be asking for the annulment.

"Have you had breakfast yet, Lord Northcote?"

"No, not yet, Lady Northcote." Catching hold of her wrist, he drew her gently to a halt. "And once again, it is Gabriel. You are to use my given name from now on; is that understood?"

She met his gaze. "If you insist."

"I do, Esme."

Taking hold of her other wrist, he pulled her arms behind her back and stepped near, angling his body so that she was pressed to him. He looked down, enjoying the way her small round breasts thrust against the fabric of her faded gray dress and the hint of sweet, supple flesh concealed within. He realized now why she was wearing such a worn-out, ugly old frock—she did it so she could tend to her rescued creatures without sullying her prettier gowns.

It reminded him of the first time they'd met. How he'd thought she was a servant and how he'd planned to talk his way underneath her skirts at his earliest opportunity.

Curious to realize that she was his wife now, and curiouser still that he, one of England's most infamous rakehells, hadn't yet managed to get under those skirts, not even after taking vows.

That was a lapse he needed to remedy soon. Very soon.

Bending his head, he took her mouth. He smiled inwardly when she gave a tiny gasp that was half surprise, half pleasure. Her fingers curled into small fists as her body instinctively arched closer to his.

"Open up," he murmured, nipping and teasing her mouth with the promise of further delights. His patience was rewarded moments later as she obediently parted her lips and invited him inside.

Without loosening his hold on her wrists, he indulged in a lazy, languid exploration, pressing unhurried kisses against her lips before indulging in far deeper play with his teeth and tongue that showed her all the intimate things he really wanted to do.

She shivered and shyly kissed him back, following his lead. Spreading his thighs, he drew her more fully into the lee of his body, his touch growing more intense, even though he knew he dared go only so far, given their present location this close to the house.

Forcing himself to maintain control, he savored all

her responses, her breathy sighs and unpracticed kisses, which only made him want to teach her more.

Toying and teasing, he used his tongue with a skill designed to tempt and enthrall. He smiled again as she trembled and kissed him harder. And for an instant, he let himself go, savoring the honey-sweet taste of her mouth and the heady fragrance of her skin, which set his blood afire.

He broke off abruptly and buried his lips against her neck, kissing her there as he released her wrists so he could wrap her in his arms. "We should go up to the house."

"Oh yes . . . I suppose so."

He kissed her mouth again, then moved to the other side of her throat to scatter kisses along her nape.

She quivered, eyes closed, a dreamy look on her face.

He caught her earlobe between his teeth, then gave it a little suckle. She jumped slightly, clearly startled.

With a chuckle, he resumed his ministrations to the tender skin of her throat. "Perhaps we should skip breakfast and go to your bedchamber instead."

He slid his hand up the length of her spine, then down again, deliberately slow.

Her eyes popped open. "My bedchamber?"

"Hmm-hmm."

"But it's morning."

"So it is—the best time of day for coupling. I prefer to see my lover rather than groping in the dark. No candles required."

He snuck a look up from under his lashes and chuckled again at her wide-eyed expression.

"We can't," she whispered.

He pressed an openmouthed kiss to the base of her throat, just above her collarbone, gratified when he felt her answering response. "I assure you, my dear, we most certainly can. Let us away." Straightening, he met her gaze.

"But my maid will be waiting for me," she said.

"Then we'll send her about her business."

She shook her head. "You don't know Mrs. Grumblethorpe. She won't approve."

"I hardly need the permission of your maid. Since we happen to be married, Mrs. Grumblethorpe can jolly well bugger off."

"Gabriel!"

"Come now," he scoffed. "You must have heard far worse language than that from your horde of brothers over the years."

"Perhaps," she admitted, "but I'm not supposed to know what any of it means."

He arched an eyebrow, suddenly curious. "*Do* you know what 'bugger off' means?"

"Of course. It means to shoo away insects. Something particularly nasty, like bedbugs or wasps, I presume."

A laugh burst from his chest, deep and unfettered, with an honest amusement he rarely experienced.

"What is so funny?"

"Nothing, my dear," he lied, as he worked to rein in his good humor. "Nothing at all." Catching hold of her hand, he turned her toward the house. "Come, let us go."

"All right, but not to . . . *you know*. Everyone must be awake by now and at breakfast. They will wonder what has become of us if we do not put in an appearance."

"I rather imagine they'll know precisely what we're up to if we do not put in an appearance. We are newlyweds, after all, even if we haven't actually consummated anything yet."

"Oh," she groaned, cheeks growing pink, "that only makes it worse."

"How have you managed to face them these past two weeks considering the reason we were forced to marry? You did do a naked drawing of me, remember? Most of them likely think I've been tumbling you for weeks now."

Her chin came up. "They do not! And that sketch is hardly the same thing as fornicating while my entire family has breakfast just down the hall. That sketch is art."

"Art, is it? Some might say it was an act of lascivious interest on the part of an overly indulged young woman with too much personal freedom."

She shook off his hold. "Too much—are you implying that I am spoiled?"

"No more than most dukes' sisters, I daresay. And at least you aren't cruel and conniving like so many of the *Ton* girls I've met. You've just been given your way in far too many respects and need a firmer hand to rein you in."

Her eyes flashed with blue fire. "Rein me in? I am not a horse, Lord Northcote."

"No, you most definitely are not." He raked his gaze over her body. "I have no interest in fucking a horse. Just my wife, who, so far, does nothing but refuse me."

Her cheeks burst with hot color; clearly she knew the meaning of that particular bad word.

He realized instantly that he ought to apologize; he hadn't meant to say anything quite so crude or insensitive. But he'd be damned if he was going to say he was sorry to some nineteen-year-old slip of a girl, even if she did happen to be his new bride.

Her hands opened and closed at her sides, and he wondered for a moment if she was thinking about slapping him—assuming she could reach that high.

Instead she backed away. "I should have listened to my instincts and refused to marry you, regardless of the cost to my reputation. How dare you speak to me like that?" She blinked, her eyes growing moist.

"Esme." He stretched a hand toward her.

She moved farther away, shaking her head. "I was going to let you come to me tonight despite my qualms, but now I have changed my mind."

"Esme," he said, her name a growl this time.

"From now on, you are to stay away. Tonight and every night. If you do not, I shall scream for all of my brothers to come and toss you out."

"You forget. You are my wife. I have every right to you and your body."

"I am not your wife yet, as you keep reminding me. I have changed my mind. I am going to Edward and tell him I want an annulment."

He covered the distance between them so quickly, she gasped in surprise. And again when he caught hold of her wrist. "You will do no such thing, madam. Rescind your threat or I shall take you into the woods right now and see to it that you are as married as you can possibly be. I presume you take my meaning?"

The color drained from her face and she nodded.

"Say the words. Take it back."

Her jaw tightened as if she still wanted to refuse. Abruptly, she gave a jerky nod. "I will not ask for an annulment."

"Good. Now, as for tonight, I shall give you another reprieve since I don't want you screaming for your brothers, as you put it. Instead, I'm going to make sure we are thoroughly alone, where there will be no interruptions, before we consummate our union."

He released her wrist, watching as his words sank in.

"Then, you mean—," she began.

"That we shall be departing Braebourne shortly, yes."

"To stay at Clay House?"

"No, my dear, nothing within an easy distance of this estate. I have sent word to have my house in Cornwall made ready for our arrival. We will depart tomorrow morning."

Her mouth opened. "Tomorrow! But that's impossible. I cannot just pick up and leave."

"Of course you can."

"No, I cannot. For one, it will not allow me time to make arrangements for my animals."

"You must have left them here at Braebourne in the past when you went to London for the Season. A smart girl like you, I'm certain you will figure something out. Besides, your family is in residence, not to mention the veritable army of servants who see to the estate. I feel certain none of them will let your beloved pets starve."

"No, of course they won't, but—"

"Good, that dilemma is solved. The rest should be easy."

"Easy? What will everyone think when we announce that we are leaving in such haste?"

"That we are a newly wedded couple who are desirous of privacy."

She shook her head. "My siblings will never believe I want to depart so quickly."

"Of course they will, because you are going to make them. Or do you want everyone to know that our marriage is a disaster before it has even begun? Do you seek yet another dreadful scandal to add to the already extensive list you're collecting of late?"

She stilled, then looked away, her lashes sweeping down. "No."

"Exactly. So put a smile on your face and let us go into the house for breakfast, where we can start convincing everyone of our perfect marital accord."

"I couldn't possibly eat."

"You can and you will. Believe me, my dear—I've been playacting at all manner of things for years. It's a talent one develops rather quickly in times of necessity. You will too."

He offered his arm and waited.

She stared at it, an expression of undisguised dislike on her face.

Without another word, she laid her hand on his sleeve and together they walked the rest of the way to the house.

Chapter 14

"Are you certain you cannot remain at Braebourne for a few days more?" Mallory asked Esme the next morning as they stood together in the entry hall. "Everyone will only be here for another week or two; then we'll all be off to our own estates. It will be Christmastide before we are together again."

Footmen moved past, hands and arms laden with Esme and Northcote's luggage, which was being secured inside the heavy traveling coach.

Other family members were gathered as well; Leo and Lawrence stood in conversation with Northcote, grinning at something he'd said, while Mama and Claire were busy overseeing the packing to make certain nothing essential would be forgotten.

If only I could feel so carefree and confident.

But rather than bolt for her room as Esme longed to do, she pinned a bright smile on her face and tried to sound enthusiastic about the upcoming trip. "I wish we could remain, but Gabriel is most eager to show me his house in Cornwall. He's calling it our honeymoon house. I hear the view is splendid, right on the sea. I have spent so little time near the ocean; I am quite excited by the prospect of listening to the waves and smelling the salt air."

She had no idea if his house—Highhaven, he'd called it—had a sea view or not, but she had to come up with some convincing reason for her supposed eagerness to leave. As for Northcote, he could scarcely wait. At his behest, Mrs. Grumblethorpe had appeared in her bed-chamber at six o'clock that morning with instructions to make haste so they could be on the road.

To her consternation, Northcote's prediction about her family's reaction to their news had proven disgustingly accurate. Even Edward and Mallory had appeared convinced that she and Northcote were getting along splendidly and were hurrying off so they could enjoy a bit of time alone as a newly married couple.

All that had been required were a few smiles and some laughs, and everyone had bought their story like a school of fish caught in a net.

Of course, it hadn't hurt that Northcote had openly taken care to touch her. Holding her hand. Idly stroking her hair or the curve of her shoulder. Resting his palm along her hip or waist while in conversation with one of her relations.

And kissing her.

He'd taken delight in that most of all.

The devil had a real knack for catching her unawares too, timing their little "moments of affection" so that they appeared spontaneous and genuine—and were always done within view of witnesses. How he managed to arrange things, she would never know, but somehow he always succeeded, selecting just the right place and time so it seemed as if they'd snuck off for a stolen moment together only to be found out.

The whole charade infuriated her. She could have called him out on it in front of her family but found herself playing along instead, smiling and acting as if she were thrilled with her new husband and their marriage. According to their story, luck had shone a radiant light upon them and granted them a grand love match, much to their mutual surprise. And for those who'd heard via the servants' grapevine that she and Northcote had yet to share a bed, it was being attributed to his restraint and consideration of her tender feelings while they got to know each other better.

Mallory and Thalia in particular had looked skeptical at first—probably because they'd been firsthand witnesses to her premarital cold feet. But soon even they had seemed convinced, happy looks in the two women's eyes as they fell for the lie.

After that, she'd had even more reason to keep up the charade, loath to wipe the looks of pleasure and relief from her family's faces. They wanted to believe the faerie tale. Who was she to ruin it with the truth?

Mallory smiled at her now, reaching out to give her a warm hug and a kiss on the cheek. "I'm so pleased that you and Northcote seem to be getting along so well. If I am not mistaken, the two of you are well on your way to being in love. He can scarcely keep his eyes off you and he never seems to let you out of his sight."

Yes, to make sure I don't decide to annul the marriage, after all—promise or no promise.

But it was already too late. She'd tied her fate to his the moment she'd spoken those two simple words in the chapel.

And then he was at her side, sliding an arm around her waist to pry her gently but firmly away from her sister. All her relations followed the two of them outside onto the wide gravel drive, where they began to exchange good-byes. She found herself passed from one loved one to another, sharing tearful hugs and kisses with her mother, then Ned, Claire, Cade, Meg, Grace and Jack, who bussed her noisily on the cheek. Next came Drake, Sebastianne, Adam, Mallory and Thalia.

Last were Leo and Lawrence, who each gave her extra-long, extra-strong bear hugs that lifted her briefly off her feet.

"If he steps out of line," Lawrence whispered in her ear, "remember that you've only to send word and we'll be on your doorstep in a trice. You may be his wife, but we'll always be your family."

She nearly broke then, the truth on her tongue, wanting to get out. But suddenly she glanced sideways and caught sight of Northcote. He waited near the coach, apart from the others.

And yet again, for reasons that continued to elude her, she couldn't bring herself to speak against him, to humiliate him, no matter the difficulties that lay between them.

So rather than take advantage of her last chance to escape, she went to the coach and allowed Northcote to hand her inside.

He'd just taken the seat across from her when Burr leapt inside. His tail waved like a silken flag as he let out a happy bark and settled against her skirts.

Northcote frowned. "I thought you were leaving your menagerie behind."

"I am, but not Burr." She stroked her hand over the dog's head. "He pines if I'm away. I wanted to bring Henry as well, but the poor dear is just too old to make the trip."

He studied the animal, his eyes narrowing suddenly. "I remember you," he said, addressing the dog. "Burr, is it?"

Burr barked and wagged in agreement.

"I suppose, in an odd way," Northcote mused aloud, "that it only makes sense for him to accompany us, considering he was there at Cray's lake that fateful day. Your silent accomplice, as it were."

She flushed slightly but made no reply.

Before he had a chance to offer another sarcastic comment, the coach set off, gravel crunching beneath the wheels and the horses' hooves.

Turning her head, she looked through the window for one final glimpse of her family, still gathered on the drive. They waved and she waved back, one last time. Her throat tightened as she sat back, her eyes squeezed closed against a sudden rush of tears.

She'd been away from Braebourne before, but never on her own and never with the knowledge that from this day forward, the estate would no longer be her home.

She would have a new home now, one that was strange and unfamiliar. Like the furry and feathered creatures she rescued, she liked the comfort of familiar surroundings, and of soothing, established routines. Now everything and everyone around her would be new, particularly the man who lounged in the seat opposite.

She opened her eyes and received a tiny shock of surprise.

Northcote was watching her.

His hawklike eyes were speculative and enigmatic, every bit as mysterious as Aeolus's had ever been.

She hoped the bird was thriving in his newly rediscovered freedom, soaring happily once more through the wide-open skies.

Odd how the two of them seemed to have switched places. Before he'd been the one in a cage. Now it was her.

After settling himself more comfortably into one corner, Northcote crossed his arms and closed his eyes.

Is he going to sleep?

When she heard the faintest of snores coming from him barely a minute later, she knew that was exactly what he'd done.

Beast.

No matter how tired she might be, sleep always eluded her when she was sitting up, whether she was seated in a cozy chair next to the fire or inside a moving coach.

She scowled at him with frustrated envy for another few moments, then turned her attention to Burr. Patting the seat beside her, she invited him to hop up next to her, which he did with alacrity. She reached into the traveling satchel near her feet and pulled out her sketchbook and a pencil.

She drew Burr, who was always a favorite subject, capturing him in state of doggy dreams. Next, she tried to sketch the passing scenery, but it went by too quickly and soon proved an exercise that was more frustrating than enjoyable.

Slowly, her sights turned to Northcote.

He was still asleep, his features bold and arresting, beautiful in their way. In sleep, he seemed more approachable, his usual mask of cynicism temporarily cast free of its mooring.

Something in her softened to see him so, together with a wish that he might look like this when he was awake.

But she supposed that was impossible.

He was who he was.

Just as she was who she was.

The hardened rake and the tenderhearted innocent shackled together for life because of a single imprudent act.

She stared down at the blank page, remembering.

Slowly, she began to draw.

It was well after sunset three days later when they reached Highhaven. The countryside was swathed in a darkness so dense it was a wonder the coachman and horses were able to find their way.

Inside the coach, Esme drew in a breath of humid, brine-scented air and listened to the sound of the sea crashing against the rocky shoreline somewhere closeby.

Northcote had set a grueling pace, stopping only to change horses and again at night to dine and let them both rest for a few hours. To her surprise and relief, they had slept in separate rooms. Yet in spite of the long journey and their present late arrival, Esme hadn't complained. Truthfully, she wasn't eager to spend yet another day inside the coach with him, where he sat mostly silent and brooding.

Or else asleep.

When he wasn't asleep, he read, while she did the same. Over the entire journey, they'd exchanged barely a handful of words, and most of those polite inquiries that one might have used with the most ordinary of acquaintances.

She peered through the coach window, anxious to see her new home, albeit a temporary one since she knew from a remark Edward had made that this was not Northcote's ancestral estate. That great house lay somewhere to the north, though precisely where she wasn't certain, and given Northcote's present taciturn humor, she wasn't about to ask.

Travel weary, Esme gazed into the night, one arm wrapped around Burr for comfort. She frowned when she caught sight of the house with its dark, unwelcoming facade.

Clearly, they were not expected.

The coachman leapt down and went to bang on the front door. Northcote followed, seemingly unperturbed by the lack of light or servants.

He tried the door but found it barred. Raising his fist, he was the one to pound this time—and keep on pounding.

"Keep yer everlastin' drawers on, will ya," grumbled a man's voice from inside nearly a minute later. "I'm comin'. I'm comin'. And I'll thank ye ta' cease tha' racket, whoever tha' devil ye might be."

From inside the house came the unmistakable sounds of locks being drawn back. Still grumbling, the man opened the door. "If ye weren't tha' devil, ye'd have a care fer tha' time. Decent folk shouldn't be disturbin' other folk at such an hour."

"I'm sure not," Northcote drawled. "Then again, I ceased being decent long ago."

"M-my lord," the older man stammered, his eyes popping wide with recognition. "Wot ye doin' here? The missus and me weren't 'spectin' ye, well, not tonight anyhow."

Northcote eyed the darkened house. "Yes, that much is evident. You did receive my letter, I trust?"

"Aye, but only jes' this mornin'. We didn't think, well, Mrs. Canby 'n' me . . . Ye said next week," he finished accusingly.

"Yes, and so I did. Lady Northcote and I had a change of plans, however, and decided to come early."

Lady Northcote and I . . .

Esme sniffed under her breath. If there was blame to go around, it lay squarely on Northcote's own head.

"Jim, who's there? What do they want?" called a female voice from somewhere deep inside the house.

Mrs. Canby, Esme presumed.

Light from another candle added its illumination to the one in the servant's hand as the woman stepped forward to join Jim Canby where he stood in the doorway.

"It's his lordship and his new lady, Jemima," the male servant explained.

"What!" The woman nearly dropped her candle, the flame flickering as she somehow managed to wring her pudgy hands and keep hold of the candle all at the same time. "But we weren't expectin' ye and the house ain't ready. Oh, I'm ever so sorry, milord. What must ye be thinkin'?" She shot a worried glance toward the coach. "What must yer lady be thinkin'?"

"The omission is mine," Northcote said. "Pray light a few candles and find us something edible for dinner. I presume there is food in the larder?"

Jemima bobbed her head of white hair with its last few lingering strands of what must once have been a glorious red. "Aye, but nothin' fancy. Jest some bread and cheese, maybe a shoulder of ham. Might have the fixin's fer a soup of some sort."

"Any of that should do nicely so long as it's hot and filling."

"Well, let me air out a bedroom first fer yer lady wife so she can refresh herself afore supper; then I'll get to bangin' some pots 'round in the kitchen."

Before Northcote had time to offer so much as "yea" or "nay," the older woman spun on her heels and disappeared back into the darkened house. Illumination burst quickly to life in the foyer and front room as candles were set ablaze.

Meanwhile, Jim hurried forward and went to help the coachman unload the luggage.

Burr leapt down from the coach, barking twice as his paws landed on the crushed shell drive. He raced in an excited circle and barked again, clearly happy to be free of the vehicle.

Esme stood to exit the coach, expecting to receive assistance from the footman.

Instead, Northcote waited below, looking serious and saturnine.

He held out a hand.

She almost refused his assistance. Then she caught sight of his expression and changed her mind. She was just too tired to argue tonight.

But he released her the moment she was on the ground, leaving her to make her way into the house alone. Burr trotted at her heels, his pink tongue lolling.

Grumbly will see to it that I have everything I need.

Then she remembered.

Mrs. Grumblethorpe wasn't with them; she had been left behind at Braebourne. Northcote had made up some excuse about the house being small and how they needed to travel light. Since they were there for their honeymoon and would have no occasion to entertain, he'd argued that she could do with the services of a local girl to attend her while they were in residence.

But she knew he'd refused to take Mrs. Grumblethorpe because of the remark Esme had made about her longtime maid not approving of his actions. He would want no interference now that he had her alone.

She shivered and trailed him inside, glad she at least had Burr.

As good as her word, Mrs. Canby showed her to a pleasantly decorated bedchamber done in refreshing shades of green and white. Despite the fact that the room was only a third of the size of her bedroom at Braebourne, it was surprisingly comfortable, with a soft woven rug to warm the wooden floors and a spacious cherrywood canopy bed that dominated the space.

A cheerful fire was crackling in the hearth by the time she was shown to the room by Mrs. Canby, who stayed only long enough to help her change out of her traveling dress before she set off downstairs for the kitchens to fix dinner.

Esme washed her hands and arms and face with the fresh water Mrs. Canby had also been kind enough to provide; then she sagged down onto the mattress. She gripped one of the wooden bedposts, then closed her eyes, fighting the odd urge to cry.

The door opened without a knock and her eyes flew open.

Northcote stood on the threshold.

Esme lunged for the counterpane, yanking it up out of its neat tuck. She held it in front of her like a shield. "What are you doing here?"

He walked in and shut the door. "Mrs. Canby told me she hasn't been able to hire a girl from the village for you yet, so I've come to play lady's maid."

"There would be no need of anyone's help if you'd just let me bring Mrs. Grumblethorpe along."

He ignored her remark and crossed to her luggage. Opening her trunk, he reached inside.

"Stop that," she said. "I can look after myself."

Again, he ignored her, pulling out a lavender evening gown embroidered with rows of tiny blue forget-me-nots. It was one of her favorite dresses, but not tonight. Not since he'd chosen it for her to wear.

"Stand up," he said. "Let's get you into this."

She wrapped the coverlet tighter around herself. "I told you I don't need your assistance. You may go."

He eyed the gown and the long row of tiny buttons that ran along the back. "Don't be absurd. You'd never manage to fasten even half of these buttons on your own."

"Then I shall choose another dress."

There must be an easier-to-fasten gown somewhere in her luggage. Maybe one of her sketching dresses?

"There are no other dresses," he said, as if he were fully aware of her thoughts. "At least not ones you can put on without an extra pair of hands. And if you're thinking about donning one of those disreputable rags you wear when you see to your animals or go painting, I'll tell you right now that I had the lot of them burned."

Her mouth dropped open. "You did not!"

"No wife of mine is going to parade around in public looking like the lowliest of scullery maids."

"How dare you. Those were my dresses and you had no right—"

"I had every right," he said, cutting her off. "I am your husband and you are a viscountess now. I expect you to look like one. Now, stand up and let me assist you into this gown so that we may go below and dine."

Her knuckles whitened as she gripped the bedclothes harder and shot him a glare.

He arched a single dark brow. "Or would you rather forgo the evening meal and get straight to bed? I can *undress* you just as easily as dress you, you know."

Words of outrage trembled on her lips. How she wished she could tell him to go straight to the devil. But she hesitated, aware by now exactly how dangerous it could be to spar with him. She'd learned early how to spot a lethal predator; she was coming to understand that he might be the most lethal one of all.

Still, she held out against him for a few seconds longer before loosening her hold on the counterpane without entirely letting it go. "You could at least turn your back."

He gave a quick laugh. "Oh, I think not. And might I remind you that I'll be seeing far more than those pretty unmentionables of yours quite soon. Now, up you come."

She considered protesting again but realized he had her neatly trapped.

Loathsome cur.

Flinging back the coverlet, she hurried to her feet and turned her back to him as quickly as possible.

She waited, wondering what he would do. But he only chuckled.

"Raise your arms."

The dress billowed around her as he lifted the gown up and over. Her head popped out seconds later as he settled the material into place with nothing more than a few quick, efficient tugs.

He really did know how to dress a woman, didn't he? Given his reputation, she supposed he'd done this for a great many women. Dozens? Hundreds?

Her forehead creased, her stomach quivering at the thought of his vast experience and her complete lack.

She held still as he set to work on the buttons, his fingers brushing ever so faintly against her corset-covered back as he moved upward.

His pace slowed as he came to the last few buttons. Five . . . four . . . three . . . two . . . one.

Breath caught in her throat as he skimmed his thumbs over the sensitive skin along the nape of her neck, hot shivers chasing after one another in crazy circles.

Leaning nearer, he pressed a kiss against the edge of her jaw and another behind her ear before he took her earlobe between his teeth. He bit, exerting just enough pressure to send her pulse ricocheting yet careful not to cause pain.

She barely had time to adjust to the novel sensation when he slid his hands down and around to boldly cup her breasts. He held her without an ounce of inhibition, cupping and exploring her flesh with a shocking kind of possession. It was as if he owned her body and could do anything he liked, which, given marriage laws and the ring on her hand, some might say he did.

Her mind turned dull as he caressed her further, her lips parting on a silent gasp. For despite the material of her dress and the confinement of her stays, his touch left her feeling naked, as if there was nothing between their skin but air.

Her nipples drew taut, the intimate place between her legs aching in a way she didn't expect or fully understand.

Then, as abruptly as their interlude had begun, he let her go.

She shuddered and fought to keep her balance, her hands clenching at her sides.

Damnable man.

How could he do that to her so easily, especially when he'd just put clothes on her rather than taking them off?

As for him, an upward glance showed him looking calm, as if he'd just been discussing the weather with her rather than brazenly fondling her breasts.

Perhaps, for him, such acts had little meaning. But for a woman . . . for her . . . it meant more.

He would be her first, her only. And when he finally took her to his bed, she needed it to mean more.

"Shall we, my dear?" he asked, offering his arm.

She stared at his coat sleeve for a moment, then accepted.

Chapter 15

Esme ate sparingly despite the excellent quality of the food; she was too worried about the night to come to really enjoy the meal.

Mrs. Canby had worked miracles, particularly considering the limited amount of time and ingredients at her disposal. Yet somehow she had put a delicious meal on the table consisting of a piping-hot cream of potato soup with bits of browned onion and black pepper; slices of fine local cheese, cured ham and crusty fresh bread. She'd even managed to whip up an apple tart with brandied whipped cream to finish.

Not wishing to injure the older woman's feelings, Esme had made an effort to try some of everything—everything, that is, except the ham.

"Is that all you're eating?" Northcote said, pointing a fork toward her plate when he noticed her lack of appetite. "Here, have some ham."

"No, thank you," she said.

"Why not? It's delicious. Or don't you like ham?"

"Actually no. I do not eat meat."

He stilled. "What do you mean, you don't eat meat? Everyone eats meat."

"I don't. I find it repugnant." She forced herself to swallow a spoonful of soup; it really was delicious.

He studied her for a moment. "This is because of all your furry creatures, I suppose? You don't like eating the little friends you've just rescued."

"Well, of course I don't. I would be the most dreadful hypocrite otherwise, don't you think? But before you grow alarmed, you needn't worry. I don't expect you to give up the consumption of animal flesh. Everyone in the family eats meat and I gave up trying to change their minds long, long ago."

"Animal flesh, hmm? I suppose that's an accurate way to describe it." He cut a piece of ham, put in his mouth, chewed and swallowed. "Delectable."

He smiled.

She applied herself to her soup.

"At least eat some of that cheese," he urged a minute later. "You do eat cheese, I presume?"

"Yes. Cheese, milk and eggs, just not the animals who produce them. I have been known to eat the occasional clam or mussel, but I always feel rather guilty afterward, so I generally refrain."

"Well, you'd better let Mrs. Canby know. She's probably planning to stock up on dead beasts at the market tomorrow and slaughter any of our chickens who have recently quit laying."

Esme set down her spoon. "I most certainly hope not. I shall tell her directly."

She made to stand up, but Northcote reached out a hand to stop her. "Sit. There's plenty of time to discuss the menu planning tomorrow. And I'll mention your aversion to the Canbys tomorrow so there is no misunderstanding."

"You would do that? When people find out about my dietary preferences, most of them think I'm either peculiar or overly softhearted."

He leaned back in his chair, nursing his glass of wine. "Well, there's no doubt you have a very soft heart, but there's nothing wrong with that. As for being peculiar, I'll reserve judgment for now."

A laugh escaped her and, without even realizing, she relaxed a little for the first time in days.

She ate more soup and a small slice of cheese before

he coaxed her to try the apple tart. It was as divine as the rest of the meal.

He refilled her glass of wine and they sat for a time in a silence that was almost companionable. Her weariness returned, her eyelids beginning to droop as a wave of sleepiness washed over her.

She came abruptly awake to the touch of his hand against the back of hers. Gently, he slid her wineglass out of harm's way. "Why don't you go upstairs? I'll join you in a bit."

Her eyelids popped wide, her sleepiness vanishing in an instant.

"Mrs. Canby will attend you." He picked up the brandy snifter at his elbow and swirled the amber liquor inside the glass.

When had he gotten that? Just how long was I asleep?

She searched for some excuse, anything to postpone her return upstairs. But nothing useful came to mind. She supposed her efforts to delay were over.

They were alone.

With a fine tremor of nerves running through her, she stood and left the room.

Mrs. Canby was waiting for her when she entered her bedchamber. Burr was there as well, wagging happily as he came forward for a pet, which she gladly bent to bestow.

The older woman greeted her with a cheerful smile. She began chatting in a quiet, pleasant voice as she helped Esme change into the nightgown and robe that had been laid out across the bed.

While the housekeeper hung her gown inside the wardrobe next to the other dresses the servant had unpacked earlier, Esme moved to the washbasin. Carefully, she bathed her face and hands, then brushed her teeth with a mint tooth powder that left her mouth tingling and fresh.

And then there was nothing left to do but go to bed.

Esme stared at the smooth, clean sheets and coverlet

that had been invitingly turned back but made no move to climb in.

Mrs. Canby extinguished all but one branch of candles, wished her good night and went to seek her own rest. Burr circled, then settled down on a rug near the fireplace and closed his eyes.

She considered inviting him to join her in bed but decided not to chance it. Not that she thought Lord Northcote would be mean to the dog, but he would surely be displeased to find his side of the bed occupied by the animal.

Her stomach jittered, her skin crawling with anxiety.

Don't be so nervous, she told herself as she cupped her hands underneath her elbows and hugged her arms to her chest. *It isn't as if he is some despicable fiend or repulsive toad.*

Quite the opposite, in fact.

Northcote—although she supposed she really ought to start calling him Gabriel since he would soon be sharing her bed—*Gabriel* was everything a man should be.

Attractive, intelligent, urbane.

Sexual and sophisticated, with a depth of experience she couldn't even begin to fathom. Surely, he must like his sex in the normal way, whatever that might be. Then again, based on some of the rumors she'd heard . . .

A fresh tremor went through her and she hugged her chest tighter.

What would he expect of her? What if he grew impatient with her inexperience? What if she couldn't give him the things he desired?

She'd seen stallions covering mares, witnessed the frenzied power, the near violence of their coupling. Surely it wouldn't be like that?

Closing her eyes, she thought of his kisses.

She liked his kisses. More than liked them actually.

And his caresses . . .

Those were wonderful despite his unsettling boldness.

Her body warmed at the memories.

Maybe she was worrying needlessly. Maybe it wouldn't be so bad.

Hurrying forward before she could change her mind, she jumped into the bed and pulled the covers up to her chin. Lying flat on her back, body rigid, she waited for him to come.

More than an hour after Esme left the dining room, Gabriel finished the last of his brandy and made his way up the stairs.

The house was dark except for the candle he carried.

He listened to the silence, punctuated only by the sounds of the sea and the gentle brush of the wind against the windows and eaves.

He hadn't brought a valet with him; he could do for himself here in the countryside. Entering the bedroom next to Esme's, he set down his candle, then stripped off his clothes. He washed, brushed his teeth and shaved, then put on a robe and slippers and let himself out into the hall.

Esme lay in bed, the covers pulled so high he couldn't tell if she was awake or asleep. Her long hair trailed over her pillow like a dark river. She didn't move or acknowledge him in any way.

Asleep, he guessed, holding back a sigh.

Her dog Burr thumped his tail in greeting, however, and briefly lifted his head from where he lay curled near the soothing warmth of the fire.

Gabriel crossed to stroke his head. Burr closed his eyes with pleasure and settled back to resume his doggy dreams.

After blowing out all but one candle in the branch of candles on her dressing table, Gabriel carried his own light over to the bed. He set it down on the end table, then turned, his hands going to the belt on his robe.

She lay staring at him, her eyes as wide as those of a doe who'd just sighted a hunter.

"So you *are* awake," he said casually, letting his

hands fall to his sides. "You were so still I figured you'd drifted off."

"No," she whispered, her voice pitched high.

He studied her, abruptly aware how young she was—not even twenty—and how innocent. It was easy to forget what it was like the first time. His own first time seemed like centuries ago.

At fourteen, he'd been seduced by the wife of one of his uncle's friends when the couple had come to visit that summer. He'd awakened one night to find her in his bed, her lips wrapped around his cock. By the time he'd gone back to school that autumn, he'd had little innocence left. Since then, he'd grown increasingly jaded, memories of the boy he'd once been dim and difficult to recall. Yet tonight, some lingering remnants resurfaced, along with an uncharacteristic compassion for Esme's virginal fears.

He sat down on the bed, facing her. "You needn't look so distressed. I'm not going to pounce on you, you know."

She didn't seem reassured. "What *are* you going to do?"

"Well, I keep hoping I'll get to make love to my wife, but we can talk for a while, if you'd rather."

Her forehead creased. "You want to talk? Now?"

He shrugged, a long, slow roll of his shoulders, as if they had all the time in the world. "Certainly. What would you care to discuss?"

She shrugged back, clearly at a loss.

"Hmm. What about fashion?" he suggested. "Most women love talking about fashion."

Her lips twitched as though she found the idea of him discussing fashion amusing. Wouldn't she be surprised to learn that he knew rather a lot about women's attire? He'd bought enough gowns for his lovers over the years that he'd picked up quite a bit of knowledge concerning fabrics, styles and all manner of feminine furbelows.

She shook her head again. "My apologies, but the

"Perhaps I can make it up to you." Bending, he dusted a kiss against her cheek, one side and the other. Then he continued on, planting a line of unhurried kisses against the skin he'd just stroked with his finger.

He heard her breathing quicken and smiled as he pressed his mouth into the curve of her throat. He licked her there in a tiny circle, savoring the fragrant taste of her skin and enjoying the hard beat of her pulse where it throbbed erratically nearby.

He suckled there, sure he would leave his mark.

Before this night was through, he planned to leave his mark all over her. But first things first.

Sliding his finger onward, he found the top button on her nightgown. She tensed as he slipped it free with the aid of his thumb. He moved to the other side of her neck and began suckling anew.

Her legs shifted beneath the sheets, her pulse beating wildly.

He opened two more buttons in quick succession, then moved on to a fourth.

Leaving the honeyed haven of her throat, he began kissing his way downward across her breastbone, where a sliver of her skin lay exposed between the open edges of her nightgown. He paused when he reached the place between her breasts just above her diaphragm. Without warning, he ran the tip of his tongue back up the flesh he'd kissed only moments earlier, leaving a wet trail in its wake.

Then he blew in a long line and heard her gasp and shiver.

"I wonder what pearls I might find awaiting me now," he murmured, as he looked up and into her eyes. They were dark and lambent, her lids heavy with a surfeit of sensation.

Slipping a hand underneath the left side of her nightgown, he cupped her breast and discovered what he sought. Just as he'd hoped, her nipple was round and firm, drawn up like a bead. He flicked it, then flicked it again, watching the heat rise in her cheeks as she caught her lower lip between her teeth and sighed.

Deciding she was ready for more, he rubbed the tender peak between his thumb and forefinger, gradually increasing the pressure until she let out another little cry.

Abruptly, he pushed back the material of her nightgown with both hands and worked it down her shoulders and onto her arms. He wedged the cloth, buttons straining so that her arms were trapped against her sides, her naked breasts fully exposed to his view.

"Ah, look," he said. "A second pearl. I am showered with a wealth of delights."

And before she could react, he bent to feast on her, fondling one breast while he opened his mouth over the other and began to lick and suckle.

Esme arched uncontrollably, her body on fire, awash in waves of need and delight.

Ah gods, the pleasure. It was indescribable, more intense than any pleasure she'd ever experienced before.

A part of her knew she should be shocked, that she ought to be cringing with dismay at the brazenly intimate things he was doing to her body. But exactly like his other kisses, this new variety was something she could not seem to resist. Everything he did to her felt too good, far too wonderful to even consider telling him to stop.

His teeth scraped against her nipple and she arched again, pressing her breast more fully into his mouth, as if she were begging for more. He smiled, then complied, suckling with more force before he gave her aching nipple the slightest little nip.

Fire flashed through her, searing her veins.

"Oh!" she said.

"'Oh' is exactly right." His voice was low and throaty. He met her eyes and smiled as if he were enjoying every one of her naive responses.

And she realized in that moment that he was.

Gabriel was the teacher and she the pupil, an acolyte

learning from the master, who was nothing less than a virtuoso of all things carnal and impure.

She twisted, trying to move her arms. But he'd imprisoned her neatly inside her nightgown, leaving her utterly at his mercy.

Her breasts quivered and she moaned as he repeated his trick of blowing on her wet flesh. He did it again, swirling the tip of his tongue around the tight bud of her other breast before teasing it afterward with a draft of cool air.

A moan sang from her as he continued to lavish her breast with the kind of attention he'd applied to the first. Hums of pleasure came from deep in his throat as he drew on her with a powerful intensity.

She shifted her legs beneath the sheets with a sudden restlessness, her body burning and feverish.

As if he knew exactly how she was feeling, he flung back the bedclothes, tossing them all the way down to her feet.

"Better?" he asked.

She nodded, unable to find the strength to reply aloud.

He leaned up and kissed her for the first time since he'd come into the room, claiming her mouth in a series of long, sultry, openmouthed kisses that made her head spin and her heart speed even faster.

Before she had so much as an inkling of his intentions, he pushed the skirt of her nightgown up around her waist, leaving her completely exposed.

He began touching her, one big hand moving in a slow exploration of her thighs and knees and calves before gliding upward to settle on the delicate skin of her stomach. He splayed his hand wide, rubbing her in a tantalizing circle before he dipped his little finger into her belly button and gave it a wiggle.

Her toes curled, her legs sliding upward and slightly apart as if they had a will of their own.

And that's when he shocked her again as he slid his hand down and settled it over the mound of dark curls between her thighs. He cupped her there with undisguised possession, as if he were letting her know that this part of her belonged to him.

That every part of her now belonged to him.

Her blood beat in a wild rhythm as he reached a finger inside her. It felt tight, too tight, and he stopped with only a knuckle at first. But then he continued, pressing inexorably onward until his finger was lodged fully inside.

She drew a sharp inhalation, then another, as he teased her inner flesh with gentle but insistent strokes. Leaning over, he kissed her again, muffling the helpless little whimpers that were coming from her throat.

Then he added another finger and began stretching her more.

An embarrassing moisture formed as she turned slick against his hand. Instinctively, she clamped her thighs tight, trying to force him out.

But he burrowed deeper, his fingers scissoring open like a fan as he insinuated his thumb into her outer folds to find a spot that made her convulse and cry out.

"There's a girl," he said against her lips, his fingers moving insistently below. "Spread those pretty thighs and let me make it even better."

But she didn't know how it could get better, as a clawing hunger built inside her that demanded appeasement.

He stroked faster, deeper, and she was lost—his to command, his to please. Her thighs fell wide, as she gave him permission to do whatever he wished.

He leaned up next to her and watched. Watched as he continued moving his fingers inside her with deft strokes. Watched as her breasts heaved and her hips bucked, taking his fingers into her now with a kind of grateful supplication.

And then light and heat spread through her in an astonishing burst, pleasure radiating out from where he cradled her and into every inch of herself.

She lay stunned, half-giddy and giggling as she wondered why in the world she'd ever been nervous about this.

About him.

This was wonderful.

This was heaven.

When, please, could she have some more?

He eased away and stood up, his hands going to the belt of his robe. When he turned back, her eyes went wide and a warning glimmer of her fears returned.

She'd seen him before, there at the lake. Seen him in all his glorious masculine beauty.

But she hadn't seen him aroused. Hadn't known he would look so powerful, so strong and tall, or that his shaft would be so large.

He was a big man, in every way.

Good heavens, she'd had trouble taking his fingers at first; how was he ever going to put *that* into her?

"You'll never fit," she blurted out as she tried to scoot off the other side of the bed. But she was still bound inside her infernal nightgown, her arms incapable of helping her stand.

Before she could go so much as another inch, he caught her around one ankle. "No," he admonished, "you're not going anywhere."

Settling a knee on the bed, he joined her. "As for fitting, you'll take me just fine. We'll just have to make sure you're ready first."

What does that mean? She frowned.

He reached up and rubbed the spot between her brows, then kissed her, taking his time to gently reclaim her mouth.

"You've liked what we've done so far, have you not?" he said a minute later.

"Yes," she admitted on a whisper.

"Then trust me to make the rest of this good for you. I can, you know."

And suddenly she realized that of all men, he was likely the best she could possibly have found to take her innocence.

"It's going to hurt, though, isn't it?"

"A little. I won't lie. You are a virgin and you're quite small. But we'll find a way to make it easy. All you have to do is trust me. I am your husband. Let me decide what it is you need. Trust me to know best."

On any other occasion she might have taken exception to his statement, since she wasn't the sort of woman who could blindly obey a man. But he was right in this instance. He was her husband and he was going to consummate their marriage tonight no matter what she said or did. And he was right as well that she had liked everything he'd done so far. So why not trust him?

She nodded. "All right. But could we at least take off this nightgown?"

He laughed. "We can tonight. There'll be plenty of occasions later for that sort of play."

Before she had time to consider his remark any further, he reached out and freed her from her gown.

After tossing it onto the floor, he pulled her into his arms and kissed her, parting her lips to thoroughly plunder the inside of her mouth. He coaxed her to join him, her responses growing more open and eager, natural and easy.

"Touch me," he said, as his mouth moved to her throat and his hands to her breasts, where he began toying with her nipples in the most stirring of ways.

"Where?" she whispered.

"Anywhere. Everywhere."

She was tentative at first, careful to confine her hands to his arms and shoulders and the top of his back. But when he started suckling her breasts again, she grew bolder, letting her fingers wander over his chest to thread into the light thatch of hair that grew there. She found one flat nipple, and with a daring she didn't know she possessed, she flicked it with her fingernail.

He shuddered and groaned, much to her delight.

She roved more freely after that, tracing the lean plane of his stomach, the curve of his hip and the hard, muscled length of his thigh. She located the slight hollow at the base of his spine and the firm roundness of his buttocks.

He liked that, especially when she stroked down to the clef where his buttocks met his thighs.

Suddenly, as if he could stand it no more, he reached out and took hold of her hand, moving it between them. With his large hand guiding hers, he wrapped her fingers around the hard length of his arousal.

She startled at the sensation, marveling at the contrast between his warm velvety skin and the rigidity of his shaft. He moved her fingers, showing her what he wanted, compelling her to tighten her grip far more than she might have imagined he would want.

Then he left her again to explore, while he continued his own sensual wanderings.

She was stroking the head of his shaft, moving her thumb over a curious bead of moisture that formed there, when he pulled her hand away and rolled her onto her back. Without preamble, he parted her thighs with his hands, then buried his face where she least expected.

"Ahh, ahh, ahh," she cried as he began licking her core as if he were enjoying some particularly savory dish. He parted her nether lips and feasted more fully, spearing her with his tongue before finding a nub of flesh and suckling in a way that made her writhe in abandon.

Thoughts slid away as her entire world narrowed to the place between her legs and the sharp, aching need he was building with relentless determination. She had no control, her body growing increasingly slick as his every touch coaxed forth more of her feminine moisture.

But he didn't seem to mind. In fact, it seemed as if his actions were specifically designed to elicit that effect, as though he wanted that part of her as wet and needy as it could possibly become.

She ached with a violent yawning desire to be filled, to be taken in ways she didn't even understand. The yearning grew, driving her half-mad and desperate, until she wondered if she might die were it not assuaged. He drove her to the brink, but just when she prayed to be cast over into blissful oblivion, he stopped.

Her eyes popped wide, a half scream of frustration issuing from her lips.

But she realized he wasn't being cruel moments later as he rolled onto his back and lifted her so that she was straddled over him.

"Take me inside you," he told her, his words harsh with need. "Take as much of me as you can manage; then I'll see to the rest."

Take him?

"I don't know how," she cried.

"It will come naturally—you'll see. Here, I'll help."

Reaching between them, he guided his shaft so that the head rubbed against the entrance to her femininity. "Press down. Feed me into you."

She tried, leaning forward with her hands braced on his chest to urge him deeper.

But he was large and her own untried passage so narrow that she could barely take more than the tip. She realized now why he'd tried to make her so slick, so she could accept him more easily, more fully.

"Rise up," he said, teeth clenched, "then come back down. Hard."

She did, lifting herself up, then bouncing down.

The move gained him another inch. She did it again and was rewarded by a bit more. But then it began to hurt, his intrusion leaving her stretched and uncomfortable, though he was still barely inside her.

"Rest a moment," he said.

She shook her head, her long hair tumbling over her shoulders and across his stomach. "Gabriel, I don't know if I can do this. Maybe we should stop."

"No, sweetheart, not when we're nearly there."

Reaching up, he swept back her hair, then cupped her cheeks with his broad palms and leaned up for a kiss. The move pushed him a fraction deeper, her cry lost against his mouth as he ravished her with his lips and tongue.

He deepened their kisses, distracting her with such sweet pleasure that before she had time to consider, the pain began to dull. Without thinking, she wiggled closer to kiss him back, to kiss him mindlessly, and as she did, he slid in a little deeper.

His hands moved to her thighs and spread her wider, then clutched her hips and buttocks to hold her tight.

Kissing her all the while, he raised her up so that he almost pulled free, then brought her down again, forcefully and without mercy.

A sharp pain stabbed through her as she was impaled, and she cried out, aware that her maidenhead had been breached. He was lodged deep and thick within her, so close she could feel his erection throbbing against her tender inner flesh. For a moment, she wasn't sure she could bear it, overwhelmed by the sensation, stretched beyond her capability.

Quite suddenly, he wrapped her inside his arms and rolled her over so she lay on her back beneath him. He'd managed the change in positions without losing any of the advantage he'd gained. Taking her mouth again with his, he slid his palms under her buttocks and shifted her up and into him so that, quite improbably, he went deeper. With a hand, he urged her to lock her legs around his waist, her arms around his back.

He pulled back, nearly all the way out, then thrust in again, his movements stealing her breath. She hung on as he set up a rhythm—in and out, then in and out again.

Closing her eyes, she steeled herself to endure, knowing he needed this no matter how painful it might be. Knowing she would bear it as his wife.

But then he bent his head again to her caress her breasts with the sweetest of suction and slid his fingers between them to tease the nub of flesh that gave her such delight.

Suddenly she was straining beneath him, inviting

him in rather than resisting, drawing him deep, as deep as he could go, as desire flared back to life. The pain eased, all but forgotten as pleasure took its place.

He thrust harder, faster, as she kissed him wildly and urged him on, instinctively moving her hips up to meet his own, to take everything he had to give. Time spun away, this moment all she knew, as her yearning escalated, hunger turning her wanton as she strained closer to a promised kind of bliss.

The air filled with keening cries that she scarcely recognized as her own, her body damp and shaking, need tormenting her as her blood boiled hot and her lungs labored for breath.

She held him tighter and let him lead her where he willed, giving herself to him, trusting he would see her safely to shore.

And then suddenly she was flying, breath sobbing from her throat as waves of delight burst free and spiraled outward, everywhere. With his touch, he'd promised her heaven, and he hadn't lied.

She floated on an ocean of bliss, holding him as he claimed his own shuddering satisfaction, the heat of his release warm and wet inside her.

Then he lay quiet in her arms.

At length, he rolled away, separating himself from her. He didn't speak as he drew the sheet up over her and left the bed.

She wanted to call him back but didn't.

Was he leaving her? Already?

Turning her head away, she fought a sudden, inexplicable urge to cry. She missed him already and had no earthly idea why.

But to her relief he returned, a basin of water and a towel in his hands, which he set down on the night table.

He eased back the sheet again, exposing her to his eyes and the night air, which felt unexpectedly cool. Vividly aware of her nakedness and her puckered nipples, she covered her breasts with her arms.

"Don't," he said, his voice raspy. "You are beautiful,

every inch of you. Don't ever hide yourself from me, particularly when we are alone. Never when we are together in our bed. Is that understood?"

She nodded and slowly lowered her arms to her sides.

After saturating the cloth in the water, he wrung it out, then laid it up high between her thighs. It stung for a moment, then began to soothe some of the soreness from her intimate flesh.

She gasped as she caught sight of the sheets for the first time. Blood was smeared across the white cotton and over her thighs as well. Gabriel was bloody as well, his flaccid shaft coated in the remains of her maidenhead.

"I'll wash after I've seen to you," he said, noticing the direction of her glance.

To her surprise, his shaft stirred under her gaze, as he grew partially aroused from nothing more than a look.

He rinsed and wrung out the cloth, then applied it to her again. "Don't worry. I know you're sore. I won't take you again tonight."

She noticed he didn't say anything about tomorrow.

Then again, if he pleasured her as thoroughly as he had tonight, she knew she wouldn't mind, even if a little discomfort was involved.

No wonder he had women throwing themselves at him. She better understood now the whispered comments she'd overheard about him in London. Realized why he was so successful at luring even the most virtuous of females into his bed. For once they had a taste of Gabriel Landsdowne, why would they ever want any other man?

Yet he was *her* husband, not theirs.

But would he cleave to his pledge to be faithful to her? Or would he grow bored once the novelty wore off and his interests turned elsewhere?

She closed her eyes, not wanting to think of all the reasons why she would never be enough.

When he'd finished wiping away her virgin's blood, he dried her, then carried the basin with its pink-tinged water over to the slop.

Pouring clean water for himself, he washed and dried himself as well.

Naked and clearly unashamed of it, he padded back to the bed and slid in next to her.

"Sleep," he commanded as he tucked her close to his side, one long arm slung over her shoulder. He curved a hand around her right breast and drifted off.

She shifted into a more comfortable position and felt him tighten his hold on her.

He was possessive, she realized, even in his sleep.

She knew he'd had carnal relations with a great many women, but had he ever actually loved one? And if he had, could he ever do so again?

Not that she wanted him to. Theirs was not a love match, whatever rumors to that effect her family was determined to circulate. So long as she and Northcote got along without quarreling, she would be satisfied.

Wouldn't she?

Frowning, she sighed and forced her eyes closed. She wouldn't sleep—she was far too keyed up—but she could doze a bit.

Less than a minute later, sleep overtook her.

Chapter 16

"What would you like to do today?" Gabriel asked over a late breakfast the next morning.

She looked up from her plate of eggs and toast and peered across the table at him. He sat relaxed in his chair, a cup of hot black coffee cradled in one hand. He seemed in fine spirits for a change; the result, she presumed, of a night of good sex and good sleep.

As for herself, she was still trying to adjust to the new intimacy in their relationship. Every time she remembered the night just past, a flush would creep into her cheeks. The reaction was only made worse by the residual tenderness between her legs, which served as a constant reminder of how it had felt to have him inside her.

If only he wouldn't look at her as if he were remembering their night together too and couldn't wait to take her again. He made her feel all tingly and self-conscious—and yes, desirous. The tips of her breasts ached, both from fresh need as well as from all the attention he'd lavished upon them last night. Worse, they were puckered up as hard as a pair of unripe berries beneath her bodice. More than once, she'd caught him looking at her breasts, then smiling up at her with knowing eyes and a silent laugh.

Jesu, but the man is a devil.

At least he hadn't pressed her to have sex again this morning, even though she knew he would have enjoyed another romp. But he'd been amazingly considerate on that score, though she couldn't claim he'd been gentlemanly, considering the way he'd embarrassed her earlier in front of Mrs. Canby.

"See to it a hot bath is drawn up for Lady Northcote."

"Of course, my lord," the housekeeper had said. "I'll prepare it myself."

"Good. And be sure to put in a healthy measure of Epsom salts. Her ladyship has reason to be sore this morn."

Esme had wanted to cuff him then and there, especially when he'd noticed the high color in her cheeks and grinned at her obvious embarrassment.

"It's nothing she won't know about anyway, given the bloody state of the sheets," he'd said as soon as they were alone.

"Perhaps, but you didn't have to make such an effort to point it out."

"I only had your well-being in mind. Besides, I'm pretty certain the Canbys know we're having sex. I suspect the bigger surprise is finding out that we didn't consummate until last night."

She laid her hands on her flaming cheeks and groaned.

With a laugh, he'd pulled her into his arms and kissed her until she forgot all about being embarrassed. Had it not been for her soreness, she knew he would have tumbled her straight back into bed and taken her again, regardless of anything the servants might have thought.

Picking up her teacup, she took a drink, grateful to find the tea cool enough not to scald. "I don't know. What is there to do here in Cornwall?"

"Well, we're not visiting the neighbors; that's for certain. And they should have sense enough to know we're on our honeymoon and stay away."

"Gabriel," she admonished softly. Though truth be known, she had no more interest in entertaining company than he.

"I could take you into town to shop," he suggested.

She shook her head. "No, not today."

"Ah, but I forget. You probably like shopping as little as you do clothes."

"I said I don't follow *fashion*. I didn't say I don't like clothes. Or shopping."

"I beg pardon, my dear, and stand corrected," he answered solemnly.

But she could tell he was teasing her. Her pulse beat a fraction faster, her stomach jittering. She rather liked this new, more cheerful Gabriel. She wondered how long he would remain.

He took a drink of his coffee. "What about a walk? There's a fine view along the sea cliffs and a gentle path that winds down to the beach not too far from here. It's all rather picturesque, presuming you enjoy that sort of thing."

"Oh yes, a walk sounds like the very thing. And Burr could do with a run."

At the sound of his name, Burr lifted his head from where he lounged underneath the table—no doubt hoping for a scrap or two despite the ample breakfast he'd already consumed.

"Ah yes, Burr. He is, of course, welcome to come along."

"I'll just go and get my hat, shall I?" she said with sudden enthusiasm.

"Don't you want to finish your breakfast first?"

She glanced down at the eggs and toast left on her plate, suddenly aware that she was still hungry. "Oh, I suppose you're right."

Reaching for her fork, she ate most of the eggs and a slice of buttered toast, then washed it all down with the tea left in her cup.

Gabriel laughed at her indecorous haste.

"Don't ever tell Mama you saw me do that," she warned him as she laid down her fork again and got to her feet.

"Never. Your secret is safe with me."

She smiled and wondered suddenly if she might enjoy this time with him after all.

Gabriel watched her go, her dog at her heels as they raced up the stairs.

What a child she can be sometimes, he thought, smiling again at her uninhibited display of enthusiasm as he poured himself a bit more coffee.

Of course, she had been anything but childlike in bed last night, her responses passionate and eager in spite of her initial trepidation. Once he'd managed to overcome her virginal fears, she had turned willing and warm in his arms, becoming as sensual and seductive as a siren of ancient myth. She might be shy and untutored, but she wasn't cold.

No, after last night, he knew there wasn't a cold bone in her entire luscious body.

With the proper instruction, she was going to make an excellent lover, and he looked forward to teaching her. In fact, he would have enjoyed nothing more than spending the entire day in bed with her, but he wasn't a monster. He knew she was sore and needed rest after his vigorous rending of her maidenhead.

God, she was tight, he thought, tighter than any woman he'd had in recent memory. Perhaps tighter than any woman he'd had *ever.* Then again, his tastes never had run to virgins, so he supposed there was that point to consider.

Still, Esme was unique, nothing short of extraordinary.

Beautiful and sweet-tempered and mine.

All mine.

His shaft turned hard despite the satisfaction he'd found with her last night. He cursed softly under his breath, well aware he would have to resist his more prurient impulses for a little while longer.

But after that . . .

Suddenly she was back, attired in a lovely green walking dress and a long silvery gray cloak. A pert little bonnet sat perched atop her silky dark hair, the matching green ribbon tied neatly at her chin. As for her shoes, he noticed that she'd opted for a pair of sensible brown half boots that looked as if they were well broken in. Most women would have chosen a pair of high heels because of how pretty they looked in spite of their unsuitability for cliff walking.

But not his Esme. As she'd told him, she was no slave to fashion.

He found he approved—and not just of her footwear.

Pushing his chair back from the table, he rose and went to her, taking her hands. "You look beautiful."

She smiled, a measure of her shyness returning. "It is only a walking dress."

"Yes, but it is you who are wearing it."

Unable to resist, he slid his arms beneath her cloak, placed his palms on her bottom and pulled her close. She gave a sharp little inhalation as he pressed her up against the erection he made no effort to hide.

With her wrapped tight inside his arms, he took her mouth, hungry and claiming. She trembled, then kissed him back, opening her mouth to accept his demands as she made tentative demands of her own.

For a second, he considered going back on his promise and carrying her upstairs for a thorough tupping. She could spend the whole day in bed getting acclimated to the sensation of having him buried deep inside her.

But he knew she wasn't ready again yet, so he broke their kiss, his lungs laboring in a way he didn't often feel. "We should go." He set her away from him. "I find I could do with that walk."

She looked at him, breathless and flushed. "Yes, me too."

And then she laughed, a high, pure sound that went straight to his heart.

Scowling, he strode out into the hall to find his coat.

The wind ruffled Esme's cloak and skirts as Gabriel helped her down the rocky path to the beach. The ocean stretched beyond like a gleaming jewel, waves crashing to shore with dollops of frothy white on top. She breathed in the cool, refreshing air, savoring its salty scent.

"I'm relieved to know that I didn't lie to Mallory after all," she remarked as they reached the flat, sandy beach and began to stroll arm in arm.

Burr, who was in his element, let out a happy bark and raced ahead, stopping every so often to sniff at some interesting find.

Gabriel arched a brow. "Lie to her in what regard?"

"About Highhaven being near the shore. I said I was looking forward to spending time at the ocean, and to my delight, I find that I am."

"So you like it?" he asked after a slight pause. "You are not sorry I brought you here?"

"No. Why would I be sorry?" She sent him a look of surprise.

"Well, there are some ladies who might find this area remote and confining, with a lack of amusements to keep them entertained."

She made a dismissive noise. "Those ladies are not me, as I am continually telling you. In fact, the next time we come here, I shall bring along my paints and paper. I would love to spend a day drawing the cliffs and the shoreline. It's quite majestic."

"Then we shall do exactly that. And perhaps if the weather is clement, I could strip off for you again and stretch out naked on the beach."

Her eyes widened for an instant before she gave him a shy smile. "Yes, perhaps you could."

Laughing, he stopped and pulled her into his arms, then found her lips for a long and very thorough kiss.

Her head was spinning by the time he let her go, her legs weak and a little wobbly as they resumed their walk. It was a good thing he'd taken hold of her arm again or else she feared she might have collapsed onto the sand.

"Are you hungry?" he asked a short while later. "Mrs.

Canby packed us a couple sandwiches and slipped them into my coat pocket just as we were leaving."

It hadn't been much more than an hour since they'd left the house, but even as she opened her mouth to refuse, she was surprised to realize that she was hungry.

Ravenous actually.

No doubt the result of a light dinner and breakfast and loads of fresh air and exercise. As for the kind of exercise, she forced herself to focus on their walk rather than everything they'd done in bed last night.

"I could do with a bite, if you could," she agreed.

He led her over to a large flat rock and helped her get comfortably settled before he took a seat next to her.

"Ham and cheese with mustard," he said as he checked the first cloth-wrapped sandwich. "Let us see what else she packed. Ah good, this one must be for you. Cheese and chutney." He passed her the second sandwich, then opened his own and took a bite.

They ate in companionable silence, content to watch the rhythmic undulation of the waves and Burr's antics as he splashed through the water, barking and chasing birds.

He padded up to them when she was nearly finished, his fur wet and sand covered, tail wagging happily. She'd eaten as much as she wanted, so she tossed him the uneaten portion of her sandwich. He wolfed it down eagerly, then stretched and gave a full body shake.

Water went everywhere.

She squealed and raised her arms to avoid the droplets but got doused anyway. "Oh, Burr," she complained.

But he just gave her an unrepentant doggy grin, then settled down to rest.

Beside her, Gabriel chuckled and brushed off a few droplets of his own. He reached into the interior pocket of his coat and withdrew a handkerchief. "Here, allow me."

Gently Gabriel blotted the moisture from her cheeks and forehead and a damp spot at the base of her throat. He watched her pulse speed faster, beating visibly underneath her skin.

Reaching out, he touched the tip of one finger to a small purple bruise that lay just below the edge of her collar. "It would appear that I've marked you."

"Oh." She started to lift a hand to the spot but let it fall back in her lap. "It doesn't hurt."

"I am glad. But perhaps it needs a bit more soothing." Leaning close, he placed his lips lightly on the mark and kissed her ever so tenderly before running his tongue over her flesh.

She shivered and closed her eyes.

Taking care, Gabriel scattered kisses over her throat and along the fine curve of her jaw. He moved upward to her ear, then lingered to tease its curved shell and the ultra-sensitive flesh just behind her lobe. Kissing her all the while, he covered one breast with his palm and searched out her nipple where it hid pebble hard beneath her gown and stays. He'd noticed her pert little nubs outlined beneath her dress at breakfast and had been pleased to know that she was as aware of him as he was of her.

When they'd left the house, he hadn't planned to seduce her, but suddenly he had to have her—at least some small bit of her, anyway. Their coupling last night, rather than appeasing him, seemed only to have increased his appetite. Maybe his hunger stemmed from the weeks of abstinence he'd endured prior to their wedding, but whatever the cause, he wanted her now.

"Lie back," he murmured against her lips.

"What?"

"Lie back. There's room without me if you're careful."

"But why? What are you doing to do?"

He gave her a lascivious grin.

"But we can't," she said in shocked tones. "Not here, out in the open."

"This is my land. No one will see us."

"But what if they do?"

"Then they'll get an eyeful, won't they?"

She frowned, considering. "Still, shouldn't we go home if we're going to—" She circled a hand to finish the unspoken part of her sentence.

He shook his head. "No, I want you now. Besides, I'm only going to pleasure you a little, like I did last night."

It took her a few moments to understand his meaning. As soon as she did, an adorable flush rose to her hairline and she squirmed. But he could tell she wanted him to proceed despite her nerves.

She hesitated another few moments, then shifted sideways and leaned back, taking care to center herself on the rock face.

Dropping down to his knees, he disappeared under her skirts and settled himself between her legs.

And with the sun shining and the waves crashing to shore, he feasted on her intimate flesh, her ragged cries carried away on the breeze as he brought her to a shattering climax.

She lay panting and replete afterward, a look of dreamy satisfaction in her soft blue eyes. "What about you?" she asked drowsily. "Don't you want to—"

"I can wait," he said, getting to his feet.

Her eyes went to the obvious bulge straining his trousers. "It doesn't look like it."

A laugh caught him, one that turned quickly to a groan as his arousal protested the movement. "Don't tempt me, my dear. I'm enough on the edge as it is."

Slowly, she sat up, reaching to readjust her bonnet, which had gone askew. He watched her hesitate, wondering what she was thinking as her already pink cheeks flamed red again. "Is there anything I . . . that is . . . could I do something to help?"

She looked so mortified, unable to even meet his eyes, that he nearly laughed again. But as the idea took hold, his shaft stiffened further and gave a violent throb of longing. Just the thought of her pretty mouth on him was enough nearly to be his undoing.

Yet despite their night together, she was still

amazingly innocent, and he didn't want to shock her unduly by introducing her to some of the more lurid pleasures. Not so soon anyway. A good man would resist the impulse and take a long walk to ease his raging erection.

But when had he ever been good?

"Actually there is," he said, his words husky with need. "But only if you want to. I won't be upset if you decide you wish to refuse."

Not much anyway.

Her eyes turned wide. "What is it?"

"The same thing I just did to you, only in reverse."

He watched the play of emotion on her face as she puzzled it out. Breaths heaved in her chest, the tops of her small breasts trembling. "Mercy. Though I suppose it only makes sense, considering."

He grinned, despite the situation. "Really, you don't have to, my dear."

"No," she said, surprising him. "I will. But you'll have to tell me how. I've never done this before."

He laughed again. "On that score, I am well aware."

Slowly, he sobered, his arousal twitching with anticipation. Reaching down, he loosened the ribbons of her bonnet and took off her hat, setting it safely aside where the wind wouldn't sweep it away in a gust. He inched closer, positioning her so he stood between her legs with the open edges of his coat arranged to provide shelter for her.

"What do I do?" she whispered, her pupils dilated with nervousness and curiosity.

"Open my falls and take me out of my drawers. Or would it be easier if I did it?"

"No, I'll try." Her fingers shook as she reached to unfasten his trouser buttons, slipping one free, then another.

His thigh muscles clenched, his balls tight and aching with a lust he couldn't remember experiencing for a very long time. For a moment he felt almost like a green boy having his first fling, the need was suddenly so intense. His thickened shaft strained against his drawers as he waited.

"Here," he said when she couldn't quite manage the buttons.

He flicked open the buttons with a practiced hand and let his heavy arousal spring free, its engorged, vein-covered length straining toward her in supplication.

Her breathing quickened and she swallowed hard. Suddenly she looked uncertain.

"Do you want to stop?" he asked, his tone guttural.

She hesitated, then shook her head. "No."

"Then take me in your mouth. Slowly at first; you don't want to go too fast."

After drawing a ragged breath, she straightened her shoulders and leaned in. She touched him first with her tongue, a tentative brush along the tip that made him jolt as if he'd been hit by electricity.

Alarmed by his reaction, she pulled back. "I'm sorry. Did I do it wrong?"

"No. God no, you did it just right." He clenched a fist at his side. "Please, continue."

A little frown of concentration creased the spot between her eyes in an expression of determination that he was beginning to recognize. She curled one little hand around his shaft to hold him steady; then she opened her mouth and licked him again, starting again with the tip, then up one side and down the other.

He shuddered, a drop of semen leaking from the slit. But rather than quail, she caught it on her tongue and swallowed. "Hmm, salty. You taste like the sea."

Glancing up, she met his eyes.

He expected her to look away. Instead, she opened her mouth and brazenly drew him in. She suckled him, her lips warm and slick around the head of his shaft, her tongue swirling this way and that with moves that made the blood turn to steam in his veins.

Taking her fingers in his, he pumped her fist over his shaft from center to base, showing her how to stroke him while she suckled. As she caressed him, she grew bolder, her eyes closing as she drew on him as if he were as sweet and delicious as a stick of hard candy.

He held himself steady, resisting the urge to thrust deeper into her mouth. "More," he groaned, as his hands came up to cup her face. "Take more."

She paused briefly, then widened her mouth and let him push another inch inside.

"That's it," he urged. "Relax and take me."

Gently, careful not to do more than she could take, he began to thrust slowly in and out of her mouth, the sounds of her moans and the wet heat of her tongue driving him to the brink. He tried to pull out, his climax upon him, but she tightened her hold and wouldn't let go.

Without meaning to, he released in her mouth, hot spurts of his seed shooting into her throat. She gulped, working hard to swallow as much as she could manage. He thrust shallowly once, twice more, then forced himself to pull free, his shaft limp, body gloriously replete.

He couldn't remember when he'd been better satisfied by a woman's mouth. Had he ever? If she weren't already his bride, he would have set her up as his mistress, since she had all the makings of a damned fine courtesan.

He waited, suddenly worried at her reaction. Had he gone too far?

But then she looked up, swallowing again as she fought to regain her breath. "Was it all right?" she whispered. "Did you like it?"

Shocked and not a little relieved, he pulled her up and into his arms. "No, I didn't like it. I *loved* it."

She smiled, shyly but with a hint of naughty delight. "Good. Is it very wrong of me to admit that I did too?"

Laughing, he kissed her. "No, sweetheart," he said when they came up for air. "It's not wrong at all. Not in the slightest."

Chapter 17

For Esme, the next three weeks passed by in a pleasant haze, each day seemingly better than the one that had come before. Without any particular consultation on the subject, she and Gabriel fell into an easy, enjoyable routine.

When the weather was clear, they took long walks and often went down to the beach, where she sketched or painted while he read a book or played a game of fetch with Burr.

The dog, who had never really bonded with anyone but her, had quickly become Gabriel's faithful and devoted slave. Were she a different sort of person, she might have been jealous. Instead, she was simply happy to see what good friends man and dog had become.

As for Gabriel's promise to strip out of his clothing for her again so she could draw him, the cooler temperatures had not been cooperative. Still, that didn't mean that she hadn't drawn him at all, her sketchbook filling almost daily with new renderings.

On other occasions, Gabriel took her to see some of the nearby tidal estuaries. She delighted in observing the tiny fish and other aquatic creatures that made the rocky, shallow pools their home. She added them to her collection of sketches as well.

Another favorite out-of-doors activity was riding. Gabriel was an excellent horseman and together they would gallop over the moors, the wind tugging at their hair and clothing like a mischievous child. On particularly sunny days, they liked to stop where the cliffs overlooked the sea and partake of one of Mrs. Canby's delicious picnic nuncheons while the majestic blue-gray waves rolled and crashed beyond.

On the days when they were not so lucky and cold rain drummed on the roof and cascaded like rivers from the eaves, she and Gabriel would stay inside, cozy-warm by the fireplace. Usually they both read or else took turns at the writing desk penning a variety of letters: she to her family and friends, and he to his friends, his steward at Ten Elms, his servants and his London man of business.

And when they weren't doing any of those things, they had sex.

Lots and lots of sex.

She'd quickly grown used to being kissed and caressed awake each morning, his mouth and hands busy arousing her so that she was slick and aching with desire by the time he sheathed himself heavily inside her.

He took her at bedtime each night as well, awakening her lust in ways she'd never imagined possible as he brought her to completion over and over again. In fact, he'd told her to stop wearing a nightgown to bed, since, in his words, "it only got in the way."

She never knew what position he might choose or when he would decide to show her a new one. Front, back, side, up, down, on her hands and knees, her legs over his shoulders, her legs hooked over his arms—he was always showing her something different.

He liked a variety of places too, not content to confine their lovemaking to her bed or his own. Chairs, tables, sofas, the floor. He'd even had her once standing up, her back pressed against the wall, her legs locked tight at his waist as he thrust hard and fast within her until she'd had to press her mouth to his shoulder so the whole house wouldn't hear her cries of fulfillment.

And then there were the times during the day when he would shock and surprise her. Like the afternoon they'd been reading on the sofa, the tea Mrs. Canby had delivered still steaming in the pot, when he'd gone over and locked the door. Picking a clean napkin up off the tray, he'd twisted it lengthwise, then told her to open her mouth.

"So you won't have them all coming down on us when I make you scream," he'd explained as he put the napkin into her mouth, then tied the ends at the back of her head. "Because that's exactly what I'm going to do. I'm going to make you climax so hard you won't be able to stand straight for the rest of the day."

And he had, using his mouth and hands on her first in ways that had left her half-dazed and frenzied with need before he'd seated her on his lap in a chair and pumped into her from behind. Using his knees to spread her wide, he'd penetrated her so deeply she'd felt as though they'd been joined into one, each thrust longer and harder and more earth-shattering than the last, until finally she reached her peak, her screams mercifully silenced by the cloth in her mouth as a dark, powerful bliss splintered her apart.

Perhaps she ought to have found him too intense, his sexual demands too much for her to satisfy. But the more times he took her, the more her own cravings grew.

She ached for him, wanting him even when he wasn't inside her. She reached for him, curling herself against him as they slept side by side at night, and again during the day, even if was only to hold his hand. She'd come to their marriage expecting nothing—actually less than nothing—and fearing the very worst.

But day by day she fell deeper under his spell, enjoying more than his touch, but his company as well. His clever mind and his sharp wit. His unexpectedly generous nature and his willingness to share—everything, that is, but personal details about himself.

Despite their closeness, she still knew almost nothing about his past or his family, whereas he knew practically everything about her own. They talked freely about her family as she regaled him with stories and anecdotes that made him smile and laugh. But the few times she'd ventured to ask questions about his own family, the most he would tell her was that his parents were dead and that he didn't see much of his other relations. She'd learned better than to ask why, since he grew moody if she pushed. And so she'd let it drop, far too happy and content to risk starting an argument with him. She didn't ask about the future and he didn't bring it up, the days drifting one into the other.

"Shall we go into town today?" he asked her over breakfast that Friday. "The market will be open and I thought you might enjoy seeing a little more of Cornwall than our own small corner. We could even have a meal at the inn if you'd like."

So far, she'd had no complaints regarding their isolation, but he was right: it might be nice to spend a few hours in a town surrounded by people again.

Smiling at him over her tea and scones, she agreed.

The main thoroughfare in Truro was crowded when they arrived. Tradesmen, shopkeepers and farmers were gathered in the market square to hawk their wares, while townspeople and visitors wandered among the wooden stands in search of produce, livestock, artisan-made goods, services and the best bargains to be had. Merchants and shop owners displayed their goods as well, in hopes of luring customers inside rather than out.

Esme watched a pair of women stop to ogle a display of hats in the window of the local millinery, while a trio of sailors disappeared inside a tavern in search of a pint and a game of cards, no doubt. With her hand tucked securely around Gabriel's arm, they wandered, enjoying the noise and smells and vibrant pulse of life.

When she paused to admire a length of fine blue-green silk that the merchant claimed had only just arrived from the Orient, Gabriel purchased ten yards. And when she oohed and aahed over a selection of toffees and sugared fruits, he bought her large handfuls of each that the candy maker was delighted to wrap in heavy paper and brightly colored ribbons.

As for Gabriel, he bought nothing for himself, though he did stop to consider a rather handsome pocket watch made from rare Cornish silver.

After moving on, much to the watchmaker's disappointment, they started in the direction of Truro's best inn, where Gabriel told her a rather decent meal could be had. He was checking the busy street for an opportunity to cross safely, when someone called his name, the sound ringing out above the throng.

"Northcote! I say, Northcote, is that you?"

Gabriel turned his head, a smile creasing his cheeks when he caught sight of a slender, brown-haired man of medium height threading his way through the crowd toward him. "Mark? Mark Dennis!"

Moving swiftly, Gabriel took several steps forward and caught hold of the other man's hand. They exchanged an enthusiastic handshake while Esme looked on. They laughed, clearly pleased by their chance meeting.

"By God, it's good to see you," Mark Dennis said. "How long has it been?"

"Two years at the very least, maybe three. But that's what comes, I suppose, of you taking a position at an estate in the north county. How are the cold wilds of England, by the by?"

"Cold and wild." Dennis laughed. "But really, I cannot complain. A younger son only has so many options, and there are far worse fates than being private secretary to an earl. Besides, we cannot all end up peers like you."

The smile faded slowly from Gabriel's face. "True. Though had I the chance, I would happily trade it all if it meant having Matthew back. He was suited for this life and would have made a far better viscount than I ever shall."

Dennis looked suddenly abashed. "Christ, what a great clod you must think me, saying something with so little sensitivity. I'll understand entirely if you wish to turn your back now and forget we ever met."

Gabriel recovered quickly. "No, never that. Besides, it would rob me of the opportunity to harass you over all your other past sins. Pray, think no more of it."

Dennis reached again for Gabriel's hand and shook once more. "You are an excellent friend, Northcote. Excellent and generous of spirit, no matter what anyone else may say to the contrary."

The two men shared another round of smiles, once again in complete accord.

Before anything more could be said, Gabriel remembered her and swung around, a look of sincere apology on his face. "Forgive my lack of manners, my dear. It was not my intention to neglect you." Reaching out, he drew her forward and slipped an arm around her waist. "Allow me to do the honors and present you to my friend and former schoolmate, Mark Dennis. Mark, my wife, Esme."

"Wife!" Dennis's expression was so surprised as to be almost comical, but he recovered quickly. "What extraordinary news." His face split into a wide smile. "I am thrilled, thrilled for you both. Lady Northcote"— he paused and made her an elegant bow—"what a genuine delight to make your acquaintance."

"It is for me as well, Mr. Dennis," she said, smiling back. "I am always happy to meet a friend of my husband's."

"Well, I don't know that you'd want to meet *all* of Northcote's friends, or that he would want you to either. But it's lovely of you to say so all the same."

She laughed, taking an instant liking to Mark Dennis. He had an open, amiable manner and a genuine warmth and irreverent intelligence that put one instantly at ease.

"So what brings you to this part of the country?" Gabriel asked.

Dennis briefly lifted his eyes skyward. "It's my great-aunt, if you must know. Every few months, she claims to be at death's door, saying how it's only a matter of days until the grim reaper pays her a call and claims her eternal soul. She's nearly blind and about as ill-tempered as a badger. But she's rich, so Mama insisted I make the pilgrimage just in case the old girl decides to leave me something substantial in her will."

He gave a humorless chuckle. "She told me only this morning that I don't have my fawning down near so well as my multitude of cousins, so I expect the only thing great-aunt will leave me is a thinner pocketbook for having made this trip. Still, if it gets my mother to quit writing, begging me to visit dear Auntie, then it will be time and funds well spent."

"Ah, the tribulations of family," Gabriel said. "Thank God I so rarely have to set eyes on mine. Now, Esme here, she's got enough relations to populate a good-sized village."

"There are not *that* many of us," she protested.

Gabriel sent her a look. "Oh, come now. You've six brothers and a sister, their assorted spouses and children, your mother, aunts and uncles and cousins, plus their spouses and children. I'd say you might even qualify as a large village. You certainly have enough people to form a cricket league."

She frowned, considering. "Well, I will admit that we do all rather fill up Braebourne at Christmastide. What a blessing the house is so vast."

"Braebourne?" Mark Dennis chimed in. "Do you mean the Duke of Clybourne's estate?"

"Indeed," Gabriel said. "Esme is the duke's youngest sister."

Dennis's brown eyes alighted with deepened interest. "Then this is even more of an honor, Lady Northcote."

"Are you acquainted with Edward?"

"The duke? No. But I have corresponded with one of your brothers, Lord Lawrence. He has been assisting my employer with some legal matters this year past."

Esme brightened. "Then I shall be sure to mention you to him when next I write. He will be vastly glad to hear that we met."

"I am not so certain of that, but you are very kind," Dennis said.

"That is Esme, kind to both man and beast." Gabriel glanced down at her, and for a moment Esme lost herself in his eyes.

Just on the edge of her vision, Mark Dennis shuffled his feet and coughed. She looked up to find him smiling at her, gentle speculation in his gaze.

Dennis set a fist on his hip. "So, you are staying at Highhaven, I presume. What brings you here this time of year, other than an eagerness for some bracing sea air, that is?"

Absently, Gabriel rubbed a hand against the small of her back. She didn't even think he realized he was doing it, he'd grown so used to touching her.

But Mark Dennis noticed.

"Actually, we're newly married and are here on our honeymoon," Gabriel said.

"Blister it." Dennis shook his head in disbelief. "Leave it to me to be the one to interrupt your private time alone together. You ought to have told me to take myself off rather than letting me blather on and on when I'm sure you've other things you'd much rather be doing."

"Of course we would not, Mr. Dennis," Esme said. "You and Gabriel are old friends, school friends, if I remember right, and it is only natural that you should wish to renew your acquaintance. In fact, why do you not join us now for a repast? Gabriel and I were just on our way to the inn for a meal. You must come with us so that the two of you can continue to catch up on everything that has happened since last you met."

"Oh no, I could not." Dennis waved away the idea with a hand. "I've intruded more than enough already."

"Honestly, we would be delighted to have you. Gabriel and I have been too much in each other's company of late and it would be good to add a new voice to the conversation. Tell him, Gabriel," she urged, "convince him he must join us."

Gabriel arched an amused brow. "You heard the lady, Mark. Do come along or Esme will never be content on the matter."

Dennis hesitated. "If you are quite sure? I really do not wish to intrude."

"Excellent. It is all settled then." Esme smiled brightly. "Gentlemen, let us away."

The men laughed, then Gabriel tucked her hand into the curve of his arm and off the three of them went.

Chapter 18

"And I told him he was standing too near the bog, but the fool wouldn't listen," Mark Dennis said nearly three hours later as he, Gabriel and Esme sat around a table at the inn's best—and only—private parlor. "So in he went, wig and all. Took half a dozen men to haul him out and another hour to clean off enough of the muck before his wife would let him back in the house."

All three of them laughed, in a fine humor after a good meal and numerous libations—spirituous in the gentlemen's case, since Esme had confined herself to tea after a single glass of wine.

Gabriel leaned back in his chair and savored a swallow of brandy from the snifter the servant had just set down. The man cleared the cheese and sweets plates from the table, then moved quietly from the room.

"I'd forgotten how much I enjoy your stories, Mark," Gabriel said. "You always were one for spinning a fine yarn."

"You as well." Dennis played absently with the stem of his wineglass. "I can't recall the last time I've laughed so much. This afternoon has been exactly the respite I needed. My thanks to you both."

"Oh, we feel the same," Esme said. "This has been lovely, and I am so pleased to have made your acquaintance."

"And I yours, Lady Northcote."

"Yes, fate was clearly smiling when she brought us

all here to Truro today," Gabriel said. "Particularly since this is the first time I've let Esme venture into the populated world since I whisked her out from under the noses of her family three weeks ago."

Esme sent him a faintly scandalized look. "Gabriel, you make it sound as if you've been keeping me captive. Which he has not, Mr. Dennis," she assured the other man.

Gabriel chuckled and caught her hand where it lay in her lap, lifting it to his lips for a kiss. "Actually, I have rather. But only because I haven't been able to bring myself to share you until now."

Pretty color spread into her cheeks in a way he adored, making Gabriel suddenly wish his friend to perdition so he could kiss her. But such pleasures would have to wait until he and Esme got back home. Maybe if there was time, they would be able to fit a quick tup in before dinner.

Esme glanced away, then across the table at Mark. "You must promise to keep in touch, Mr. Dennis, and plan a stay with us when you next have a few days' leave from the demands of your employer."

"That is most kind of you, Lady Northcote." Dennis looked touched by her obvious sincerity. "I shall look forward to that occasion with eager anticipation."

Esme smiled. "Esme."

Dennis smiled back. "Esme. And if your husband has no objection, please call me Mark."

"She would likely call you Mark now even if I *did* object, so do as you both please," Gabriel said.

Esme gave Gabriel a wry look, while Dennis chuckled around a sip of his wine.

"Now, if you gentlemen will excuse me," Esme said, "I shall leave you to enjoy your libations. There is a hat I saw in one of the shop windows that I think might suit my sister, and I have a sudden fancy to inspect it more closely."

"You're going shopping?" Gabriel asked, still in possession of her hand. "Wait, and I will accompany you."

She shook her head and got to her feet. "You will

only be bored. Stay and enjoy talking to Mr. Dennis a while more. The shop is just a few doors away."

He and Dennis rose to their feet. "Even so, I do not like you going alone," Gabriel said. "Have one of the serving girls accompany you."

"As you like."

Gabriel rang for the proprietor, who had been attending them since their arrival, and made his request for a girl to accompany Esme.

"Gladly, your lordship." The man gave a bow. "I'll ask me own daughter to walk with her ladyship. She's a good, honest girl, Trudy is. You'll like her, my lady."

"I am sure I shall. There"—she turned back to Gabriel—"happy now?"

"Reasonably." Regardless of their audience, he gave her a quick kiss. "Don't be long."

"I shall not."

Once Esme and the innkeeper departed, he and Dennis resumed their seats.

Mark Dennis settled back, a broad smile on his face.

"What?" Gabriel asked.

Dennis shrugged. "Nothing. Just you."

"What about me?"

"Only that it's nice to see you happy for a change. You chose well when you set your sights on Esme Byron."

Gabriel sipped his brandy, deciding not to reveal the truth—that not only had he not chosen her, but that technically speaking she had been the one to set her sights on him as he lay naked and asleep. But Dennis was right. If he had to get trapped in the parson's noose, he could have fared a great deal worse than Esme.

Inwardly, he smiled, seeing her lovely face in his mind's eye. Then Dennis began speaking again, pulling him from his reverie.

"After what happened with Amanda all those years ago, I never thought you'd let yourself care for another woman. It's good to know you have finally found someone with whom to share your life."

Gabriel's hand tightened around his brandy glass. "I

believe we agreed *years ago* that you were never to mention that woman's name in my hearing."

Dennis's smile faltered. "Well, and so I did. But I cannot see what difference it makes now, not with you married and so clearly in love with your bride."

"What did you say?" Gabriel froze.

"I said you're in love. It's as clear as the nose on your rather overly long face. Surely you have realized."

In love? With Esme?

A jolt shot through Gabriel's system as if he'd been hit by a particularly violent lightning bolt.

He set down his drink with an audible chink. "I do not know what you imagine you can see, but you are mistaken." His voice was like ice.

Mark Dennis stared. "Well, I do not believe I am, but as you prefer."

"What I *prefer* on this subject is for you to leave it alone since it is none of your business. My wife and I rub along quite tolerably; she makes an excellent companion and is a fine addition to my bed. Anything more is irrelevant."

He drummed a pair of fingers against the tabletop. "As for Amanda Coyning, or whatever her current last name may be, I am lucky to have escaped her avaricious clutches. If I am not in error, she is on her third husband now, each one older, richer, and more dimwitted than the last. That way she can ensure their hasty demise and keep her coffers well supplied with gold."

Gabriel drew in a breath, gazing with unseeing eyes toward the window. "There was a time when I detested my uncle for interfering and ruining my chance to wed her. But in hindsight, he did me a great service. He thought he was inflicting yet another grave injury, but ultimately, it would seem he was doing a kindness, however unintended. Ah, the follies of being nineteen and fancying oneself in love."

"Gabriel, I am sorry. I didn't mean to dredge up old wounds," Dennis said, looking painfully uncomfortable.

"You have dredged up nothing, old friend. My

feelings for the former Miss Coyning are long dead, and as wintry as the grave. In fact, I don't think I ever actually loved her despite my youthful declarations and the weeks of agonized moping I spent after she jilted me and flung herself into the arms of her first wealthy catch. Really, I should be grateful to her as well for teaching me an important lesson."

"Which is?"

"Why, simply that love between a man and a woman is nothing but fantasy. There is lust and pleasure and, if one is lucky, friendship and respect. Anything else is complete delusion."

"I know you're a cynic, but surely even you do not really believe that."

"I believe exactly that, so do not speak to me again about how I love my wife. She is a pleasing young woman who will someday be the mother of my children. I shall honor her for that when the day comes. But love? There is no love, and I will thank you not to bring up the subject again."

Dennis looked troubled, but rather than argue further, he nodded. "Your marriage is your own concern, of course. I shall offer no observations about it in future."

Gabriel inclined his head at the other man's tacit apology, then tossed back the last of his brandy. "So, what news from the rest of our old cronies at Eton? I've heard nothing from any of them lately except Selworth, and I never did care much for anything he has to say."

Mark Dennis laughed, their easy friendship restored, and off he went in a new conversational direction.

Esme returned to the inn, the innkeeper's daughter, Trudy, chattering cheerfully away at her side. She was well pleased with the outing and delighted by her purchase, even though it was not a hat.

In truth, the bonnet for Mallory had been just an excuse. Her real goal had been the silver pocket watch that Gabriel had so admired when they had been shopping earlier. The watchmaker remembered her, beaming when she'd told him that she wished to purchase the watch for her husband. Luckily, Gabriel had just recently given her a generous amount of pin money, saying that even if she had no real need of it for her everyday expenses, she should nonetheless have some cash at her disposal to do with as she saw fit.

"I am not one of these men who use money as a way to manipulate their wives," he'd told her as he handed her the pound notes. "If this is not sufficient, you've only to ask for more. You will not find me ungenerous."

Her eyes had widened at the amount. "I can see that I won't. You are extremely generous. Thank you." Stretching up on her toes, she'd kissed him. He'd kissed her back, and moments later, money had been the last thing on her mind.

Until today, when he'd mentioned their outing to Truro. She was glad now she'd thought to put some of the cash in her reticule. To her delight, it had been just enough to cover the cost of the pocket watch, which she planned to surprise Gabriel with as a Christmas present.

She hugged the secret close to her chest as she walked down the hallway to the private parlor, the paper-wrapped watch hidden securely in the depths of her reticule. She paused, hearing the low, rich tones of the men's voices. Gabriel was saying something about Eton as she pushed open the door.

Gabriel and Mark Dennis swung their heads around as she entered the room, peculiar expressions on their faces—Dennis's curiously uneasy, while Gabriel's was disturbingly remote. Both men stood as she came farther inside.

"So, you are back." Gabriel ran his eyes over her assessingly. "Where is the hat?"

She grew still, taken aback by his tone, which was critical and cold. He looked oddly cynical, with a hard glint in his eyes that she hadn't seen since the days before their marriage.

A tiny shiver went down her spine.

Deciding she must be imagining things, she forced

a happy smile. "The hats did not impress on closer inspection, so I decided to purchase something else for Mallory. I found a lovely bit of lace that I thought she could use to trim a dress or shawl. With Honiton only in the next county, I suppose I shouldn't have been surprised to have found such excellent-quality lace here. The woman from whom I bought it is a true artisan."

"How nice." Gabriel looked away, frowning as if he were displeased, or worse, bored. "Well, if you're finished shopping for the day, we ought to start for home. I don't want to be traveling at dusk."

Since it was midafternoon, she didn't think there was much risk of that. But clearly he wished to leave. Had he and Mark Dennis had an argument while she was gone? Something had certainly occurred to put him in such a precarious humor.

"Of course," she agreed quietly. "We can leave whenever you wish."

He turned toward his friend and held out a hand. "Mark, safe travels. It was good seeing you again. Look me up when next you are in London."

Esme frowned. What did he mean? When *he* was next in London?

But of course, he must mean the two of them and he had simply misspoken, she decided. They had been married only a little over three weeks, so she supposed it was only natural that he was not yet used to referring to them as a couple.

Dennis took the offered hand and shook. "I shall make a point of it, yes."

When Gabriel said nothing further, Dennis turned to her and bowed. "Lady Northcote, what a great pleasure it has been. I am glad we had this opportunity to meet. Thank you for a most enchanting nuncheon."

Esme smiled, relaxing slightly for the first time since she had entered the room. "The pleasure was mine as well. I am already looking forward to the next time we meet. And remember—call me Esme."

"You are kindness itself, Esme. I wish you health and every happiness."

He bowed again, then was gone.

Silence descended.

"Wait here," Gabriel said abruptly. "I have to settle up with the innkeeper; then we shall depart."

She laid a hand on his sleeve. "What is it, Gabriel?" she said softly. "You seem upset. Did something go amiss between you and Mr. Dennis?"

His mouth and brows tightened for a fleeting instant before the look vanished as quickly as it had appeared. "Of course not. What could possibly have gone amiss?"

"You just seem out of sorts, is all."

"If I do, it must be from nuncheon. I ate far too much rich food and drink."

To her recollection, he hadn't eaten anything richer than what he usually consumed at home. He was one of the most robust men she knew, with a constitution to match—stomach included. But why would he lie? Maybe he really was feeling unwell. It would certainly account for his erratic temper.

"Poor dear," she said. "When we arrive home, I shall brew you a posset to settle your stomach. It's a remedy I learned from Meg and it always works wonders."

For a moment it looked as if he were going to refuse; then he nodded. "Yes, that would be most agreeable. Why don't you have a seat while I'm gone? I shall only be a few minutes."

But as she sat alone, waiting for him, her disquiet returned, setting her own stomach atremble.

Chapter 19

Dinner that evening was a miserable affair.

Although she and Gabriel carried on a conversation, their words were all polite small talk, with none of their usual relaxed banter or the lighthearted verbal jousting she had so come to enjoy.

She attempted, more than once, to ascertain the cause of his abrupt change in mood. But he rebuffed her each time, telling her she was mistaken and that nothing was wrong.

Finally, she gave up, hoping that whatever it was would pass, and quickly.

Even though she found herself doubting again that his difficulty was related to his stomach, she fixed him a posset containing peppermint, licorice root and basil not long after they'd arrived home. He'd thanked her, then drunk it down in a few quick gulps, handing her back the cup as if relieved to be free of her ministrations.

It was with a kind of relief that she went upstairs to bed early.

After her maid helped her change out of her gown, Esme bathed, then brushed her teeth and hair and crawled into bed. Lying in the semidarkness cast by the fireplace, she waited for him to join her.

And waited.

And waited.

She was just drifting off to sleep when he let himself

into the room, closing the door behind him. Quietly, he eased between the sheets.

"Gabriel," she murmured sleepily, more relieved than she had realized that he was there.

Leaning over, he kissed her. "I'm sorry, Esme. I know I've been a bear today."

Reaching up a hand, she stroked his cheek, some of her sleepiness fading. "It's all right. We all get blue deviled sometimes."

He stared at her, something mournful and distant in his tawny eyes.

And abruptly she was afraid. "Gabriel?"

He kissed her again, his touch devoid of passion. "You are tired. Go to sleep."

"No, I'm not." She stroked a hand over his chest and arm. "Really."

But rather than gather her close as he always did, he rolled onto his side away from her. "Good night, Esme."

Her chest ached with disbelief, words lodged in her throat so tight she could not speak.

And for the first time since coming to Highhaven, he did not make love to her.

"Pack your belongings," he told her over breakfast the next morning. "We've been here for weeks. It is time we departed."

She laid down her spoon, the porridge she'd been trying to make herself eat turning even colder in its bowl.

Earlier this morning when she'd awakened, Gabriel hadn't been in their bed, nor had he roused her near dawn to make love, as was his habit. After ringing for her maid, she'd bathed and dressed, then gone downstairs to the breakfast room, Burr trailing faithfully at her side. At least he wasn't avoiding her like Gabriel was.

Finally, ten minutes after she'd sat down at the table, Gabriel had joined her. He'd offered a brief greeting— no kiss—then tucked wordlessly into the plate of food Mrs. Canby laid before him.

Once the housekeeper had gone, Esme tried again

to ask what was troubling him. But he brushed her off with a shrug and told her to eat her meal.

She'd wanted to press him further, half-angry, half-alarmed by the change in him, and painfully aware of the wall he'd put up to keep her out. It was a distance she neither understood nor approved. Whatever had happened yesterday, it was something that had clearly not been resolved by a night's rest.

"Leave? To go where?" she asked, one hand fisted in her lap.

He raised his coffee cup to his lips. "To Ten Elms, my estate in Derbyshire. Make whatever preparations you require. We will set out tomorrow morning at first light."

"But—"

"Yes?" He met her gaze, his expression remote, chilling. "Can you not be ready by then?"

"No, it is not that. It is only . . ." She glanced down, twisting her napkin between her fingers before she looked up again. "Gabriel, what have I done? Why are you so angry with me?" She spoke fast, her words running together with sudden desperation. "Just tell me so we can resolve whatever it might be. I cannot make amends if you will not even tell me what it is that has distressed you."

For an instant, she saw a softening and an odd hint of longing, as if he might yet bend and tell her why he had become a stranger to her overnight. But then the wall up again, the cool mask lowering again across his face.

"You have done nothing and I am not angry with you," he said. "You mistake the matter, my dear. You need to remember that not everything in the world is about you."

His words struck her like a slap. "Then what is it about?"

He looked away, reaching for the coffeepot to pour himself a fresh cup. "I am just weary of this place and have business that can no longer be put off. It is as simple as that."

Weary of you, he meant.

Had his unexpected meeting with Mark Dennis reminded him of his former life and of all the things he was now missing? She mustn't forget that he hadn't wanted to marry her. She had never been his choice. Until today, she had almost forgotten that fact.

"I thought you liked it here," she said dully. "That we were having fun."

"I did. We were. But surely even you must realize that our honeymoon cannot last forever. As they say, all good things must come to an end sometime."

The warmth drained from her cheeks, a sick suspicion forming inside her that it wasn't just their honeymoon to which he was referring.

Abruptly she pushed back her chair, the legs screeching discordantly across the wooden floor.

Burr leapt to his feet, whining faintly as he sensed her distress.

"I have a great deal to do if we are to depart tomorrow," she said, careful to keep her head turned away so he could not see the devastation on her face. "I shall be abovestairs if you have need of me."

She hurried toward the door, Burr on her heels.

"Esme," Gabriel called.

But she didn't stop. She couldn't, not without him seeing the tears filling her eyes. Racing out into the hall, she took the stairs as quickly as her feet could carry her.

Gabriel dropped back into his chair and rubbed a hand over his jaw, only barely keeping himself from following her.

He'd seen the shock and confusion on her face, read the hurt in her eyes, especially when he'd made those last few cutting remarks.

He knew he was acting like a brute, but he could see no other way around it. He needed space, a bit of separation between them, so he could get his emotions under proper control again. This thing between them—whatever it might be—was dangerous and had to be stopped.

For as much as he'd snapped and jabbed at his old friend, Mark Dennis had done him a service; he had made him see things with clearer eyes.

It might appear cruel now. It might even hurt him and Esme both. But in the long run, she would come to agree that it was all for the best.

Esme fancied herself in love with him. He could see that now. But it was an illusion and nothing that would last once the romantic bubble between them burst and faded away.

Even now, he remembered how it felt—that giddy flush of first love, that golden haze of passion and joy that seemed as if it knew no bounds.

He'd loved Amanda Coyning, or at least imagined he had, and thought she'd loved him back. For a few brief, shining moments, it had seemed as if heaven had come down to earth in the form of a single bright angel named Amanda.

But then his uncle had informed her that should she and Gabriel wed, he would be cut off, without so much as a ha'penny to his name. The only things he could offer her would be an incomplete university degree and a small, isolated house in the wilds of southwestern England where no one of any great import ever ventured.

She'd dropped him like a plague carrier, ending their engagement without so much as a tear as she gave back the small ring that had been all he'd been able to afford at the time.

Determined to marry well, she'd quickly found a very wealthy, very old baronet who had been delighted to offer a ring in exchange for the pleasure of having a pretty young thing like her in his bed.

Her rejection had been devastating and had left Gabriel's heart bloodied and battered. But time and distance had healed the wound, leaving his eyes wide-open to the puerile fantasy known as love. He'd vowed then never to let himself be so weak and gullible again.

Not that Esme was trying to dupe him; she had none of Amanda's cunning charm or vicious duplicity. Still, it was time to put an end to the pleasurable idyll in which they'd been living these past few weeks. He'd let himself get too close to her; that was all. Allowed himself to indulge his passions too deeply, too freely.

Obsession was what Mark Dennis had seen, not love. And he would manage that obsession by putting some much-needed space between them. Time and a change of scenery would put everything back in the proper perspective. It would bring clarity and allow them both to set new boundaries in their marriage and stop confusing sex with affection and lust with love.

He could have tried to explain it all to her but knew she would fail to see the truth. She was too inexperienced in such matters to realize that feelings changed, and that whatever infatuation she might feel for him now, it would not be how she felt next month or even next year.

So he would make the hard choice for her.

As for himself, he would vanquish the gnawing hunger he had for her, a craving that still rode him like a beast. As for the deep closeness that had developed between them, it would mellow into comfortable affection with time, the kind that would allow them to coexist and eventually raise a family together without all the messy inconvenience and ridiculousness of so-called love.

That had been his parents' mistake, their marriage beset by vicious arguments and jealous rages, horrible door-slamming, vase-throwing fights so loud every person in the house had heard them and cringed.

As a small boy he'd been confused, even frightened, by the tumultuous swings in their relationship. One minute they would be wrapped around each other, lost in a world that excluded everyone but themselves. The next they would be screaming, hurling vile insults and recriminations meant not just to wound but to eviscerate. Later, as an adult, he'd come to understand more of the details of his parents' ill-fated union, learning of their impassioned, whirlwind romance as well as the affairs and infidelities that had followed.

He'd been a fool in his youth to think anything good could ever come of love.

He would not be a fool again.

Chapter 20

Five long, hard, unforgiving days of travel later, the coach pulled up to the front entrance of Ten Elms.

As had been the case with Highhaven, the staff were not waiting at the ready to welcome their master and mistress home. But at least, Esme thought as she climbed stiffly down from the coach, Burr leaping out behind her, it was not full night this time but rather midday, a weak autumn sun spreading comforting light in every direction.

The house stretched wide and tall before her, the facade cut from blocks of muted gray limestone that rose three stories high to a slate-covered roof. Multiple chimneys dotted the structure, while multipaned windows gleamed in the muted light.

Yet despite the grand Baroque style of the house, it cast a faintly neglected air, like a once graceful lady whose beauty had faded after the splendor of her youth. Still, the house looked solid and capable of providing her with a bed and bath and hopefully a decent meal.

Without bothering to comment on the state of her new home, she trailed Gabriel to the front door, which opened to reveal a surprised-looking young man who appeared to have only just finished buttoning his black livery jacket.

"My lord, my lady, welcome," the young man said in a slightly breathless tone that made Esme wonder if he had just raced upstairs from the servants' hall to meet them.

"Where is Starr?" Gabriel strode past him, a scowl

on his face that did nothing to alleviate the servant's obvious unease.

After five days of seeing the same scowl, Esme was used to it. Silently, she followed him in.

"Mr. Starr is away, my lord. Visiting his sister."

"And Mrs. Foy? Is she absent as well?" Gabriel said, cutting him off.

The servant shook his head. "No. She is upstairs, making up your rooms." He wrung his hands. "If we had received word of your impending arrival sooner, everything would have been ready."

"Not to worry," Esme said, giving him a little smile as she drew off her gloves. "His lordship makes a habit of not informing his staff of his travel plans, so it is only natural that you are all aflutter trying to accommodate. I am Lady Northcote, by the way. And you are?"

"David, my lady."

"Well, David, I thank you for greeting us. Now, if you would be so obliging, I would be vastly grateful for a cup of tea, a sandwich—cheese and cucumber, if possible—and a dish of water for my dog. Do you think that could be arranged?"

"Certainly. I'll see to it right away."

"Since my bedchamber is as yet being prepared, where should I wait?"

"In the drawing room, of course," Gabriel said with a wry twist of his lips. Sweeping a hand toward a hallway that led off to the right, he motioned for her to precede him.

Repressing a sigh, she moved across the spacious marble foyer in the direction he had indicated.

She located the drawing room with little difficulty, the chamber pleasant but old-fashioned. The heavy green draperies and antique furnishings clearly had originated several decades earlier.

A slightly stale scent hung in the air as well, as if the room had not been occupied in a very long time. She suspected the dust sheets had only recently been removed, perhaps even within the past hour.

Rather than take a seat, she went to the window and looked out, pleased to find a spacious lawn with a garden that managed to be pretty despite its slightly overgrown appearance. Ranged across the gently rolling hills were thick stands of trees, burnished in crisp autumn colors of red, gold and orange. Nearer the house stood a number of immense elms planted carefully along a lovely winding path that led up to a small Roman-inspired folly.

She counted and found precisely ten.

"How long has it been since you were last here?" she asked, not looking around but aware of him standing somewhere behind her.

"I'm not entirely sure. A year, maybe more. I don't come often. Why?"

"I just wondered, since the house doesn't seem much loved."

"No, there was never much of that here."

And doubtless will not be again, she thought.

Over the past few days the rift between them had not healed, much to her sorrow. Although Gabriel was unfailingly polite—too much so on some occasions—the coach ride to Ten Elms had been nearly as unendurable as that first dreadful journey from Braebourne to Highhaven. Yet on that occasion, she'd had no expectations of enjoying his company. This time she had been keenly aware of its loss.

And yet in spite of his emotional distance, some small part of her continued to hope that he would warm to her again. That she would wake up one morning to find the old Gabriel in her bed, kissing and teasing her to laughter while he made her heart and body sing from the pleasure of his warm, lusty embrace.

But she didn't see how that was even a possibility when he no longer came to her bed. All along the way to Ten Elms, he'd gotten separate rooms for them at the inns where they had stopped for the night. Initially, he'd made some excuse about them both needing a proper night's rest since they were traveling such a long distance. But she knew that lack of sleep had nothing to do with the situation. Instead, she feared it was a case of him being tired of her.

Of course she could have gone to him; there was a time when he would have delighted in her being the one to initiate their lovemaking. But as much as she longed to bridge the distance between them, even if only in a physical way, she knew she wouldn't be able to bear it if he rejected her.

So she did nothing. Just as she said nothing either.

A quiet knock came at the door. To her relief, Esme turned to see a kitchen maid enter with a laden silver tray. The wide-eyed girl set it down on the tea table, bobbed a curtsy, then hurried back out again, all without once looking at either of them.

"Your servants seem a bit nervous," she said once the girl had left.

"Do they? I hadn't noticed."

Likely not, if he always spent his time scowling when he came here. It didn't take a genius to realize that he didn't much care for Ten Elms. Was it because of his brother and the memory of his loss that he had a dislike of the place? Or was it something more?

A bowl of water had been sent up for Burr. She put it down on the floor and watched as he lapped happily. She didn't usually feed and water her animals in the drawing room, but until he got settled here, she wanted to make sure he had everything he required.

Burr seen to, she took a seat on the sofa and proceeded to serve, arranging sandwiches and cakes on plates and pouring cups of tea for them both.

After passing a filled plate to Gabriel, she began eating her own.

Neither of them spoke.

Another knock came nearly fifteen minutes later.

Esme looked around to watch a slender woman with a sleek bun of downy white hair enter the room. The heavy fabric of her black bombazine rustled as she walked, a set of keys jangling at her waist. Somewhere in her late fifties or early sixties, the woman had a narrow face, clear gray eyes and a thin mouth set in a stern pucker.

She stopped, her hands clasped at her waist. "My lord. My lady, I am Mrs. Foy, the housekeeper. Pardon the delay in attending to you personally. As David was to have informed you, I have been upstairs seeing to the preparation of your rooms. They are ready and await you at your convenience."

"Thank you, Mrs. Foy," Gabriel said, offering the woman no more than a cursory glance. "We shall ring when we have need of you again."

Her thin lips tightened. "Very good, my lord. My lady, would you care to inspect the menu for dinner? Cook is doing her best to accommodate on such short notice. I believe she plans to serve chicken this evening."

"Oh, actually, chicken will do very well for his lordship, but I shall require a dish without meat."

"Without meat?" the woman repeated, looking even more pinched. "Such as, may I inquire?"

"Vegetables, bread, noodles, soup made without meat stock, cheese, milk, fruit. Anything, really, so long as it is not made from killed meat."

The housekeeper sniffed, then gave an aggrieved nod. "I shall inform Cook as to your . . . preferences. Now, if there is nothing further?"

Esme hesitated for a moment, then set down her plate. "Actually, Mrs. Foy, I will have you show me to my room now. I would like to change out of my traveling clothes and take a hot bath, if one can be prepared."

"Very good. If you will follow me."

Gabriel stood as she left the room but made no effort to follow. Unlike her, he knew his way around the house.

Dinner—at least her dinner—consisted of cream of mushroom soup, fried potatoes and onions, buttered carrots, purple beets, bread and butter.

Dessert was an apple tart with brandied whipped cream and a slice of golden cheddar cheese.

Gabriel had been served all of that in addition to the aforementioned roast chicken, which he consumed with apparent enjoyment. Throughout the meal, he drank wine, followed by coffee and a glass of port. She had a glass of wine and tea.

Despite the somewhat plain nature of the food, it was quite good and more than plentiful.

Their conversation during the course of the meal was politely desultory, confined to casual topics, such as the weather and the meal, each of them careful to avoid anything that might touch on the personal.

Weary from the long days of travel and the strain that lay between them, she excused herself early and went upstairs, Burr trotting at her heels.

One of the housemaids came to assist her since the maid she'd had in Cornwall had not wanted to accompany her so far north.

She thought longingly of Mrs. Grumblethorpe and wished she could send for her. But just before she'd left Highhaven, she'd had a letter from Edward telling her that her old nurse had asked to be pensioned out and that she had gone to live in Kent near her brother and his wife.

She was happy for Mrs. Grumblethorpe, since no one was more deserving of a rest and a place where she would spend her later years at her ease. Yet the departure of her old companion left Esme feeling lonely and oddly adrift, as if one more tie to her old life had just been severed forever.

After bidding the housemaid good night, she climbed into bed and blew out her bedside candle, pitching the room into near blackness that was relieved by only the fire burning low in the grate.

She wasn't certain how much time had passed or exactly what disturbed her, but suddenly she was awake, her eyes opening again to the darkness.

And then he was there beside her, bending near as he slid his fingers into her hair and plundered her mouth with long, drugging, openmouthed kisses. He tasted of brandy and heat and unbridled need.

"Gabriel," she whispered.

But he hushed her and stripped off her nightgown, leaving her naked beneath his questing hands and hungry mouth.

"Let me," he murmured against her ear as his fingers found all of her most sensitive places and worked them with irresistible skill. "Just let me."

And she did, quivering while keening gasps issued uncontrollably from her throat. His touch fanned the flames of her desire, driving her hard and fast as he forced her body to accept his demands in ways that left her aching and enslaved.

With no further preliminaries, he parted her legs and thrust heavily inside her, filling her completely.

"Take me," he commanded as he pulled back, then thrust again. "Take all of me."

Reaching down, he positioned her again, opening her wider, arching her hips and angling her knees higher, so that on his next thrust she did take more. Her entire body shook, his thick shaft buried so deep it seemed for a moment as if they had joined into one.

She closed her eyes and held on, giving herself into his keeping as he rocked them both to a stunning, mind-shattering completion.

But even as she floated, her inner muscles twitching with the pleasurable aftereffects, she realized he wasn't through. Inside her, she felt him turn stiff again, his erection as hard as if they hadn't just finished coupling.

"Turn over," he said gruffly.

Pulling out, he rolled her onto her stomach, then gave her bottom a stinging smack with the flat of his hand. He did it again, then a third time.

Her already satiated need sprang abruptly back to life, hunger burning like wildfire. Her breasts ached, the tips tight nubs.

"On your knees."

He smacked her bottom twice more as she scrambled to obey, her skin hot and stinging where he'd struck her.

Using his knees, he parted her thighs and sheathed himself to the hilt with a single powerful thrust.

"Aaah," she cried as her inner flesh stretched to receive him.

Almost impossibly, he was bigger than before, thicker. He throbbed within her so that she seemed to feel him everywhere all at once.

He started to move, swift and sure, one arm curved over her shoulder, the other underneath her stomach so that her back was pressed tightly against his chest.

Finding her breasts, he kneaded one, then the other, rolling and pinching her nipples between his thumb and forefinger. He kissed her cheek and throat, and the length of her shoulder before nuzzling the spot at her nape. Opening his mouth, he fixed his teeth on her and bit down.

She went over on a sharp, high-pitched cry, her dripping sheath spasming around him.

But he was far from done.

Driving them both at a relentless pace, he brought her to another explosive climax, his fingers working the flesh between her legs while he continued to pump heavily inside her, every stroke lodging him deeper than the last.

She screamed as pleasure burst like a lightning storm inside her, rattling her bones and searing her blood until it all but threatened to tear her apart.

Her brain went blank, her entire body limp and satiated.

With her cradled securely inside his hold, he thrust once, twice, three times more, before roaring out as he claimed his own powerful release.

Together they fell forward against the sheets.

Minutes passed as she drifted.

She mumbled, sleepy and satisfied, when he rolled them onto their backs and tucked her gently against his side, one of his hands moving in a slow glide up and down her arm.

She snuggled closer and smiled, everything hazy and

dreamlike. "I love you," she murmured, her lips brushing against his chest as she spoke.

The hand on her arm stilled briefly before resuming its lazy slide. "I know you do." As soft as a butterfly's wing, he kissed her forehead. "Forgive me, Esme."

He spoke in a whisper, his words so quiet she wondered if she'd actually heard them at all.

But then sleep claimed her and she had no more time to think, lost in the blissful oblivion of dreams.

Chapter 21

Esme awakened with a smile on her face, reaching her arms over her head to indulge in a quivering, full-body stretch. Breathing deeply, she caught Gabriel's heady masculine scent, which lay all over the sheets and pillows.

It seemed to be imprinted on her as well.

Her skin.

Her hair.

Her body.

He'd possessed her last night, shown her heights of pleasure that still radiated in her soul.

She sighed, happy and relieved that their estrangement was over, that he'd finally returned to their bed.

Sliding a foot sideways, she sought him out. But all she found was empty space.

Disappointed, she opened her eyes and sighed again. In spite of the way he'd exhausted her last night, she wouldn't have minded indulging in another energetic bout of love play this morning.

Maybe they could manage a little something before nuncheon, she thought as she sat up, grinning at the naughty idea.

Lord, he's turned me wicked.

But she liked it, just as she liked him.

Loved him.

A memory suddenly came to her of saying those words.

I love you.

Was it a dream or had she really said that to him last night? Had she confessed the feeling that had been growing quietly within her these past few weeks like a vine twining around her heart?

Letting her eyes slide shut, palms open in her lap, she knew she had.

But what was it he had said back?

I know you do, not *I love you too.* And there had been something more.

Forgive me.

Forgive him for what?

For their recent disharmony and the cool way he'd treated her lately?

Or for wanting her when he wasn't in love . . . at least not yet.

For she had to believe that he would love her someday; otherwise, she wasn't sure she would be able to bear it.

To be married for life to a man who did not love her and never would? It was no more than she'd expected when they had wed. But that was before she'd known his kiss and lain in his arms. Before she'd seen the man he was and found herself wanting to know more, wanting to know everything there was to understand about the complex, interesting, intelligent, beautiful, enigmatic soul who was Gabriel Landsdowne.

Flinging back the sheets, she leapt lithely out of bed, pausing to give the tail-wagging Burr an enthusiastic rub before continuing on into the adjoining dressing room.

After seeing to her personal needs, she washed with the water in the pitcher and brushed her teeth, then slipped into a robe and rang for the girl who was acting as her maid.

The servant knocked, waiting until Esme called permission before shouldering her way inside, a small tea tray in her hands. "Good morning, my lady."

"Good morning. Oh, how lovely." Esme came forward once the maid set the tray on the small table near the window. Taking up the blue-and-white china teapot, she poured herself a steaming cup of fragrant black breakfast tea, the liquid the color of rich walnut. After adding a dollop of milk, she took a sip.

Delicious.

Next she reached for a scone. Breaking off an edge, she popped it into her mouth, the flavor bursting delightfully in her mouth.

"Will you be wanting any particular gown today, milady?" The maid stood, hands folded patiently at her waist.

Esme chewed another bite of scone, then waved a hand. "Any day dress will suffice. One of my warmer gowns, I think. It seems rather chilly in here." She glanced toward the fireplace and the logs that had turned to ash in the grate overnight. "Or is the rest of the house warmer?"

The maid's eyes grew a bit round. "No, milady, the fires aren't laid 'til evening this time of year."

Esme's brows puckered with a tiny frown. The fires at Braebourne, especially the ones in the family quarters, were kept lit and well tended at all times of day once autumn set in and the weather began to turn cool. The house was always quite pleasant, never demanding anything more than a shawl or a light woolen dress.

Highhaven had been maintained at a pleasant temperature as well; she'd never been cold. But admittedly, Ten Elms was a much larger estate. Perhaps Gabriel simply didn't want the expense of heating so large a space when he was so rarely here. Then again, while they were in residence, there surely could be no great harm in lighting a few more fires for a few hours more. She would have to speak to him about the issue.

"Definitely one of my wool day dresses, then. Maybe a blue one." Gabriel always liked her in blue. He said it complemented her eyes.

The girl nodded and went to lay out her dress.

Esme finished the scone and washed it down with tea. A quick check of the mantel clock showed it was late, after ten o'clock; otherwise, she would have waited so that she could have joined Gabriel downstairs for breakfast. But she supposed, given the hour, that he had eaten already.

Burr wagged, casting doggy eyes at the second, uneaten scone on her plate. She hesitated, since she was planning to get him his own late breakfast as soon as she was dressed.

"Oh, what will it hurt? You're such a good boy, you deserve a treat every once in a while." Breaking the scone in half, she fed it to him in two bites, which he wolfed down with obvious excitement.

"Conniver," she said on a laugh.

He barked and waved his tail.

Smiling, Esme wandered into the dressing room to find her clothes neatly laid out. The maid helped her into her undergarments and a blue wool day dress; then Esme took a seat at her dressing table so the girl could brush and pin up her hair.

"Ye've lovely hair, milady."

"Oh, thank you. Paula, is it?"

"Yes, ma'am." The girl gave her a shy smile in the mirror.

"I appreciate you helping me on such short notice."

Pink rose into Paula's cheeks. "Oh, you're more than welcome, my lady. It's an honor to serve you."

Silence fell as Paula worked, brushing and twisting Esme's thick hair into a neat arrangement at the back of her head.

"Pretty," Esme pronounced, checking the finished hairstyle in the mirror.

Paula blushed again, clearly pleased.

"Is his lordship about?" Esme stood and turned. "I was hoping he might be along to see me by now, but perhaps he's busy taking care of business matters."

The color leached out of the girl's cheeks. "Oh! Oh, mercy, forgive me, my lady. I forgot."

"Forgot what?"

"Mrs. Foy asked me to give this to you. Said it was

from his lordship and not to delay." Reaching into her apron, she withdrew a letter.

Esme accepted the missive. "Well, you've remembered now. No harm done."

"Will there be anything else?"

When Esme shook her head, the servant bobbed a curtsy and withdrew. As soon as she was gone, Esme broke the wax seal and opened the note.

What she read made the color drain out of her own cheeks.

"Left for London," it said. *"No idea when I will be back . . . Do anything you like to the house. Send the bills to me at Cavendish Square. Yours, Northcote."*

Yours, Northcote!

He'd made passionate love to her last night, taken her until neither of them had had the strength or breath left in their bodies to move, and he signed his letter, *Northcote?*

She stood, her fingers trembling against the paper, feeling like the very epitome of a fool. Slowly, she crumpled the note inside her fist and squeezed, her nails cutting into her palm.

Lifting her arm, she made to fling the note into the fire, only then remembering there wasn't one burning, the grate cold and filled with ash.

Every bit as dead and lifeless as her heart.

From inside the coach, Gabriel stared absently out at the passing autumn landscape, his thoughts miles away, back at Ten Elms with Esme.

No matter how he tried, he couldn't get the memory of her out of his mind, the satiny smoothness of her skin, the delicate sweetness of her scent, the honeyed taste of her kisses. She'd claimed him last night, every bit as much as he'd claimed her, so much so that he very nearly rapped on the ceiling and ordered the coachman to turn around and go back.

He fisted his hand on his thigh and forced himself to resist.

Obsession—that's all it is, he told himself, as he had days ago in Cornwall. A surfeit of sexual intoxication coupled with an unhealthy amount of isolation.

Once he got back to London, her hold on him would fade. A few days, a couple of weeks at most, and Esme Byron Landsdowne would cease to be the focus of his world.

He'd been enamored of women before, although never quite to the extent he seemed to be with Esme. But just as his interest in all his previous lovers had waned, her allure would fade as well. By the time he saw her again, she would be out of his system and he could proceed with their marriage in a rational, even comfortable way.

In the meantime, he would use their time apart to see to the business he'd told her he had been neglecting—an excuse that hadn't all been a lie.

Thanks to his marriage to Esme, he was no longer in debt.

Only last week, the inheritance money due to him as a result of his tying the knot had been released by the estate attorneys. It was more than enough to pay off the mortgage on Cavendish Square and leave him with a comfortable fortune, besides. Then there was Esme's dowry, which served as a kind of additional boon.

At the time of their wedding, he'd half expected the duke and her brothers to find some way to withhold her dowry. As a practicing lawyer, Lawrence, in particular, could have found some clever means of squeezing him out. Instead, Clybourne had been surprisingly generous about the marriage portion, transferring a substantial sum into his accounts, no questions asked.

Not that they'd given him all of Esme's money. Quite the opposite, in fact, the size of her dowry staggering even by aristocratic standards. As agreed to in the settlement, the vast majority of her money was tied up in trust, to be passed directly to her in the event of divorce or his death, then on to any children they might produce.

It was an arrangement some men would have loathed, but he was no fortune hunter, so he didn't mind.

Besides, if he wanted, he could invest in some much-needed improvements to the farms and tenant lands at Ten Elms and conceivably earn himself yet another tidy sum. There was money to be made in new farming methods that his uncle had never had the foresight to implement, for all his supposed brilliance in having once managed the estate. It would almost be worth spending time at Ten Elms, if only to prove himself a better custodian than his blighted uncle.

But that would have to wait for now, be put off until he got his feelings for Esme under proper regulation.

As for what her family would think when they learned that he'd left her behind at Ten Elms, he couldn't say. He doubted they would be pleased, not with him and Esme married less than a month and him off to London while she stayed alone at his ancestral home in Derbyshire.

He scowled, guilt riding him at what they would all surely view as abandonment, Esme included. He wondered what she was thinking, now that she'd had his note.

Probably that he was a cad and a bounder, a heartless blackguard who had shamelessly abused her innocence and destroyed her youthful trust.

I love you.

Her whispered words resonated in his mind, chiding him even now. A secret part of him had thrilled to hear them, wanting her softness, craving her comfort and devotion.

But devotion changed and love went away; he, of all people, had learned that lesson only too well, both as a boy and as a man. Love was weakness and he would drive its nascent tendrils from his soul before it had a chance to dig in and take root.

And Esme?

She would recover. A few weeks apart and she would be glad he'd had the sense to put a stop to their lust-filled fantasy.

Until then, he hoped she didn't suffer too much. Actually, he rather expected that she would pack her bags and go to Braebourne, where she could vilify him to her heart's content, surrounded by the comfort of her old home and family.

And if she does not?

His scowl deepened and he drummed his fingers against his thigh.

He would not feel guilty, not much anyway. Besides, what did she really expect? She'd known he had a black heart when she'd married him. He was only acting true to form.

Reaching for the book he'd brought with him, he opened it and began to read, determined to drive her from his mind, even if only for a short while.

Esme flung open her wardrobe and reached for the nearest dress, pulling it out and stuffing it into her open portmanteau. She was too angry to even call for her maid to do the packing. She would take just enough clothes and toiletries to make the journey to Braebourne, then send for the rest of her belongings after she arrived.

Burr watched from where he lay on the dressing room floor, his head on his paws.

"What?" she asked him, as she wadded up another dress and thrust it into the case. "Why are you looking at me like that? I'm not the one who ran out on my wife after less than a month of marriage."

Burr stayed silent, his liquid brown eyes watching her with quiet concern.

"He left me, Burr. He left us. And without even having the decency to tell me to my face that he was going. 'Doesn't know when he'll be back.'" She repeated it in a sarcastic singsong. "Well, he can stay away forever as far as I'm concerned."

She blinked away the tears that stung her eyes.

Burr whimpered softly.

She stopped, her arms full of stockings and chemises.

"You think I'm wrong, then, do you? That I'm running away? That I'm giving up too soon?"

Abruptly, she sank down onto a low stool. "Oh, Burr, why did he leave? And just when I thought everything was better between us. I don't understand. Do you think it's because I told him I love him? Did I scare him away?"

With a sniff, she wiped her damp eyes with the edge of a stocking. Burr ambled over and laid his head on her knee, thumping his tail twice on the floor.

She laid the clothes aside, then stroked his soft fur. "What should I do, Burr? If I leave now, everyone will know that my marriage is a failure. And my brothers . . . God, they'll go wild if they know he's left me. They'll probably go after him and drag him back, even if he doesn't want to come. Although knowing Gabriel he'll tell them all to go to perdition and it will just make everything that much worse."

Burr's eyes closed with pleasure as she scratched his head. "No, I suppose, as bad as it is, that I need to be brave and remain here. What was it he said? Do whatever I like with the house? It would serve him right if I take him up on that offer. I can already think of several improvements to make. As for the area, Derbyshire seems a lovely place. Only imagine all of the new hills and fields where you and I can roam."

She drew a shaky breath and fought back a fresh wave of tears. "Oh, I'm so angry with him, Burr. I could gladly throttle that man. I wish I didn't love him, but I do, even if he doesn't love me back. Even if he never loves me back."

The dam burst and she began to cry in earnest.

She cried until she felt as if she had no more tears left to shed.

Rising to her feet, she went to the basin and washed her face with cool water.

Feeling more composed, she returned the dresses to the wardrobe and her stockings and chemises to the dresser drawers, then went to the small secretary that stood in the corner of her bedchamber.

After seating herself in the chair, she withdrew a sheet of paper and began to write. If she was going to stay here and try to make this her home, then she wanted it to feel like home, and that meant having all her beloved pets around her, as well as the rest of her clothes and possessions.

And if she truly made this a home, the next time Gabriel returned, he would find a warm, welcoming place he would never wish to leave again and a wife he would realize he'd been a fool to desert.

Chapter 22

A strong early December wind blew, lumbering clouds threatening rain when Esme rode up to the stables at Ten Elms almost six weeks later.

A groom came forward to help her dismount, then led her mare away while she headed back to the house. Burr trotted at her heels along with Haydn and Handel, who had arrived a month earlier, together with the rest of what her family had always affectionately dubbed her "menagerie."

Even Poppy, her rabbit, had been sent north. Despite her recovery, the decision had been made that Poppy should not be set free again for fear of predators. Instead, Esme had installed her in a quiet area of the garden here at Ten Elms, where she would have plenty of room to hop and graze. She had even seen to it that a special weatherproof bunny hutch was built that would keep the little animal warm and safe this winter.

To her surprise and delight, Lawrence had accompanied her furry creatures on the journey, along with Charles, the footman, who had been seeing to their daily care, and a stableboy whose principal job it was to carry water and change bedding in the travel baskets.

"Lawrence," she'd exclaimed when she'd seen her brother pull up in the coach. "What are you doing here? You didn't say a word."

"I thought I'd surprise you." He'd swung her into his arms and given her a big hug and kiss on the cheek.

"You thought you'd check up on me, you mean."

He gave an unapologetic shrug, grinning as they walked into the house. "Everyone was leaving Brae-bourne when your letter arrived. Since I'm the last unshackled sibling, I volunteered to accompany your animals north and find out how you're doing." Standing back, he surveyed her where they now stood together in the drawing room. "So, how are you doing? You look well enough, though a touch pale perhaps."

She smiled, fighting not to let her recent unhappiness show. "Just fine."

"And that husband of yours? Where is he, by the way? Off taking care of estate business?"

"In a manner of speaking. He's . . . actually he's in London."

"London? What's he doing there? Why didn't he take you with him?"

And that's when she'd broken down, tears spilling over her cheeks as she confessed the truth. Together, they'd huddled next to each other on the sofa, one of Lawrence's long arms wrapped around her shoulders.

"He ought to be horsewhipped, leaving you here alone like this," he said when she was done. "We should never have encouraged you to marry him."

She shook her head. "No, it was my choice to go through with the wedding, and he's been good to me, really."

"By deserting you?" He stood up to pace. "When Edward hears about this, he'll be livid."

"Which is why you aren't going to tell him." She dried her cheeks with his handkerchief, then balled the cloth up inside her hand.

"Of course I'm going to tell him. He needs to know what that blighter has done."

"No, he does not," she stated in a hard tone. "This is between Gabriel and me, and I don't want any interference."

"Esme—"

"Swear to me that you'll stay out of this and won't tell

the family. Gabriel is my husband and it is up to the two of us to resolve our difficulties, whatever they may be."

He studied her, his blue eyes widening slightly. "Christ, you're in love with him, aren't you?"

"And what if I am?" She lifted her chin defiantly. "Anyway, you should be glad. At least my marriage isn't turning out to be the loveless union all of you feared it might be."

He arched a golden brow. "Perhaps not, but I don't think the idea was for the affection to only be on one side. At least let me have the satisfaction of going next door to his town house when I get back to London so I can punch him a few times. Obviously he needs to be reminded that he has a wife."

She smiled, amused despite herself. "I doubt he's forgotten. But no, you are not allowed to injure him. Now, swear."

In the end, he'd sworn, but not before reminding her of one last consideration.

"You know, with him in London, there may be talk."

Her forehead creased. "Surely not this time of year, what with everyone away."

"Not everyone *is* away. Leo and Thalia are at Bright-vale for the time being, but it's an easy matter for them to drive into Town. And when they see him there and you not there, it'll only be a matter of putting two and two together."

Her scowl deepened. "Oh, very well, go ahead and tell Leo—"

"Which means Thalia will know too. Believe me—he tells her everything."

She sighed. "Fine. You may confide in Leo and Thalia, but no one else. And make them swear that they won't pass it along, even if you have to get it written in blood first."

He grinned. "Shame they don't let women enter into the professions. I suspect you'd make a fine attorney."

"I shall take that as a compliment."

"It is meant as one."

Lawrence had stayed for the next week and had even allowed himself to be drafted into helping select new draperies for the study, the library and Gabriel's bedchamber, since she wanted a man's opinion on the rooms.

And then, once again, she was alone.

Charles, however, had decided to stay when she offered him a position in the household as first footman at twice the salary he had been earning at Braebourne. Not that she was planning to make a habit of poaching servants from Edward and Claire, but she couldn't pass up the opportunity to have at least one faithful ally in the house. Besides, Charles was one of the kindest, most good-natured people with whom she had ever been acquainted. She had long trusted her animals to his care and she now gladly trusted her new home to him as well.

As for the butler, Mr. Starr—who had returned from his visit to his sister only days after her arrival—he was as old and crotchety as Mrs. Foy was severe and reproving. Despite their being unfailingly polite—at least on the surface—the pair was proving to be a real impediment to her efforts to bring new life and warmth to Ten Elms. Whenever she tried to change something, even something as insignificant as the kind of tea served at breakfast, they would tell her that it "was not the way things were done here at Ten Elms" and that they would have to check with the master, who, of course, was away from home.

She had learned, via Charles, that nothing had changed in the running of the household in the ten years since Gabriel's uncle had last been in charge. And since Gabriel spent so little time in the house, he had never bothered to change anything after assuming the peerage, leaving the servants to do as they had always done.

The situation infuriated her enough that she had written to Gabriel about it. He had written back, telling her to make whatever changes she liked and that he would inform Mr. Starr and Mrs. Foy to follow her orders.

Only they were not and Gabriel wasn't here to make them.

As she walked now toward the house, the dogs still trotting happily at her heels, she thought about the other letters she'd received from Gabriel.

They arrived roughly once a week, brief missives that inquired after her health and whether she had ample funds and provisions.

Often they were accompanied by a hamper full of choice goods from London—cheeses, sweetmeats and fine wines, exotic fruits, such as pineapples and oranges, intriguing root vegetables and newly harvested nuts.

There were also sundries like fine-milled soap and violet-scented powder, ribbons, lace and once an entire bolt of the most beautiful deep blue cashmere, which she had immediately set about having made into a warm day dress and matching pelisse. There were also paints and paintbrushes and paper, enough so she had no worries of running short.

She never quite knew what to make of his gifts and whether he sent them out of thoughtfulness or guilt. Either way, she could not help but love them because they had come from him.

It was pathetic, she supposed, since she knew she ought to be angry with him. But she couldn't seem to muster the appropriate amount of fury. She didn't want to fight Gabriel; she just wanted him back.

And then there was his last letter, the one in which he had asked her something new.

"Are you with child?"

Her cheeks had first flushed, then grown cool as a fresh wave of sadness engulfed her.

"No," she had written back, *"I am not."*

She found herself wondering even now if he would be on his way home to her if the answer had been yes. Then again, perhaps he might come anyway, if for no other reason than to continue the attempt to produce an heir.

It was, after all, the one thing that would most certainly bring them back together—or at least bring him back to her bed eventually.

Her chest ached, knowing he would likely leave again

once he did succeed in getting her with child. But the time spent in his arms might almost be worth the cost.

With her boots crunching on the gravel drive, she walked toward the front door. And that's when she saw it.

The coach.

Without stopping to consider, she raced inside.

Is he here? she wondered, heart pounding. *Has he come back at last?*

She went first to the drawing room but found it empty. Next she tried the library, but there was nothing but shelves of books inside. Realizing that he must have gone upstairs to his bedchamber to change out of his traveling clothes, she whirled around and started for the stairs, the dogs chasing after her as if it were a game.

Suddenly she heard a sound coming from the end of the corridor where his study was located. Smiling, she changed direction again and hurried toward it.

"Gabriel?" she said as she reached the doorway. "Are you home?"

But the man who looked up at her entrance wasn't Gabriel.

"Who are you?" She wrapped a hand around the doorframe, the dogs clustered protectively around her skirts. "And what are you doing in my husband's office?"

The stranger looked up from where he stood behind Gabriel's desk, an arrogant tilt to his fine-boned face. He was older, somewhere in his fifties, were she to guess, of medium height and slender build. His hair was pale blond turned mostly white. But it was his icy blue eyes that were his most striking feature; just looking into them made her shiver.

Where were the servants? she thought. How had he gotten this far inside the house with no one taking notice? Suddenly she was glad of her canine escort.

"Hello there," he said with an unconcerned drawl, as if she hadn't just caught him where he was not supposed to be. "You must be the new Lady Northcote."

"I am. And who might you be?"

He made her a short bow. "Sidney Landsdowne. I

am Gabriel's uncle on his father's side. Your uncle now too, it would seem."

His uncle? She hadn't known Gabriel even had an uncle. Then again, she knew almost nothing about his family, only that his brother and parents were no longer living. But apparently he did have relations. How many she still had no idea.

She relaxed, but only a bit, as she sank into a curtsy. "Oh, well, hello, this is an unexpected surprise. How nice to finally meet some of Gabriel's family."

"Yes, I was in the area and thought I ought to call and pay my respects. My apologies for not sending word to you earlier that I planned to drop in, but it was all rather last-minute."

"Ah, I see."

But she didn't, not really. Sending a note was an easy enough thing to do, particularly when meeting someone for the first time, even a new relation. But maybe he was only passing through and it had been a spur-of-the-minute decision as he said. Then again, she had been in residence for six weeks and married to Gabriel even longer. Surely he could have sent a letter welcoming her to the family before now. Only he hadn't actually welcomed her, had he?

"Gabriel isn't here, I am afraid," she said.

"Is he not? How . . . unfortunate." He smiled, but the look didn't do anything to warm his eyes. Nor did he seem particularly surprised by the news that Gabriel was not in residence.

Had he already known that Gabriel was away?

No, I am just imagining things, she told herself, shaking off the reaction.

"Forgive the way I am dressed. I have only just returned from riding."

Landsdowne waved a dismissive hand. "You look lovely. The fault is entirely mine for surprising you so unexpectedly."

"Why do we not go to the drawing room and I shall order tea. I will only be gone a few minutes to change."

"Of course. That sounds most agreeable."

Still, he made no move to leave.

"Mr. Landsdowne? If you don't mind my asking, what are you doing here in the study?"

"Uncle Sidney," he said in an ingratiating tone. "Please, there is no need for formality. After all, we are family now, are we not? Esme, is it not?"

"Yes." She paused, suddenly aware of the fact that the dogs hadn't moved so much as an inch from her side. Burr, in particular, was always ready to make new friends, be they animal or human. But in this instance, he had kept his place, positioned so that he was almost touching her.

Esme reached down to pet him. "But you still haven't said, Uncle Sidney. What are you doing in here?"

Something dark flashed in his gaze, a flicker so quick she wondered if it had been a trick of the light. Then he smiled again. "This used to be my office back when I managed the estate for both my late brother and late nephew, so I sometimes forget it is not still mine. I was your husband's guardian when he was a boy; did you know that?"

"No, I didn't realize."

"Hmm, at one point I controlled the entirety of Ten Elms."

It sounded like he wished he still did.

"A shame Gabriel takes so little interest in what was once a great estate," he continued. "But, of course, he has far too much liking for London, does he not, your husband?"

What was that supposed to mean? Did he know that Gabriel was in London? *Had* he known, even before she told him Gabriel was away?

Landsdowne ran a finger over the desk near the ledger that lay open on its surface. Only then did she notice the heavy leather book.

Had he been looking at the accounts before she'd come in?

And come to think, who had let him into the house to begin with? Starr and Mrs. Foy always seemed to be hovering nearby, even when she was wishing them to perdition. Yet today they were nowhere to be found. And where were Charles and David and the other footmen?

As if noticing the direction of her gaze, Landsdowne snapped the book closed. "Old habits, like I said. But come, shall we adjourn for that tea?"

"Yes, I think that would be a good idea."

He waited to let her precede him from the room, then followed her out. Suddenly she wished she hadn't mentioned going upstairs to change her clothes. The idea of leaving him unattended in the house made her feel strangely uneasy.

They had just walked out into the corridor when Charles suddenly appeared. He was slightly out of breath and looked curiously harried. "Forgive me, my lady, for not being here when you got back from your ride. Mrs. Foy sent me off to the village on an errand. I only just now returned."

"No harm done," she said. "I have been getting acquainted with Mr. Landsdowne, Lord Northcote's uncle. We were just on our way to the drawing room to take tea. Could you ask David to let Cook know to make up the tray?"

"Of course, my lady."

"In the meantime, would you be so good as to show Mr. Landsdowne to the drawing room." She turned back to the older man. "If you'll pardon me for a few minutes, Uncle Sidney, I will just nip upstairs to change."

"Certainly, Esme. Please, take your time."

But time was the last thing she was going to squander.

Hurrying upstairs with the dogs following, she rang for Paula, then went into her dressing room to select a gown. Two of the cats watched with sleepy feline gazes as her maid arrived to help her wash quickly and slip into an afternoon gown of soft chestnut-colored wool.

A check of the hall clock showed that a mere fifteen minutes had passed. Pausing to smooth her gown and collect her nerves, she took a deep breath and walked into the drawing room.

It was with relief that she noticed Charles standing at attention on the far side of the room. Clearly, he had understood her silent message, exactly as she'd hoped.

Landsdowne got to his feet at her entrance. "That was speedy."

"Yes, with six older brothers, I've learned over the years not to dawdle too long over my wardrobe." She took a place on the sofa while he resumed the chair opposite.

"That's right. You are a Byron," he drawled in an unctuous tone, as though he didn't entirely approve.

She wasn't used to people slighting her family—at least not to her face. Generally, they were more likely to fawn rather than cast aspersions.

She was saved from the necessity of replying when the tea tray arrived moments later. To her surprise, Mrs. Foy was the one to bring it in, rather than a maid. On previous occasions, the housekeeper had made it quite plain that such duties were beneath her, but apparently not today. Esme could only assume it was because Mr. Landsdowne was the guest.

"Welcome again, sir," the housekeeper said. "It is so good to have you here at Ten Elms once more."

"Indeed, it is good to be back. It rouses memories of days long past."

"Oh, it does, sir, it does."

"Thank you, Mrs. Foy. You were always so attentive. This all looks most excellent," he said.

The housekeeper smiled; Esme had never before seen her smile.

Clearly, Landsdowne and Mrs. Foy knew each other well. In fact, she must have been his housekeeper back when Gabriel's uncle had been in control of the estate. And Starr must have been his butler. Suddenly, Esme understood whose orders they were still following whenever she attempted to change something—and they weren't Gabriel's.

Since coming here, she'd learned that Gabriel was rarely in residence. Rather than hire new servants, he must have left the old ones in place, staff who clearly had an old allegiance.

As Esme watched, Landsdowne and Foy exchanged a curiously conspiratorial look that made her wonder if this was not his first visit back since Gabriel had become the viscount.

"Yes, thank you, Mrs. Foy," she said, interrupting the silent exchange. "That will be all for now."

The housekeeper's smile disappeared. "Of course, my lady."

Once the older woman left, Esme served the tea and sandwiches. They all contained meat, so she took a sweet biscuit for herself instead.

They ate and talked at a leisurely pace, Landsdowne commenting on the weather and the habits of the fauna and flora in the area.

"Delicious," he pronounced after a time. "I wonder if we could have some more of the ham and chicken sandwiches?" He glanced toward Charles, who stood quietly off to one side of the room. "Perhaps this young man might be so good as to procure a few more?"

Esme realized she could hardly refuse. Besides, "Uncle Sidney" had been a pleasant enough companion these past twenty minutes. Perhaps she had misjudged him earlier.

"Of course." She nodded to Charles. "Please inform Cook that Mr. Landsdowne would like more of the ham and chicken. And a fresh pot of tea as well."

"Very good, milady." With a bow, the footman departed.

"I'm sure it won't take above a few minutes."

"No matter." He leaned back in his chair. "We've time."

She resisted the urge to frown, hoping he wasn't hinting that she should invite him to lodge here at Ten Elms overnight.

"So," he said conversationally, "what exactly has your husband told you about us? The Landsdowne side of the family, that is?"

He met her gaze, his eyes that same unnerving arctic blue.

"Oh, not a great deal, I'm afraid." She placed her cup onto its saucer. "Only that he lost his parents and older brother some years ago."

"And nothing else?"

"No, not really. Gabriel is a very private sort of man."

"Is he? How interesting that you think so." Landsdowne took a sip of his tea. "I cannot say I am surprised, though, that he hasn't confided in you. His is hardly a tale suited to delicate sensibilities, and yet, had he any decency, he would have told you the truth. Then again, Gabriel has never been a decent man."

"What is it exactly that you think he ought to have told me?"

"Why only that his mother was a loose-moraled bit of baggage who led his father to his death."

Her cup rattled as she set it onto the tea table. "That is a most disturbing accusation."

"It's not an accusation. It is a fact. His mother was nothing but a whore. Her affairs were legendary. I am surprised the rumors never reached your ears, since even young misses gossip about such things despite everyone pretending otherwise. But I forget, do I not, that you and my nephew married in rather a hurry? Something to do with a lurid drawing, if I was rightly informed."

Esme's spine grew rigid. Suddenly she didn't think very highly of Sidney Landsdowne again.

"You must have noticed that none of us attended the wedding," he went on. "Oh yes, we were informed and chose not to give credence to yet another one of Gabriel's sordid peccadilloes. He's spent his life disgracing this family, but then, like mother, like son, I've always said."

"That is quite enough."

His eyes narrowed. "Oh, I think not. After all, have you no interest in knowing just what sort of man you married?"

Her fingers balled into a fist in her lap. "I already

know everything I need to about my husband. He is a good man."

Landsdowne tossed his head back on a laugh, the sound as chilling as his cold gaze. "*Good?* Now, there's a word that was never associated with my nephew. Yes, he's so good he abandoned you here, alone, in this house. Don't think I don't know all about it."

"Do you? Did Mrs. Foy tell you, perhaps?"

He arched a brow. "My, but you're a smart one, aren't you? Yes, Mrs. Foy keeps me informed on occasion about things she thinks might be of interest. As for your absent bridegroom, he is back in London, up to all his old profligate ways, whatever he may be telling you otherwise."

Her hands turned cold, fingers trembling suddenly.

"He's the very devil, miss, and no mistake about it." Landsdowne's voice deepened as he leaned closer. "Why, I could tell you stories that would curl your pretty hair. I tried to curb his excesses at an early age; I was the only one to recognize the evil in him. But even regular beatings couldn't drive the sinful pride and determined wickedness from that boy's soul."

She gasped, her eyes gone wide with undisguised horror. "You beat Gabriel when he was a child?"

"Of course I did, once he became my ward. My brother was always far too indulgent with him, so someone needed to try to drive the wickedness out. But it would seem I was too late; the damage had already been done."

Esme stared, knowing suddenly that she was looking at a monster.

"Then again," Landsdowne continued, "my brother was far too indulgent with everyone, especially that tart wife of his. Rather than putting a halt to her loose ways, he gave her free rein until her scandals drove him to madness."

He paused, his voice dropping to a near whisper. "He killed her—did you know that? Chased after her in a jealous rage when she ran away with one of her lovers. When he caught up to them, he shot the pair of them dead, right there where they lay naked in each other's arms. But rather than say good riddance to that worthless bitch, he turned the gun on himself and took his own life."

His eyes burned, and he appeared half-mad himself. Esme shrank back.

"I blame her," he raged softly. "Her and her useless brat. Her little angel, Gabriel. That's what she always called him. *Her little angel.* At least she did when she bothered to remember his existence. I've always wondered which one of her lovers was actually his father."

"What?" Shock ran like a live charge through Esme's veins.

"That's right." He smiled with a kind of grim glee, baring his teeth. "He's a bastard, and in more ways than temperament. Oh, my brother never believed it, naive fool that he was. Said Gabriel took after his mother and he had no doubts of her fidelity, not then, at least. But all the evidence was there, right before his very eyes, if only he'd chosen to pay attention.

"The Landsdownes are blond." He gestured toward his own head of hair, which must have been golden in his youth. "We have always been blond and blue-eyed, all the way back to the very first Landsdownes who fought on the Lancastrian side during the Wars of the Roses. Go to the portrait gallery and you will see. Blond, every one of them, until him."

He sneered. "Gabriel, who looks nothing like any of his paternal family. He was always a changeling. Brown hair and those damned yellow eyes. And tall. He outstripped his brother by nearly a foot by the time they were out of leading strings. But none of it really mattered until Matthew perished. Matthew, who was meant to be the heir. Matthew, who was the real Landsdowne, not that impostor who stole this family's birthright, the noble title of Northcote."

Esme sat unmoving, stunned. She'd been in the family portrait gallery more than once since her arrival, drawn, of course, to the glorious art. Now that Landsdowne pointed it out, she had noticed a preponderance of blond hair and blue eyes among the subjects. But even if Gabriel's coloring was darker than that of most of his ancestors, it only meant that he took after his mother, not that he was illegitimate.

She'd seen the Gainsborough painting of the late Lady Northcote and remembered being struck by how very alike Gabriel was to her. She'd seen portraits of his father and brother as well, identified by tiny metal nameplates. Curiously enough, there was no portrait of Sidney Landsdowne. Had Gabriel removed it? She wouldn't blame him if he had, considering all that she had just learned.

"What is it you want, Mr. Landsdowne?" she asked bluntly. "Why have you come here when you so clearly hate my husband?"

Her question seemed to catch him off guard, and he refocused his attention. He smiled, looking for a moment like a kindly uncle rather than the brute he actually was.

"Why, to help you, dear lady. To warn you."

"Warn me about what?" She tilted her head, a shiver running over her skin.

"That devil you've wed, of course. I wish I could have done something to prevent your nuptials, but it was already too late by the time I learned you were to wed. He had already compromised you too thoroughly to attempt an intercession." He shifted in his chair. "I did intercede once before, though, several years ago. I congratulate myself even now in preventing his efforts to marry a lovely young woman named Amanda. But with my assistance, she was saved from your present sad fate."

Gabriel had wanted to marry someone else years ago? Who was she? And had he loved her?

Forcing herself not to think of such things, she straightened her spine and looked Landsdowne in the eye. "I don't consider my present fate to be a sad one."

"Oh, come now," he scoffed. "My nephew has already abandoned you here so he can return to all his iniquitous pursuits in the city. This is only the beginning of a life of misery for you, and if you would only think on it, you would see that you need to leave now, while you still can. He hasn't bred you yet, has he?"

"I beg your pardon?"

"Got you with child, girl. Or is that why the two of you wed in the first place?" His gaze went to her stomach, inspecting for a telltale shape.

She bristled outwardly. "It was not, and I'll thank you to keep a civil tongue in your head, sir."

"Civil or not, you would do well to pack your bags and hurry back to the bosom of your family. A man such as your brother the duke ought to be able to protect you. Though why he let you marry a profligate like my accursed nephew, I shall never understand."

"Get out!"

"What?"

She got to her feet. "I said, get out. Be gone now and do not ever think of coming back. I promise you will be shown the door."

"Well, I never—" Landsdowne leapt up, blustering.

"Of course you have," she said. "No wonder Gabriel refuses to even speak of you. You are a cruel, vile man who clearly feeds off his own hatred and jealousy. Rather than being kind to my husband when he was nothing but a defenseless child, you abused and degraded him when you ought to have shown him love. Having spent a mere hour in your company, I can safely say that I have no wish ever to see you again."

A menacing expression came over Landsdowne's face, cold brutality in his eyes. Was this how he'd looked years ago when he'd beaten Gabriel? Was this what Gabriel had faced every day for years before he'd finally grown old enough to escape his uncle's vindictive grasp?

"I can see now that you are beyond assistance," Landsdowne told her. "He has already polluted your mind and no doubt corrupted your body as well. You deserve him."

She drew herself up proudly. "You are right. I do.

Now I must ask you once more to leave. Or do I need to have one of the servants escort you out?"

"Oh, and which one would that be?" he taunted. "All of them are still loyal to me."

"Not all." From the corner of her eye, she noticed that Charles had returned, the plate of sandwiches in his hand. He set them down. "My lady. May I be of assistance?"

"Yes, you may. Charles, Mr. Landsdowne was just leaving. If you would be so good as to show him out."

The footman stepped to one side, waiting for Landsdowne to walk past.

Landsdowne glared. "Insolent chit. You will receive no further welcome from me or mine."

"Good. If they are yours, then I want no welcome. Good day, sir."

After chuffing out a breath, he spun on his heels and stalked away. Charles followed.

It was only once he'd gone that she realized she was trembling, head to foot. Laying a hand across her stomach, she sank back down onto the sofa, afraid otherwise that her knees might give out.

In the distance, she heard the front door close and, a minute later, the sound of coach wheels driving away.

Charles returned. "He is gone, my lady. Will there be anything else?"

She took a moment more to collect herself, then nodded. Before she could let herself collapse, she had one more thing to do.

"Yes, actually, there is. Please tell Mrs. Foy and Mr. Starr that I wish to see them immediately."

If he wondered why, he didn't give any indication. "Very good, milady."

"Oh, and take those sandwiches away. I have no use for them."

Charles picked up the tea tray and left.

Esme waited, hands folded in her lap.

Mrs. Foy and Starr entered the room a short while later.

"You asked to speak with us, my lady?" Mrs. Foy said in her usual cool tone.

"I did." She looked at them, studying the pair with fresh eyes. "Mr. Starr, was it you who let Mr. Landsdowne into the house this afternoon, then left him unattended to roam at will?"

Starr and Foy exchanged looks. "I greeted him on his arrival, yes. But you were out at the time, my lady," Mr. Starr said. "Mr. Landsdowne is his lordship's uncle. I did not see any harm in leaving him unattended, as it were."

She turned to the housekeeper. "Mrs. Foy, I am given to understand that you and Mr. Landsdowne are in the habit of corresponding with one another. Is that true?"

"Well, I write to him on occasion. But I have known Mr. Sidney for a great many years, since the time when he was a young man."

"And this correspondence? Did it by chance involve information related to Lord Northcote and myself? Personal information that only someone in this household would be privy to?"

Mrs. Foy puffed out her bony chest. "I may have mentioned a few details here and there, but nothing of significance. As Mr. Starr said, Mr. Landsdowne is family."

"Family who detests Lord Northcote and seeks only to do him harm. To do me harm."

"Why, I—," Mrs. Foy exclaimed.

"You are dismissed," Esme said quietly. "Both of you."

Two sets of eyes popped wide, and Mr. Starr's and Mrs. Foy's mouths opened and closed like a pair of fish caught on a line. "But, milady—," Mr. Starr sputtered.

"You have no right," Mrs. Foy declared. "It is up to the master to decide such things."

Esme sat calmly, her hands still clasped in her lap. "Of course. And what do you think your master will decide when I tell him that you have been spying on him all these years and that you've been conspiring against him with his uncle, the man who used to beat him as a child?"

Mrs. Foy opened her mouth, but nothing came out, her gaze lowering to the floor.

"Pack your belongings and leave this house," Esme said firmly. "I expect both of you to be gone by nightfall."

"Nightfall?" Mr. Starr looked stunned, while Mrs. Foy's cheeks turned a sallower color than usual. "But where are we to go?"

"The village inn comes to mind. Otherwise, perhaps Mr. Landsdowne is still in the vicinity and he can find accommodations for you. I would suggest you ask him for a character as well, since you shall receive none from me or his lordship."

Rising to her feet, Esme crossed the room and tugged the bell pull. Both Charles and David arrived in the doorway almost immediately, making her think that they must have been waiting outside in the hall all this time. Most likely they had heard every word.

"Charles, David, Mr. Starr and Mrs. Foy are leaving us. Please see to it they do so without any fuss. Mrs. Foy, your keys."

Esme held out her hand and waited.

The housekeeper sent her a bitter, resentful look, but did as she was ordered.

Esme nodded, her gaze returning to the footmen. "Have the dogcart readied to take them into the village."

"Very good, my lady," Charles said, David nodding his agreement.

"Oh, and Charles?" she added. "Once you have taken care of this matter, please come see me. I have something more to discuss."

"Of course, Lady Esme. I mean, Lady Northcote."

She smiled and let him go on his way.

A knock came at the library door nearly two hours later. Esme looked up from the book she had been trying, and failing, to read, her mind far too full of other thoughts.

Charles walked into the room.

"Is it done?" she asked without preamble.

He nodded. "Mr. Starr and Mrs. Foy drove away not five minutes ago. In a right dudgeon they were too. I kept an eye on Mr. Starr while one of the kitchen maids watched Mrs. Foy pack. Went through her baggage myself when she was done. Never heard such foul language from a woman in my life. Makes me wonder if she ever worked in Billingsgate as a fishwife."

Esme sighed and set her book aside. "Thank you, Charles, for your help. You have been a godsend."

"It's always a privilege to serve you, my lady. The house will be far better off without those two in it. They were a grim pair, making life miserable for all of us while they complained of one thing after the next. You did the right thing, giving them the boot."

She frowned. "Yes, but it would seem I am now without a housekeeper or a butler."

"You'll find someone soon. I've no doubt."

"As to that, it brings me to the reason why I asked you to come see me. How many years of service do you have?"

"Sixteen years, my lady. I started as a hall boy at Braebourne when I was just a lad. Worked my way up to second footman there and first with you."

"That seems a lengthy amount of time, or at least it does to me. What would you say to becoming butler here at Ten Elms?"

Charles's eyebrows went high. "Butler? But, my lady, I don't know if I'm prepared. I'm not even thirty. That's young for the butler of a great house."

"And I am only nineteen and already mistress here. Besides, I think you would make an excellent butler."

"I thank you for the confidence, but I must warn you, I still have a great deal to learn."

"Then we shall learn together." She smiled widely. "Charles, or should I call you Bell now? I know you will do a splendid job as butler. But most importantly, I know that I can trust you, and that his lordship will be able to trust you as well. I want no one in this house who is either unkind or disloyal, and I will be counting on you to help me pick the right staff. I want to make this house a home again. Will you stand by my side, now when I need you most?"

Charles straightened his shoulders, a look of pride and determination on his face. "I will, your ladyship. I will not let you down."

"Good." Relief coursed through her. "First things first: weed out anyone you think may still be in the pockets of Starr and Mrs. Foy."

"Consider it done. I've one or two in mind, but the house is so short staffed that it's not a problem. David is a good lad. And you've no worries with Paula. She's already belowstairs celebrating Mrs. Foy's and Mr. Starr's departures."

Esme nodded. "Hire whomever you require, as many staff as you think are needed."

"I know a few likely people, and I'll write to Mr. Croft. He may have some suggestions."

"So long as we don't steal them all from Braebourne, he ought to be amenable. Thank Croft and tell him I said he was to assist you."

Charles grinned at that. "Yes, ma'am."

"In the meantime, I am going down to London. I shall leave you in charge of the workmen and the pets I decide not to bring along with me. If any difficulties crop up, you have only to write."

"Going to see his lordship?"

"Yes. I am."

Whether he wants me there or not. I'm going to get my husband back.

Chapter 23

"Will there be anything further, my lord?" a footman asked nine days later as he finished pouring a fresh cup of coffee for Gabriel, then cleared away his empty breakfast plate.

Gabriel glanced up from the newspaper he was reading. "No, thank you. That will be all for now."

The footman withdrew, leaving him alone in the morning room that overlooked the garden at the rear of his town house in Cavendish Square.

From the corner of his eye, he watched a little brown wren land on a tree branch outside. It hopped a few inches on small bird feet before pausing to sing out a flourish of notes, its tiny feathered throat moving as it warbled a sweet song.

Then, as abruptly as it had arrived, it flew off again.

How Esme and her cats would have delighted in the small show. He could easily imagine the way she would have smiled, could hear the joyful sound of her laughter as she marveled at the simple yet beautiful sight. His eyes slid closed for a few moments as he thought of her.

Suddenly he came back to himself and the present moment.

Scowling heavily, he returned to his newspaper, forcing himself to continue the article he'd been reading.

But try as he might, the prose didn't hold his attention, his thoughts drifting away as they did so frequently these days—to Esme, of course.

Always to Esme.

He'd assumed he would be over her by now. Nearly two months had passed since they'd parted, which ought to have been more than enough time for the heat of his desire to burn out. In the past, he'd never had trouble shaking off a woman's hold. Even his youthful love for Amanda had turned instantly to hate, then, not long after, to disdainful indifference.

Yet each day, Esme continued to plague him. Small, entirely random things would spark some memory of her or leave him wanting to share a comment or observation he knew she might enjoy. He would see and hear things when he was out and about in the city that brought her to mind—artwork and architecture, books and music, and the scents of ink and paper and paint in particular.

And animals. Everywhere, there were animals. Carriage horses and birds, stray dogs and alley cats, creatures that she would surely have longed to rescue from their plight. It had gotten so bad that he wasn't even taking the pleasure he used to feel when he ate meat, especially if it still bore a strong resemblance to the animal from whence it had come. One evening at a dinner party with some male cronies of his, the chef had served whole fish. But when he'd looked at it lying on the serving platter, he'd had to omit that part of the meal, unable to eat the damned thing because of its sad stare, accusing even in death.

But of all the times he could not shake free of her memory, nighttime was worst. He would lie awake in his bed, tossing and turning, his body racked with desire. And when he finally did fall asleep, she would come to him in dreams, leaving him empty and aching when he woke again, bereft to find her gone.

Each day he told himself that *today* would be the end of his need for her, that he would outlast these cravings and free himself from her hold if only he gave it a little more time.

He considered taking other women to his bed, figuring that if he bedded enough females, one of them would surely succeed in driving Esme from his mind. But every time he was on the verge of saying yes to the overtures of some willing doxy, he would turn her away. He'd given Esme his word that he would be faithful to her, and he could not break it. But even if he no longer cared whether he violated his promise, he knew deep down there was a far greater deterrent and that was the simple fact that he didn't want another woman.

The damned truth of it was that he wanted his wife.

He wanted Esme.

Tossing the newspaper aside, he reached for his cup of coffee, only to put it down again when he realized it had turned cold.

Blast, she is driving me mad.

Only think how his friends would laugh if they knew that he, a man reputed to be one of the most heartless rakehells in all of London, had been brought to this state—ensnared in a paroxysm of lust and longing, and all for his own wife!

Not that he couldn't have her if he wanted. All he needed to do was return to Ten Elms and take his fill.

Come to think, maybe that was exactly what he should do.

Christmas was coming soon, true, and it was possible she might already have left for Braebourne to spend the holiday with her family. Then again, if he departed now, maybe he could catch her while she was still at Ten Elms. After all, Christmas would serve as a perfectly reasonable excuse for his return to the estate.

There was also the fact that she was not yet with child. The begetting of an heir provided him with yet another sound reason to return to her bed. If she balked—and she might, given the abrupt manner in which he'd left her—he could always remind her that as his wife, she was obligated to give him progeny.

Perhaps if he were very lucky, it would take months to get her pregnant. Only imagine all the days and nights he would have to satisfy his needs. And maybe, if he took his time and regulated his appetites, he would finally be able to satiate his unwanted obsession with her once and for all.

He'd just pushed back his chair and risen to his feet when he heard an odd commotion coming from the front of the house that included what sounded like several barking dogs and meowing cats, of all things.

He went out into the corridor to investigate.

"Do be careful with them," Esme said over a fresh round of yips, barks and meows. There appeared to be—one, two, three, four dogs, if his count was correct. He recognized Burr, but the rest were new, to him at least, the small pack running hither and thither around the entrance hall, tails wagging with unfettered excitement. There also seemed to be more than one cat, each confined inside its own basket.

"They are generally very well behaved, but the trip has unsettled them," Esme informed Pike, his usually stoic butler, and one of the footmen, who both looked as if hell had just been unleashed upon them.

Gabriel didn't entirely disagree.

"Pray take the cats upstairs, open their baskets, and let them be quiet for a while. Oh, and be sure to close the doors. I don't want them running loose in the house and disappearing somewhere before they have time to acclimate. David can help you."

David, whom Gabriel recognized as one of the footmen from Ten Elms, stepped forward. In the servant's hands were a pair of baskets. The third basket waited on the marble floor. Inside was a short-haired black cat with one green eye, which was currently peering with suspicion through the wicker.

"Not to worry, my lady. I'll see to it they're settled," David said. He looked at the other servants. "If one of you could show me the way?"

Pike regained his usual stalwart composure. "Your pardon, madam, but who are you precisely?"

Esme's eyes rounded and she opened her mouth.

But before she could reply, Gabriel stepped forward. "This is Lady Northcote, your new mistress. Esme, meet Pike, my butler, and Nathan, one of the footmen."

For the second time in one day, Pike's imperturbable exterior cracked ever so slightly around the edges. He recovered so quickly, however, that the slip was all but unnoticeable.

Pike bowed. "My lady, it is an honor. Forgive me for not realizing immediately who you were."

Esme smiled, her generous nature allowing her to instantly forgive. Gabriel wondered if she would be quite so generous with him.

"That is quite all right," she said. "Usually it is Lord Northcote who discomposes the servants with his untimely arrival, but it would seem to be my turn this time."

At just that moment, as if the animal had only then noticed him, Burr bolted toward Gabriel, his canine nails clicking on the floor. The dog let out a happy howl, his entire body quivering with overwhelming excitement. Gabriel reached down automatically to pet the ecstatic dog, smiling at the exuberance of the greeting. He couldn't remember the last time anyone had been so thrilled to see him. He didn't even mind the mass of dog hair being transferred to his trouser legs.

"How are you, boy?" he said. "It's good to see you too. Oh, you're a good dog, aren't you? Yes, you are."

The dog gave a delighted bark and wiggled harder while the servants looked on with obvious bemusement. Because, for all his notoriously wild ways and past peccadilloes, Gabriel knew he had never been the sort to engage in open displays of affection.

"He's missed you," Esme remarked, drawing off her gloves as she walked forward.

Gabriel glanced up and found himself unable to look away, struck by her fresh, guileless charm and radiant beauty. She was simply effervescent; it was as if a sweet spring breeze had just blown into the house and back into his life.

"What about you?" he said softly before he thought better of it. "Have you missed me too?"

She met his gaze, her eyes intensely blue. "If I have, you will find I am not nearly as demonstrative with my affection as Burr."

Inwardly, he winced. Then again, he supposed it was only to be expected considering the way he'd treated her of late.

She turned her head. "Pike?"

"Yes, milady?"

"I should like a pot of tea if it could be managed and something to eat. I presume my rooms will need to be readied, so I will take it down here while I wait."

"Serve in the library," Gabriel told the other man. "It will be more comfortable than the drawing room. And inform the chef that her ladyship doesn't eat meat, though cheese, eggs and milk are welcome."

If Pike found this last instruction unusual, he didn't show it, merely nodded and went to make the proper arrangements.

Suddenly they were alone, except for the dogs, of course, who trailed after them like a small furry entourage.

"What are you doing here, Esme?" Gabriel asked as he led her across the foyer and down a corridor toward the library. "You sent no word that you were coming. Is something amiss at Ten Elms?"

"Not precisely. I thought it would be easier if I just came ahead. You're not the only one who can be full of surprises."

"Apparently not. And what do you mean by 'not precisely'?"

"I'll tell you after I eat."

He preceded her into the library only to turn back moments later when he realized that she had come to a full stop not far from the entrance.

"Gracious," she murmured.

Her eyes were fixed on a large oil painting that was prominently displayed on a central wall, one of the few, that is, not taken up by the shelves and shelves of books that lined the entire room. But it wasn't the painting so much as the subject matter that had undoubtedly solicited her remark.

He looked at the artwork and its depiction of a scene from ancient myth. Naked nymphs and satyrs cavorted around a lake while Bacchus and several equally unclothed handmaidens drank wine and frolicked with the god as he sat on his throne. There was a great deal of sexual imagery in the trees, plants and wildlife as well, if one chose to pay close attention.

The painting had entirely slipped his mind when he'd decided to bring Esme into the library. Ladies, at least not the proper sort, weren't generally in the habit of visiting his town house. Since the day he'd taken possession of Landsdowne House, it had been a bachelor's residence. But no more, he supposed, now that he was married. Esme might even want to rearrange some of the art displayed in the more public areas of the house in order to protect the delicate sensibilities of her female family and friends. Presuming she would be staying here more than a few days, that was, which was a matter that had yet to be decided.

"I presume this is part of your erotic art collection?" she mused aloud. "It is most beautifully done; only look at the masterful brushwork and the lush, luminous colors. Curiously enough, it reminds me of Boucher, though I suppose it was done by a less well-known artist."

He lifted a brow. "I am impressed, madam, since Boucher is exactly who painted the work. You do indeed know your art. The provenance says he did this painting as a private commission for a wealthy, anonymous patron. I acquired it at an equally private auction a few years ago and have enjoyed viewing it ever since."

"Well, if this painting is representative of your collection, I would guess that all the works must have scandalous, clandestine origins due to the lurid nature of the subject matter."

"Actually, this is one of the less provocative pieces," he informed her. "The majority of my collection is housed in a separate gallery devoted strictly to erotic art and literature. A couple of the maids won't even go inside to clean."

Esme turned her gaze on him. "Is it really that bad?"

"Or that good, depending on your point of view." He grinned. "I'll show it to you sometime, if you'd like. After all, you are an art lover. Come to think, perhaps I should frame the naked sketch you did of me and add it to the collection. Or would you prefer to keep it and hang it on your bedroom wall?"

"I believe I will leave it exactly where it is, else the entire house know what you look like without clothing. Although knowing you, you'd likely be as proud as Bacchus here, and every bit as shameless."

His grin widened. "Yes, but only because certain parts of me actually do rival the gods."

A faint dusting of pink trailed up her neck and into her cheeks.

He laughed, then nearly groaned as a sudden rush of desire flooded through him. He was just about to reach for her when Pike arrived, the tea tray in his hands.

"Oh good," she said, moving away, "I am famished."

Slightly disgruntled, Gabriel followed her over to a comfortable grouping of chairs and sofas and took a seat. The dogs clustered around her—two coal black Scotties with impish gleams in their eyes and a rather elderly looking brindle spaniel who put his paws on the sofa and silently begged to come up. Esme happily complied, reaching down to lift the old dog onto the sofa, where he curled into a contented ball against her hip.

While she rinsed and dried her hands with the water and towel Pike had brought, Burr sidled over to Gabriel, his flag of a tail waving as usual. The dog sat, then laid his head on Gabriel's knee, looking up at him with unbridled devotion.

Animals are so open and honest, he thought, as he reached out to stroke Burr's silky head. *If only the same could be said of people.* Although he supposed there were a rare few who surprised him every once in a while.

Like Esme.

He looked at her and felt his chest squeeze tight.

"Tea?" she asked, her blue eyes as open and unguarded as her dog's.

He shook his head, then glanced away.

He'd almost forgotten what it was like to be near her. She was as bright and radiant as an August sun, bringing light and warmth into even the darkest of places.

And yet the darkness was comfortable and familiar to him; he understood the dark, for all its bleak failings. It was the light that puzzled him, the light that could make even the bravest of men afraid. For how could any man bear to go back to the dark, once he'd given himself fully to the light?

Scowling heavily, he found himself wishing suddenly that she hadn't come. Yet, contrarily, he was so glad she had.

He waited, idly stroking Burr's head while Esme ate. Neither of them said much, content to be silent while she enjoyed her meal of cheese-and-watercress sandwiches, fruit compote and walnuts cracked fresh from their shells.

"So," he said once she was finished. "Time to explain. What are you doing here, my dear? Frankly, I assumed you might be on your way to Braebourne by now to celebrate the holidays with your myriad kith and kin. Won't they be looking for you to join them? Or are you still planning to journey onward after you tell me what it is you meant by 'not precisely' when I asked if there was some difficulty at Ten Elms?"

"Oh, that." She set her teacup aside.

"Yes, that. What has occurred?"

"Nothing dreadful, really. The house hasn't burned down or anything."

"I cannot say I would find that such a bad thing if it had, but please, go on."

She smoothed a hand over the skirt of her dark green velvet traveling gown. "Well, it began when your uncle decided to pay me an unexpected visit. You Landsdownes all seem to have that in common, curiously enough."

"He did what?" Gabriel sat up abruptly in his chair, inadvertently dislodging Burr from his knee. The dog moved away to join his fellows.

"I returned from a ride to find him in your office, looking at one of your ledger books," Esme continued. "Being he is your family, I couldn't very well just toss him out—"

"That's precisely what you should have done."

"I invited him to stay for tea, little knowing what he was really like. He is not a nice man. If the rest of your relations are anything similar, I can well understand why you do not keep in touch."

A sudden film of rage blurred Gabriel's eyes. "Did he hurt you?"

"No, nothing like that," she reassured him. "He just said some rather ugly things, mostly about you. He also let slip the fact that he's been spying on you for years with the help of Mrs. Foy and Starr. Did you have any idea? Apparently they have all been keeping up a correspondence."

His hands fisted on his knees. "No, of course I did not know. My steward oversees only the tenants and the land, so I am certain he did not know what was going on inside the house. I left the management of that to Starr and Foy. Had I realized what was actually taking place, those two would have been out the door quicker than I can whistle. I assure you they will be gone as soon as a messenger can be dispatched."

"Oh, no need. I have dismissed them already. I even took pains to make certain they are not lingering in the village, but to my relief they have moved on. I elevated Charles to the position of butler, so the house is being well looked after. But I still have need of a new housekeeper. I thought I could search for one while I am here in the city."

"Who is Charles?"

"Oh, he is one of the footmen from Braebourne. He accompanied Lawrence when he came to see me last month, and I ended up luring him away from Claire and Edward. He's excellent with the animals."

For Esme, anyone who was "excellent with the animals" was excellent in all regards, although if he'd been a footman at Braebourne he was clearly honest and well trained.

"And my uncle?" he asked grimly. "What of him?"

"Oh, I booted him out as well, once I'd had more than enough of his hateful bile. I don't think he likes me any better at this point than he does you."

"You actually forced him to leave?"

"Yes, with Charles's help, of course. I mean, Bell. I really do need to remember to use his last name now that he is the butler at Ten Elms."

Suddenly Gabriel liked this Charles—or Bell—a great deal better.

Christ, he could kick himself for having left Esme alone at Ten Elms. He never would have if he'd had any idea his villain of an uncle might show up to harass her.

In future, he would need to take more care.

"So is that when you decided to come here?" It surprised him that she hadn't gone straight to Braebourne and the protection of her brothers. It pleased him that she had come here to him. "You aren't afraid to be at the estate now, are you?"

"Oh no. I feel perfectly safe there. The servants know to turn your uncle away from now on, and I really don't imagine he'll be back."

I shall make certain of that, Gabriel promised himself silently.

"But he did say one thing that made sense."

"Oh? And what might that be?" His voice was grim, knowing that anything his uncle suggested couldn't be good.

She folded her hands together. "He was very aware that we have not been living together the past few weeks and told me that other people are starting to notice as well. I wouldn't have paid any attention to it were it not for the fact that Lawrence as much as said the same thing to me earlier. Our hasty marriage stirred up enough talk. We don't need to give all the tale-tellers even more to wag their tongues about."

"Let them wag. I've never cared what people think and I'm not about to start now."

"In the main, I would agree. But we are not the only ones involved. It will affect my family too, and they have already done enough to put a good face on our union without us messing it all up again."

He flexed his fingers against his thighs. "Which means what exactly?"

"I thought I would stay here for a while, possibly until the Season begins. Once people see us together, and in accord, the speculation will die down. They'll all grow bored and move on to the next cause célèbre."

His eyes narrowed. "You seem awfully knowledge-able about such matters for a young woman who was in the schoolroom not so very long ago."

"Only because my family has already weathered more than its fair share of scandals. I may not have been directly involved at the time, but one cannot help but hear things."

"Even through closed doors?"

A little smile played over her lips. "Especially through closed doors."

Briefly, he smiled, then leaned back to consider everything she'd just said. "And what of Christmas? Are you expecting us to travel to Braebourne?"

She shook her head. "No. I've already written to Mama and Edward asking them to excuse us this year. I explained that we want to spend our first Christmas together alone. So don't worry that you'll be put to the trouble of playacting again like we did before we left for our honeymoon. We'll have a quiet holiday. You'll hardly even know I'm here."

Oh, I'll know.

How could he not when her presence alone was enough to fill every room with life, as if the house and everyone in it had been half-asleep until she'd burst through the door?

He let his gaze move over her, drinking in her effervescent beauty all over again, while his blood sang with familiar longing.

Should he go along with her plan? He couldn't immediately come up with a reason not to do so.

Before she'd arrived, he'd already decided to join her again at Ten Elms. So why not in London? He could slake his passions with her here just as easily as he could in the country. And maybe she was right. Maybe it would be a good thing to quash the gossip before it got horribly out of hand.

"Very well," he said. "We'll do it your way for now. Welcome to Landsdowne House, my dear."

Esme hugged her pleasure and relief to herself as she made her way upstairs to the viscountess's suite of rooms. Her plan had worked even better than she'd imagined. She'd feared Gabriel might balk at the idea of her moving in or, worse, try to send her back to Ten Elms.

Instead he had agreed.

She'd been prepared to use whatever persuasion might prove necessary, but in the end, he hadn't been all that hard to convince.

Yet that had been the easy part.

Now the real work would begin.

First, she would have to find some means of healing the damage to their marriage. Perhaps she had been guilty of expecting too much of him—more, she realized now, than he had been capable of giving. Her own emotions were always open, her ability to love freely expressed and plain for all to see. She'd had the benefit of being raised with love, always secure inside a family circle whose affection and support were unquestioning and fixed.

But not Gabriel.

He'd suffered unimaginable loss at a very young age. Been abandoned and betrayed, then abused and deceived by those who ought to have protected him, who should have loved him without condition or reserve.

She understood now that he kept a great deal of

himself hidden, locked away behind a guise of cool indifference that no one was allowed to look behind.

But she saw.

She knew there was more to him than the black-hearted hedonist he'd spent years convincing the world that he was. Perhaps he even believed it himself.

But she didn't.

She knew there was a goodness buried inside him, a kindness he tried hard to conceal.

She'd felt it.

There was love inside him too; he only needed someone to help him find a way to let it out.

And that would be her second task—to make a home with him and show him what it was like to be loved without fear or reservation.

She'd realized before that she had scared him off by openly confessing her love. This time she would not be so obvious. Instead, she would give him the freedom he needed to be comfortable with her while she found ways to quietly demonstrate her devotion.

She had worked with enough wounded animals in her time to know that you couldn't smother and push them too fast to accept you or they would remain wary of even the most tender care. Gentle, consistent handling and affection were the keys to their hearts. She just prayed they would prove the keys to Gabriel's heart as well.

And if she somehow managed to perform a miracle and earn his trust, what then? Would he be willing to make their marriage a true union of partners rather than one of necessity and convenience? Would he want to be with her, freely and of his own accord, rather than turn his back on everything they could have together?

Even now, she knew that she owed it to them both to try.

For what choice did she really have, when she loved him so much? When it was her future and her very happiness that were at stake?

Chapter 24

Gabriel was surprised by how easily she welcomed him back into her bed. Considering the way he'd run off with only a brief note to explain his abrupt departure from Ten Elms last autumn, he'd assumed he would have to use some clever methods of seduction to get past her bruised feelings.

Instead, she'd lain in her bed watching him as he'd taken off his robe, then slipped in beside her. Sliding his arms around her, he'd kissed her. Hungrily, she'd kissed him back, meeting his demands with ardent demands of her own.

After a while, she'd pushed him onto his back, then sat up on her knees and pulled her nightgown off over her head, leaving her naked to his view. Leaning close, she ran her hands over his chest and arms and stomach before sliding lower.

"You asked me earlier if I missed you," she said in a sultry voice, as she curled her fingers around his stiff, aching shaft. "I did. My bed has been lonely without you."

She stroked him with her hand until he moaned low in his throat. Then she bent and took him into her mouth, her long dark hair pooling in silky waves over his stomach and thighs.

She worked him until he was shaking and on the edge of release before raising herself to straddle him. Legs parted, she sheathed him deep inside her body, cradling him inside her slick velvet warmth. His hands went to her hips and he took her, driving deep and hard, hips thrusting until they built each other into a frenzy.

When it was over, she said nothing, and neither did he.

Content. Replete.

But instead of cuddling as she always had before, Esme put on her nightgown, then rolled onto her side away from him.

"Good night, Gabriel. Sleep well." She yawned and pulled up the covers. "Close the door on your way out unless you want the cats and dogs in bed with you."

It took him a few moments to come to terms with the fact that she was kicking him out. Slowly, he climbed out of bed. Collecting his robe, he shrugged into it.

"Good night, Esme."

Feeling oddly cold and alone, he went to his room.

Christmas Day dawned cold and clear, the ground white and sparkling with a blanket of snow that had fallen overnight.

Gabriel awakened alone again, as he had each morning for the past week. Lying quietly in his bed, he listened to the faint sounds coming from Esme's dressing room next door.

Generally, he left her to her own devices during the day, each of them separately occupied until they had dinner together, then met again later in bed.

Since her arrival she had stayed busy in her efforts to bring Ten Elms into the modern age. According to Nathan, who accompanied her on all of her outings, she had been meeting with vendors and merchants, craftsmen and even a couple of architects, as she made selections on everything from paint and wall coverings to rugs, furniture, lamps, china and silverware.

She'd asked Gabriel once if he was quite certain he didn't object to the expense, but he'd waved off her concerns, telling her to just send the bills to him and to buy whatever she liked.

When Gabriel had asked Nathan about the shopping

expeditions, the footman explained that her ladyship bought only the highest-quality goods and services, but that she wasn't above seeking out an excellent bargain. With a laugh, the footman had told him that it was the merchants who needed to beware of being fleeced, not the other way around. Esme might look like a hothouse rose, but when it came to business, she was as shrewd as they came.

Gabriel was aware that she was also quietly insinuating herself into his London household as its new mistress. For although she hadn't initiated any permanent changes to Landsdowne House, her touch could already be felt in every corner of the residence, from the fragrant, freshly cut holly and pine boughs that wrapped the mantelpieces and banisters, to the array of new meatless dishes his chef was being inspired to create, to the smiles on the faces of the servants as they went about their duties. He'd even caught Pike whistling a holiday tune under his breath the previous day as the butler stood arranging the floral centerpieces for the dining room table.

In only a week, Esme had brought a warmth and vibrancy to the house that it had never before had. And yet when it came to him and Esme, there seemed to be more distance between them than ever.

She didn't turn him away when he came to her bed each night. In fact, she always welcomed him with a generous, fiery passion that never failed to steal his breath and leave his body wrung out and thoroughly replete. He had never expected to find such passion with his wife, especially considering the circumstances of their union. Yet she made it clear that she no longer wished to sleep with him, turning away once they were done making love, her silence the signal for him to leave.

He ought to have been thrilled, he knew. After all, a pleasant, nonconfrontational relationship with regular, satisfying sex was exactly what he'd wanted. It was the perfect marriage, offering companionship without all the messy emotional entanglements that led to dissatisfaction and disillusionment.

So why did he mind that she no longer wanted to sleep in his arms?

Why was it tearing at him that she had yet to tell him again that she loved him?

Had he been right and her admission of love had been nothing more than naive infatuation? Or had she actually cared for him but he'd killed the nascent tendrils of her devotion when he'd deserted her?

Whichever it was, he didn't like it. No, he didn't like it at all, although what he was going to do about it, he couldn't yet decide.

Tossing back the covers, he reached for his robe, then got out of bed.

A fluffy white cat, whose name he thought was Mozart, of all things, sat in a chair, where the creature had obviously been watching him for some time.

"How did you get in here?" he asked.

The cat blinked his green eyes but made no reply.

He walked closer, then reached out and gently scratched the top of the cat's head. Mozart's eyes slitted and he began to purr.

"I'll bet you could tell me what she's thinking, especially since she lets you sleep with her."

Mozart purred louder.

"Braggart."

Leaving the cat, Gabriel started toward his dressing room, then changed his mind. Moving instead to the connecting door between his room and Esme's, he gave a quick rap and went inside.

Esme sat at the table that stood in front of her sitting room's large window. Beyond, she had a lovely view of the snow-covered garden, where a stone fountain with its impish cupid was bedecked in white.

Steam wafted from the cup of tea she'd just poured, one of the scones from the basket Paula had brought her sitting on a small blue-and-white china plate.

She heard the knock and looked up. Her pulse gave a little hop as she watched Gabriel walk inside. He was still in his robe, his hair tousled from sleep.

He looked mouthwateringly divine.

This was the first time he'd joined her in her rooms for breakfast. Usually, he was up and out of the house before she awakened. But perhaps even Gabriel relaxed on Christmas Day. Then again, nearly everything was closed, so there wasn't a great deal for him to do but stay abed and sleep late.

"I thought I heard you up," he said as he came forward and dropped into the chair opposite. "That looks good." He nodded toward the scone.

Without asking, she took another one out of the basket, set it on a plate and passed it to him. "Would you care for tea or shall I send down for coffee?"

"Tea will do."

While she poured, he buttered the pastry and bit in, making a sound of pleasure low in his throat. "One of your cats is in my room," he said conversationally.

"Oh, do you want me to go in and get her?"

Gabriel shook his head. "Him. And no, he's fine, except for the cat fur. But I presume the maids will sweep it up."

"Yes, I am sure they shall."

Esme hid a quiet smile as she raised her teacup to her lips.

Despite an occasional grumble from him about all the "furry interlopers in the house," she could tell that Gabriel liked the dogs and cats. She'd caught him more than once petting one of them when he didn't think anyone else was watching. And the dogs always raced to greet him when he'd been out and returned to Landsdowne House.

"Happy Christmas, by the way," she said quietly.

"Oh. Right. Happy Christmas."

Then he went back to eating.

She supposed, given what she'd learned, that Christmases hadn't been very festive for him, not even as a child.

She thought of her own childhood Christmases at Brae-bourne, how joyous and lively they had always been, the house filled to bursting with noise, laughter and frivolity.

And family, of course. Lots and lots of family.

She was missing everyone today but glad that she was here with Gabriel. Maybe, if he would let her, she could show him how very special the holiday could be.

"So what shall we do today?" she asked in a bright voice.

He paused midbite. "Do?"

"Why, yes. I was thinking after church that we might take a ride in the park. Or I hear there is a holiday fair going on near the Thames. That might be entertaining."

"Yes, if you like having your pockets picked. Such events are notoriously riddled with thieves looking for a few unsuspecting pigeons to pluck."

She doubted any thief with an ounce of sense would come within ten feet of Gabriel, since he was one of the least "unsuspecting" individuals she had ever known. It would be rather like a mouse trying to get the better of a sharp-clawed cat.

"Well, just the ride in the park, then."

"It's too cold and slick. And it might snow again."

From the look of the near cloudless sky, she didn't think so, but she decided not to argue.

He drank the last of the tea in his cup. "As for church, I don't attend and am not about to start. Considering my less than saintly behavior, I would probably be turned to ash the moment I set foot over the threshold."

"I rather doubt that," she said with amusement. "And it's not as if I attend regularly either, but Christmas service is always nice. Come with me. It will be fun."

"'Fun' and 'church' are not two words that I ever associate together." With a shake of his head, he leaned back in his chair. "Forgive me, my dear, but you will have to count me out of that plan as well."

"What about playing some games, then?" she suggested. "I realize there are only the two of us, but speculation and charades are always amusing."

"You want me to play charades? Really, Esme?"

She tossed up her hands and let out an exasperated huff of breath. "Fine, then what would you propose, since I can see there is no pleasing you today?"

"Hmm, what to do?" he mused aloud. "I have an idea."

She tried her best not to be irritated. "Oh? And what might that be?"

As she watched, a wicked glint sparked to life in his golden eyes, a familiar look that could signal only one thing.

"Oh no." She shook her head and started to get up from her chair. "We are not doing *that* right now."

Reaching out, he caught hold of her wrist and pulled her toward him. "Doing what?"

"You know *what*. Now, behave."

"I *am* behaving, exactly like I always do."

"Gabriel, it's Christmas Day."

"Yes, it is, and I want to open my present."

Before she had any further chance to react, he pulled her onto his lap and began plundering her mouth, leading her into a dance that was dark and feverish with passion.

She didn't protest, never able to resist him once he'd laid his hands on her. She should curse herself for being so weak, she supposed, but how could she when his touch was always so sublime? And when he was the only man she knew she would ever want.

Tunneling her fingers into his hair, she kissed him back, circling her tongue around his in a wet, silken slide. He groaned and palmed one of her breasts through her nightgown, pushing her robe off so it dropped to the floor. He arched her over his arm, then broke off their kiss so he could suckle her breasts, not bothering to take off the gown but finding her through the material.

She grew wet, and not just where his mouth was on her breasts. Restlessly, she shifted her legs and cupped his head to press him nearer. He hummed low in his throat and teased her with his teeth in ways that made her shudder.

Suddenly, he stopped and stood her on her feet. Her knees were pleasurably wobbly. She expected him to take her to bed, but he shoved the dishes aside instead and lifted her up on the table. He pushed her nightgown up to her waist, then sat back down in his chair.

"Spread your legs," he said.

"Gabriel, maybe we should—"

"Spread them."

An anticipatory shiver went through her, and she parted her legs.

"Wider."

She opened them more, exposing her inner flesh to the cool air of the room.

"Good girl."

He reached behind her and she heard the china rattle.

What is he doing?

To her astonishment, she saw that he was holding the jam pot. Her eyes widened as he dipped two fingers in and scooped out some of the thick sugary jelly.

It glistened, red and viscous.

"What are you— Oh my God," she cried, her delicate flesh contracting as he began to smear the sticky confection over her nether lips.

She shuddered, then shuddered again as he used his fingers to paint her with a slow, thorough attentiveness, pausing to scoop out more of the jam so that she was slick and sticky. Her breasts ached, tips puckering, blood beating in wild strokes as he teased her slit from base to top in a way that was nothing short of torture.

Then he set the jam pot aside.

Meeting and holding her gaze, he sucked the jam off his fingers, first one, then the next, sucking slowly as he laved them clean. "Hmm, red currant. My favorite."

Slipping his hands under her thighs, he angled them even wider and buried his head in between.

She peaked almost instantly, her need already so great that his first few licks were enough to send her over the edge. Crying out, she dug her fingers into the table linens, barely caring when she heard some of the dishware tumble off onto the floor.

But he wasn't done. Instead, he was only just beginning, licking and lapping and nipping and suckling as though determined to cleanse every last bit of stickiness from her. She closed her eyes, her hips arching instinctively as he built her hunger again, until she thought she might go mad. She grew wet, then wetter still, but he swallowed every drop with unbridled greed, as if he couldn't get enough.

She climaxed powerfully, screaming as the bliss hit her. Pleasure unfurled, searing her from the inside out, as her mind went blank.

Before she had time to recover even a little, he scooped her up into his arms. Her body hung limp as he carried her in several quick strides to his bedroom, Mozart running out on hurried feet.

Gabriel shut the door.

Laying her on the bed, he stripped her bare, then did the same for himself, flinging their clothes onto the floor. Setting a knee onto the mattress, he moved over her, pausing only long enough to nudge her thighs apart before he thrust hard and deep inside her.

He captured her wrists and pulled her arms over her head, so that she was pinned beneath him, completely taken. He pressed his mouth to hers, then along the column of her throat. "Tell me again what you said that last night," he murmured, moving to catch her earlobe between his teeth.

"What night?" she asked, lost in a sea of pleasure. "What do you mean?"

"That night at Ten Elms before I left." He grazed the other side of her jaw, feathering kisses at random. "You said something to me, or don't you remember?"

Her eyes went wide, meeting his own as he raised his head. And she could tell, there in the bright light of day, that he could see she understood. That she did indeed remember the words.

I love you.

When she didn't speak, he plundered her lips, taking her mouth with an unexpected kind of demand. "Tell me. Say it again."

"Gabriel."

Easing partially out of her, he thrust again, stealing her breath, possessing more than her body alone. "Say it," he urged.

But she couldn't, even though she felt the emotion in every cell of her body.

"Why?" she whispered.

"Because I want to hear the words on your lips again. Tell me you love me, Esme. Say it."

He pumped inside her again, gaining another inch, then another, building her need higher with each new touch, every kiss and caress, until she was aching and near desperation, coiled on a razor's edge of desire.

"Tell me." He circled his hips and rubbed the ultra-sensitive tips of her breasts against his chest with a sensual skill that made her quake. Yet just when she thought she would claim her release, he denied her, letting her know he was the one in control.

"I have to know," he said again. "Do you love me?"

His fingers intertwined with her own, their hands held tightly together as he stroked her passion another degree higher, then another, tormenting her with a promised ecstasy only he could provide.

And suddenly she broke.

"Yes," she cried, the words wrung from her throat. "Yes, I love you. *Love you.*"

And he smiled.

Then he was kissing her wildly and thrusting inside her with a need he could not contain.

She arched, her heels digging into the mattress, her hands gripping his own as if he were a lifeline. Abruptly she peaked and joy crashed through her, spinning her in dizzying circles until she didn't know where her body ended and heaven began.

He claimed his own release almost immediately after, his hips moving fast and sure, teeth clenched as he climaxed forcefully inside her, so powerfully she felt the warmth of him in her womb.

They lay together for a long while after, neither of them moving or speaking. Lazily, he rolled onto his back, careful to keep them joined as he cupped a palm over her bare bottom to hold her tight.

She floated, not knowing what to say, not sure if she understood what he wanted from her, now that he'd made her confess her love for him again. Yet he still had not said the words back.

Suddenly, she wondered if he ever would.

But when she raised her head, she saw a happy gleam in his tawny eyes that she'd never seen before, something she sensed was from more than just sex.

At least she hoped it was.

He kissed her slowly, threading his fingers into her hair. "Now, admit it. Wasn't this better than going to church?"

Her eyes widened at his unrepentant blasphemy; then she laughed. "Maybe you *would* have been turned to ash had we gone to service, since you are a wicked, wicked man."

A wide grin spread over his face. "Indeed, I am, my dear, but you love me anyway. Isn't that right?"

Her own smile faded. "Yes, I do."

Even if I shouldn't.

Even if you will one day break my heart.

The remainder of the day stretched out at a leisurely pace. After lingering in bed for a while more, they rose and took a bath together, which led to another vigorous round of lovemaking that left the floor of the bathing chamber slick with soapy water.

Rather than calling for her maid, Gabriel helped her dress in a simple, yet pretty gown made of green velveteen. She brushed her long sable hair and was about to twist it up to pin it atop her head when he stopped her. "Leave it down today," he urged, leaning down to kiss the sensitive nape of her neck.

She hesitated, since ladies of good standing did not

leave their hair down in public. But as she and Gabriel were not receiving callers today, and the rest of her family was at Braebourne, she didn't see how it could hurt.

Locating a pretty red ribbon, she tied it back, allowing the loose waves to trail down her back nearly to her hips.

They ate dinner in the dining room, seated next to each other rather than at opposite ends of the long, festively decorated table. Great silver epergnes arranged with red-tipped holly, orange bittersweet and brown pinecones perfumed the air, while equally fragrant beeswax candles provided the illumination.

The chef outdid himself, as one delectable dish after another was brought up from the kitchens. For Gabriel, there was a succulent roast goose with figs and a tender glazed ham, while she dined on a pair of clever cheese dishes, one made with cream and potatoes and another from Italy that combined cheese-filled flat noodles smothered with a wonderful rosemary butter sauce.

Accompanying all of that was a plentiful array of vegetables, spiced and stewed fruits and freshly baked breads with creamy butter. And for dessert, there was a flaming plum pudding with a cognac whipped cream so strong it threatened to leave her tipsy.

Presents were handed out to the servants, who would have the following day off from work for Boxing Day; then she and Gabriel returned upstairs to her sitting room again, where they would exchange presents of their own.

He surprised her with an exquisitely fashioned painter's easel made of polished mahogany and a leather case filled with tiny jars of ground pigment that she would be able to use for oil painting. She marveled at them, lifting the glass jars up to the candlelight, the colors reflecting like a rainbow.

She tossed her arms around his neck and kissed him enthusiastically. "Thank you."

"If I'd known this would be the response, I would have bought you art supplies weeks ago." Laughing, he kissed her back until she pulled away to remind him that he had yet to open his own present.

"It's not much," she said, fingers woven together in her lap as she watched him tug the ribbon free of the box in his hands. "But I hope you like it."

He gave her a little smile, then took off the lid.

For several long moments, he said nothing, just sat gazing into the box. She worried her lower lip between her teeth, wondering if she'd misjudged.

"When did you get this?" he asked, his voice thick and unusually deep.

"In Cornwall, that day we went to Truro. The merchant assured me that it is genuine Cornish silver, which he says is quite rare now, since the last silver mines there closed decades ago." She paused, wondering again what he was thinking. "I'm sure you already have a timepiece, likely far more modern and better made than this one, but I'd seen you admiring it so I thought it might be something you would enjoy."

Suddenly he looked up, his eyes fierce and as luminous as molten gold. "I had no idea that you'd done this. How did you manage?"

"Oh, it was when I told you I was hat shopping for Mallory. I bought this then."

He rubbed a thumb over the back, a fleeting shadow of remembrance darkening his face.

She remembered that day too and the way he'd changed so drastically after meeting with his friend, though she still did not know why.

"It's only a trifle," she began, "so I'll understand if you do not like it. We can look for something else tomorrow or—"

Before she could say another word, she was locked in his arms, her ribs aching slightly from the tight embrace. "No, I don't want anything else. This is perfect. No one has ever—" He broke off.

She reached up and touched his cheek, a layer of evening bristle already roughening his skin. "No one has ever what?"

But he only shook his head, his throat working as he swallowed.

And she understood. No one had ever bought him anything simply because he liked it. No one had ever given him a gift meant exclusively to please and which demanded nothing of him in return. What a sad childhood he must have known. What an emotionally isolated life he must have spent since.

Very carefully, he put the watch back in its box and set it on the table. Taking her hand, he drew her to her feet and led her into her bedroom, where the room was lit by only the fire.

Slowly, tenderly, he undressed her, saving the ribbon in her hair for last. She helped him undress next, sliding his coat and shirt from his shoulders and arms, pulling off his trousers, shoes and stockings.

He pulled back the covers and they sank together onto the bed, kissing and caressing as if the night would last forever and they had no reason to rush. She sighed at his gentleness and moaned from his strength, sure in those moments that he must love her, even if he could not yet say the words.

Afterward, he pulled her to him just when she would normally have rolled away, twining her in his arms in a way that left her no room to escape. He didn't ask if she had any objections to his staying tonight, just cupped his hand around one of her breasts in a gesture of blatant possession and closed his eyes to sleep.

But she had no complaints, her heart warm and hopeful locked inside his embrace. Snuggling closer, she closed her eyes as well and smiled.

Chapter 25

She and Gabriel didn't speak again about everything that had happened on Christmas, but their relationship changed from that day forward.

He slept with her each night, and although they still maintained separate schedules during the day, there were also times when he accompanied her on one of her outings. He'd even been willing to provide his opinion on new rugs and draperies for his bedchamber at Ten Elms.

With winter upon them, they often stayed inside, where she used the easel and paints he had bought her. She began with a couple of small studies of the cats and dogs, then moved on to a grander piece with Gabriel as the subject. Despite his teasing complaints at having to wear clothes in this painting, he proved to be a good model, willing to sit quietly as he posed for the portrait.

"You need a painting done of you as the viscount," she remarked one afternoon. "I couldn't help but notice that there isn't one in the gallery, either here or at Ten Elms."

"A wise choice on my part, it would seem, since my uncle would surely have had it burned during one of his clandestine visits to the estate."

Esme had laughed at the time, but sadly she wasn't sure he was wrong.

Lawrence returned to his town house next door in mid-January and began joining them for dinner at least twice a week. And in February, Leo and Thalia and Drake, Sebastianne and little August came back to the city. The seven of them made a merry group on those evenings when all of the adults dined together at one of their respective homes, and Esme delighted in doting on August, who was already showing signs of being every bit as smart as his father.

At Esme's request, Sebastianne and Thalia offered their opinions and lent their expertise in her efforts to refurbish not only Ten Elms, but Landsdowne House as well.

"The rooms are all tastefully done but rather masculine," Thalia commented one gray February afternoon. "There's nothing of *you* here, Esme. It needs your woman's touch."

Sebastianne had agreed. "Precisely, starting with finding new homes for some of Gabriel's more lurid paintings. We French take a far more mature view of sex and nudity than you English, so were it up to me, I would leave them. But I fear if any respectable English ladies visit the town house, they just might be overwhelmed by the sight and faint dead away."

"Hmm, you are right. Still, it might almost be worth the uproar just to see the reaction." Esme grinned.

"How true," Sebastianne agreed, while Thalia smiled, shook her head and joined in their laughter.

Still, Esme hesitated, wondering if Gabriel would object. But when she broached the subject, he surprised her.

"They've stayed up far longer than I ever imagined they would now that you're in residence," he said. "Move whichever works you think might shock your female friends and acquaintances who will surely come to call."

With Pike's help, she relocated a couple of the more prominently displayed pieces to private areas of the house. But she left the Boucher in the library. Ladies weren't likely to venture in there, and besides, she liked the painting; it made her smile every time she went in the room.

As March arrived, the temperatures began to moderate, tiny buds formed on the trees, grass began to green, and into the city came an influx of the *Ton*, returning from their country estates in anticipation of the new Season.

Esme exchanged frequent letters with all her immediate family, and so knew not to expect any of the rest of them in Town anytime soon. With so many young children between them, Edward, Claire, Cade, Meg, Jack, Grace, Adam and Mallory had all decided that it was far easier to stay at their respective estates rather than moving their families to London for a few weeks. Everyone, they agreed, would meet in late summer at Braebourne for a nice long visit.

Neither Esme nor Gabriel had plans to fully participate in the Season either, but invitations began to arrive at the house, along with an occasional caller. A few were genuine friends, whom she and Gabriel welcomed gladly. But others dropped by out of curiosity, eager to meet the sinfully infamous Lord Northcote and his equally notorious new wife.

To Esme's consternation, gossip about their hasty marriage and the naughty pictorial reason for it continued to circulate. But the more she and Gabriel were seen together around Town, the less anyone continued to pay attention, exactly as she had once predicted.

Actually, had it not been for that, she would likely have gone back to Ten Elms, particularly since there were so many new improvements taking place at the house that she longed to see. But if she left now, she wasn't completely certain Gabriel would accompany her, and she was afraid to push the issue and find out for sure.

For in spite of their new closeness and the fact that he seemed to relish any outward expressions of her love, he never expressed the sentiment himself. Even now, she still did not truly know what he felt for her.

Oh, he liked her. Of that she had not the least bit of doubt. But love . . .

It was a hope she continued to hold in her heart, waiting patiently for the day he would kiss her and say, *I love you too.*

So for the time being she was resigned to staying in Town and taking part in at least some of the activities of the Season. Which meant clothes shopping with Sebastianne, Thalia and Claire, who had decided to come up to Town after all, but only for a week.

"Edward has business with the Lords, so I thought I would come along," Claire said cheerfully, as they stood in the modiste's shop a day after her and Edward's arrival. "Oh, it is so good to see you. You look wonderful, by the way. I can tell marriage suits you, or should I say your husband suits you. I am glad it has turned out to be a happy match, after all."

Esme nodded, feeling oddly and unaccountably shy. "What makes you so sure?"

Claire arched a pale eyebrow. "Anyone can tell. They have only to look at the pair of you. Gabriel could barely keep his eyes off you today when we all came to collect you. It did my heart good to see, I must confess."

Claire had turned away then to offer an opinion on a length of material Thalia was considering. But Esme didn't move. Hugging the comment to herself, she prayed that Claire was right.

A week later, Gabriel and Esme attended a ball together, her very first as Viscountess Northcote. It was a smaller affair, since the Season had not yet officially begun, but exactly the kind of party best suited for her introduction into Society as his wife.

The *do* was being hosted by an old university friend of his, Lord Cooper, a man who luckily had never done anything bad enough to be painted with the same black brush that tarnished Gabriel's own less than savory reputation.

In fact, since Esme's arrival in London, he had been careful not to bring her into company with the more hardened members of his old crowd, a set known for their licentiousness and sin. They were an often crude and tawdry bunch on the whole, and he wanted her to have nothing whatsoever to do with them. He used to take immense pleasure in flouting Society's rules—the more unsavory the act, the better, he'd always said. But now that he had Esme to consider, he found himself unwilling to do anything that might embarrass her or besmirch her reputation. And so, over the winter, he'd begun turning down invitations to join his former friends in one sort of revelry or another. Much to their astonished disbelief, he was no longer interested in their sordid amusements, and had recently vowed to cultivate—or recultivate—a new group of friends. Attending the ball of Lord Cooper and his wife was just such an attempt, and when he came face-to-face with his old friend, he found himself genuinely happy to see him.

"Thank you for having us," Gabriel said as Esme spoke animatedly with Lady Cooper.

"Of course. It is our pleasure." Cooper inclined his head. "I was glad to see you at the club the other day. It has been too long since we had a chance to sit and talk."

"Indeed, it has."

Cooper's eyes strayed toward Esme. "I can see what has been holding your attention of late. Your new bride is quite exquisite. I am happy for you both."

Gabriel watched Esme as well and agreed. Esme *was* exquisite, not only in beauty but in mind and spirit too. Rather than getting over her as he'd once planned, he found himself more ensnared than ever. But it wasn't just the passion that continued to burn between them; he enjoyed her company too.

To his surprise, he realized that he found as much pleasure and contentment sitting with her, reading or talking in front of the fire on a cold winter's night, as he ever had indulging in wild parties and excesses. Were he being strictly honest, he supposed he'd used those pursuits to blunt his pain and fill the voids in his life. But now that he had Esme, the old hurts didn't seem to trouble him so much anymore.

She loved him; she told him so nearly every day, usually at his urging, since he had an almost endless need to hear her say the words. Pathetic, he knew, especially for a man who'd once professed not to believe in such emotions. But she and her love warmed him from the inside out, and he could no longer do without either one.

And what of me? Do I love her?

He swallowed, the truth staring him in the face no matter how much he wanted to deny it.

Yes, God help me, I do—even if part of him still feared everything it might mean. But like a drowning man, he supposed he was finally surrendering to the inevitability of his fate.

He met Cooper's gaze again, the other man's eyes twinkling with sympathetic amusement.

"Not a word," Gabriel warned, annoyed to realize that everyone he encountered seemed to recognize the emotion he felt long before he was able to see it himself.

But Cooper only laughed. "I have to admit it's rather refreshing to see the mighty fall, but not to worry—your secret is safe with me."

"This is lovely," Esme murmured nearly an hour later as she and Gabriel danced a second set together—a waltz this time, to her delight. "I could dance with you all night, but I suppose we ought to separate for a little while lest everyone begin remarking about how gauche we are for being in each other's pockets."

He spun her in a circle. "Let them remark. They're all talking about us anyway."

"Are they?" Surreptitiously, she glanced around and discovered he was right. People were watching them, some with speculation, others with disapproval and even envy. "Even so, we're supposed to be lessening the talk, not increasing it."

The dance ended. Arm in arm, they left the dance floor.

"Go join the men for a bit," she encouraged. "I'm

sure there must be a card or billiards game taking place somewhere in the house."

"So you want me to gamble?"

"Of course, so long as you don't lose," she said teasingly.

He laughed.

Leaning up on her toes, she kissed his cheek. "Come collect me for supper."

"Aren't you worried it will invite more comment if I take you in to supper?"

"I don't want to eat with someone else. I want to be with you."

His gold eyes turned molten, and for a few seconds she thought he might actually kiss her right there in front of everyone at the ball. Leaning close, he put his mouth against her ear. "If you aren't careful, I just might carry you off to a secluded spot and have my wicked way with you. But in deference to the occasion, I shall strive to be good. For now."

Her pulse hurried faster. "Go on, before I change my mind." She laid a gloved hand on his shoulder and pushed. He didn't budge so much as an inch.

Chuckling, he nipped her earlobe, then sauntered away toward the card room.

As soon as he was gone, she wished him back. The few people she knew were very casual acquaintances and the rest strangers. None of her family were in attendance.

Young August was down with a cold, so Sebastianne and Drake had stayed home to nurse him. Edward and Claire had gone back to Braebourne, while Leo and Thalia were at Brightvale again. And Lawrence was busy working on a legal case and could not be drawn away.

She was about to walk across the ballroom to join the matrons who'd arranged themselves on a nearby row of chairs, when a man stepped into her path. Glancing upward, she looked into a familiar pair of eyes.

"Lord Eversley."

"Lady Esme, I thought it was you." He made her an elegant bow.

She curtsied back.

"Although it is Lady Northcote now, is it not?" he said.

"Yes, it is."

"Allow me to offer you my best wishes on your marriage."

"Thank you."

They stood awkwardly for a moment.

"I—"

"How—"

They spoke at the same instant, their words overlapping. They both laughed, awkwardly again.

"You were saying?" she began.

"No, please, you first."

"Oh, nothing important. I was only going to remark that we have not seen each other in quite some time."

His smile fell away. "No, not since last summer, at Braebourne. I was not able . . . that is, I . . . my dear lady, you must allow me to offer you my sincerest apology."

"Apology?" Her forehead creased in genuine puzzlement. "Why, whatever for?"

"For my behavior after that evening. For the way I ran off without even bidding you a farewell. For not staying long enough to allow you to offer an explanation for something which I have since come to realize was entirely innocent on your part."

"Oh, not entirely innocent, Lord Eversley," she said with a faint chuckle. "I did draw Lord Northcote, after all. I have an impetuous streak, you see, that sometimes leads me into all sorts of dire predicaments. I am sure you were shocked, and justifiably so."

"I was, I confess, but my behavior was still inexcusable. I ought to have stayed. It would have been the gentlemanly thing to do. You probably wish you need have nothing more to do with me."

"Not at all. We were always friends, were we not? And everything has worked out well in the end."

"Has it?" He frowned, his eyes moving quickly in the direction of the gaming rooms before moving back to hers. "Forgive my impertinence, but are you happy?"

"I am, yes." She smiled softly, her thoughts drifting to her husband. "Very happy."

He studied her, then relaxed, his shoulders visibly easing. "I have worried over the matter, you know, fearing that you felt you had no other choice."

Actually, at the time, she had felt that she did not have any other choice but to marry Gabriel or be ruined. But as she had just told Eversley, everything had worked out well in the end. Worked out as it was surely meant to be.

"I love my husband, Lord Eversley. Truly, trouble yourself no more on the subject."

Suddenly, he smiled. "You have always been so generous of spirit, Lady Esme. I mean, Lady Northcote. I hope that you might be generous again and say we may continue to be friends."

"I should like nothing better."

They shared another companionable smile.

"Only look, a new set is forming. May I have the honor of this next dance?" he asked.

"Oh, I . . ." What excuse could she possibly give? Then again, why should she and Lord Eversley not dance? The awkwardness was past. It was time to turn over a new leaf. "Yes, thank you. I would be delighted."

Taking her hand, he led her out onto the dance floor.

After nearly an hour, Gabriel walked back into the ballroom. He'd won a nice bit of cash, but the play bored him, his mind far too frequently on Esme rather than the cards in his hands.

She'd promised him supper together, so he'd come to collect her early. If the gossips wanted to wag their tongues about him dancing attendance on his wife, let them. Far worse things had been said of him and would no doubt be said again.

He stood scanning the ballroom in search of her

when the last person on earth with whom he wished to converse slipped up beside him.

"Why, if it isn't Gabriel Landsdowne in the flesh. Who would ever have thought to find you at such a respectable entertainment? I was so surprised when I realized it was you that I had to come over and say hello."

He looked down at the woman at his side. Amanda Coyning, older yet still beautiful in a cold, serpentine kind of way. He couldn't remember the last time they'd spoken—sometime after she'd betrayed him by breaking off their engagement but long enough ago that he had no real recollection of the date or occasion.

Then, of course, there had been the night roughly six years ago when she'd been between husbands and had tried to interest him in a tryst. He'd rebuffed her with a cutting, and very public, refusal that had made her shake with humiliation and rage. She'd hated him ever since.

"How do you do, Amanda? Or should I say Lady—" He broke off. "What is it now? I've lost track of all your last names; you've had so many."

"Nibblehampton," she said stiffly.

"Good Lord, he must be rolling in money for you to put up with that ridiculous surname."

"Actually, he is amazingly kind, like you used to be a long time ago."

"A *very* long time ago." His lips twitched with wry amusement. "What do you want, Amanda?"

"Why is it I have to want something?" She pouted.

"Because if you didn't, you wouldn't be you."

And suddenly he realized how true that statement was. Amanda always had been the sort who continually craved more, even when she'd been a girl. No matter how much she had, be it tea biscuits or precious gemstones, it was never enough to suit. When he thought back, he remembered that she'd always been wheedling some gift from him, usually something he hadn't been comfortably able to afford. Because he'd been young and she'd been so pretty, he'd been willing to overlook her shortcomings, choosing to see only her outward beauty while making excuses for the ugly selfishness that lay inside.

But Esme wasn't like that. Even if she someday lost all her looks and became as wrinkled and bent as an old crone, she would still be beautiful, because that's what she was inside. Esme sparkled like diamonds, while Amanda was nothing but paste.

He looked at Amanda and felt something he'd never felt for her before.

Pity.

With a touch of sadness.

For she would never know real love or happiness. Emotionally, she would live alone and die alone, as empty and unmourned as any person could be.

He already knew he'd been a fool to have ever thought he loved her. But tonight he realized he hadn't even known what real love was. Now he did, now that he had Esme.

His old anger toward Amanda fell away. She'd wounded him, but it didn't hurt anymore. It would never hurt again.

"As I said, I was surprised to see you here," Amanda drawled. "Entertainments such as this aren't really your style."

"Or yours."

She shrugged. "My husband's daughter-in-law is a friend of Lady Cooper and persuaded me to come. Since it is so early in the Season, I thought it might be a good way to pass the evening. Little did I realize I would find you here along with your new bride. By the way, if you are looking for her, she is out on the dance floor. Ah, there she is now, if I am not mistaken."

Gabriel's eyes were drawn across the room to where Esme was indeed dancing, her skirts whirling as she moved to the music.

Amanda idly tapped a fan against one palm. "If I am also not mistaken, her partner is Lord Eversley. He's a former beau of hers who paid avid court to her last

Season. When he was invited to Braebourne last autumn, everyone assumed an engagement between them was all but settled. Imagine the shock when she married you instead, and under less than usual circumstances. There was a scandal of some sort, I believe?"

He tried to ignore Amanda's venom; her real goal in seeking him out having just been revealed. But the damage was already done, since he could not unhear her words.

He turned deliberately indifferent eyes upon her. "My wife is a beautiful woman. I am sure she had many beaux last Season, but I am the man she chose to wed. Now, if you will excuse me, Lady Nibblehampton." He executed a quick bow and strode away before she could say anything else.

The dance had just finished by the time he reached Esme and her former beau. They came off the dance floor, the man laughing at something she had said.

So that was Eversley, was it? Now that Gabriel saw him, he didn't like the look of the fellow, and most particularly the admiring way he was gazing at Esme. She'd told him that Eversley had meant nothing to her. But what of Eversley? Did he feel the same?

Gabriel scowled at the thought.

Esme stopped when she saw Gabriel, her smile brightening as he drew near. "Well, hello," she said. "I wasn't expecting you back so soon. You didn't run into bad luck at the tables, did you?"

"Not a bit. I won quite handily, as it happens. But you promised me supper, so I have come to collect you."

"Goodness, is it that time already?" She opened her fan and waved it in front of her pink cheeks, Lord Eversley waiting beside her. "Oh, forgive me, Lord Eversley," she said, turning her gaze toward the other man, "but have you met my husband, Lord Northcote? Gabriel, this is Lord Eversley."

The men exchanged bows.

"A pleasure," Eversley said.

"Indeed."

Their eyes locked as they surveyed each other. Eversley looked away first.

Gabriel offered his arm. "If you are ready, my dear, shall we go in?"

"Oh, yes, of course." Before taking his arm, though, she turned to Eversley. "Thank you for the dance. I am glad we had an opportunity to renew our acquaintance."

"As am I." Eversley smiled. "I look forward to seeing you again soon."

Before he could go on, Gabriel secured her hand on his arm and led her away. "So, he's the one, is he?"

"The one?" She looked puzzled.

"The man you told me about before we were married. The suitor everyone assumed you would wed."

"Oh, that. Well, people assume a great many things that never come to pass."

"Your family included?"

She stopped and turned to face him. "Yes, even my family on occasion."

"Then what's he doing sniffing around you again?"

Her eyes widened. "He's not *sniffing*. He asked me to dance. This is a ball, Gabriel. Dancing is one of the things people do at balls."

"Hmmph." He curved an arm around her waist and drew her near. "Well, in future I would prefer you dance only with me."

She smiled. "I wouldn't mind that in the slightest. But as we discussed earlier, we're trying to steer people's attention away from us, rather than focus it on us even more. Eversley is an old acquaintance, Gabriel, nothing more. And Society being what it is, I was bound to cross paths with him at some point."

"I suppose so."

But she was right and he was quite likely overreacting. She must have had many suitors last Season. If he complained about them all, he would spend the next several weeks in an angry lather. Still, as much as she said that Eversley was as harmless as one of her pets, Gabriel didn't believe it. Eversley was a man, after all, and Esme was a beautiful woman. Besides, he'd seen the way Eversley had looked at her. The way any normal warm-blooded man would look at her.

He waited to see if she would say more. When she didn't, he decided to let the matter drop.

"Can we go in to supper now?" she asked. "I'm starved. I hope they serve something other than lobster patties and caviar."

He linked their arms again and started toward the dining room. "Never fear, my dear. I won't let you starve. I shall go to the kitchens myself if need be and raid the larder for bread and cheese."

She laughed and leaned against him. "My hero."

Chapter 26

The Season officially began twelve days later, just after Easter Sunday. Invitations flooded in, and callers knocked on the front door of Landsdowne House with far greater frequency than either she or Gabriel might have wished. Their days of peaceful togetherness were over, at least for the near future. They spent their days and evenings at one entertainment or another, even though they hadn't planned to participate in the tumult.

They did ride together each morning, savoring the early hour, when the park was green and uncrowded as they cantered from one end to the other. And they slept together at night, curling into each other's arms even on the rare occasions when they did not make love.

But by mid-April, Esme was longing to go home to Ten Elms. She didn't voice her wish to Gabriel, though, unsure if he would come with her and unwilling to chance his refusal if he would not. And so she stayed in London, had lunch and tea with friends and attended parties with Gabriel in the evening, all the while craving the serenity of the countryside and the single-minded focus of losing herself in her painting, which she had also had to temporarily put on hold.

She had another reason for wanting to leave the city, though it was a suspicion rather than a fact at the moment. But she'd been feeling overly tired of late and a little queasy at the unlikeliest times of day. At first, she'd put her symptoms down to too little sleep and the demands of the Season.

But recently she'd begun to wonder if there might be another reason. A happier reason. Namely, she thought she might be with child. It was an idea that filled her with equal measures of joy and trepidation. After all, what did she know about being a mother? But the more the idea took hold, the more she wanted it to be true.

Still, she decided not to say anything to Gabriel, at least not until she knew for certain. She assumed he would be pleased, but what if he wasn't? He still had not professed any kind of love for her, but each day with him was better than the last. He seemed, well, almost happy, and she wanted nothing to disrupt their marital bliss.

The only dark cloud to mar their newfound contentment was an occasional sighting of Sidney Landsdowne and his family. She'd experienced an almost electric jolt the first time their paths had crossed at a soirée, roughly two weeks after the start of the Season.

She'd just finished having a cozy chat with another young matron with whom she'd made her come-out last Season when she turned around and found herself standing barely two feet away from Gabriel's despicable uncle. She'd darted a glance to her side, wanting to flee, but a lifetime of etiquette had kept her rooted to the spot. Giving Gabriel's uncle the cut direct, no matter how hateful he might be, would be sure to unleash a firestorm of gossip among the *Ton*. And so, despite her personal repugnance for the man, she'd forced a smile and sunk into a curtsy.

Sidney Landsdowne bowed politely in return, his pale features betraying not so much as a hint of the enmity that had passed between them during their last unpleasant encounter, at Ten Elms.

"Niece," he said.

"Uncle," she replied.

His eyes were as blue as an icy lake as they swept over her. "You are looking well. City life must obviously agree with you."

"Indeed, it does. And you as well. Are you newly arrived in Town?"

"We've been in residence a short while. We arrived in time for Gillian to be presented to the queen. But come, allow me to make you known to more of your new family. My wife, Enid, and daughter, Gillian. Alas, my sons, your cousins, are not here in London at present or I would introduce them as well."

It was only then that Esme noticed the pair of blond women waiting as silent as wraiths nearby. The older woman's thin lips were set in a sour pucker of barely veiled disapproval, her eyes as glacial a blue as her husband's. As for her cousin Gillian, Esme couldn't tell much yet. The girl was a pretty, diminutive blonde whose looks reminded Esme of some of the portraits in the gallery at Ten Elms. To Esme's surprise, Gillian gave her a tentative smile. Esme gave her one in return, wondering if the other girl might be shy rather than cold like her parents.

Landsdowne's gaze moved over Esme, then stopped as his eyes fixed suddenly on the emerald necklace around her throat before traveling up to the tiara in her hair. "Are those some of the Landsdowne jewels?"

Instinctively, Esme touched her fingers to the necklace. "Why yes, I believe they are. Gabriel gave them to me only recently. They're quite lovely, don't you think?"

"No, I don't think." Landsdowne looked suddenly murderous.

Esme took a step back.

"Look what he's done to them." Sidney's hands turned to fists.

"Are you surprised to discover that he's ruined them?" Enid said, speaking for the first time. "I told you, you ought to have buried the jewels somewhere and told him they'd been lost."

Esme listened, dismayed by the reaction and confused by the remarks.

Suddenly, a familiar arm curved around her waist.

It was with relief that she felt Gabriel pull her into the protection of his hold.

"What are you doing, Uncle?" Gabriel said in a deceptively smooth voice that was low enough not to carry beyond their group. "I thought I was quite clear when we had our little talk last week that you were not to engage my wife in conversation. Or have you forgotten already?"

Gillian's eyes grew round. Clearly she wasn't used to people reprimanding her father.

"People would think it odd had I not spoken to her, Northcote." Sidney's hands flexed at his sides. "Enid and Gillian as well. Just keeping up the social pretense and all that."

"Well, the pretense has been satisfied. Aunt. Cousin Gillian." Gabriel inclined his head, then turned to Esme. "Come, let us away. I believe a dance is about to begin."

"Not so fast, boy." Sidney couldn't hide the sneer that moved across his face. "Those jewels have been in the family for over two hundred years."

"And they are still in the family. They just got a bit of much-needed refurbishment."

Sidney's eyes wheeled in his head as if he were on the verge of an apoplexy.

"Smile, Uncle. Remember the family reputation, tarnished though it may be," Gabriel said softly. "People are beginning to stare."

Enid stepped closer to Sidney and took his arm. "Much as it pains me to agree, he is right. Let us go find some refreshments."

"Listen to Aunt Enid," Gabriel said. "After all, you have Cousin Gillian to consider. You wouldn't want people talking and spoiling her Season, now, would you?"

"I wish I could take my belt to you," Sidney said on a near whisper.

Gabriel stiffened. "I know, but I'm no longer the defenseless boy I once was. You no longer frighten me, Uncle, so I would have a care if I were you. From now on, let us agree to keep our distance, most particularly you from my wife. If I see you harassing her again, I promise you won't like the hell I will rain down upon you."

Gillian squeaked and covered her mouth with a hand while Enid's thin lips nearly disappeared in a tight line of displeasure. As for Sidney, he still looked as if he'd like to strike Gabriel.

"Fine," Sidney said suddenly. "So long as you abide by your word on that other matter we previously discussed, Northcote." Sidney's eyes brushed quickly over his daughter, who looked on in alarmed confusion. "Believe me. It will be a pleasure to pretend you and your new bride do not exist."

"Likewise." Gabriel tightened his hold on Esme.

"Enid. Gillian. Come." Turning on his heel, Sidney stalked away, the two women following obediently.

"Good heavens, what an unpleasant man he is," Esme said as she and Gabriel moved away in the opposite direction. "Your aunt isn't a great deal better."

"No. She and my uncle are well suited when it comes to their vile temperaments."

Esme frowned. "Surprisingly, Gillian seems like a sweet girl. I feel rather sorry for her."

"As you ought, with parents like those. Luckily, they've always doted on her, from what I've been able to observe, so other than being strictly raised, I believe she is well treated."

Esme was relieved to hear that. "What was that other cryptic remark your uncle made regarding Gillian? Have the two of you been discussing her?"

Gabriel met her gaze, turning her toward him as they reached the edge of the dance floor. "It's nothing over which you need to be concerned. Just more of his usual blustering. All is well."

Esme studied him, then nodded. "If you say so. I do think I'll put in a good word about Gillian with some of the ladies I know here in Town. She shouldn't be made to suffer just because you and I do not get along with her parents."

Gabriel smiled. "You have far too tender a heart, my dear. Forever trying to help others. If only Gillian knew she has a new champion in you."

"I shall know." Esme moved into his arms as the music began. "Sometimes just knowing is more than enough."

Esme was standing inside Hatchards bookstore one afternoon during the third week of April, looking over the new works of fiction they had in stock, when the bell rang on the front door. Idly, she glanced up and saw Lord Eversley walk inside. Moments later, he noticed her too. A smile creased his face as he approached.

Although she didn't see him often, they had spoken a few times since renewing their acquaintance at the Coopers' ball. He was always an amiable companion and to her relief seemed to have gotten past whatever romantic hopes he might once have harbored for her. Instead, he had been true to his word to be a friend.

"Lady Northcote." He bowed. "What a happy coincidence, finding you here. I didn't realize you were a reader."

She curtsied in return. "Yes, on occasion, I have been known to pick up a book. I am pleased to see that you do the same."

"I do. Although today I am here on an errand for a friend."

After a couple of minutes of casual conversation, he turned to give his friend's order to the clerk, while she made her own literary selection. They stood chatting pleasantly afterward as her purchases were being wrapped up.

"Are you in a hurry to return home now?" he asked as they walked out of the shop and stepped onto the pavement.

"Not a hurry, no. Why do you ask?"

"Oh, no reason." He tugged at the cuff of one sleeve, appearing suddenly uncertain. "Well, that's not strictly true, but I ought not to have raised the subject."

"It would seem you already have, though I do not know to what subject you are referring."

"It's only that I could use a lady's opinion, since I've no knack for doing these things on my own and all my female relations are out of Town at present."

Torn between exasperation and amusement at his rambling, she reached out and briefly touched his arm. "Lord Eversley, please, I beseech you. Just tell me what you require."

He stopped and met her gaze. "Forgive me, dear lady. My nerves are getting the best of me. You see, I am planning to ask a certain young lady to marry me."

"Oh." She smiled. "How wonderful. My felicitations. Might I ask the name of the lucky girl, or would you prefer to keep it a secret?"

He studied her. "Well, I suppose there's no harm, considering we have you to thank for our happiness, at least in part."

"Me? How can I possibly be responsible?"

"Why because you brought us to one another's attention, of course. Or rather you helped bring her to *my* attention."

Her forehead creased. "In what way? Who is the young woman with whom you are smitten?"

"Lettice Waxhaven."

Her eyebrows shot to the top of her head and her mouth dropped open.

"I'd met her before, of course, but I'd never really taken the time to get to know her," Eversley continued, too busy talking to notice what Esme was sure must be a look of utter stupefaction on her face.

"We shared a coach, she and her mother and I, when we left Braebourne," he said. "Lettice and I got to talking. She's really quite a wonderful girl, very giving and thoughtful. And so sporty. Did you know she loves lawn bowling and archery? I had no idea we shared so many interests in common."

Esme would never have associated any of those descriptions with mean, spiteful Lettice Waxhaven. But maybe she hadn't really gotten to know the real Lettice either. Perhaps jealousy had caused the other girl to behave the way she had around Esme. Because if there was one thing she remembered about Lettice, it was the fact that she had been desperately in love with Lord Eversley.

And now it would appear he was in love with her too and about to pop the question.

"Well, I am delighted for you both," she said. "But I really don't see how I can be of assistance."

"As I said, if you can spare the time, I'm on my way now to pick out an engagement ring. I realize it's a dreadful imposition, but if you could help me, I would be immensely grateful."

"Oh, I'm not sure that's such a good idea. I don't really know Lettice's taste," she hedged.

"But you're a woman. Anything you choose would have to be better than anything I'd select."

She hesitated, worrying her lower lip between her teeth as she decided whether or not to be completely honest. "Eversley, I know you mean well, but I don't think Lettice would like knowing it was me who helped choose her wedding ring."

"Why not?"

"Well, she doesn't really like me."

He brushed off her remark. "Of course she does. She even told me how sorry she is for what happened that night at Braebourne. How she didn't really mean to bump into you and that she's felt dreadful about it ever since."

Esme rather doubted that tale. On the other hand, she supposed that if it were not for Lettice Waxhaven's actions, her drawing of Gabriel would never have been revealed. And if the drawing hadn't been revealed she would never have met and married Gabriel and fallen in love. When she considered it in that light, she supposed she was the one who owed Lettice a debt of gratitude. Still . . .

"Very well," she said, "but swear you won't tell her

I helped you. A lady likes to think her groom made the choice all by himself."

A wide grin creased his cheeks. "You always have been a bang-up girl, Lady Northcote. If I weren't marrying Lettice, I believe I would kiss you."

She laughed and took a step back. "Yes, well, please don't. My husband would most definitely take exception."

Eversley shivered. "Indeed. Northcote is one man I would never want to cross."

"Where is this jewelers?"

"Only a few blocks away. We can walk if you'd like?"

She nodded. "Yes, that sounds lovely. I'll have my coachman follow us there."

Gabriel left Brooks's club, but rather than taking his curricle home, he decided to walk, sending his tiger on ahead without him. It was a fine spring day and he was eager to stretch his legs. The city thrummed around him, vibrant with life and bustle and noise. But as much as he enjoyed the city, he was beginning to grow tired of the constant busyness and the demands on both his time and Esme's.

He thought back to the peace and serenity of Highhaven, of the blissful weeks he and Esme had spent there during their honeymoon. He wondered what she would say to the idea of going back, leaving the city and Season behind and escaping to their own private retreat by the sea.

Despite her obvious popularity among the *Ton*, and the pleasure she seemed to take at the various entertainments they attended, he'd sensed a growing restlessness in her lately. She seemed oddly secretive at times, drifting off, lost in her own thoughts when she didn't think he noticed. He told himself it was nothing, that she was only tired from the pace of their current social obligations. But he couldn't help wondering if it might be something more.

I should suggest a trip to Highhaven. A change of scene would do both of us good.

He turned a corner and continued on another pair of blocks. He was looking ahead, studying the other passersby, when he caught sight of a familiar coach and team of horses.

Esme had told him she was going shopping. She must be in one of the stores.

He was about to cross the street to find her, when the door to a jeweler's shop opened and out she came.

Only she wasn't alone.

She was with a man. A man he recognized.

Eversley.

Gabriel's hands fisted at his sides as he watched her smile and laugh with her former beau. Eversley laughed as well, then moved closer to her, taking her arm as they both stepped out of the way of a couple trying to walk past them.

For a moment she and Eversley looked cozy and conspiratorial, as if they were both in on something only the two of them knew. They turned then and moved toward the carriage. Eversley took her hand and bent over it before assisting her inside.

Gabriel stepped back, sliding into the concealment of a building where he would not be seen. He waited until her carriage drove away.

And that's when the pain hit, his stomach roiling as if he'd just taken a brutal punch to the gut.

And he supposed in a way he had.

Yet despite the evidence before his eyes, he couldn't believe she would betray him. Not his Esme.

Then again, he'd been deceived before. Quite suddenly he didn't know what to think.

Blindly, he turned away and started to walk.

Chapter 27

It was well after midnight when Esme heard a key scrape in the lock and the quiet click of the front door as it opened and closed again.

Leaping to her feet, she hurried out of the drawing room where she had been waiting for the last several hours and into the hallway. Relief flooded through her at the sight of Gabriel as he set his hat and gloves on the hall table. Moving quickly forward, she wrapped her arms around him and pressed her face to his chest, breathing in his warm, familiar scent. "Gabriel, thank God you're home. I've been so worried."

She waited for his arms to come around her, for him to explain what had happened and why he was so late in returning. Instead, he remained stiff, his arms hanging loosely at his sides.

She looked up. "Where have you been? I expected you hours ago. Your driver said you left your club around three this afternoon. I sent him back out later to look for you, but no one seemed to have any idea where you might have gone."

He pulled away from her and stepped free. "I've been walking." His voice sounded dull and tired and wrong.

Very wrong.

A shiver went through her. "All this time you've been walking? Where did you go?"

He shrugged, not meeting her eyes. "Around the city. I don't know. I'm going to my study."

Turning, he crossed the vestibule and started down the corridor, his footsteps echoing on the cool marble. She stared after him for a long, silent minute, then followed.

He was pouring a drink by the time she entered the room—whiskey from the looks of it. Raising the glass to his mouth, he tossed it back, then picked up the decanter again to pour another. He replaced the stopper with a noisy clink but didn't acknowledge her.

As she stood watching him, she remembered another time when he had changed abruptly for no apparent reason. When he had closed her off. When he had left.

"What is it?" she asked softly. "What has happened?"

He ignored her and drank more whiskey.

"Won't you talk to me? I've been frantic all evening, wondering what could have happened to you. I imagined all sorts of dreadful things. That you had taken ill or were in an accident or had even been set upon by thieves and murdered."

His eyes met hers, his own derisive. "Thieves, Esme? Murder? Really? I had no idea you were so dramatic, but then again, you are an artist, I suppose. And here I assumed you'd still be out, dancing the night away, and would barely have even noticed my absence."

Her lips parted on an astonished inhalation. "You know I wouldn't go out for the evening without you. We were promised at the Nugents' tonight, but I sent a note 'round and made our excuses."

"You needn't have done. You ought to have attended. I'm sure it wouldn't have been difficult for you to find some willing gentleman to escort you."

A muscle flexed in his jaw, his eyes turning darker.

She crossed her arms over her chest. "What is that supposed to signify, since I presume you do not mean one of my brothers?"

He flexed his fingers and slammed the glass down on his desk, oblivious to the alcohol that splashed over the side. "No, I damned well do not. I saw you today," he said accusingly.

"Saw me? Saw me where?"

"With him. *Eversley.*"

She was so astonished, a laugh rippled from her throat.

Gabriel's eyes shot fire. "So you think it's funny, do you? The two of you looked awfully cozy, snuggling up together outside that shop."

"Do you mean Hatchards?"

"No, I mean that jewelry shop. Was he buying you some trinket? I've watched him slaver over you like a besotted puppy ever since he came to Town. Don't think you can hide it from me. As we both know, he was one of your beaux and the two of you were expected to wed, but you had to take me instead when you thought you would be ruined. He wouldn't step up then, but perhaps he's regretting his decision. Perhaps you're regretting yours as well."

All humor fell away, her hands and heart turning cold. "I regret nothing. And you, my lord, are a ridiculous, jealous fool."

A muscle twitched near his right eye this time, his jaw clenched so tight she wouldn't have been surprised to hear it snap. "How dare you."

"No, how dare *you*. Accusing me of deceiving you, when I have been nothing but faithful and honest. Condemning me on the flimsiest of excuses too, I might add."

"Excuses? I saw you," he charged, his voice deep and grim.

"You saw me what? You saw me speak with a gentleman of my acquaintance on a public street in full view of the world. Watched me get into my carriage and drive home. Alone. Is that what you saw? Now I have a question for you. Why were you spying on me?"

He scowled. "I wasn't spying. I was walking back from the club when I happened to see you come out of that shop. And if it's all so innocent, what were you doing in there with him?"

She let out a huff of exasperation. "I was helping him choose an engagement ring for the young woman he hopes to marry. He asked for my assistance, as a friend, and I gave it. If you don't believe me, you can ask Nathan. He was there the entire time and knows everywhere I went and everyone I saw. He probably heard every blasted word we spoke as well."

"You shouldn't have male friends."

"And you should stop treating me as if I'm your mother or that girl, that Amanda, who broke your heart and left me to pay for it."

He flinched as if she'd struck him, something harsh and bleak darkening his eyes. In that instant she wondered if she'd gone too far. But she wasn't going to back down. Not when their very future was at stake.

"What do you know about my mother and that other . . . person you mentioned?" he demanded coldly. "Obviously some little bee has been busy filling your ears with all sorts of juicy details. Who was it?"

A little shiver of nerves went through her. "It doesn't matter who it was."

"Some gossip here in London, was it?" he pressed. "Or perhaps one of your chatty friends, the ones you have in for tea? Or, no . . . wait . . . I believe I have it. Was it my uncle?"

The answer must have shown in her eyes, because he nodded at his last guess. "Ah yes, of course, it would be dear uncle Sidney. I am only surprised you haven't said something about it before now."

"I knew it must be distressing for you, so I didn't see the point."

"Didn't want to offer your pity, you mean."

"No, Gabriel, that's not—"

"But, please, let's make sure you've heard the whole sordid tale. What did he tell you? Did he mention that my mother was little better than a whore and how my father drove himself to madness over her, then blew his brains out after he murdered her and her latest lover? What else did he share with you?"

"Nothing. Don't—," she beseeched quietly.

"Did he tell you his favorite part? That he thinks I'm some by-blow spawn from one of my mother's many lovers? That I look like her but not like my father, who probably wasn't my father at all, since I am nothing like anyone on the Landsdowne side of the family? How I'm not worthy to bear the Northcote title and am nothing but a misbegotten devil that he tried but failed to fix by means of a belt and the back of his hand?"

"Stop, Gabriel." Tears filled her eyes. "Please, stop."

"No," he said relentlessly, "you brought it up, so let's get it all out in the open. Let's have the truth, so you'll know exactly who it is you've married."

She heard the echo of his uncle's cruel words, understood the damage he'd carried inside him like an unhealed wound. She wanted to take him in her arms and comfort him, as he should have been loved and comforted as a boy. Instead, she stayed where she was, afraid he would interpret her action as the pity he claimed she felt rather than love.

"Gabriel, I do know who you are, and none of the rest matters to me." She drew a breath. "You are a decent, brave, intelligent man who hides his kindness away where others cannot see it. But I do see it. It is in the kindness you show the servants and the animals. I feel it every time you kiss and touch me.

"You were treated abominably as a child, first by parents who ought to have loved and protected you rather than destroying each other in pursuit of their own selfish desires. Then again by a monster who should have cared for you and nurtured you when you were grieving rather than hurting you even more. You lost your brother and were betrayed by a girl to whom you had promised your love and by whom you had it cruelly rejected. But in spite of all that, you're the man you are today. A man with a good heart even if he wants the world to think it is black."

"Maybe it is black and you are mistaken," he said.

She shook her head. "No. In all the ways that count,

you are a good man, Gabriel Landsdowne. You're not a saint, but who wants a saint? Only think what a great bore you would be then."

The corner of his mouth twitched, a glimmer of the darkness receding from his eyes.

She stepped closer. "And even if it's true about your parentage, which I don't believe, it doesn't change who you are. Even if you showed me incontrovertible proof that you were another man's son, it would make no difference to the way I feel."

"And what is that? You say you love me, Esme, but . . ."

"Yes, but what?"

He frowned and looked away.

She swallowed, a lump in her throat. "And now we circle back around to what started all of this between us tonight. You do not trust me."

His eyes met hers again. "I do."

"No. If you did, I would not be standing here trying to defend myself against something I did not do and will never do. I trust you to be faithful to me when I know every time we go to a ball there must be at least one or two of your old paramours in the room. When I know you were talking with Amanda, your old love, at a ball only a few weeks ago."

He looked startled. "She is nothing to me, Esme. What you saw was nothing. She approached me, then baited me about you and Eversley when you were dancing with him. You know you are the only woman I love," he told her gruffly. "The only woman I want in my bed."

Her heart beat double. "Do you truly love me? You never say."

Striding forward, he took her in his arms. "Of course I do. If I didn't, do you think I would have spent half the day and night walking all over London? Dazed and sick to imagine you with another man."

She reached up and stroked his cheek. "Oh, Gabriel, I feared you might never feel that way for me, that you might never say the words."

"Well, I'm saying them now. I love you."

"Then why can you not trust me when you know I love you too?"

He scowled. "Because it's not that easy. I don't want to you being with other men, even as friends. It makes me jealous."

"But you don't need to be. You're the only man I want. Can't you see you have nothing to be jealous about?"

"Are you sure?" He gave her a long look. "You've been quiet lately, secretive, as if you're keeping something from me. If it's not Eversley, then what is it?"

"Oh, that," she said surprised by his perception.

His eyes narrowed. "Yes, *that*. Tell me, Esme. What is it?"

She opened her mouth, then shut it again. For as much as she longed to share her hopeful suspicions with him about her possible pregnancy, she wanted it to be a happy occasion when she shared her news, not one filled with acrimony and discord.

Clearly, telling him now might end their argument, might even heal the breach between them. But only temporarily, only until the next time he decided he didn't like the way she was behaving around another man.

"It is something I want to share with you, but not right now," she said.

"Why not now? What is it?"

She shook her head. "No, I'm not telling you, not tonight."

"Then when?"

"When I think the time is right."

"And when will that be?"

"I don't know. You'll have to wait."

He lowered his arms and stepped away, his jaw tight again. "So let me rightly understand this. You have a secret, something you're hiding from me, but you won't say what?"

She crossed her arms. "That's right. You'll just have to trust me."

"Oh, so that's it, is it? This is some kind of test? You can keep secrets but I'm just supposed to trust you?"

"Yes, you are. You keep secrets, and don't claim you don't. If you didn't, you would have told me you're still on speaking terms with Amanda whatever her name is—"

"Nibblehampton."

"What?"

"Her current surname is Nibblehampton."

"Good God."

"Exactly."

For a second, Esme nearly let the humor of the name overtake her. But then Gabriel continued.

"And I'm not on speaking terms with her," he said. "She speaks to me and I try to get away."

"Well, you obviously didn't try hard enough the last time you communicated."

"So I'm supposed to pour my heart out to you about everything I've ever done and everyone I've ever spoken to in my entire blasted life?"

"No, of course not. But you can't expect me to tell you every last thing either."

"Why not? I thought you trusted me!" he taunted.

"I do. It's you who doesn't trust me!" she yelled back.

Sudden silence fell between them, the clock over the mantelpiece ticking in a steady rhythm.

Only then did she realize she was trembling. She'd never had a fight with him before, not like this one. She wasn't sure whether to scream at him again or allow herself to give in to tears. Instead, she turned and started for the door.

"Where are you going?" he demanded.

"To bed." She wrapped a hand around the doorframe and looked back at him. "I think you should sleep in your own room tonight."

His eyes narrowed dangerously. "Oh, you do, do you?"

"Yes," she said softly. "And there is another thing."

"What might that be? Another *secret*?" he added mockingly.

"In a way. I've been thinking about it for a while, but I'm tired of London. I want to go home."

His face turned pale. "You're leaving me?"

"No," she said softly. "I will never leave you, not the way you mean. But I need some time and I think the countryside would do me good." *Would do us both good,* she thought, but she didn't say the words.

His expression grew shuttered. "So you're going to Braebourne? Planning to complain to your brothers about how badly I treat you?"

She sighed. "You don't treat me badly, Gabriel, and when I say home, I mean our home. Ten Elms. Come with me. I want you to."

But once again he had closed himself off from her. "Good night, Esme."

"Good night."

Yet even as she said the words, she knew they meant good-bye.

It took her the next two days to pack and make her excuses for the various engagements she had been scheduled to attend. There were also her dogs and cats to consider, whose needs had to be carefully coordinated for the trip. She also went next door to Lawrence's town house to explain her abrupt departure to him and ended up sobbing on his shoulder while he offered to go next door and beat sense into her idiot husband.

But once again, she told him no. This was her marriage and these were her difficulties to work out.

Gabriel was barely speaking to her, not even joining her for meals. He was also sleeping in his room, having done as she'd asked, though now she wished she could take it back. She would give anything to sleep inside the circle of his arms again.

But even though she knew that all she needed to do was apologize and tell him about the baby—which she was even more certain was a reality, given that she had missed her menses for the second month in a row—she knew she could not knuckle under. It was a gamble, perhaps a foolish one, but he needed to come to her. He needed to show he trusted her now, or their marriage would forever be one long series of jealousies and fights, with him always thinking the worst of her whenever he had even the slightest doubt about her devotion.

She worried anew that she was doing the wrong thing and almost changed her mind as she was standing in the hallway on the morning of the third day, preparing to depart.

But then she saw him, looking as black and cross as a thundercloud as he watched her give a few last directions to the servants.

The hall cleared and she and Gabriel were alone.

"You're leaving, then, are you?" he said darkly.

"Yes." She drew on her gloves, fighting not to let him see how her hands trembled. "I will send you word when we arrive."

He nodded and didn't meet her eyes. "Safe travels, then. I've told the coachman not to push too hard, no matter how eager you may be to arrive as quickly as possible."

"Thank you. That was most thoughtful."

"You are welcome."

Has it really come to this? The two of us talking as politely as strangers once again.

"Well, you had best be on your way."

She nodded and he started to turn away.

"Gabriel," she called.

He looked back, meeting her eyes for the first time in days.

"Come with me. We can delay a bit while you pack a bag. It will be no trouble."

Emotion raced across his features, an inner war being fought as he struggled to decide.

"Tell me what you're keeping from me first," he challenged.

"I will. Once you prove you trust me enough to let me tell you in my own time."

Their eyes met and clashed again.

Gabriel's jaw tightened and he looked away. "Good journey."

Blinking back tears she knew would turn into sobs once she got into the coach, she raised her chin and walked out of the house.

Gabriel nearly went after her to stop the coach from leaving.

Instead, he forced himself to walk to his study, where he sat, hands squeezed into fists on his thighs. He hurt so badly it felt as if the skin were being peeled from his body.

She wanted to leave? Let her leave.

She wanted to keep secrets from him? Let her keep them.

He'd lived thirty-three years without Esme Byron Landsdowne in his life, and he would live the next thirty-three-plus just fine without her.

Then abruptly he sagged, his muscles going slack, as he hunched over.

Who am I trying to fool?

Live without Esme?

He wouldn't make it a day.

But she was wrong and she needed to learn that. Trust her? How the bloody hell was he supposed to trust her when she flirted with other men, then ran off for home the minute he called her on it?

Only she didn't flirt with other men and he knew that. She was friendly, yes, but, then, she was friendly to everyone. She treated the old men with the same kind of polite attention she showered on the young ones, with no particular difference. There was no special regard there, no heated looks and coy smiles. Those she reserved exclusively for him.

As for Eversley, the bastard's wedding announcement had been in that morning's edition of the *Times*, exactly as Esme had said. His supposed rival was engaged with the ring she had apparently helped him pick out.

But if he chased after Esme now, what did that say? After all, a man had his pride.

No, he would not bend. She was the one who should come back to him.

So why did he suddenly feel like he was the one being taught the lesson, not her?

Chapter 28

Gabriel forced himself not to go after her, one day sliding miserably into the next. Six days after she left, he received a brief note from her, advising him of her safe arrival at Ten Elms.

He sat down to write back, but couldn't, the words either too few or far too many. In the end, he sent her no note at all, balling up his various ink-stained efforts and tossing them into the waste bin for the servants to discard.

As each new day dawned, his temper grew a bit more frayed, his appetite worse, his sleep fragmented and unrefreshing as he tried futilely to find rest in his empty bed.

The house felt empty and unnervingly quiet without the dogs barking and the cats underfoot. Much to his irritation, he found he missed them too, especially Burr and Mozart, who had been in the habit of trailing him into his office and arranging themselves at his feet—or in Mozart's case, on his desk—while he handled correspondence and various matters of business.

Now it was just him in the room, him in the house.

Except for the servants, of course, who'd taken lately to giving him a wide berth as often as they could manage. He'd even bitten Pike's head off the other afternoon when the butler had mentioned something about a delivery arriving for her ladyship and ought he to send it to her in the country?

"Hell and damnation, man, do your blasted job and leave me out of it," he'd raged, as he'd poured himself another draught of the whiskey that was serving as his nuncheon.

Pike had drawn himself up, clearly offended. "Very good, milord. Should I tell Chef to serve dinner this evening, or will you be drinking that as well?"

He'd thrown his glass at Pike, his aim poor, luckily, as the crystal shattered against the wall behind the butler's head. Pike hadn't flinched, just gave him a look of pity. "At the risk of being dismissed, might I remind you that her ladyship would want you to eat."

Gabriel had sighed and nodded, quietly ashamed of his behavior. "Fine, serve dinner."

Pike had not been dismissed.

Gabriel was sequestered in his study four days later, the draperies drawn against the late-morning light. He'd barely slept all night, his face was unshaven and he was still wearing yesterday's clothes. Unexpectedly, a knock came at the door.

He scowled blackly, having left strict instructions that he was not to be disturbed. "I told you I am not receiving," he said harshly as the door opened.

"You didn't tell me."

He looked around and watched Lawrence Byron walk into the room.

"What are you doing here?" Gabriel demanded in a sullen voice.

Lawrence moved deeper into the room and sank down into an armchair across from him. "I've just come to see if you're still among the living. No one has caught a glimpse of you in days, and Pike says you're as surly as a badger who's been poked with a stick."

"Pike talks too much."

Maybe I will sack him, after all. Ever since Esme had come into the house, Pike had turned into a bossy old woman.

Only Esme isn't here anymore.

The thought slashed through him like a knife.

"Get out, Byron," he said without temper, too tired to muster much fire.

"Oh, I'm *Byron* now, am I?" Lawrence settled back into the chair, clearly planning to stay awhile. "And here I thought we were as close as brothers these days. Although I am known to bicker with my brothers far more than I do my friends. You can get away with saying all manner of shabby rubbish to your family that you'd never dare try on your friends for fear of them kicking your arse."

"I'd like to kick your arse, right out of that chair," Gabriel grumbled.

Lawrence grinned, then leaned forward, a serious expression replacing his smile. "Look, Gabriel, this has to stop."

"What has to stop?"

"This." Lawrence gestured with a hand to the whole of Gabriel. "This fight between you and Esme; it's hurting you both. You're so miserable you're making yourself sick, and she's not doing well either."

"What do you mean?" A sudden thought hit him. "Is Esme ill?"

"It's nothing serious; at least that's what she assures me. She told me not to worry, but you know how quickly these things can progress. It's hard not to be concerned. I thought you should know."

Gabriel's skin turned cold, his body rigid with anxiety. "Of course I should know. Why hasn't she written to tell me herself?"

"Well, she said she thinks it will pass with time and she didn't want to trouble you."

He leapt to his feet, hands fisted at his sides. "Not trouble me? She's my wife and I love her. Of course she should trouble me if she's sick. I'm the first person she ought to have told."

"My thoughts exactly. You should be with her at Ten Elms. And her birthday is only a few days away, you know. If you leave now, you can be there in time to spend the day with her. I can't think of any sadder way to pass one's own birthday than alone and sick in bed."

"You're right. Thank you, Lawrence. I won't forget this."

"I don't doubt you will," Lawrence murmured.

But Gabriel was no longer listening. Shouting for Pike, he strode from the room.

Lawrence watched Gabriel leave, listened to the servants spring into action in order to prepare for their master's hurried departure.

He hoped his gambit worked.

Usually he stayed out of other people's business, even when family was involved—actually, particularly when family was involved.

But Esme was his baby sister and she was desperately unhappy at the moment. The only way he could see to make her happy again was to get her and Gabriel back together, and if that meant a bit of truth stretching, then so be it. Not that he'd lied, precisely. Esme *was* feeling tired and nauseous, just not for the reasons Gabriel thought.

Lawrence smiled and prayed that Gabriel was as smart as he thought and didn't muck this up.

Esme awakened, morning light streaming through the curtains. Despite her low spirits, she forced herself to get out of bed—or rather her body forced her as she raced for the nearest basin and proceeded to vomit what little remained of last night's supper. Once the worst was over, she washed her mouth with clean water, then crawled back into bed.

May sixth, she thought. *My birthday. And I'll be spending it alone.*

But then she laid a hand on her stomach and amended her statement. She wouldn't be alone. She had the baby with her.

She'd had the doctor out to visit not long after her arrival at Ten Elms, and he had confirmed her suspicions.

She was definitely with child.

If she'd had any remaining doubt, it would have been

put to rest by the bouts of nausea and vomiting she was experiencing. In general, though, the sickness came upon her in the morning, then promptly disappeared to trouble her no more until the following dawn. And except for morning, her appetite remained good, so she wasn't suffering in that way.

No, her suffering came from another source entirely, one that made her ache with a deep, unremitting pain.

She and Gabriel were estranged, more deeply than at any other time during their marriage. She'd hoped by now he would have come to her, or sent for her, writing to say that he was sorry and could they begin again. But he hadn't written, not even a note. Though she supposed given everything they had said already, what more was there to discuss?

Feeling better, physically at least, she got out of bed again and rang for her maid. Once she was bathed and dressed in a blue-and-white-spotted muslin that her maid had hoped would lift her spirits, but didn't, she went downstairs for the day.

She had no more work to do on the house. It was finished, everything new and sparklingly clean. The rooms gleamed with crisp new coats of paint, new rugs, draperies and wall hangings, lamps, fixtures, furniture and more. All the tradesmen she'd hired had done exceptional work, clearing out everything that had been dark and gloomy and replacing it with cheer and sunlight. It was a house that breathed now, a house that was ready to be a home.

The servants were an asset now as well. Bell was an even better butler than she'd hoped, and with the assistance of the new housekeeper, Mrs. Liss, he had the place running like a finely tuned clock.

With nothing domestic to oversee, at least not that morning, she considered painting; she was still trying to finish Gabriel's portrait. But the smell of the oil paints made her queasy and the subject matter made her sad, so she vetoed that idea, scouring her mind for another option.

Maybe she would do something simple, take a walk in the garden, then sit for a while in the sunshine and read. It was a beautiful day, and no matter how low, and lonely, she might be feeling, the fresh air would do her good.

She called for the dogs to accompany her, since they loved any chance to run, sniff the plants and chase any squirrels that might cross their path. Putting on her bonnet and pelisse, she went outside.

Chapter 29

"Good day, how may I be of service?" asked a sharply dressed man who stood at the front door of Ten Elms.

From his appearance, Gabriel would guess he was the butler, yet he looked far too young for the job. But Gabriel didn't have time to worry over such things right now. All he wanted was to see Esme.

He met the servant's gaze. "You can start by letting me inside. I am Northcote."

The man's eyes widened. "Lord Northcote? Forgive me for not knowing you immediately. I am Bell. The butler."

"Ah, so you're Bell. The one who is good with the animals."

"Yes, my lord," the servant replied with a tilt to his mouth. "That would be me."

Done with the small talk, Gabriel moved inside, thrusting his hat and coat at the other man, who hastily accepted them. For a moment, Gabriel barely recognized the place, it looked so different. So light and airy. So inviting. Not at all like the Ten Elms he had always known.

He turned again to the butler. "Where is my wife? Upstairs?"

"No, my lord, I believe she is out in the garden."

Gabriel stopped. The garden? What was she doing outside? Then again, invalids often took fresh air in order to convalesce. Not that Esme was an invalid—not yet, anyway.

Scowling heavily, he strode back outside, ignoring Bell's offer to return his coat. His boots crunched as he made his way to the side of the house and the gardens that had always reminded him of a boneyard in the autumn and winter.

But no more, he saw, as he drew nearer, the garden alive with flowers and greenery, a great deal of it new. The elms, however, were still in place, rising tall and majestic from their place of honor.

Then he saw her, seated on a bench, her head bent over a book. The dogs were nestled at her feet. They leapt up at his arrival and raced toward him, Burr in the lead, tail waving like a banner. He petted their heads and said soft hellos.

When he straightened, Esme was looking at him, her blue eyes wide with surprise and the slightest bit of wariness, as if she wasn't certain how to react. Her cheeks were flushed with pretty color.

Or was it fever?

If so, she shouldn't be out of doors.

He strode forward, needing to be near her.

"Gabriel." She set down her book and smiled. "You're here."

"I am," he said, encouraged by her greeting. "I came as soon as I could. Lawrence told me you've been sick."

Her smile fell away, her shoulders stiffening beneath her pelisse. "Oh, he did, did he? I suppose he told you everything. I knew I should never have confided in him, and I wouldn't have if I'd known he would go blabbing. Well, if that's the only reason you're here, you can go straight away again."

Reaching for her book, she picked it up and opened it again.

Rather than being deterred, he sank down next to her on the bench. "So, you wanted to hide this from me? Not tell me how sick you are? He said the doctor came by."

"He did, yes."

"And what did he say? What treatment has he prescribed?"

"No treatment. Only that I need to rest if I am tired."

"Well, then let's get you back inside. The servants shouldn't have permitted you to sit out here in this cold air and take a chill."

"It's May, Gabriel, not January. I am fine right where I am. My pelisse is actually a little too warm."

"Nonetheless, I don't want you to tax your strength." He put a hand under her elbow to coax her to her feet, but she resisted.

She tilted her head and gave him a probing look. "So, you came because you think I'm ill? No other reason?"

"What other reason do I need? You're my wife and I love you. I came as quickly as I could, fearing you might worsen and I'd be too late."

"Oh, Gabriel." Flinging her book aside, she put her arms around him. "I'm not sick, not the way you fear."

"Are you certain?" He searched her face.

"Very sure. I'm sorry you've been so worried. I shall chastise Lawrence when next I write."

He pulled her closer. "You ought to have told me yourself. You ought not to have thought you couldn't share this with me. Esme, I'm sorry for everything. For my stupid jealousy and my idiotic pride. I should never have let you go. I wanted to stop you the day you left London, but I held back. I was an idiot, exactly like you said. It's been absolute hell without you."

"It's been hell for me too," she murmured, her eyes shining. "I've missed you so much."

Relief and hope spread through his chest. "So do you think you can forgive me? I can't promise I'll never be jealous again, but I'll try. I'll give it everything I have not to let my temper and my insecurities get the better of me. Because I do trust you. I love you. And whatever this secret of yours is, you can tell when you're ready, or never at all. It's your decision. Just say you'll take me back. Just tell me we'll never be apart again."

She laughed and pressed closer. "Of course I'll take you back. And I never want to be apart again either. I love you, Gabriel. You're my first, my last, my only."

He kissed her, taking her lips with a sweet force that filled his body with pleasure and his heart with joy. And he did feel joy and relief, such as he had never known. He'd thought trusting her with his love would be a weakness, but now he knew it would only give him strength.

Her fingers tunneled into his hair and she kissed him with a heady ardor that made the world fade away. She was his world, and from this moment forward, he would want no other.

Esme was floating, part of her wondering if this was real or a dream. But if it was a dream, then she never wanted to wake up again. Gabriel had said such beautiful, wonderful things, and he meant them. He loved her. He trusted her. Now it was time to trust him too, because she didn't like keeping secrets. From now on, she would keep nothing from him, most especially the one thing she longed to share with him the most.

But instead of drawing away, she kissed him back, fervently, endlessly, her toes curling with giddy pleasure until she lost all sense of time and place. Toasty warm from passion and the heat of his body pressed to hers, she barely felt the sudden sharp breeze that gusted over them.

But he must have as he eased back, ending their kiss. "We should go inside."

"Yes." She nodded dazedly. "Let's go in. Let's go to bed."

He arched a brow. "Bed is where you belong, but we'll wait to make love again. I want to make certain you're well first."

"Gabriel, about that. It's not what you think."

"It's not? You have been sick, haven't you?"

"Yes, but—"

"No buts; we need to get you well."

"I am well, or at least as well as any woman in my condition."

"Your condition?" He studied her for a long moment, sudden speculation warming his eyes. "Esme, this doesn't have anything to do with your secret, does it?"

She nodded, a little smile curving her lips. "Yes. I wanted to tell you sooner, but I didn't know for certain then, and I wanted it to be a happy occasion when I shared the news, not when we were in the middle of a horrible fight. That's why I wouldn't tell you, even though I've been dying to for ages now."

Emotions chased over his face, little pieces appearing to fit together as he puzzled out her jumble of words. "Esme, are you . . . are you with child?"

She nodded again. "Yes."

He looked stunned.

"Well? What do you think?" she asked with sudden nervousness.

He looked at her for a few seconds more, then stood up and pulled her into his arms. Holding her high against him, he swung her in a slow circle and kissed her and kissed her and kissed her some more.

When he finally let her come up for air and set her on her feet, she blinked dizzily up at him, watching as he laughed with a carefree happiness she'd never seen before.

"So, you're pleased?" she said, glad his arms were still secure around her.

"Pleased? Oh, sweetheart, I'm ecstatic. Over the moon. Thrilled. There aren't enough superlatives to describe how I feel."

She laughed, warmth blossoming inside her. She hadn't known she could be any happier, but now she was.

"So that's what you've been keeping from me?" he said with good-natured accusation. "That's what you told your damned brother before you told me?"

She gave him a sheepish smile. "Well, only because I went over to his town house after our fight and it all came tumbling out. I didn't mean to tell him. I've been feeling guilty about it ever since. Forgive me, Gabriel."

"Of course. I would forgive you anything." He pressed his mouth to hers again. "I love you, Esme."

"I love you too."

He laid a hand over her stomach. "So this is why you've been ill?"

She nodded. "Morning sickness. Not the most pleasant way to begin the day, but it usually gets better and I feel wonderful by evening."

"Damned Lawrence. Remind me to murder him when I see him again. He ought to have told me that you're increasing, not make me think you're at death's door."

"I made him swear not to tell you, or anyone else, so he was only honoring my request. But I'm sorry he had you so worried." She rested a palm against his chest, over the place where his heart beat, sure and strong. "Then again, if not for him, we probably wouldn't be standing here together now."

Gabriel took a moment to consider, his features softening. "That's true. I suppose when you look at it that way, I should be grateful. Maybe I'll just beat him up a little instead of actually killing him."

She laughed, knowing he was teasing. At least she hoped he was teasing.

Then he grinned at her, his old naughty grin that never failed to send delicious shivers down her spine. "Lawrence did remind me of something else."

"Oh? What is that?" she asked.

Gabriel tucked her closer against him. "That today is your birthday."

"You're right. It is."

He pressed his lips to hers. "Happy birthday, my love. Though in my rush to arrive, I didn't have time to get you a present, but I'll buy you anything your heart desires. Just tell me what it is you want."

She smiled, her whole body aglow with happiness and love. Tenderly, she kissed him again. "Nothing. I already have everything I want, right here in my arms and here inside me." She took his hand and placed it against her stomach, where their child grew.

Smiling, he leaned his forehead to hers, then found her mouth once again, adoration and love in his every touch.

"Now," she said a few breathless minutes later, "take me inside where it's warm, so you can have your wicked way with me again."

He threw back his head and laughed, then fit her close against his side as he turned them toward the house. "My darling Esme, it will be my pleasure."

Epilogue

Esme rapped quickly on the door to Gabriel's study and went inside without bothering to wait for an answer.

Gabriel was seated behind an imposing mahogany desk, the windows on both sides of the elegant, but thoroughly masculine, room flung open to let in what amounted to no more than a minuscule breeze; the summer day was a hot one. He'd stripped off his coat, leaving him in shirtsleeves and waistcoat.

At her entrance, Gabriel looked up from the papers he was reading and smiled when he saw her. Across from him was Mr. Hay, the steward for Ten Elms, whom Esme only then noticed.

Mr. Hay rose from his chair and bowed to her, his brown hair curling more than usual, no doubt due to the humidity. Everyone in the neighborhood was eager for a storm to break and cool things off, even if only temporarily.

"Oh, forgive the interruption, gentlemen; I didn't realize you were meeting. I thought his lordship was alone. I will leave and come back later."

"Nonsense, my dear," Gabriel said as he laid down the page in his hand. "Hay and I were nearly finished, weren't we, Hay?"

The steward looked as if that was news to him, but he nodded. "Yes, just so, my lord. We can continue whenever you prefer. I told Mr. Bracken that I would ride over to his farm today and inspect his fruit trees. Something to do with a new pear he is developing."

Gabriel stood as well. "If his pears are as good as the cherries we had from his orchard, then tell him I look forward to his efforts."

"As do I," Esme said. "Give Mrs. Bracken my best as well, will you? And thank her again for the skin salve. It has worked wonders."

Hay nodded. "It will be my pleasure, my lady." Then with another bow, he was gone, taking care to quietly close the door behind him.

"What is this about skin salve?" Gabriel asked. "I know you've become a favorite among the tenants and they're always giving you gifts, but I didn't realize you've taken to accepting medicaments from them in return."

"I haven't, not really," Esme said, moving deeper into the room. "But when Mrs. Bracken learned that I'm increasing, she insisted I take a jar of her home-made cream. She tells me all four of her daughters have used it during their pregnancies and not one of them has a single skin mark."

"Is that so?" Coming close, he took her hand and led her back to his desk, where he resumed his seat, then drew her down onto his lap. He laid a hand over the ripe curve of her belly, which was quite clearly beginning to show beneath the airy willow green muslin of her gown. He loved touching her burgeoning stomach, especially when they lay in bed together. His newest favorite pastime was pressing his hand to her stomach and waiting to feel the baby kick. That and enjoying the increase in her breast size, a physical change of which he was extremely admiring.

"You're certain this salve is safe?" he asked.

"Quite sure. I asked her for the ingredients, and it's mostly olive oil and flower essences with a touch of something secret that she assured me was quite harmless, but highly efficacious."

"Probably pig tallow."

Esme's mouth rounded in horror. "Oh, good heavens, I hope not."

He laughed and hugged her closer. "I'm teasing you. Everyone for twenty miles around knows you adore animals and that you don't eat meat. I am sure Mrs. Bracken wouldn't give you anything that might offend, especially after you nursed her favorite little dog back to health last month."

Esme frowned, hoping he really was teasing about the pig tallow. But then she brushed off her concerns, remembering how kindly Mrs. Bracken always was and what care she took never to serve anything with meat when Esme stopped by on one of her visits to the estate farms and leaseholders' cottages.

"So?" Gabriel said, pressing a kiss to her lips. "Why are you here? Or did you just miss me and couldn't bear to stay away?"

She smiled and kissed him back. "Of course I missed you, even if it's only been two hours since we last saw one another for nuncheon. But that is not why I'm here."

"Why, then?" He frowned suddenly, his fingers splaying wider against her stomach. "Nothing is amiss, is it? You're not feeling ill?"

"Of course not. I feel wonderful these days, now that my morning sickness has passed." She smiled gently and laid her hand over Gabriel's far larger one. "The doctor says everything is progressing exactly as it ought. Come late November, your son will be here."

"Or my daughter. Don't be so certain it's a boy."

Esme plucked at her skirt. "You won't mind if the baby is a girl?"

"Not at all. I'm with your brother Jack. I would be entirely content with a whole houseful of girls."

"But you need an heir."

He shook his head. "My uncle or cousins would be

thrilled to inherit, so no, I don't actually require an heir. I just want a healthy child, whatever the sex."

"Well, in that case, we're *definitely* having a boy. Your uncle is not getting his hands on this house again. Especially not after all the work I've put into it."

Gabriel laughed, then sobered again. "You do make an excellent point. The house looks splendid, and all because of you. I actually look forward to coming back here when I've been over to the village or out riding the fields with Hay. I used to hate this house, but not anymore, not when I know you're inside waiting for me when I return."

"It's our home. You and me and the baby. And the animals, of course."

He smiled. "Of course."

She saw him flick a glance toward Burr lying in a patch of cool shade on one side of his desk and a pair of the cats stretched out in a pool of sunlight beneath a nearby window.

"Oh, and the servants," she added.

"Yes, let us not forget them."

"Did I tell you that I heard from Mrs. Grumble-thorpe?" Esme offered eagerly. "She has agreed to come out of retirement and take up the position of nurse for the baby. She'll be here as soon as we return from our holiday at Braebourne."

She and Gabriel planned to depart for Braebourne in two more weeks, where they intended to remain until the end of September.

His frown returned. "Are you sure we shouldn't just stay at Braebourne until after the birth? Your whole family will be there to see you through your labor. We've discussed this before, and I still don't like the idea of you traveling when you'll be so far along."

Esme's jaw firmed in what Gabriel had taken to calling her "stubborn face."

"Yes, we have discussed this before and your child and heir will be born here at Ten Elms."

"Esme—"

"No, my mind is made up and I will not be swayed on this point. As for the trip to Braebourne, Mallory has traveled all over creation before her babies were born and no harm ever came to any of them. We shall leave Braebourne weeks before the baby is due. It will all turn out splendidly."

Esme knew she had won the argument again when Gabriel gave a resigned sigh. "At least your mother will be returning with us," he said. "If you go into labor early, she'll know what to do."

"She will indeed." Leaning forward, she kissed him. "Besides, I suspect you could help me through the birth on your own, if necessary. You're very resourceful."

"Resourceful, am I?" He laughed. "Well, no matter how resourceful you may think me, I'd rather leave your labor and delivery in far more capable hands than my own."

"So you don't want to be with me during the birth?"

He arched a brow, a faint hint of alarm in his eyes. "Do you want me to be?"

She thought for a moment, then nodded. "You were there when we made our child. You should be there for his birth. But only to hold my hand. You can let my mother and the doctor take care of the rest."

"Hand-holding, hmm? I think I could manage that, presuming your mother and the doctor don't kick me out first."

"I won't let them."

He chuckled. "Of that I have no doubt. Very well, my love, I will be there with you when our baby is born." He kissed her gently. "I will always be with you, Esme Landsdowne. I love you. You're my whole life now."

"As you are mine." Laying a hand against his cheek, she pressed her mouth to his, love and happiness flooding through her as it did on a daily basis now.

She was about to suggest they retreat upstairs for an afternoon "nap" when she heard a crinkling sound coming from the pocket in her gown.

"Oh," she said, easing back. "I nearly forgot."

"Forgot what?" he murmured, his eyes lambent with barely banked desire.

"The reason I came to find you."

He blinked, then laid his lips against her neck. "It wasn't to tell me about your old nurse returning?" he asked absently.

"No, it's something else entirely. Something I found when I was going through the attics."

He head came up, his eyes narrowing dangerously. "What do you mean, going through the attics? When were you doing that?"

Guilty color stained her cheeks. "This morning when you were out surveying the lake dredging. All I did was stand around while the footmen moved furniture and opened a few trunks for me. Since we're refurbishing the third-floor nursery, I wanted to see if there might be some old toys or other useful things for the baby. I actually discovered a wonderful old chest that would be perfect for extra blankets and such."

"You can order new toys and new chests from London. There's no need for you to tire yourself with such needless enterprises."

"I wasn't tired in the least, and honestly, the servants did all the work for me. While I was up there, I happened across a couple of other interesting finds. One, curiously enough, is a portrait of your uncle. Did you put that up there?"

He scowled. "No. Foy or Starr must have done, since I ordered the damned thing burned. I'll tell Bell to toss it on the rubbish heap at his earliest convenience."

"Yes, well, much as I agree with the sentiments, and believe me I do, I suppose we ought to retain the painting in the interest of family history. I could scribble a note and paste it on the reverse saying what a vile man he is, just so future generations know."

He smirked. "Sidney would hate that. Yes, let's do it."

She smiled back, then grew serious again. "There was something else."

"Oh? And what might that be?"

She climbed off his lap, then reached into her pocket to withdraw a letter, the paper fragile and yellowed with age. "This was inside the drawer of a writing desk, stuffed away in the back. I very nearly missed it."

Gabriel looked at the letter but made no move to take it from her.

"There was a second letter for your brother," she continued, "but this one is for you."

"Me?"

"Yes, it's . . . I believe it is from your mother."

Surprise moved across his features.

"I didn't read it," Esme hastened to explain, "at least not much of it, once I realized who it was from. I wasn't sure . . . but have you ever seen it before?"

After a brief hesitation, he took the delicate missive from her hand, then slowly folded open the page. His eyes widened ever so slightly and he swallowed. "No."

"My dearest Gabriel, please forgive me for what I am about to do . . . ," Esme knew it began.

He bent his head over the letter and began to read.

She watched, feeling like a bit of an intruder all of a sudden. But just when she wondered if she ought to give him some time alone, he reached out and took hold of her wrist and drew her nearer, so her legs pressed against his own.

"She was going to send for us, Matthew and me," he said in a low voice. "Once she got settled, she wanted us to live with her, even if my father objected. She said she loved me, loved Matthew, and that she was sorry for not being a better mother." He paused, his fingers tight against the paper. "All these years, I didn't think she cared about me at all."

"Of course she cared. You were her son. Of course she loved you. I'm sure your father loved you too, whatever he may have ended up doing in a moment of thoughtless rage."

"I suppose they were very unhappy together there at the end," he mused. "I guess I've never really seen them as ordinary people, who were both good as well as bad."

He laid the letter on his desk, then slid his arms around her so she stood with their baby between them.

She stroked his hair. "Perhaps I shouldn't have shown the letter to you, but I thought you had a right to know that she was thinking of you before she left. That she loved you."

He pressed his cheek to her rounded stomach for a moment before looking up. "No, you were right to show it to me. I presume Sidney made sure neither Matthew nor I ever saw the letters. Or perhaps it was my father. Maybe that's how he discovered she had left him."

"Oh, Gabriel." Tears filled her eyes.

He reached up and brushed the dampness from her lashes with a thumb. "Don't cry, sweetheart."

"But I've made you sad. I didn't mean to."

He shook his head and smiled. "You haven't. You couldn't. You make me happy every day. You're the light of my life and I cannot do without you."

"Nor I you. I love you, Gabriel. Now and always."

With a gentle tug, he drew her down onto his knee again, pausing to kiss her. "Thank you."

She met his eyes with surprise. "For what?"

"For seeing past my hardened, sinful exterior to the man underneath. For loving me despite my many faults."

"You have no faults, not in my eyes."

"I do, but it is kind of you to overlook them."

"As you overlook mine."

"Now, there we disagree, since you are perfection itself," he said. "You are everything that is good and generous and kind, and I thank my lucky stars each and every day that you came into my life. Thank you for saving me, Esme. Without you, I would never have known real happiness." He laid his palm on her belly again. "Without *you*, I would never have had a home again, or a family."

Wrapping her arms around his shoulders, she kissed him with unfettered devotion. "Without you, I would never have been truly happy either. I was adrift until we met. As for family, you have a huge one now. There are so many of us, you may come to regret joining the clan, especially when they all descend on us for the birth."

His earlier look of unease returned. "You think all seven of your siblings and their broods will be here? At Ten Elms?"

"Yes, I suspect so. Good thing we have a home with so many rooms. But what is it they say? The more, the merrier?"

He considered that for a moment, as a smile creased his face.

He laughed. "Right you are, my dear. Let us have more of everything—more love and more happiness and more babies! And we shall be merry for all the rest of our days."

Then he kissed her again, and made her very merry indeed.

Don't miss Tracy Anne Warren's

The Bedding Proposal

Available now.
Continue reading for a preview.

"This party is duller than a Sunday sermon," Lord Leopold Byron complained with a sigh.

From where he stood with his elbow crooked idly atop the fireplace mantelpiece, he surveyed the other guests. Not for the first time, he wondered why he'd bothered to accept this evening's invitation; the only amusing activity was drinking, and he could have done that anywhere. At least the champagne was a palatable vintage. Taking consolation from the thought, he drank from the crystal flute balanced in his other hand.

At the opposite end of their host's mantelpiece stood his twin brother, Lord Lawrence Byron. Given that they were identical, Leo supposed they must make a picture, particularly dressed as they both were in black silk evening breeches and black cutaway coats with crisp white shirts, waistcoats and cravats.

Lawrence looked at him and raised an eyebrow, its color two shades darker than his golden brown hair, which fell past his jaw; Leo also tended to wear his hair slightly long. "Just be glad you aren't actually in church," he said.

"If I were, at least I'd be able to catch up on my sleep. Rather handy, being able to doze off with my eyes open; fools the vicar every time. Tough to do standing up, though."

"I can manage in a pinch, so long as there's a convenient wall to lean against. Last time I tried it, though, I started snoring. Great-aunt Augusta caught me and boxed my ears."

Leo chuckled in sympathy. "She may be pushing eighty, but the old gal can still pack a wallop."

Lawrence nodded. "I'll wager she could make even the great Tom Cribb shake in his boots."

Both men grinned for a moment at the image of their formidable aunt taking on one of England's fiercest boxers.

"You can't expect London to be terribly exciting this time of year," Lawrence said, "what with most of the *Ton* off at their country estates. I don't know why you didn't stay at Braebourne with everyone else for another few weeks."

"What? And leave you rattling around Town all by yourself? I know you've taken it into your head to actually do something with your legal studies, but coming back to London early in order to set up your own practice? It's beyond the pale, even for you."

Lawrence gave him a wry half smile. "At least one of us values his education. I happen to like the law; I find it fascinating. And might I remind you that you also studied the law, same as me?"

"Just because I earned a degree in jurisprudence doesn't mean I want to spend the rest of my life pitching my oars into legal waters. You know I studied the law only because I couldn't stomach anything else. Now that the war's over, the military holds little appeal. As for taking ecclesiastical orders—" He broke off on a dramatic shudder. "Not even Mama can see me in a vicar's collar with a Bible tucked under my arm."

Lawrence laughed. "*No one* could see you in a vicar's collar with a Bible under your arm. The very idea is sacrilegious."

"You're right," Leo said. "I prefer to live a gentleman's life, as befits the son of a duke. And thanks to some sound financial advice, courtesy of our inestimable brother-in-law, Adam, and our brother Jack's friend Pendragon, I can afford to do so, even if I am the fifth youngest of six sons."

"Only by two minutes," his twin reminded. "You know, I've always wondered if the nursemaid didn't switch us in our cribs and I'm actually the elder."

"Not likely, considering I'm the brains behind the majority of our greatest schemes."

"The brains, are you? I'll admit you've got a God-given flair for making mischief that few others can match, but I'll thank you to remember who it is who always manages to talk our way out of the thicket when we land ass-first in trouble."

"You do have a knack for turning a story on its head." Leo drank more champagne. "Which leads me back to this career nonsense of yours. You invested successfully with Pendragon, same as me, so I know you don't need the blunt. Why, then, do you want a job? You know as well as I do that gentlemen don't engage in trade."

"It's not trade. The law is a perfectly honorable profession," Lawrence said as he fiddled with his watch fob; it was a gesture Leo knew always indicated defensiveness on his twin's part. "As for my reasons, it keeps me from being *bored*—unlike you."

Leo rolled his eyes. "God, save me. Next you'll be telling me I should join you in chambers and hang my shingle up next to yours. Or worse, take up a cause and run for Parliament. I can see it now: the Right Honourable Lord Leopold, standing on behalf of Gloucester." He shook his head, smiling at the absurdity of the idea.

But his twin didn't return his grin. "Might be good for you. You're five-and-twenty now. You could do with some purposeful direction."

"The only direction I need is to be pointed toward a fresh glass of wine," Leo said, tossing back the last of his champagne. "That and a proper bit of entertainment."

"A woman, you mean? Maybe you shouldn't have broken things off so soon with that pretty little opera dancer you were seeing over the summer. She was a prime bit o' muslin."

Leo scowled. "Oh, she was pretty enough and most definitely limber, but after a couple of weeks, the attraction began to wear thin. Outside the bedroom, we had absolutely nothing in common. Her favorite topics were clothes and jewels and the latest amorous intrigues going on backstage at Covent Garden. It got so that I had begun making excuses not to visit her."

He paused and briefly drummed his fingers against the mantelpiece. "I knew enough was enough when she started hinting that she wanted to quit dancing so I could take her on a tour of the Continent. As if I'd consign myself to spending weeks alone in her company. I'd rather be clapped in irons and paraded naked through the streets than endure such tedium."

Lawrence chuckled. "I hadn't realized the situation was quite so dire."

"That's because you were too busy with your own flirtations." Slowly, Leo turned his empty glass between his fingers. "No, if I wanted to set up another mistress, she'd have to be someone unique, someone incomparable, who other men would go to great lengths to possess. Someone like—"

And suddenly, from across the room, a woman caught his eye.

Her hair was as dark as a winter night, upswept in a simple yet refined twist that showcased the delicate creamy white column of her throat. Around her neck hung a plain gold chain with a cameo that nestled between her breasts like a cherished lover. Despite the surprisingly modest décolletage of her silk evening gown, the cut served only to enhance the lush curves of her shapely figure, while the brilliant emerald hue of the material cast no illusions regarding her sensuality and allure.

He knew who she must be, of course. He'd heard talk that she might make an appearance tonight—none other than the infamous Lady Thalia Lennox.

Ever since the firestorm of scandal that had erupted

around her nearly six years earlier, she'd become both disgraced and notorious. Even he, who had been no more than a green youth reveling in one of his first years about Town, had been aware of the uproar at the time.

The gossip had ignited first over her much-publicized affair, then exploded during the divorce proceedings that followed. Divorces were virtually unheard of among the *Ton*, and extremely difficult to obtain due to the necessity of three separate trials and an Act of Parliament. Nevertheless, her cuckolded husband, Lord Kemp, had sued against her and been granted a termination of their marriage.

And while a taint of scandal continued to trail Lord Kemp even to this day, the proceedings had turned Lady Thalia into a social outcast. Once a darling of the *Ton*, she now dwelled along the fringes of genteel respectability, invited out only by those who either were dishonored themselves or simply didn't care what anyone thought of them—or so said the gossips who continued to relay stories of her alleged exploits.

This evening's supper party was hosted by a marquess who was separated from his wife, lived openly with his mistress and most definitely didn't give a fig about other people's opinions.

Frankly, his host was one of the reasons Leo had attended tonight's revel, as Leo had assumed the party would be wilder and more amusing than it had turned out to be thus far. But now that he knew Thalia Lennox was among the guests, his expectations for a lively evening were reinvigorated.

"You were saying? Someone like who?" Lawrence asked, picking up on the sentence Leo had never finished.

"Her." Leo set his glass aside.

Lawrence's gaze moved across the room. "Good Lord, surely you aren't thinking what I think you're thinking?"

"And what would that be?" he said, not taking his eyes off Thalia, who was conversing with an elderly roué who couldn't seem to lift his gaze higher than her admittedly magnificent breasts.

"We were discussing women, and, if I'm not mistaken, that's the scandalous Lady K. over there. You must be out of your mind to even consider making a play for her."

"Why? She's stunning. One of the most enchanting women I've ever beheld. And I believe she goes by her maiden name of Lennox these days."

"However she's called, she uses men like toys and discards them once they're broken, to say nothing of the fact that she's several years your senior."

Leo couldn't repress a slowly forming grin as he turned to his twin. "Just look at her. She can't be that much older, even if she has been married and divorced. As for her using me like a toy, I look forward to being played with. Anywhere. Anytime."

Lawrence shook his head. "I'll be the first to admit she's attractive, and I can see why you'd be tempted, but do yourself a favor and find another opera dancer. Or better yet, go visit one of the bawdy houses. You can slake your thirsts there without causing any lasting damage."

"Ah, but where is the challenge in that?" Leo said. "I want a woman who can't be had simply for the price of a coin. A spirited female with some good solid kick to her."

"The only kick you're going to get is in your posterior when she boots you out of her way. My guess is she won't look at you twice."

Leo raised a brow. "Oh, she will. Care to wager on it?"

Lawrence narrowed his eyes. "All right. Ten quid."

"Make it twenty. Ten's hardly worth the effort."

"Twenty, it is."

They shook, sealing the bet.

Lawrence stepped back and crossed his arms. "Go on. Amaze me, Don Juan."

Leo brushed the sleeves of his coat and tugged its hem to a precise angle. "Take the carriage home if you get tired of waiting. I'm sure I'll be otherwise occupied tonight."

With that, he set off in search of his quarry.

*   *   *

I should never have come here tonight, Lady Thalia
Lennox thought as she forced herself not to flinch
beneath the leering stare of Lord Teaksbury. She didn't
believe he had met her eyes once since they had begun
conversing.

*Old lecher. How dare he stare at my breasts as if I'm
some doxy selling her wares?* Then again, after nearly
six years of enduring such crude behavior from men of
her acquaintance, one would think she would be well
used to it by now.

As for the ladies of the *Ton*, they generally looked
through her, as if she were some transparent ghost who
had drifted into their midst. Or worse, they pointedly
turned their backs. She had grown inured to their snubs
as well—for the most part, at least.

Still, she had hoped tonight might prove different,
since her host, the Marquess of Elmore, had known his
own share of personal pain and tended to acquire
friends of a more liberal and tolerant persuasion. But
even here, people saw her not for the person she was,
but for who they assumed her to be.

Ordinarily, she tossed aside invitations such as the one
for tonight's supper party—not that she received all that
many invitations these days. But she supposed the real
reason she had come tonight was a simple enough one.

She was lonely.

Her two friends, Jane Frost and Mathilda Cathcart—
the only ones out of all her acquaintance who had stuck
by her after the divorce—were in the countryside. They
had each invited her to join them at their separate estates, but she knew her attendance at the usual autumn
house parties put each woman in an awkward and difficult position. Plus, neither of their husbands approved
of their continued association with her, their friendship
limited to occasional quiet meals when they were in
Town, and the back-and-forth exchange of letters.

No, she was quite alone and quite lonely.

Ironic, she mused, considering the constant parade

of lovers she supposedly entertained—at least according to the gossip mavens and scandal pages that still liked to prattle on about her. Given their reports of her behavior, one would imagine her town house door scarcely ever closed for all the men going in and out—or perhaps it was only her bedroom door that was always in need of oil for the hinges?

She felt her fingers tighten against the glass of lemonade in her hand, wondering why she was dwelling on such unpleasantness tonight. Better to put thoughts like those aside, since they did nothing but leave the bitter taste of regret in her mouth.

A hot bath and a good book—that's what I need this evening, she decided. That, and to tell the old reprobate still leering at her to take his eyes and his person somewhere else.

If only she hadn't given in to the temptation to wear emerald green tonight, perhaps she wouldn't have ended up being ogled by a loathsome toad like Teaksbury. But she'd always loved this dress, which had been languishing in the back of her wardrobe for ages. And honestly she was tired of being condemned no matter what she wore or how she behaved. *In for a penny, in for a pound,* she'd thought when she made the selection. Now, however, she wished she'd stuck to her usual somber dark blue or black, no matter how dreary those shades might seem.

Ah well, I shall be leaving shortly, so what does it really matter?

"Why, that's absolutely fascinating," Thalia said with false politeness as she cut Teaksbury off midsentence. "You'll have to excuse me now, Lord Teaksbury. After all, I wouldn't want to be accused of monopolizing your company tonight."

Teaksbury opened his mouth—no doubt to assure her that he didn't mind in the least. But she had already set down her glass, turned on a flourish of emerald skirts and started toward the door.